The People Of The Wolf

by

Jack F. Reich

Bloomington, IN   Milton Keynes, UK

authorHOUSE®

AuthorHouse™
1663 Liberty Drive, Suite 200
Bloomington, IN 47403
www.authorhouse.com
Phone: 1-800-839-8640

AuthorHouse™ UK Ltd.
500 Avebury Boulevard
Central Milton Keynes, MK9 2BE
www.authorhouse.co.uk
Phone: 08001974150

First published by AuthorHouse 8/15/2006

ISBN: 1-4259-5294-1 (sc)
ISBN: 1-4259-5295-X (dj)

Library of Congress Control Number: 2006931986

Printed in the United States of America
Bloomington, Indiana

This book is printed on acid-free paper.

Chapter 1

Sun Boy had failed to bring his torch back to the high plains of the Moreau River country this sun. Clouds were low, with the color of "old man when gone." Every now and again little pieces of sleet fell, giving the appearance of a veil of white to the far hills. Wind, oh yes, the ever-present wind came sliding like a snake over the land, pressing all things down in its path and shaking all else. It gathered dust where it could and picked up tumble weeds and other particles where it could not. It started in the snow clad peaks of the Rocky Mountains far to the west. Then, sliding down the eastern slopes it gathered speed as it came, moving the smoke flaps on the lodges of the Crow. Wind was snapping the door flaps of the Sioux while raising the dust clouds in the fields of the growers to the east along the big rivers. It was late September and the wind had teeth in it. A raw damp chill that ached the bones and formed goose bumps all the way down the backside, it ruffled the long hair on the buffalo and tossed the manes and tails of the horses. It pushed the long grass to the southeast bending it down, breaking off seed pods. It was cold, and getting colder.

Curly and Cubby were six years old and in the prime of their lives. They were big and well muscled, weighing over one hundred and twenty pounds each. Tall Elk's band of Sioux was still under their protection and had little warfare the past few years; due to the fact it made no sense to try to surprise them. It just could not be done. The pack had grown in numbers as well, now numbering thirty-two wolves. The She Wolf had never mated again when her mate was killed. That

1

was that, but she had remained the overall brains of the pack. Curly was the new leader. When a tough problem came up Curly made the choice after first getting a nod from mother. Her wisdom was always sought after first.

Curly and Cubby had taken their male pups born this year on a long swing down country. A hunting trip as well as a test for endurance and to see if the enemy tribes were planning a raid, for Tall Elk's Sioux by far had the best horse herd on the plains.

Eagle was flying overhead, having problems with the wind. She sat down on a branch of a stunted tree and waited for the pack to come up. Eagle was a magnificent bird. Her head was snow white with white feathers laying flat against her dark gray body edged with black, with some brown low down near her golden legs. Her eyes were far seeing and bright. They set just back from her golden hooked beak. Her tail was snow white, tipped with black and gray.

Curly and the pack had come up and Ling Lang presented eagle with a young rabbit. Ling Lang was Cubby's son. He was named after his father's brother who died after fighting big cat who would have killed a colt out of Golden Star. Ling Lang put himself in front of the colt and fought well. The big tom was too much for him and before the pack got there he had his belly ripped out. His neck torn and was bleeding too much. Moon Boy put two arrows in the lion's heart and carried Ling Lang back to the lodge. Three suns later, Ling Lang was resting in a cotton wood tree. He lived by the law and had died by the law. Eagle thanked Ling Lang for the rabbit he opened it and quickly ate the warm meat.

Curly asked, "What did you see, Eagle, while floating high in the sky?"

Eagle looked wise then spoke, "Far to the south and some west was a large group of warriors. They had gathered from mixed tribes. They are under a strong Crow chief, Black Thunder Rolling On The Mountain. He is a large man and full of hate. He is hungry for revenge for all the Crow braves Tall Elk killed." Eagle thought long then said, "I don't think they will come soon." Eagle went on to say they wait for more braves to join them they know if they fail this time no one will ever go on the war trail again against Tall Elk and his Sioux. Eagle then said, "My son is watching and I go now to join him. If they start this way I will tell you."

Curly took the lead. All seven wolves moved as one. Their strides were long and sure in spite of the wind; they covered ground. Their bodies could have been made of spring steel. They were tireless. Sundown came and went.

At moonrise they killed a sleepy buffalo calf and devoured large chunks of hot meat. Then they were gone, leaving the rest to the lesser meat eaters. They had news and their band had to be told. Curly knew they would play a major part in the war and Eagles too. At first light they were at Tall Elk's lodge.

Cubby gave the short bark and Tall Elk and Moon Boy appeared. Curly said, "We have run in the light of the sun just past and all of the dark past. We have news and we could eat some meat and rest a little then we will tell all." The wind had almost spent itself, but it was cold in the morning light. All the braves and bigger boys were standing or sitting on their buffalo robes. Some of the young women too were sitting on robes. All knew the important of the first light gathering.

Curly and Cubby came and sat down, one on each side of Moon Boy. Curly spoke first, "A large band of braves from mixed bands of crow, have joined a strong war chief called Black Thunder Rolling On The Mountain."

Cubby now spoke, "Black Thunder hates Tall Elk for all the Crow braves now dead, because of Tall Elk. Some of the dead are his relatives. He also wants our horses and he knows of our breeding of horses. And they are the best on the plains."

Curly spoke, "He wants Tall Elk's women too. They will be his slaves and also his sons. He thinks they control the pack. No one controls us. We do as we do out of love for you. We also love Eagles too."

Tall Elk spoke quietly, "How many come?"

"We do not know" Cubby and Curly said, "Bald eagle and her son watch now and other eagles will go soon to help. We called Sniff, Dusty Rose and Fatty to bring their groups too. We will be ready. We will have seventy-five or eighty wolves and many a Crow will die in his sleep and never know what hit them."

Urgently, Tall Elk spoke, and with a deep sense of authority, "Some of you could go hunt meat. We will need much food; others look to your bows, arrows, lances, your knives and axes."

Skunk said, "Some of you could help with the arrows. I will put new grandfather snake poison on the tips. Some of you may need a new bow. I will do that too."

"Get the feel of your weapons," Tall Elk commanded, "It has been a long time since we needed them, thanks to our pack and eagles. I was hoping for no more wars. I am sorry that we again have to kill. So many of them have already died and some of us to, because of hate. We have worked hard and long, for what is ours. We should not just give it away. They would kill us anyway for being weak, AND WE ARE NOT WEAK! Ho!"

"Ho," all shouted. "We are strong." With that, the band dispersed went to do what each did best. At sun down, when the cooking fires were being kindled, the she wolf with twenty or so of her grandkids came into camp and went to Tall Elk's lodge. She asked if there was something they could do that would help.

"Yes," Tall Elk considered, "Ten of you could go to the horse herd and see to it that no one comes to take horses. You could change guards every five hours or so. The rest of you could ring the camp and do as you did so well six snows past. Are you hungry?"

"No," said the she wolf, "we were at the buffalo kill and we had enough there."

A big three year old male wolf came to stand by Moon Boy, "my name is Shadow and I will be your friend. The same as my father is. My father is Cubby and I can make the same terrible sound as he can." With this he opened his mouth and out came a sound that would spoil milk, turn blood to water and make even the stoutest hearted brave want to make water.

The she wolf said, "Shadow that caught me off guard. That makes me want to find a little hole and go in. Warn me next time or I may soil myself." All smiled but in fact it was anything but funny and funny was not one of them. Tall Elk did go make water. He said he was going to anyway but the she wolf wondered if this was truthful.

The next sun came and the next. No word came from eagle. Tall Elk and Moon Boy were getting nervous. "There must be nothing to report, or Eagle would have told us". Tall Elk said, "All was ready in the Sioux camp."

Skunk had put poison on all the arrows and even asked braves to go with him to find snakes, for more poison. All of Skunk's bows were in use. All quivers were filled and in some cases two were filled.

War horses stood by each braves lodge. Thirty or forty wolves were out, some hiding. Some were out on patrol but all watching. At sun's highest point, three dots were coming from the southwest. Bald Eagle got there first. She glided in so graceful on cupped wings it made your teeth hurt. She sat down by Tall Elk's lodge and asked for meat and water for her and the others. When she had eaten all she wanted she told them all was in turmoil at the Crow camp. More of them ride away, some suns then ride in.

Eagle said, "He sees us in the sky and doesn't know if we are with you or just riding the air currents. He shot an arrow at me the other sun and it made it about half way then fell back down poking his horse in the flank. The horse bucked him down and Black Thunder was mad. He lost his arrows when his horse stepped on them."

Bald Eagle's son ruffled his feathers, spread his wings and refolded them then he spoke, "I feel Black Thunder will come soon. He must or give up his war. If more braves ride home than stay, his power is weak. If this is so, he must start with what he has or be disgraced. I will rest. Then I will start back but before I go, I have a plan. Let them get thirty or forty miles from you. Then send some of the pack. Thirty maybe circle their camp, not too close - let one wolf howl, then two, now two on the backside, then two on each side now all the pack at once. Then silence. Be still for as long as it takes to breathe twenty times. Then have Cubby and Shadow give their terrible sound two or three times. This will be the end of the war, I think. If they come it will be without rest and many will go sleep in trees for a very long time."

Chapter 2

Black Thunder Rolling On The Mountain sat in front of his shelter in his makeshift camp. Since first light he had watched three or more eagles drawing lazy circles in the clear blue sky. Then seven eagles would circle. Then three were gone and four rode the air currents; it was maddening. Black Thunder knew they were the Sioux scouts. They watched his every move and he could do nothing about it. Then two or three braves had rode in from Bent Feathers band of crow and told how this Tall Elk, Sioux chief, had brought Bent Feather to his camp and killed him in front of the entire crow camp. All sun he had heard of the wolf pack, who could talk with the Sioux as freely as he could speak with the braves. He looked at his warriors. It was time to go and go now. There were fifty or more braves waiting to follow him to war with the Sioux, to seek the blood of the war leader Tall Elk.

Black Thunder grabbed his weapons and settled his war feathers. Then he tied the string around his neck, leaped on his bay war horse and dashed out of camp going north by east. The crow braves, who had sat long enough, followed as fast as they could get ready. All except for the eight who sat by the dying fires and looked long at each other.

"He will kill them all." said Brown Otter.

"He has no plan except to kill Sioux." spoke Slow Bear.

"I think he is crazy," said Blue Bird, "let them go, all of them. Let us go quick or he will come back and call us cowards. Then I will kill him."

Bald Eagle watched them go, forty three in all. Eight had not gone but had put out the fires, got on their horses and went west on their back trail to their home camps. They were the smart ones. Four eagles were going as fast as they could go to tell Tall Elk. The crow war party was on their way. At just past midway to sundown, Black Thunder pulled his heaving stud horse in to blow. No sense in killing the horses. The Sioux were not going anywhere and he wanted the braves to bunch up. He wanted to see if any late comers had caught up but no, they were not all there: eight or nine were missing. He asked a brave, "Where are the others?"

"Blue Dogs horse went lame and he had no other, so is leading him back," a young brave said, "Brown Otter, Slow Bear and Blue Bird and five more went home."

Black Thunder was full of rage. The raid had just started. He had lost nine braves and he had no way to know how many Sioux rode with Tall Elk and the wolves, how many of them? How did the wolves figure in the fight? Would they just scout or would they kill braves too? If they did, he would have a hard time controlling the war party. From being a bad sun, on the raid it got worse: out of nowhere came Bald Eagle. She dove at Black Thunder's head with the speed of light screaming out her rage. She put her talons in his head dress tearing away most of it. Black Thunder notched an arrow to kill eagle. He was off balance and when his stud lunged he fell off his horse. He released the arrow by accident which struck the left hind leg of Frog's pinto mare that kicked Black Thunder in the belly. When the dust had settled and some of the fog had left Black Thunder's brain, the mare was standing on three legs and unable to travel, unless at a slow pace. Frog had worked the arrow out of his horse's hind leg, and gave it to Black Thunder, who cleaned it and put it in his quiver. When he took off his head dress he saw the blood. A talon had made a long cut in his head.

No one had a horse for Frog to ride, so Black Thunder took the war party north at a canter. He was glad. Frog may not have said so but he saw only bad luck for the others. Black Thunder was so full of hate, he never thought of the braves or their horses. All he saw was killing Tall Elk, taking his women and getting the wolf pack under his command.

Bald Eagle! Black Thunder would kill that eagle for making him look foolish in front of the war party causing him to shed first blood on the raid. She would suffer long and hard if he caught her. He reached to fix his war bonnet and remembered it was gone and was mad all over again.

Fast Fox shook his head and looked at Bull's Tail. He was going to have a talk with Black Thunder when they stopped to water and graze the horses. Fast Fox was one of the chief's oldest friends and had been with him on many a raid. Black Thunder was a good leader, most of the time, but not this time. If the braves thought him weak or going crazy they would just ride away from Black Thunder and he would too.

Fast Fox saw the shimmer of water in a large ash draw up ahead. He moved up by the chief and pointed, "Water! Let us water the horses and us too. It is near sundown and we should eat. I am hungry and so are the mounts. We should rest. The tired braves do not fight well and I will talk with you, and you had better hear my words. I have spoken."

Black Thunder looked long at his old friend, "make camp by the water and someone go kill meat we will eat and rest too. Now Fast Fox are you happy?"

"No, many words still must be said and you must hear them all. When that is done and you hear them well, then I will be happy."

The night camp was a good one. It was well watered with sweet cold water running out of old rocks, well cleaned and with plenty of moss. A spot much loved by all kinds of wildlife who just now were disturbed by all the new comers. Deer snorted, ducks quacked, and birds chattered noisily in the near darkness. The old stream bed was soft with much sand washed by many years of time and was a good place to sleep. Fires were crackling on piles of dry twigs that lay everywhere. A buffalo calf roasted above the fire, and some meat was drying on racks for sun to come.

Fast Fox sat down by Black Thunder, "My chief," he began "this entire raid you have been mad for this or that. Never have you said how glad you were to have so many with you from all the bands. All you can say and think is to kill Sioux to get their horses, their women and the wolf pack. Why is the pack with them? Because, they want to be! No one could make them stay. If we win they will be just gone, eagles

9

too. The Sioux have good horses. Why? They have been breeding them for a long time. Cutting the lesser studs only and using the best for breeding. Why do they have much to eat? They grow fields of food. Instead of raiding and fighting maybe we should try trading and asking questions of new ways to live better. If you will not hear me, then go to the braves and tell them you are proud to have them with you and not many will ride home again. The Sioux are great fighters and know we come. They will be ready. I, Fast Fox, have spoken." With that he found his robe and fell into a deep sleep.

Black Thunder sat for a long time knowing Fast Fox was right, but how to change? The raid was going, and if he said stop, let us go home, no one would ever hear him again and who would blame them? Could he stand that? No! Much better to die in battle but did he have the right to lead the others to their death? To trade for young stallions was a good idea too, but they had nothing to trade the Sioux would want. Seed for growing crops was a good idea also. Other Crow had thought of that before but no one had done anything about that either. He knew of good spots along water ways to grow crops. Black Thunder got up and put more dry wood on the drying fires. Soon the meat strips were dripping fat and grease in the fire. Then he went to his robe and slept fitfully.

Bald Eagle sailed into Tall Elk's camp on the Moreau River. Tall Elk and Moon Boy were there. "I have brought you this." It was most of Black Thunders war bonnet. "I, Eagle, took it off Black Thunder's head and he tried to put an arrow in me. His bay stud lunged then he fell off and the arrow hit a pinto in her hind leg. She now stands on three legs. One more that can't fight us. They camp now some fifty miles from where they started. Call the pack - they were there."

"Curly, the Crow will camp when sun falls off the world near Fox Ridge after full dark. Run off as many horses as you can. They will be tired, but keep them coming. A crow on foot is not much of a fighter. Then after they are relaxed, howl to them as my son said. There are forty now; when you are finished there should be less. Take as many of yours as you feel is enough. Take the older wolves. No young ones should go. Tall Elk, if you look at the war bonnet you will see blood. It is Black Thunder's blood. I cut him with my talon. He shed first blood on his raid. The feathers came from my uncle. Black Thunder killed him. Take three of them and tie them to your war bridle. It will bring you luck. Give two to Moon Boy and the rest use later as you need them. Now Curly, I, and two more eagles will fly overhead. If I see anything you need to know I will tell you," Eagle said.

When sun boy brought his torch back to earth, Black Thunder was up on his bay stallion. "Braves of the Crow people, I want to tell you that I am proud to have so many of you with me from other bands. My raid has not been smooth. Not enough of you came at one time so we did not start. Then some went back and others had horses go lame. I put an arrow in Frog's pinto and now some of you may feel we are too few. I go anyway. I will feel glad to have you with me. Some of you will never ride again. The Sioux are good fighters and we go to their home lands. The wolves and eagles make it more dangerous. It has not been heard of before, this thing of animals talking to people. Bird's Wing, son of Yellow Tail told us first and no one believed him. Bent Feather, a chief, told us and we did not believe. Now I believe. That is why I wanted this raid - it is to get control of the pack and eagles. In camp last night Fast Fox my friend told me that he thought the pack that helped the Sioux because they wanted to. Not because they had to. I believe Fast Fox speaks with a straight tongue as always. I do not know what is in front of us. I plan to talk to Tall Elk. If I can I will make less war talk and more peace talk. If I can, too many Crow bones may lay in the sun. Now maybe the time to be big has come and we will be able to be not at war so much. Maybe then we can see our young ones grow to be great in our tribe. Not deposit our bones in other lands. I Black Thunder have spoken."

Curly picked thirty eight older wolves to go. Leaving the rest of the wolves under the direction of the she wolf to circle the Sioux home, making the web so tight that a mouse would have a hard time getting past. The thirty-eight ran under a cloudy sky and left no more signs of their passing. They ran as a cloud shadow falls over the land, and missing nothing. They ran low to the ground. Like velvet over spring steel, their long strides never missed a step. Twenty miles came and went, then forty. Around midway to sun down they killed an old cow buffalo with a bad foot. All ate well but not too well because they had a job to do, and they meant to do it well, even then most of the meat was eaten. They watered close to Fox Ridge, went up on the butte to watch and wait.

Bald Eagle slid out of the sky and perched by Curly. "They are coming but slower than I thought. They may not use your water - two miles more there is an ash draw well watered, with grassy hill sides that is maybe where the horses will be. They will be on a picket rope, seven or eight to a rope and one brave with each bunch. They ride many stallions, so stay down wind of them, or they will catch your scent. Let them make water and feed maybe two hours. Cut one or two of the brave's legs deep, and if you do well, they will be walking and it will slow them down. They are close now so stay out of sight of the butte sky line; I will watch."

Eagle lifted up and went north then south to watch. The Crow came in a bunch at a slow canter, past the water the pack used on up to the ash draw; it looked like they would pass it then a brave loped over to look waved and they all went in to the camp place. The camp place was not as good as the one last sun but good enough; it had less wood, more rocks, and the ground was harder. Two braves dragged in a young dry buffalo cow that slid over the grass well enough leaving a blood trail from a cut throat. Fires were lit and the cow was cut up and the smell of hump ribs filled the wooded draw with well being. Some of the braves ate liver raw. Others cooked it some but most wanted hump ribs, or steak. The horses were watered and put on picket ropes to graze on the lush hill side grass. Only two braves tended them. Cooking fires now became drying fires, and meat was put on racks to cook and dry, as the wood burned down more was put on so it was a never ending cycle.

All the braves were in their robes sleeping. The wolves chewed the ropes wherever tied to anything. All the tenders had gone to find their robes, so they had an easy time of it. The wolves chased the horses north at a dead run for ten miles or so and then let them slack off to blow; then at a trot then a slow canter on into the night. When the Crow came out of their robes it was all history. The horses were just gone, to the last one. It was too dark to see the hand in front of their faces so they went back to their robes. No one said anything because there was just nothing to say. An hour later the nightmare began. On the north side of camp a wolf howled, long and mournful. A short time later a second howled then on the left two more howled, now on the right two more howled, to the south two more. Then all thirty eight howled as one: the sound was maddening. The noise got the braves out of their robes and got the fires going again, put arrows to strings, formed circles. They stood, poised, with arrows out. There was nothing, no sound. For ten minutes nothing then Cubby growled his horrible sound once, twice, three times, and the braves fell over each other soiled themselves, and even the wolves looked around for places to hide.

Over on the other side of camp, Shadow made himself known. Braves covered themselves with anything they could find to get under cover. Curly gave a signal and all ran north to pick up the horses, where they had left them. The war was over and no one had shot an arrow.

Curly and the pack picked up the Crow horse herd grazing by water, about where they left them. They spooked when the pack came up but Curly soon had them under control and moving in the direction of Tall Elk's camp. Two wolves went to tell Tall Elk the horses were coming, as they did an hour after sun up. Tall Elk and some braves got ropes on them so they could be looked at more closely. All fine horses, many stallions.

"I think", Curly said "they are ready to talk peace. Maybe we should go and see?"

Tall Elk called a short meeting. "I would like seventy of you to ride with me and Moon Boy. We go talk to the crow; we will take forty of our lesser horses. Take your best horses and war gear. We go as soon as you are ready! Curly can you and yours go?" Tall Elk said.

"Yes we will go- how many?" Curly asked.

"All that will." Tall Elk said proudly "I want to show them not to bother us again in war." Forty old horses were brought in. Sixty-five wolves, six eagles, seventy three-Sioux and Crow- Sioux moved out of camp. Moon Boy had his horse, Golden Star, his bow by Skunk, arrows, ax and knife. The Sioux warriors moved out at a fast canter covering ground at rapid pace. When the horses warmed up the speed would be increased to a full gallop. Thunder rolled from the horse's unshod hooves. A dust cloud billowed up in their passing and all lesser prairie dwellers got out of the way or got run over. Their mothers never raised any dumb children, so rabbits, prairie chickens, prairie dogs just got out of the way.

At first light, Black Thunder Rolling On The Mountain and the war party were up and looking at what took place. It was clear the wolves had cut the ropes taking the horse herd north. They should have been tired after their run the sun just past; maybe they had not gone far, they would see. Now they would eat, fires were lit, and they cut more meat off the buffalo cow. Soon the aroma of roasting meat was filling the wooded draw. Hungry men in the open air ate well and thought of little else. The work of this sun would come in good time; why rush it and besides that the horses were gone. The horses would have to be found before they could go one way or the other or walk all the way back. That was not a good plan. They cut the rest of the meat and cooked it. What was left over would be dried and taken with them because it was hard to hunt without horses. And buffalo were unpredictable. Many an unhorsed brave had been killed by buffalo in the past. The hide should be saved too. They could carry the meat in the skin if it was done right, and Fast Fox saw to this. So this is why they were in camp longer than they should have been but there were forty of them. They were well armed and on the war path; whom should they fear?

Tall Elk and seventy-three Sioux were all around them, with long powerful bows at half cock and sixty-five wolves filling in the open spaces between. The six eagles were landing in trees also.

"You! Black Thunder, you should have feared me, Tall Elk." Tall elk said forcefully, "You should have stayed in your own country! Has it grown too little for you? Sioux are with us here, who once were Crow; they know your talk they will speak for us all but first put all your bows, arrows, knives and axes here on the ground now!" They did it. "You now belong to the mighty Sioux. I could kill you all but I don't think I will. You are too good to die Black Thunder; you have Fast Fox with you and he has more smarts in him then the rest of you put together." Tall Elk looked at Buffalo Tongue and nodded the Sioux words were now in Crow.

"Black Thunder you came to kill us all, take our horses, our pack and eagles." Buffalo Tongue said in Crow, "Eagle took the only blood shed on this raid YOURS. Wolf pack took all your horses and brought them to us and never shot an arrow. The wolves don't need weapons. They themselves are weapons and they are with us because they want to be. We don't own them or the eagles either. Fast Fox tell us why you are here? Why did you come with Black Thunder?"

"I came to keep him out of trouble. He sometimes is like a newborn; he gets mad over nothing and does dumb things. Then he is sorry." said Fast Fox sadly.

"When you go back maybe some of us will go with you. Do you have yellow gravel in your streams?" Buffalo Tongue continued to say.

"Yes" said Fast Fox.

"We would like some of it. We have a brave who can make things out of anything. It is said when the yellow gravel is made hot it forms a soft hard lump; that can then be made to look like an eagle or a horse or anything only little or to put around your neck, for good luck." Tall Elk looked at Buffalo Tongue as he put it in Crow.

Tall Elk then spoke, "Black Thunder I have changed my thinking. I think you are a great chief. You came to kill but now you take back riches beyond your dreams and you will bring us twenty of your best young mares; we will put them with Golden Star and Golden Light. They are two of our best stallions and then in the spring they will be yours to do with as you choose." Tall Elk paused then spoke, "In the spring, bring the pack horses and bags to fill with seeds to plant by your water ways. We will show you how. Your young and old will keep out the buffalo, horses, elk and even deer out of the fields so your crops can grow. You must tend them with your knives take out the weeds. That is everything but the plant you want. If it is too dry you must water them- by filling water skins from the stream and pouring the water on to your plants. Do this well and your bellies will be full. When the big snow is on the ground you're young and old will be happy and they will sing songs to your far seeing leadership. Your raid you lost but you won the WAR. You are a good chief." Tall Elk looked to Buffalo Tongue and he put it in Crow.

Now Black Thunder stood up to speak. "I, Black Thunder, am honored. I did come to kill, this is the only way I know to get the things we need, no one ever showed me a different way, now I see it is much better to talk and be friends and to trade for the things you need. I never thought of the enemies having feelings for their belongings or their families I was wrong. My heart is black and on the ground, for my feelings. My mother told me to walk a mile in the other's foot wear, and see how it would feel to be him, such a little law - how could I have forgot such a simple rule? Now I am a chief, and braves look to me for leadership and I am not worthy of their trust. I thought only of myself. I never thought the Sioux would trade for something as worthless as the yellow gravel in many of our streams. I think they are just being kind. What if others some sun come and want it to? Maybe it has a value, I don't know, for now I am happy to trade for the gold and our lives."

Tall Elk said "bring the old horses; now each of you gets a mount," they did. "Now five of you get your bows and arrows your knives and ax, this is so you can hunt meat. Fast Fox come with us. I would know more of your wisdom. Get your bow, knife and ax. You others ride home and in two full moons bring the twenty young mares to be covered by our stallions and the yellow gravel in bags. Then in the spring when grass is greening, come for the seeds. Be glad I am tired of killing, or not any of you would be going home, never come to kill again, we are friends now and will live in peace. Go now and they went".

"Moon Boy, you and your braves get their war things, Skunk may want to see. Fast Fox come. Ride with me we will talk as we go and get to know each other, you are welcome to stay as long as you like or be a Sioux Crow as Buffalo Tongue is." Bald Eagle came and said, "I will watch and see if they go home, if not I will tell you." Tall Elk nodded. Fast Fox looked at his host, "You spoke to eagle and she understood"

"Yes of course. We all talk freely; that is why we can not be surprised, we knew of your gathering long before you started. Did you not see eagles over head? They watched you come and go. They saw on some suns more ride away then ride in, they saw the chief was weak and how badly he treated his braves. I am surprised you came at all. Moon Boy take your braves and go kill three buffalo by water, take your wolves too, and then we will eat, all of us." They were gone. "Now let us go too, so they did. The main group rode out of night camp on the back trail to the main camp at a slower pace, they topped a ridge and saw Moon Boys braves killing buffalo far below on a flat by a water shed. By the time they got there fires were lighted and hump ribs were cooking as was other choice cuts.

Tall Elk and Fast Fox sat near the cooking fires, enjoying the warmth and the aroma coming from the crackling sizzling buffalo meat that flavor had no comparison to anything on earth. Fast Fox was looking at the wolf pack who was noisily consuming a large old bull buffalo from which Moon Boy's braves had removed the hide.

"How is it that the Sioux have gained the love and help from a pack of wolves, that all others believed wild brutes? Also, that they have such knowledge as to speak to humans and plan to defeat other humans in war by running off the riding stock of the Crow war party leaving them unhorsed in a strange land, unable to go forward or back? Eagles, even worse, could observe from high in the sky, and know what the Crow was doing and just glide over and tell the Sioux all things. No wonder they were unbeatable in war. How can this be? I, Fast Fox have been fast in thinking all my life and am considered wise by others, but in the things just now spoke of, I am a new born." Fast Fox said and looked long at Tall Elk. He spread his hands in a gesture of confusion and waited for Tall Elk to speak.

Tall Elk took a large bite of dripping hump ribs, looked wise and spoke, "Seven snows past, this band of Sioux came to this land in the Moreau River country to live, in our band was a brave so bad no one wanted to be near him. Eagle Claw killed one of the wolves, just to see him die. The she wolf waited until her pups could help, then they killed him. When we killed meat we always gave some to them, so they could see all humans were not bad, they are our spirit guides. A spring blizzard came just before good weather, and would have killed my son Moon Boy, but the pack found him in the snow, and brought him to me safe."

"After the blizzard was over Moon Boy and I took meat to their den and I went back to our lodge to wait and see - after a time had past, two he wolves came to sit by Moon Boy and one of them began to speak understandably. 'I am Curly. I will be your friend; I will always run on your right, what I see you will see what I hear you will hear what I smell you will smell.'"

"The other wolf also spoke, 'I am Cubby. I am Curly's brother. I, too, will be your friend and I will be on your left side, and you will know all I know, the same as Curly.' It was discovered they could talk to each other. Soon he could talk to them all. As you know Moon Boy doesn't see well, but now Moon Boy can speak to all things. The she wolf did a favor for Eagle once a long time past; now she is one of us too, as is others of her clan. Now you know, when Moon Boy rides one of his horses he sees with as many pairs of eyes as he has with him. He can tune into others in the pack such as Sniff's wolf pack many miles away, and Eagles too. So he could be here and know what is going on in any direction and if he speaks, he could send the wolves to do anything, to anyone."

Fast Fox was so amazed that he had no comeback, "I, Fast Fox, will be a Sioux Crow. I will go get my family and we will join you very soon. I will need a better horse then this pile of soup bones; he cannot catch his own shadow." Tall Elk asked Fast Fox, "Do you have horses at your Crow camp?"

"Yes. I have many horses." Said Fast Fox.

"Do you have any yellow gravel?" said Tall Elk.

"Yes I have some. I got it because I thought it good to look at."

"I want you to bring all you can. I would like to see what One Skunk will do with it."

With that they got on the horses and rode for home camp on the Moreau River. Most of the better meat was tied in the skins to be eaten at their supper meal; no one left good food - it was not done.

Chapter 3

When they got home it was near dark. After giving the meat and hides to the women Tall Elk took Fast Fox to see Skunk and solemnly said, "Skunk, this is Fast Fox, a new Sioux. He is now one of us. Do you have a strong bow? He may need one to make meat or hit a horse thief, but I don't see any do you?"

"No, but he may see his shadow."

"That is good to hit if not too close to his toe," Skunk got up went to the store lodge and brought back a bow, a massive thing, and a quiver of arrows. Be careful what you shoot at or you will hunt arrows all sun; this bow sends them very far."

"I thank you Skunk. I will use them well." Said Fast Fox.

"Also each arrow has grandfather's snake poison on each arrow tip; don't cut yourself or it will make you sick, and I will have to go find a young cow buffalo with a long slobbery tongue and much milk to make you well again." Fast Fox had a funny look on his face and all smiled. Skunk was at it again; he was funny even when he did not mean to be.

Fast Fox would soon go to get his family from the land of the Crow, and he said he would bring back some of the yellow gravel that is in their stream beds, Tall Elk told Skunk, "I have asked him to- for you to work with. When it is made hot it runs to make soft hard lumps, you could work with them to make charms to put around your neck to use as good luck charm." Skunk looked troubled. "My chief," and Skunk spoke in Sioux with no hand signs so Fast Fox could not know.

"Do you remember when we found the very old remains of a man in our potato cooler?"

"Yes," Tall Elk said thoughtfully.

Skunk said, "We agreed not to speak of it to anyone not even our family and not our wives; because we felt there was a great mystery involved here that we have no understanding of. Where did the gold and the head piece, with the red stone set in it that when the sun hit it red fire shot from it that blinded us come from? What of the long knifes that is so hard and sharp and the gold flat round pieces, with faces on them. I tell you there have been men in our lands before in the long ago not like us."

"When and if they come again and see the charms around our necks and our arms they will want them, not for the charms but the gold. Then they will want to know of our place we find the yellow gravel and when we cannot show them, they will be crazy and kill us to make us talk. Then we will kill them, but they may have ways to kill we know nothing of like the long knife or more evil than that. What then, Tall Elk my chief, have you thought of that?"

"No," Tall Elk said slowly, "I never thought of that. I just wanted to see what you could do with this yellow gravel."

"I will make more charms, my chief, but not many. I will make something for you and for me and two or three more, but there must not be many or too many people will know of them and they will talk. Then they will become curious and when they find out we take the yellow gravel from the lands of the Crow we will get the Crow in trouble and we don't want that. This is what I am thinking."

Tall Elk thought long then said, "Skunk as always you speak with a straight tongue. I have never thought other than that; we will not use the yellow gravel. We have hidden it and will save it for times in the way ahead when we need it."

Fast Fox asked Tall Elk for two good horses. "I will go soon to get my family." So his own black stud horse and one other from the Crow horse herd was given him.

Tall Elk said, "Moon Boy ask twenty-five braves and twenty wolves to go with you, also eagles go with Fast Fox to get his family. Take two robes each; it may get cold. Take bags to bring back the yellow gravel. Also take your good war gear, many arrows and some lances."

Moon Boy called the pack. "Curly, get Cubby and twenty wolves to go help get Fast Fox's family and Shadow's too. We go as soon as all are ready. At full light, twenty-seven Sioux and twenty-two wolves with four eagles up high were ten miles gone into Crow land, moving at a rolling lope. Golden Star was running up front with Curly on the right and Cubby on the left, moving at a gait that all others tried to match, but none could. They ran, heads low, missing nothing. The eagles scattered out, able to see everything when the sun was tall. Moon Boy slowed the big stallion down to blow, and at a seep the horses got some water. The grass was good and they grazed a little. The wolves pulled down a buffalo calf too small to winter well and the braves ate dry meat. The eagles sat down and ate meat with Curly. As soon as most of the horses had made water and left horse apples, the party of Sioux continued on. At dusk, all were in night camp in a grassy meadow; fresh hump ribs cooked over the open fire gave off an aroma that made hungry braves eat like they just discovered food.

An hour before first light, an eagle screamed and three wolves snarled. The men were putting gear on horses and getting bows strung. Curly said, "Hurry! Fast old boar grizzly is almost here, and he is faster then he looks. He wants a horse!" The wolves fanned out to slow the bear. When the horses caught the bears scent they were frantic, bucking and running into each other. It was still too dark to see wolves slashing at the bear's back, flanks and hump. He turned on them and was slashed in new places; he was hungry and now he was mad. Eagle dove at his head and cut a long groove above his left eye; blood got in his eye and spoiled his sight. Now an arrow was in his throat, then two more cutting off his wind, and now a long hard something pierced his side. The bear grew tired. A nap, oh yes, a good nap sounded good. So he lay down and slept, never to awaken. When it was over two braves were bucked down, one with a cut on his side, the other a banged head. One young wolf was dead; her neck broken by the bear's paw. The bear would have to sleep without his fur coat, but what could he expect? He messed with the bull and got the horn, it happens almost every time.

Light was coming from the east; you could see in the little meadow and soon it would be light enough to work. Old Grizzly Bear would be skinned and the hide tanned. His claws and teeth would be saved for a necklace, and the meat would be left for whatever eater came along; maybe the pack would eat some of the carcass. Curly was sad because the little she wolf was one of his, not old enough to fight Grizzly bear but had done her part well. Life is short, shorter for some than others, and the best thing to do with death is run and leave it behind. Fast Fox and Moon Boy fixed a place in a tree and put little she wolf in it, mounted their horses and rode south by a little west deeper in to the land of the Crow; the sun had now begun.

Old Grizzly Bear's fur coat was taken from him, even his head fur, then he was scraped and his brains were mixed with wood ash and put on the hide. It is said that every animal has just enough brains to tan his own hide. At night camp, the hide would be reopened and scraped again then pegged out to dry overnight, and by then it should be tanned good enough to be finished by the women when they got back. Maybe Fast Fox's women could do it.

The early light was cool and fresh. The horses moved out well. Golden Star danced sideways for a mile or so wanting to run; he did not like what they left behind at night camp. Horses hated the smell of bear and he could still smell bear, and the bear's hide was on one of the horses. The stallion knew it could not harm him, but it was there. Curly ran on his right and Cubby ran on his left one of them every once in a while reminded the stallion to run well and not hurt Moon Boy or else. He knew what else meant to and was careful not to misstep or step in a badger hole every one loved his rider, him too and his mother had not raised any dumb colts.

Sun had passed mid point when Moon Boy pulled the big stud down to a fast trot, a pace they could all hold until moonrise, and asked Eagle if she saw water and game. "Yes, over that ridge to your right is a good spring with buffalo and elk watering at it."

"Good! We eat elk then," he said to the two wolves. "Go one on each side and bring the elk to us. We will be on this side of the ridge, on either side of that gap kill two young bulls if you can," he told the braves. "If anyone needs a big rack of horns, kill one old bull too." They strung their bows as seven or eight elk came trotting over the crest of the hill looking back at the wolves. They let them pass then shot arrows at the heart, just behind the front leg. Three were down: one old bull, one young bull, and one cow. The rest ran down the draw and were gone. The braves bled them and retrieved the arrows from the carcasses, then drug them to the water. The rest of them made fire, so it was done. Moon Boy thought of Skunk, how he ate elk, but they had no cooking pot. Sticks were driven in the ground on all four sides, and hard sticks placed across on the forked sticks to form meat holders.

The elk were skinned and the skins pegged out, for scraped elk skin was in demand for the making of leggings and other garments. The leather was soft and yet was strong as well as warm, and the meat was good. Round steaks were soon sizzling, crackling over the fire. It was hung as they were. They needed to be turned often, and they had ten fires lighted so it was a full time job for somebody. Sage was rubbed on the meat for more flavor as well as other herbs. Eagles had liver and the wolves had the rest as well as other parts they liked so no one went hungry. Bear skin was opened up pegged out and scraped again, someone was going to have a warm sleeping robe, but as of yet no one had claimed it, or the claws.

Moon Boy asked Fast Fox "how far are we from your camp?"

Fast Fox considered the question, "maybe one sun or a little more I am not sure. It is in the foothills on a fast stream with much tall timber with shorter trees by the water. In the stream there are fish the color of the rainbow that are good to eat, we put much moss on them and roast them in the coals of the fire, I will cook some for you."

Moon Boy said, "We will rest until moon up. Then ride at night because we are close to the Fast Fox camp. We don't need any more of old bear at first light or the horses either; I want to see him first." So they got their robes and rested, then at moon up they were gone.

It was cool, but they had their robes; the horses wanted to run so they did. Around sun up they saw a stream with timber and a smudge of smoke coming up out the lower trees. The Crow lodges were in sight, many of them - a large camp. Fast Fox stopped at a big lodge, with a small fox red in color painted all over it. They had arrived at the Crow lodge of Fast Fox.

The arrival of the Sioux, sitting on splendid horses ringed by twenty-one wolves and six eagles, high and low, some gliding in to perch on tree branch made quite a sight. Soon the crow people were looking with astonishment at the sight. Fast Fox held up his hand and said, "Ho! I am Fast Fox, of this camp of Crow, and I rode with Black Thunder our war chief, to fight Tall Elks Sioux. Now I have come back, the war is over and we lost, but Tall Elk gave us our lives back and killed no one. He could have killed us all, but he said I am tired of killing you now we will be friends and fight no more forever. In the spring he will give us seeds to plant so we can eat well, when snows come. We will send twenty of our best mares to be covered by their best stallions. One of them is Golden Star now ridden by Moon Boy, Tall Elks sun."

"You also see part of the wolf pack and eagles too they guard the Sioux night and light; no war party can ever surprise them. Moon Boy speaks to them as I can speak to you. Moon Boy doesn't see well, so when he rides, Curly is on his right and Cubby is on his left, others out front some in back. He sees with their eyes and hears with their ears. He does something no body has ever done, he sees all at the same time. Eagles too tell him what is coming and what is behind and on two sides, and they speak from the sky high up and he hears them. Tall Elk knew of our coming before we started and all they ask is some bags of our yellow gravel, for one of them would make some charms out of it."

When they go back, I, Fast Fox, and my lodges go with them, for we will be Sioux Crow as is Buffalo Tongue, Stands Tall, Runs Fast, Horse Dung and Drinks Plenty Snakes Tail was killed fighting Crow, and he was Crow. While they are here they are our guests, and will be treated as guests; see that you hear my words or you will answer to me, Fast Fox. I have spoken. Now some of you go catch fish with the rainbow color on them. Others go wash out yellow gravel and big lumps too. Put them in bags to go back with them. Moon Boy will be in my lodge, and the pack get food for eagles and the pack likes their meat not cooked. Some of you show where to put horses on grass. Go now, do as I say".

A tall young woman stood by Fast Fox. 'This is Morning Light, my wife." A girl came to stand by her mother, "and this is Plum Leaf my daughter." The girl smiled at Moon Boy, and offered her hand. All could see the lightning that passed between them. Fast Fox said, "I see we will cut lodge poles soon for a new lodge".

"Ho!" all said. "We will do it!" Soon several large rainbow trout were brought to the fire all ready for the coals wrapped in moss. The inwards were given to Curly and the pack along with lesser fish too. Eagles got some also. All the Sioux braves were now in a guest lodge and the horses were put out to grass and two eagles were flying to Tall Elks camp to tell the news of Moon Boys needing lodge poles soon. Maybe it's too fast. We sometimes waste much time, on things that are clear. Why not? They would have Tall Elk, Fast Fox, the mothers near by and Skunk and Rose Bud too along with many others to help if help was needed.

Chapter 4

There was one that was in the shadows who did not approve. Weasel Tongue saw his dreams of Plum Leaf being his some sun wife falling down around him, like old ashes from a cold fire. He put an arrow to his string and glared at Moon Boy. He was not aware of three wolves standing not two feet from him when he brought the bow up. Curly had his right wrist and Cubby his left. Snap, snap two bones broke. He was taken to the fire by Curly and Cubby while Shadow brought the bow and arrow and dropped them by Fast Fox's feet. "Do we kill it?" asked Curly. "No, not yet, we will leave it to Fast Fox to decide."

Fast Fox picked up the boy's bow and put it on the fire, arrow too. "Weasel Tongue, did you not hear my words? I said they were our guests and would be treated with honor. Why did you try to kill Moon Boy?"

Weasel Tongue looked at Plum Leaf and said, "I would have asked her to my lodge some sun."

"And I, Fast Fox, would have said no. No cowards will be in my family ever." By now the bow was ashes and a tall brave came to stand by Fast Fox.

"I, Tall Pine, am sorry to say I am his father, but I will take him, and heal him then send him away. I to will have no coward to shame our family." Tall Pine said, "You, Weasel Tongue, will have your own brush shelter - you are not welcome in my lodge and you have disgraced me and your family in front of important guests in our camp. You did this for a girl who can't stand to look at you?" The father then hit him to the ground, "Now lie there so I can make a shelter then someone will splint your arms. I don't know why. You are dead now; you just don't know it. YOU WILL GET WELL AND TRY TO KILL Moon Boy, and then the wolves will kill you; it would be better if you die now. I would kill you now but that would make me as bad as you, so you will have to wait, but in the end it will be the same." Old Bear came and set the bones tied them in place and never said a word. He put a peace of jerky in Weasel Tongue's mouth and walked away. Weasel Tongue wiggled into the shelter, found an old robe got under it, and was sorry but that don't feed the bull dog, you have to answer for what you do both then and now. Then there was no judge and no jails, but punishment was ever bit as harsh or more than now and longer lasting. Here in his camp where he grew up no one would look at him. No one would talk to him or help in any way. He thought of his little black and white mare: she had foaled and he knew he had got milk from her in the past as a joke, but now that he needed to would she let him? He would see.

Fast Fox served the rainbows on wooden platters. It was hot, flakey and so good, with herbs and plums cooked together. Morning Light had made a dish of cooked greens that Moon Boy had never heard of but he thought it the best ever. After the meal Fast Fox and Moon Boy went to set by the fire to talk. "What will happen to Weasel Tongue?"

"He will get well, find others of his kind and come hunting you. He will not rest until you, or he is dead."

Curly, Cubby, Shadow, and Ling Lang came to the fire and sat down, Fast Fox asked if they were hungry they licked lips and said yes. So the supper leftovers were brought out and to make a long story short, they licked the platters clean. On the light of the new sun Bald Eagle and one other eagle arrived, gliding in on wings so light that they sat down like a feather. Meat was given them, they told them the camp was happy and could not wait to see Plum Leaf, and even now lodge covers were being put together; it will be a large lodge for many guests, suitable for a sub chief.

Curly and Cubby found Fast Fox and Moon Boy. They told them Weasel Tongue was with the horse herd, trying to get milk from the mares. "He is very hungry and he has soil all over him. I think we should kill him."

"No." said Fast Fox, "Let him suffer more, but go get him - I would talk with him." Soon they had him and he was a sight: dirty was not the word for it; he was filthy and bruised from being kicked by the mares. Fast Fox said, "Here" and put a large piece of jerky in his mouth. Weasel Tongue ate it hungrily, his eyes asked for more so more was given. "Now go to the water and soak off your stink, then the wolves will bring you back here then we will see. Go now." Later Weasel Tongue was back, not so dirty and not as stinky but not good. Fast Fox gave him a buffalo robe with a hole for his head to go through. "Now hear me, go to Old Bear and he will feed you. When you can use your arms some, get your horse, and go west to other Crow camp. One of the eagles will watch if you come to our camp we will send wolves, you will be left as you fall, to rot in the sun. Now go, I don't want to see you more".

Yellow gravel diggers had found much, even some large pieces of hard lumps that must have gotten hot at some time in the long ago: five big bags full and it was heavy, all one horse could pack. Fast Fox's lodge was down and packed, all his horses were on ropes and two of his horses had the yellow gravel packed on them in buffalo robes. Five other lodges were in line, ready to start and when Moon Boy pointed and so they did. The lodges moved well over the tall grass, level ground a fast trot to a long lope, and when sun was at mid point, all stopped to water the horses. Tired horses were changed to new ones. Now they were moving again, at midway to sundown the drag horses were changed once more.

At sundown, two cow buffalo were drug in, fires were lighted, and soon meat was cooking. The women did the cooking. They were camped near a lake bed; the water was not as good as the rushing streams of the crow last camp, but usable as you might say it was wet. The horses liked it and went to feeding on short grass that grew in abundance, everywhere. Wood was in short supply so they used buffalo chips to cook with and some sage twigs - it did not smell as good as dry wood, but the fire was just as hot only the flames not as tall. Curly and Cubby would stand guard and the pack, changing off so all could sleep. This was land with many large prairie rattlesnakes, Moon Boy had to be guarded and Shadow was with him now, for the snake was known to be sneaky and liked to get near warm bodies. Then when the body moved, snake would strike, and for Moon Boy, that could not be.

First light found the camp moving, the land rolling but mostly flat with few rocks to slow them down. The short grass acted like a carpet and the lodge poles slid nicely over it. It was so open, no place to be caught out in if an early storm came up. Air was cool and no movement.

Moon Boy called Eagle and asked her how far to some wooded draw with shelter, wood, and water, after a time Eagle was back. "You will find such a place near sundown, if you push the horses hard." Soon they were in full flight and when the drag horses were laboring they were changed, and so they rushed all sun, stopping only to put new pull horses on the lodges. At mid-point to sundown they came to a long ash draw with wood and water, and just in time. Low clouds were riding a rising wind and mist was falling and getting cold. The six lodges were set up, something they would not have done normally on the move but now all would have a place to sleep out of the storm and in comfort. Good fires were lighted and three mule bucks became the night meal. Eagles and the pack ate the inwards and spare parts. The deer meat was cooked. Some of it cooked as deer stew to be eaten later. Fast Fox was scraping the deer hides and cutting off usable parts of the antlers for knife handles and decorations, as mule deer horns were not plentiful in the land of the Crow.

Morning Light was skilled in making food more palatable; she knew of plants that could be used or added to the cooking of wild meats that made an otherwise plain meal so good braves would fight to lick the container clean. Wild grapes mixed with wild onion and just a hint of sage was such an added ingredient. If mint could be found she added that too. Moon Boy had helped Fast Fox gather large rocks to ring the fireplace to make cooking easier for the women, and now he could not get enough of watching Plum Leaf glide gracefully around the fire helping her mother. Fast Fox observed this and smiled to himself remembering how he had done the same with his wife not so long passed. "Moon Boy do you know of a place where trees grow tall? We will need them soon, I think." Fast Fox said with a smile on his face.

Moon Boy jumped as if a bee had stung him, "yes, on the Grand River there is such a place where young cotton woods grew so thick so fast there was no room to send branches, so they went straight up. Many are in this place."

"Good, then you and I will go there and get some for your new lodge, yours, and Plum Leaf's. I, Fast Fox, have spoken."

Moon Boy leaped up and out the door, found Curly and Cubby, dropped to his knees, his arms around their necks and "I will take a wife - are you happy?"

"Yes, now we will have another baby to tend and look after; no rest for us poor wolves." They looked away with tongues in the corner of their mouths and grinned at each other well pleased.

There were changes coming too, that no one could stop any more than stop a rushing flood after a sudden heavy, downpour upstream. They would be in the form of goods the Sioux could not make but wanted: firewater, gunpowder, clothing made of cloth, sweets like candy, steel like traps, guns and the worst, money. Gold! It was on their packs even now. It would be a long time before it really got here. Moon Boy's great grand children would know of it and have to deal with it, but for now life was still life, and it was good in the Moreau River country on the high plains, where wind blew free and you lived the best you could and were happy with what you had.

Chapter 5

More wood was needed and heavy wood to build up the fires in the quickly set lodges. Wind was coming under flaps and it was colder; the men went out and tried to put soil or anything that was handy to stop the wind and it helped, and it was far better inside then outside. Horses were on good grass and had found shelter in the trees and would be fine- but snow was falling it came out of the dark sky and settled on everything, most of it melting as it landed making wet sleeping for all outside. Curly and the pack curled up by the lodges and found warmth coming from inside. They were still on guard and rested with one eye open so to speak. Old bear or big cat could be near and they did not want to let them get to close. At first light the snow had stopped but the wind had not quite so eagle had gone ahead. Soon she was back, "Snow is on the ground for maybe two or three miles on your march, then gone. Load up and go, the weather will be good the rest of this sun but will come again soon you should reach the Moreau River camp by when the sun falls off the world to the west by early dark."

They got loaded and were gone from night camp before one could take thirty lone breaths. They moved well with water skins full and wood to get fires going, soon the snow was gone and the land slid away under the horses' hooves in a long lope. Thunder rolled and dust spiraled up and miles slid by around twenty-five to thirty miles per hour. Most of the horses knew where they were going and pulled at the reins to go even faster. Fast Fox's son Blue Jay was up on a big pie bald roan stud. That was too much horse for him at five summers but he felt important and would not have got off for a bowl of his favorite food.

Now when they got to The Sioux Camp they had a full two hours of sun light left. So Fast Fox's lodge was set up the right way this time with many hands helping. A pile of wood was gathered so a fire was lighted in the new set lodge of Fast Fox. Plum Leaf was hugged and hugged again by Tall Elk, Sweat Grass, Doves Tail and Eagle Plume, and then it was Skunk's turn. Rose Bud was next along with Moon Boy's boy braves and all of the bands leaders and anyone else who could get an arm around her. By this time the other five lodges of new comers were in place, set up by the same group as set up the Fast Fox lodge. Then they were made known to all, "I am Straight Hand and this is my family."

"I am Two Pines and here I stand a Sioux brave."

"I am Bob Tail Horse. I can throw an ax very well and I can cook well."

Skunk said "Good. I will help you."

Curly groaned inwardly and muttered, "Now we are lost, between dodging flying axes; us wolves will look like fur balls with tails after eating all their culinary oversights." He sighed, "But someone has to do it."

Cubby laughed until tears came, "count me in - I will do my best".

Skunk said, "if you can do better then you help cook."

"Nope we learned to eat, never learned to cook." All grinned until their faces disappeared, you wolf boys are as bad as Skunk, and then laughter went around the entire gathering.

"I am Bent Arrow and I will do my best to be a good Sioux."

"I am Coyote," and he giggled and it sounded just like a Coyote and everyone could see how he got his name.

Moon Boy and Fast Fox banked up around the outside of the lodge to keep out the ever present wind, so it would be snug and warm inside or as much as possible. Tall Elk stood and raised his arms, "I, Tall Elk, welcome you all as new Sioux. May you never regret your choice to join us, and may we live our lives in good humor and may our bellies be full, and our wives fat." At this a cheer went around the gathering that could be heard far off that made the two coyotes calling to each other be still and wonder what the humans were up to.

Sand was found to be best for the banking of lodges, so a group of youth got robes and carried sand from the river to put around the new lodges, it looked like fun so older braves got involved and soon all the lodges were banked to over flowing. Why stop now, they were having so much fun, other older lodges needed some, so they got banked too. Then a drum was brought out and singing started, soon older women fixed good things to eat and by the time moon came up to spill its silvery light over all, a celebration was in full swing. No one really knew just how it got started but such a welcoming of new members had never happened before. Curly, not to be out done stood up on his hind legs skipped over to Plum Leaf his front paws extended, she got the idea and held the paws and they did something that resembled a two step around the fire two or three times.

"Sure," said Moon Boy laughing, "you are trying to steal her away from me. You do look good together though."

Skunk shook his head in amazement, "now I have seen every thing. Soon Curly will be wearing a head dress and holding council meetings, and Tall Elk will be asking advice."

Tall Elk softly said, "I do that now and our pack's advice has saved us many times."

All said "Ho."

When sun had brought light back to the home camp of Tall Elks band of Sioux, there was much activity. Horses were caught and made ready to ride to the Grand River, the purpose to cut lodge poles. Fast Fox and Moon Boy were going with most of his boy braves- Tall Elk, Looking Back Horse, Iron People, were some of the ones going. Taken Alive, Yellow Footed Dog, Skunk You Can Not See, Buffalo Tongue and One Skunk were going along with many more. Curly, Cubby, Shadow, and Pounce were going; Pounce was Sniff's son and had stayed with his uncles to train and to look after Moon Boy; he was eager to learn, quick and intelligent but all wolf. Pounce was very large; he weighed over one hundred and sixty pounds and resembled the late Ling Lang in color and in movement. He loped like the mule deer. He was fleet of foot, sure and quick, and he never missed a step when running and could run down a deer or even an antelope. Put it another way, if you were out in the dark, Pounce is one you would not want to meet if you wanted to be a grandfather. Not that he was all bad, but he was not that good either, but with Moon Boy he was kind and gentle. Most times you had to step over him, but hurt his boss and you had better be on a tall horse with a down hill start, and that would not help much.

Blue Jay, Fast Fox's five year old son wanted to go so they caught a small horse for him to ride. No good, he said the big pie bald roan stud was his horse, and he would ride him or walk. Fast Fox looked at him long a frown on his face, and told him to go get him then. The boy made a sound and the big stud came on the run, head up tail and main streaming back, then he slid to a stop and lowered his head the boy leaped up behind his ears. The roan's head was up and the boy sat on his back, just behind the mane; it was done faster then I can tell you. Fast Fox mouth was open, and he was not the only one. "Want your bridle?" Blue Jay smiled and said, "No he knows were to go - I tell him with my knees." Skunk went to the seed lodge and came back with a lesser bow and arrows, "a Crow bow taken from one not so lucky. Any Sioux who can mount that fast I want on my right." Blue Jay grinned so big all you could see was teeth.

Curly gave a nod and two young wolves were by Blue Jay, Moon Boy said "this is Fang and he will help you; he will be on your right. This is Sees All, he to will help you, and he will be on your left- I will teach you to talk to them, they will see what you can not see, they will hear things you can not, hear them well, for only truth will they tell you." The stallion and the wolves touched noses and the bond was complete. Three eagles made lazy turns in the blue, carefully watching all.

Tall Elk pointed north, and the Black Stallion with white forelegs exploded into motion that would have left a less experienced rider setting in midair, and in two bounds the ground was just a blur. Golden Star had him in one bound and took the lead, and the tall pie bald roan was a fraction slower but not by much. All could see the old king's blood ran in them all. Every move was calculated to speed, and thunder rolled out from under the twelve hooves, already a half mile down range. Other horses were fast too but could never stay up with the three that were nearly out of sight. Tall Elk signed to slow the studs down so the rest could catch up. Golden Star was just warming up and wanted to run, but the tall pie bald roan had spent himself and was glad to blow; the black had plenty of bottom left but slowed anyway.

Skunk came up on his paint stud and just shook his head. "That horse of yours is too fast for his own good - he would fly if he had wings. I told you he would be faster than the old king and he is. NOW HOLD HIM IN or you will have all the lodge poles cut as the rest of us are just seeing the Grand River breaks." Iron People said "my old butt would be flat if we go any faster, then I would fart sideways." "I Looking Back Horse, said that would be good then he could smell himself more, and give me better air," and all smiled. Pounce snarled then Cubby made his horrible growl the rest of the pack was there all fanned out. In the wolves' path there stood Lord Grizzly, old silver tip. Old bear looked one way then the other getting their scent.

His eyes were weak but his nose was sharp: wolves, braves and horses and a lot of stallions, he had been kicked when he was young by a wild stud, and he had hurt all summer. Old bear uttered a long, low growl that made your stomach tighten up and your eyes open wide. Twenty-eight pack members all at the same time returned the challenge, then so many humans. He had felt the sharp flying sticks before too. He was brave but not stupid so he turned to go, but at his leisure. Too late, for twenty some arrows slammed into him broadside, any three would have killed him: two in his heart, four in his neck, one in his wind and one in his main blood line. Sun disappeared, and it was dark. He was tired so he fell over and went to sleep for a very long time.

Skunk prodded bear, no movement, but they waited longer. "I think he has crossed over. Pull the arrows." Some were easy; others had sunk up to the feathers and a few had buried themselves past the feathers. "Turn him on his back." Four braves started skinning, first up the legs then up the middle up the neck, then over the head and then they just rolled him out of his hide. He was scraped and pegged his brains were mixed with wood ashes while they got his claws and teeth loose. "Get your arrows" said Skunk, and they did, all were found but the two Tall Elk shot, and later they were found inside the bear going almost though his body - what a bow! Skunk got a bag and carved off bear fat to be rendered later good for cuts, rashes, burns, and also pains in the joints. The hide was wrapped up and tied on a horse then on to the stand of tall cottonwood trees to cut lodge poles.

Sixteen poles twelve foot long and two poles fourteen feet long were cut to be used for smoke poles. Eighteen poles were cut to size and trimmed by twenty braves, then peeled, put on piles and lashed together ready for moving. Skunk was in an ash and oak grove - he just could not stay out of them, and he found some bow wood of oak and ash so he took them. His helpers stacked them up; the cutters got lodge poles for others too, not just for Moon Boy so they had quite a pile. Camp was an open spot - no one had forgotten old silver tip and maybe there were more of his kind nearby. All hoped no; one was too many and they had been lucky. Lord Grizzly was by far the most dangerous meat eater on the plains and he was bad tempered and unpredictable. He may just walk away or come at you with blinding speed, and it is said his teeth hurt him most of the time, which would account for his quick rage. Upon encountering him, you just left him alone and gave him the path, every time.

Camp was set up, fires were lighted and a cow buffalo brought in, and as an afterthought Skunk You Can Not See killed a spike bull elk with One Skunk in mind - all knew he preferred elk to anything. They were skinned and the hides pegged out, along with old silver tip. All agreed that Moon Boy should get the bear skins for his new lodge that would be set beside Tall Elk's and Fast Fox's. Eagle was asked to look over the river bottom up and down to see if any bears were close to camp. "Not very close, but up river is a she-bear and a cub; they are feeding on a buffalo kill that is bad and very rotten, but they don't seem to mind. The wind is coming from the Northwest and she keeps testing it, as if she is expecting another bear to come and join her. I can't see any. I think you are safe but I will check on them."

Shadow and Pounce were with Moon Boy. Fang and Sees All were with Blue Jay. Grandfather rattlesnakes were many on the Grand River and they did not want them hurt by the poison old snake liked to give so freely. Curly and Cubby each took half the pack and made a swing around the camp, because Grizzly Bears made them nervous when too close, and they were too hard to stop quickly. Curly and Cubby and the rest of the pack got back from their scout to find the meat cooking and their shares in piles ready to eat: liver, lung, and kidney along with any other parts of the innards they wanted so all was at peace in night camp on the Grand River.

Fires were built up, and were placed so fire light flickered everywhere, holding the darkness back and unwanted prowlers too. Fire was of the humans, who most of the wild brothers either hated or feared, for they had little flying twigs that came from nowhere and went in and hurt, and then you were sick. The wild ones knew nothing of being sick except you were fine then a twig hit and the darkness came in the middle of a full sun, and shortly you were no more. The buffalo were so strong and big. They did not care of flying twigs and then they were dead. They still were not afraid. Pounce was nervous and he came wide awake out of a deep sleep, and tested the air, too much smoke and camp smell, so he tuned his ears to many camp sounds. He went to Shadow and spoke. "Come with me and get one more, something is out of the ordinary - we must see." They slid out of camp staying low going from dark place to dark spot looking, smelling and hearing nothing, they turned east, staying just under the crest of the south breaks then crossed the river. Pounce went in cover on the north side, every sense tuned. Shadow slid up by him and motioned for him to come. "Look at what Drupe Ear found!"

In a wide sandy wash was a snug camp with three forms in robes sleeping. "Shadow, go get the braves, the pack and we will see." At first light the forms were stirring and what they saw was anything but reassuring. They were looking at twenty-six Sioux with bows at half cock and twenty-four wolves with three eagles setting down. "I am Tall Elk chief of the Sioux and if you move at all you will die. You are caught." This he said with sign talk, "now put your weapons on the ground. Don't hold back anything or you die." Two bows and arrows were put on the ground but the knives were not flint or the ax either. They were of the hard shiny material. They found these with the old one. The third one was different from the others; when he got up the Sioux almost fell off their horses. He was tall, thin and he had hair on his face. His eyes were as blue as the sky on a clear sun; he started to take out the two axes from his belt and one of the others made a sign. He put them on the ground. Then took out two knives, a pouch from around his neck then he took out a horn tied with leather strings and last from out of his robe came a long, round something of the silver blue color. All of them got off their horses, stricken with curiosity and murmuring among themselves in amazement.

Now Tall Elk said "Tie them hard," and it was done. When they were tying the strange one, they got another shock. His skin was white, not as white as snow but white! One Skunk was running his hands over his garments, found a leather bag, and in was the round gold pieces with faces on them and he showed them to Tall Elk. "I told you some sun they would come again. I told you. Now what do we do?" Tall Elk said in sign, "Who are you, and from where do you come?" One made the sign to untie him, so his hands were freed.

"We two are Cheyenne from the south many suns; the other with hair on face comes from the east and north forty suns or more by the Great Lakes. He wants to build a place to trade somewhere on the plains." said one of the Cheyenne braves.

"What will he trade?" Tall Elk asked.

"Furs, he would give very much for that wolf by you." was answered back. In an instant, Tall Elk hit him in the mouth hard then spoke, "That wolf can talk to us; he is the one who found you in your sleep. He is better than you many times. Pounce, get me that stick, the little one with a fork at one end." It was done. Shock showed on the white man's face, "You would ask me to sell him to you? Cubby, show him what you think."

The wolf walked over to the Cheyenne, looked long at him and made that terribly fearsome sound then cut his face twice. "If you kill just one of them many of you will die for a long time."

"Now tell my words to the hair-faced one, and tell true or you will get what he gets. We will tie him over a very slow fire this one, until his brains cook and his eyes pop out of his head, and then we will leave him so all can see what we do to people who kill us for our furs. Now tell him." The bearded man was told. The white man turned and more white; sweat formed on his face.

"Tell him I will pay more than it is worth; tell him damn you!" said the white man. The Cheyenne speaker softly said, "They know nothing of money- you waste your time."

Tall Elk said, "Get his goods we will look." They got the bags and opened them.

Skunk said, "I will be in charge of this." Such an array of good came to light as never had been seen before: bags of little beads - every color they knew of and many more, long needles and little string to put the beads on with and looking glass to see themselves with. There were buttons and ribbons and a tool to cut the string. Skunk closed this bag and opened another. Knives! And small axes all of the hard shiny material filled the bags to the top. "We will look when we have more time."

"Who is chief here?" Tall Elk said with authority.

The Cheyenne looked at the strange one. Skunk spoke in sign, "why are you two here?"

"To help him talk to you; do you know our tongue?"

Skunk probed, "No, just the sign and Crow?"

"Let me hear it." Crow was spoken, "yes I know that one; Buffalo Tongue will talk - he was a Crow but now he is Sioux."

"How many of his kind?" Buffalo Tongue asked.

"Many; but not here - all the way east where the sun rises beyond plains and further beyond the forests, by a great water."

"Will more come?"

"Yes, maybe but not soon."

"If we let you and other Cheyenne live where will you go?"

"We will go back to our people far south."

"Then get your horses, but first do you know how that works?" Fast Fox pointed to the gun.

"Yes, but it takes much time and makes much sound do it." Cheyenne brave said. So the old gun was loaded and the Cheyenne pointed at a nearby tree and pulled the trigger. A sharp thunder stung the ears of all in the party, and all jumped in their skin a little. As the breeze carried the smoky haze away, the braves crowded around the tree in amazement. All looked at the fresh hole in the tree. What magic this was!

Calmly, Fast Fox asked, "What makes it thunder?"

"Gun powder." Replied the Cheyenne carefully.

"How do they make it?"

"I don't know."

"Can he get more?" Fast Fox was always thinking.

"Yes but not here."

"Has he more in his pack?"

"Some, I think."

"Look!"

So the Cheyenne began digging quickly and nervously through the leather bags. Two more horns of powder were there, and Tall Elk, who had been watching everything intently, asked, "Is there more to know?"

"This is the flint - turn it in about sixty booms. Here is the shot in the bag, one to a boom." The Cheyenne took out heavy bars of gray something, and explained in Crow, "This what the shot is made from; this is a mold, you need to put this pot in your fire to get it hot, then pour the melted metal in the mold, and when cool take the balls out and put them in the shot bag. When you are out of the bars, go back to arrows. Use it only when you have to, one more thing - hear me well: put powder down this hole, now drop one ball then take this rod and tamp it in place. Put this patch and tamp it; now put a little power in this part called a flash pan. Now look down the barrel at what you want to kill, then pull this trigger and a little fire will make it boom."

"I don't know why you want it - you could shoot ten arrows in the time it takes to get this ready to shoot again," snorted Skunk, "while your enemies come running closer to kill you."

Tall Elk turned away from the Cheyenne and stared with a hard look and the white man. "Tell the hair face why he is to die; tell him we would all be dead many times over had we not been warned by the wolves. Tell him we speak freely to them as brothers every sun and he wants us to sell them for money so you can kill them for the furs? I tell you white one; you will never be the reason for another wolf or anything to die again for his fur. You are as evil as big cat, and when you get this money what will you do with it? Will you eat it? Burn it to keep warm? Or bury it in the ground, so you can forget where you put it. What of the family - will you give them food? No, you would not - you would try to kill all. Take away all he is wearing. We free the Cheyenne so they can go south."

"We will go," the Cheyenne pause, "but first let us see you kill him."

"Why are you so bloody in your mind?" asked Skunk. "You helped him and now you want him dead; I want to know why."

"He is bad. We feared him so we helped him in fear of our lives"

Moon Boy said, "Pounce come to help me. He shall say how he dies, this white one. Pounce, how shall it be?"

Pounce growled low and eyed the bearded man, "Give him to the pack. We will do it; then we will know it is done right."

The wolves immediately began circling the white man, slowly at first, then gaining in speed. Instinctively, the man knew he was about to die. "No! Not that! I have not been that bad! I will quit furs! I did not know wolves could know so much!"

"Come, pack," said Pounce, "let us kill him." The whirling wolves began to speed up. At first, the wolves were out of reach, then faster and closer. The hair-faced one turned with them. "Stop!" He screamed. "Let me talk to you- I thought all animals were stupid, and were just put on earth to eat, to make money on and for man's entertainment. I did not know, or realize that wolves, horses, and eagles helped man out of love and had brains to think with and feelings to guide them. I am young as white men go and have much money. I could bring much food for you, build you houses."

"Stop!" Pounce shouted. "We don't want food dried in bags! We have the great herds to feed us and we take only the old and weak that keeps the herd strong. What you mean is you would come again, with many of your kind and many thunder sticks that say boom and kill five times as far as Skunk's best bow can send an arrow." Curly said, "Let me speak. Pounce has mostly said it all; you still wanted more. You killed all the beaver, all the mink and the otter all the animals of the streams so great gullies formed and washed away the land." Cubby asked to talk.

"I saw you from far off killing all the buffalo in a great herd, in my dream vision just for the skins. You put all of their hides in piles to rot, because you had no way to move them. I saw the buffalo dead - so many no one could eat them all no matter how many wolves came. I saw you bring many of your kind to live on our prairie and they had nothing to do so they tore up the long grass and planted plants that could not grow. So the wind blew them away and the people too. Great clouds of dust covered everything. Then in my dream I saw you standing there laughing with your hands full of money you made from the suffering of the land and all that walks upon it. Now how much more bad can one white one be?"

The hair-faced white one looked all around, he said "I see you have up your minds- so I will tell you all, red men and wolves of my vision, my kind will come again, many of them and trading posts will be built, I don't know when but it is coming." Pounce said, "You speak with forked tongue I think. Come wolves, we have a dirty job to do." And so they killed him. The wolves dug a very deep hole, covered it and patted the dirt down. They didn't want to see him more and it was done.

Two Cheyenne braves looked on in disbelief at what took place and said, "Now we are free of him - he would have killed us."

"Why did you not just leave him," asked Skunk.

"We wanted the gun, but he was very good with it and the throwing axes are well-balanced. He could hit anything with them." said one of the Cheyenne braves. Tall Elk walked over and picked them up; they were perfectly balanced and sharp. "I will take the axes," he said. Moon Boy got a long shinny knife.

Skunk said, "I will keep the thunder stick. I know somewhat how it works."

"Remember to keep the powder dry or it will not work and the gun too, or it will get red flakes called rust. When you get back, rub bear on it that will help keep the rust off, bear grease I mean." said the Cheyenne. Skunk turned to the captives, "Where are your horses? And packs?"

"We have them up in the brush."

"Go get them." Tall Elk said.

The Cheyenne moved quickly, glad to still be alive.

"What do they call you?" The first Cheyenne said, "I am Antelope, and He is Lone Bear."

"Get your bows and quivers - I would like to look at one of your arrows." He looked then passed it to Skunk.

Skunk looked; the points were different, but about the same as theirs. "Do your bows send the arrow far?"

"Yes, but I think yours are better."

"Put the packs on horses - we need to go. Come with us to our camp and you may stay a little if you like." Blue Jay mounted the pie bald roan and the two Cheyenne smiled. No one looked back at the dry wash and no one was sorry. In suns to come they would be, but Tall Elk and his Sioux could not and neither can I; no one knows the future, we do what seems best and live as good as we can.

Chapter 6

They were late in starting, but what had happened at first light had an effect that would reshape their entire world as they knew it, a turning point, if you will, one that could not be retraced. For on the horizon, that sun had appeared a new kind of human being who not only looked different, but was different in every way. Tall Elk's wealth was fine horses, a seed lodge full of food, a wolf pack, eagles and a band of people who loved and respected him and each other. The blue eyed hair faced white one wanted wealth also. Quick wealth: furs, gold and land but mostly gold to be put in a bank and drawn on for more riches all his time could afford. He made one more mistake, his biggest, for he was harsh toward the ones that helped him. They feared him, and when he later needed them, they gave him no help. "Do unto others as you would have them do unto you" was around then for it is a quote from the Bible, but it was not a part of his vocabulary and he suffered because of it.

Lodge poles were lashed five to load, and looped around the horse's shoulders with ropes short enough so the front ends carried. They didn't like it very well but after some time got used to the bumping and lined out for the Moreau River camp. Once they got on the flat lands they made better time, the poles were not heavy but were bulky and dusty.

Tall Elk and Moon Boy dropped back to watch the lodge poles slide by, looking at the ropes around the horses to see if rubbing had not caused discomfort. Everything looked fine, so Tall Elk waved them up in speed to a long lope. Golden Star wanted to run so Moon Boy let him go for a short time. As he came up by Antelope and Long Bear, who were talking to Buffalo Tongue, Antelope said, "I believe that is the best stallion I have ever seen - he is smooth gaited and no jar at all."

Curly looked up and smiled "Cubby and I have taught him all we know." Golden Star looked down and snorted, "Then why am I so dumb yet?" Cubby said, "Maybe you are a slow learner?" Curly gave a short yip and Pounce was running by his side. "Ask Skunk to drop back," and soon Skunk was running near. "Skunk!" Curly said, "Could you fix a looking glass to put on a stick around Cubby's neck so he can see himself run?"

"Yes, but why?" said skunk.

"He will watch so well that he will stumble over a grasshopper dropping then we can all laugh to see him fall." All thought it funny but Cubby, who after a long stride or two smiled too. The grave in the wash on the Grand River was forgotten, left behind like the vanishing dust from the horses' hooves.

"Antelope are you and Long Bear staying a little?" asked Skunk.

"Yes, for a small time."

"Good. I want you to show me how the thunder stick works some more."

"Thunder sticks in themselves mean nothing, but the ones that will bring them are anything like one the pack killed will mean much pain to all our people on the plains. They have things we will want and we will not be able to make so we will trade, and when we have nothing to trade, we will still want more. Then we will work for them, like Lone Bear and I did, but they will give us very little for what we do. We got a shiny knife and an ax for helping them for more than a season, and we could not leave or he would have killed us."

Sun was past midpoint to sun down and the lodge pole cutters still moved south in rapid movement or as fast as the horses could travel. All were in a hurry to get to home camp for one reason or another. Skunk wanted to get in his lodge and with the new bags, the gun, and the five bags of gold. He had done nothing with any of the white man's things yet and would sort out all he knew of the past suns and try to make sense out of it. He knew killing the white one was wrong. He should have been questioned more, made to talk. Now he was gone; too late to worry about that but he had wanted to kill Pounce, Curly, Cubby, and Shadow for their fur. Now Skunk knew what the round gold was, it was money and the wolf's fur was money, and he would much rather have the good humor and the companionship of the wolves than money to cling and clang in a bag. Anyone who said they preferred the gold would be crazy and Skunk would have nothing more to do with them.

They were turning down the long ridges up above mule deer draw and the horses knew that they would be munching sweet grass soon and picked up the tempo themselves, soon they were in front of Tall Elks lodge.

Skunk motioned to June Bug to come help him unload, and told him to get two more so he did. Skunk took the gun and the boys carried the packs and the bow wood. "June Bug, go get me some firewood then rub down the stud and turn him to grass- I need to think." Skunk covered the five bags of gold and leaned on them, wondering what their value would be in the white man's world. He thought of the pot to melt the gray bars for the thunder sticks, and wondered if it would not work. He would try melting the yellow gravel.

Light had returned to the Sioux camp on the Moreau River. Everyone knew something of the lodge cutting adventure on the Grand River, and they were waiting to know all as it would touch all of their lives in suns to come. Tall Elk called the camp crier, "Tell all the camp to come to my lodge - I have news to tell." A short time later most of the camp was on hand to hear the news of the trip, wolves too. Pounce, Shadow and Drupe Ear, were uneasy because they felt strangers were near so they slipped out of camp and found them in a dry wash east of the camp. "Two Cheyenne from far south are now with us: Antelope and Long Bear. The other a stranger from forty suns east and some north by the Great Lakes; he was bad: he held the two Cheyenne as his slaves. His eyes were as blue as the sky in mid summer, and he had hair on his face, and his skin was white. He wanted to build a trading post where he would trade furs of ours, for things he had. He wanted to kill Pounce, Shadow, Curly, and Cubby because he liked their furs. He wanted to trade for the furs. We told him they were our brothers and they saved the camp many times from our enemies. He did not believe so the pack killed him and put him deep in the ground."

"He had many things with him that now belong to us. He had this," and Skunk held up the gun. "This is a thunder stick. It can kill far off; five times as Skunk's best bow can send an arrow. Antelope show them." A log was put far off by a bank of dirt. Antelope loaded and fired. Boom! A cloud of smoke billowed up and everyone jumped. Two boys ran to the log and all could see the round hole. In one side and out the other, at least five or six times the distance of a bow shot of the best bow. A boy went to the place were the log was and picked up a flat gray something and brought it to Skunk; it was the lead ball that had made the hole. "Good." he said, "I will remold it and it can fly again." Sweet Grass asked if there was more to see. "Yes, there is much more but not for war. The reflecting things could catch the sunlight and send a signal back but eagles do that." Skunk showed her one, "Now look at it and you will see yourself," She did and dropped it with a startled sound. "Do I look like that?"

"Yes, very pretty," smiled Skunk. She gave it to Doves Tail who looked at it and said, "oh my!" Then she pushed back a lock of hair or two, and then showed Eagle Plume who strutted, around looked at his father and said, "Moon Boy was part of a war party at six. When do I get a horse to ride? Can you talk to wolves?"

"Yes. Golden light has a gold and white filly, just two seasons old; she is very alert, intelligent, and very fast. You will learn to ride quick or be on the ground a lot. Curly, will you have two of the pack be assigned to Eagle Plume to protect him and guide him as he rides?"

"I will ask my son Sly and Cubby's son Little Bit who is small but strong and wise."

Tall Elk asked Blue Jay to call the big pie bald stud, and as soon as they could hear the thunder of hooves, the stud was there, and Blue Jay was on his back. Tall Elk put Eagle Plume up behind Blue Jay, and gave him a rawhide rope, and told them to get Eagle Plume's horse, and then come back.

They found the filly and she was glad to see them, but was not sure about the wolves until the wolves informed her that they were there to help the boys and her too. They told her there were many things to see. At a full gallop, they would see problems that could arise and then tell her and Eagle Plume. They must hear all at one time then act, because they would always tell truth. Sly asked the filly how she felt about old grandfather rattlesnake and told her it was late in the year now but he could be out yet. "If we see him in time we will tell you. Most of the time he will say if you are too near, but if you spook, Eagle Plume may fall on him, and the snake is always ready to give his poison. The filly said, "Now that I know that I will not jump."

Eagle Plume spoke softly to the horse, "Lower your head and I will get on behind your ears, and then lift me up. I will set on your back." She did and he sat on her back. "Now let us go to see father." said Eagle Plume.

Tall Elk was there. "Your filly is beautiful. What did you name her?"

"She is Wind in My Ear."

Doves Tail came and patted her long neck then spoke earnestly to the horse, "Take good care of my son - he is young and restless."

Skunk gave Eagle Plume a bow with many arrows. "This is a bow by Skunk - it is the best. The arrows have meadowlark feather to guide them and they will sing as they fly so all will know them." Then Skunk gave Eagle Plume a belt knife made of flint. "This I made for you. Go and get meat for our evening meal and I will cook it, and then, Sioux brave, we will talk more." Skunk said.

Two young boys rode west by north to mule deer draw on two proud prancing horses; they felt as tall as two shadows on a full sun just before it falls off the world to the west. Four wolves looked for deer; it was Little Bit who found them grazing among the trees. Two arrows flew and two deer fell; they were cleaned and the wolves with one eagle ate what was left over. Blue Jay sat his tall stud on the downhill side. Eagle Plume handed him the hind legs and pushed the other pulled up went the deer. Now it was Eagle Plume's turn, and the wolves got the hind legs and Eagle Plum pulled. It was harder but the deer was on Wind's back. Now let us eat deer with Skunk. There were never two prouder boys than the two who sat their horses by Skunk's lodge, "Skunk! We have meat! Will you cook?" Three mothers and two sisters skinned the deer and helped Skunk get the meat in the pot. Two proud fathers and Skunk sat on robes and grinned as good smells filled the air.

Moon Boy joined the others and said, "I see my brother is now a brave of the Sioux. He has learned to put a deer on a filly with the help of our friends Sly and Little Bit and maybe Fang and Sees All too." First he talked to wolves as well Wind In Her Ear. "Very good! I, Moon Boy, am proud to be his brother. I have spoken." Others tasted the first kill of the boys too. Looking Back Horse said 'it was as good as deer killed by Moon Boy in his sixth summer'. The arrows were tipped with luck to fly so true Eagle Plume got an arrow out of his quiver and showed him arrows made by Skunk guided by meadowlark feathers that sing as they fly. All smiled to see the look of pleasure that crossed the face of Skunk to hear the words spoken. Kind words are as easy to say as harsh, but sound as nice as flowers smell on a soft wind. Buffalo Tongue and Bent Arrow had a little; Bent Arrow had been given an ax he and threw it at a log one sun so hard that it split the log open revealing an old arrow point driven in the wood when the tree was young. The wood had grown around it, hiding it. The point was different from any Stone Breaker had ever seen, so he studied it long and hard: it had wavy edges with a groove down its middle. He made some like it for Skunk to try, and when Skunk shot a buffalo the arrow went out of sight and caused so much inner damage the buffalo was dead almost at once.

At first light a group of braves helped Moon Boy select sixteen lodge poles and two longer smoke poles, they were lashed together stood up then holes were dug to put the ends in. Now the holes were packed and made tight, as you remember women had been working on the lodge cover since Eagle reported Plum Leaf and Moon Boys love for each other, the first half was laid out final adjustments were made then hoisted in place now it was tied in place. The second half was up it fit perfectly it was lashed. The smoke poles adjusted the door was put on, opening to the southeast. Moon Boy's braves got out the sand robes and banked the lodge. Tall Elk and Fast Fox got poles then tamped the sand, so no openings were left. Round rocks, all ready gathered were placed around the fire pit. Burning wood was gotten from Tall Elks fire and from Fast Fox fire to light the first fire in the new lodge of Moon Boy and Plum Leaf. Iron People and Taken Alive had made a back rest for Moon Boy it was covered with beaver skins and otter to make it soft. People also had cut cider bows to put under the buffalos robes. Then one bear skin was put over that. The other bear skin was over that to cover with, as an after thought other buffalo robes over that. The bringing together of the young people was simple and beautiful. Tall Elk and Fast Fox held a robe and draped it around them, then opened the lodge door let them enter then closed the door behind them, that was that. Curly and Cubby were on each side of the door on guard on skins, I would not have tried to borrow anything that night, would you? They had a way of doing things that makes sense to me. They just hung a light skin from the lodge poles so it touched the ground part way or all the way around the air behind stayed cooler to help keep meat longer and was some place to store things. Plum Leaf was fixing that, Moon Boy hung up his bows and quivers of arrows. He placed his lance put his axes where he could get them fast.

When Moon Boy opened the door flap water skins in hand, his boy braves took them and let us do that. Skunk and Rose Bud were coming with bundles of something too. Skunk said, "robes to set on for your guests. Rose Bud had pillows made from goose and duck feathers in light deer skins, decorated to look like roses. Plum Leaf was so happy she hugged and kissed Rose Bud many times, Skunk too. Eagle Plum was embarrassed with all the hugging and kissing everyone was doing; he threw a rock at a passing gopher the rock missed and took a bad bound, hitting Stone Breaker in his left foot. Stone Breaker picked it up, looked at it got his tools and went to work on it; he was one never to miss an opportunity. Tall Elk seeing the entire happening, he walked over to the old brave "what are you doing with that rock?"

"I don't know, but it came from nowhere and hit my foot. I was thinking maybe someone wanted me to make a throwing rock out of it." Tall Elk smiled then said, "I know you will do well - you are over halfway done now."

Antelope and Long Bear the Cheyenne braves were showing signs of wanting to go south to their homelands. Antelope told Skunk, "let us go hunt buffalo with the thunder stick so we know you can load it, kill with it and reload it again. Also you must keep it and the powder dry or it will not work. We know nothing of how they make the powder. The white one never told us, and you can't go get more because you don't know who to ask or where to go."

Twenty or so braves were needed to go get meat, and so Skunk organized the hunt for first light. Moon Boy, Tall Elk, Fast Fox, Looking Back Horse, Buffalo Tongue, Horse Dung, Iron People, Fast

Horse, Skunk You Can Not See, the two Cheyenne, most of the boy braves, Yellow Footed Dog, Spotted Owl, June Bug, Circle Eagle, the two small boys and the wolves assembled themselves for the hunt. Bald Eagle had found a large herd moving south by mule deer draw so it was certain where they would go in morning.

All the Sioux mentioned plus a few more were mounted with bow, ax, and knife with pack horses ready to hunt. Skunk handed the thunder stick to his son then mounted his paint stud, and retrieved the gun. His bow and quiver were tied on already and he had already decided that he would use the gun only for a few shots just to see how it worked and to make sure he could reload. He rode west, and the rest followed, the wolves fanned on two sides and in front six or seven eagles seeing all from high up. It was a fine late fall day with sun in the sky so blue you could see yourself in it; the air was warm but had a cool feeling at the same time, and the horizons shimmered with mirages that made shapes dance and leap. It was like a fine wine. They were past mule deer draw moving at a good pace - not fast, but not slow either. Eagle came in and said the buffalo were just ahead so the hunters got their bows strung, lances ready and fanned out. They were after dry cows and young bulls, and they would take no tough old bulls or wet cows.

Bow strings snapped and lances drove deep. The mighty buffalo seemed larger than usual and the herd was so large it spread out so far that the buffalo seemed not to see the danger. So the harvest continued. Most of the meat would be dried and stored, nothing would go to waste; nothing ever did. Skunk got on a hilltop, dismounted, loaded the thunder stick, and primed it. He looked down the barrel to where the front leg was fixed on an old bull, then raised it a little for windage and touched it off. Boom! The bull just slumped and fell. The distance was four times an arrow flight. Skunk thought to himself, "I think the evil to kill many people is now what I hold in my hands. If the whites come in great numbers with their thunder sticks, we will kill them quickly; there is no other way."

Skinning and bleeding had begun. The buffalo had just grazed on, leaving the dead to lie as they had fallen. No one could remember a larger herd; it was awesome. Meat was placed on skins, then loaded onto drags, and when it was all that could be hauled, the horses were put to one side, and when six were loaded they were returned to camp by a boy brought for that reason. It would be slow work but it was needed. No one minded too much; after all, it was food for everyone to eat. They were at last down to Skunk's old bull, so Fast Horse asked, "What do you want to do with him, Skunk?" Skunk answered, "I want his hide, his horns, his feet and what killed him."

Curley and Cubby groaned, "If I eat any more and had to run I would have to roll." Pounce and Shadow said, "I feel like a fur ball with a tail," Eagle said, "I don't think I can fly. Can I ride on your back Pounce?" "Why not I think I can do that, but don't spur me or I may faint." The she wolf lay on her side and laughed until tears came, "just look at you wolves! If a bunch of mice came by and wanted to fight they would win, and I am responsible for you all. Burp!" Then all laughed. "That's alright Grandma, I won't tell if you don't," Bald Eagle's son sailed in and sat by his mother, "I would say you ate too many grapes and drank too much water, mother. I wish I had drunk too much - I think I would be feeling better than I do now. Why did you stop, mother? I am sure you could have eaten two or three more if you had tried." Bald Eagle just looked at her son, "now you be nice or I will spank you at seven thousand feet," he grinned but said no more, for she could do it and do it well.

Chapter 7

Somehow they all made it back to camp. Bald Eagle caught an updraft, was airborne, and then she felt better so she went up around eight hundred feet and simply glided. The buffalo had never run but they were working south, for it was late in the year. Snow could come at any time then hunting would become more difficult. The buffalo would not all leave, but the biggest end of the herd would go. In camp, racks of meat were drying everywhere you looked; the cooking pots were bubbling and Skunk had a container in hand sampling this pot or that one. He said he was making sure it was all good, but all knew he was making sure he got enough to eat. Skunk was clever, but they saw though that one and just smiled at each other and winked.

When the sun was two hands up, the Cheyenne were gone. They had meat and Tall Elk gave them two stallions from the Crow plus the ones they had. Antelope said they would be back in the spring to hunt and maybe fish the big rainbows in Fast Fox's streams. Antelope thanked them again for saving their lives. The white one was like Eagle Claw - he only wanted to kill, the next ones maybe as bad, what then. They still would have to be killed but if they had good help, then some of them would die too and they would have thunder sticks. No need to worry now; it may be a long time before they got here and the furs they most prized were mink, otter, and beaver and they were few along the Moreau River.

Moon Boy could see that the smaller wood was getting harder to find around the lodges. So he asked his braves to get two horses, ropes, axes, some young women, and boys with lashings. They would pull some wood from nearby. He got four horses. Eagle Plume and Blue Jay wanted to come too; so they rode to a nearby draw and put wood together. They tied it and took it to the camp. By now others were unloading; the wood pile was growing by leaps and bounds. Moon Boy had piles of smaller wood tied so he just picked them up and ran the short distance to camp, by now others were doing the same. Curly and Cubby looked on, dumbfounded. "What is the boss doing?"

"Firewood," said Pounce, "food for the fire. We can help." Each found a good-sized limb balanced it and took it to Moon Boy's lodge. Now they were all there and firewood piled up as by magic. Plum Leaf came out to see what the commotion was about, then said, "I will help you stack it up and we will make a windbreak too." So she did.

Light was fading so Moon Boy held up his arms and said, "Enough. Turn the horses out to grass and let us stack it up so all can get at it." The ropes and axes were put away then they all helped stack wood. When Moon Boy looked at his lodge he almost dropped the arm load he was taking home. He had forgotten the pack was getting wood too, and there was Tall Elk, Fast Fox and Skunk stacking wood, and the pack still bringing in more! "Stop!" He said laughing. "Stop, we have enough for all snow time now." Then he hugged them all, "Thank you my brothers. Come in and set on robes I will build up the fire. I think we can spare the wood." Curly, Cubby, and Pounce sat by the door, and Pounce said, "The rest of the pack went to eat buffalo at the place we made meat. They will circle around to see what has been there - we think big cat may be near. If he is, we will know very soon because some of us can see well. We know where he likes to sleep. We will see his hair caught on tree bark; others will smell him and I know how he thinks. We left sign for him to read; we said no horse or else go eat rabbit. He knows what 'or else' means too, and so we will see."

Tall Elk, Fast Fox, and Skunk sat on robes around the fire. Curly, Cubby and Pounce had come in to but felt not quite comfortable, Moon Boy had wanted them to set by the fire, but they liked open air better. Curly got up and informed his friends presently, "I must go find a hill to answer the call of the wild." The other two said they would help, and they were out the door just that fast. Skunk spoke, "the thunder stick feels cold in my hands. It is not warm like my bow and I find no good feeling when it booms. Bull buffalo was dead. He never knew what hit him - he just crumpled then rolled over. I think I will not use it much because it makes too much sound. Also, I have looked at it long and can not make one piece of it. We don't have what it is made of and the little beads - we can't make them either, or the things that makes your face look back at you. Fast Fox what is your wisdom on this?"

"If they come again, we will stay away from them or be their friends during the day, but kill them when they sleep at night. Or one more thing we could do is to get behind them and put arrows in their backs as they look at the ones in front."

Tall Elk spoke, "We know of plants that grow in our lands that could help too. Put them on the arrows with the snake poison and the two together should kill them faster. Maybe we worry too much. It may be a long time before they come again so let us live as the Great Spirit meant for us to live: walk softly, smile a lot and carry a large war club. That means make little noise, be friendly, and if that don't work hit them between eyes hard." All smiled, Skunk laughed long, "Tall Elk my friend that was funny. I am glad you are finding some humor at last."

Sweet Grass and Dove's Tail brought good things to eat. Just as Morning Light came in with more, Rose Bud had brought something to eat for everybody. Plum Leaf boiled potatoes and put them on wooden platters, and then dished buffalo stew over them and when the potatoes were mashed down you had mashed potatoes and gravy, a wonderful surprise. No one had ever tasted anything like it before and it was that good. Fast Fox was acting just as a proud father should, telling everyone how he had told Plum Leaf when little, to fix potatoes and stew just that way. Morning Light said "windy one, we never had potatoes until we came here."

Chapter 8

F ar to the south and some west, on north slopes of the snow-clad Black Hills was the old camp of Fast Fox the Crow, now Sioux. It was a place of joy and contentment for Weasel Tongue, for here Plum Leaf had been kind to him sometimes, and he knew she could make the simplest food taste like a dream come true. She had given a bite or two to him and it was there he had fallen in love with her. Moon Boy, just a young Sioux, had brought Fast Fox home to the camp. Just because the Sioux sat upon a fine golden stallion, and was surrounded by a pack of wolves on the ground and eagles in the sky, she, Plum Leaf, had fallen in love with him. Moon Boy was younger than Weasel Tongue by several years - yes he was the son of that bad Sioux chief, Tall Elk who had defeated the Great War chief, Black Thunder Rolling On The Mountain, and never shot an arrow. The Crow braves would never live that down. Then he killed no one, but he gave them seed to plant to grow food and stud for twenty mares.

It was all wrong. The Sioux were getting good treatment in their camp. Yes, he had heard Fast Fox's words but who was he anyway, certainly not a chief. Weasel Tongue had came back with bow and arrows in hand. Yes, he had seen the wolves in the shadows looking at him, but they were just animals. Big dogs if you will. He could kick them out of his way and there sat the Sioux in full light of the fire. Weasel Tongue lifted the bow for a kill and then the wolves broke his arms. He screamed as he was drug to the fire, and then a wolf put his good bow on the fire. He shuddered at the memory.

Now he sat in the lodge of Old Bear which was just big enough for one person, and he was looking at him again. "You are a sorry thing Weasel Tongue, because of you, your father my friend will not talk to me. I am low on food too. I don't hunt well but I must try or I will be hungry. If I get too low you go without. You had better get well soon. I told Fast Fox I would help you. I have. You are filthy again. Go to the water and get clean or get out of my lodge. You stink." Weasel Tongue was bitter. He had been hiding that fact from Old Bear so he could stay longer. He got handfuls of moss and cleaned himself in the water. He felt a fish, a big one, he somehow got it on the bank and got some moss, put a stick though the gills and took it to the lodge of Old Bear. He was not home so Weasel Tongue built up the fire, put moss around the fish and put it in the coals to cook.

When it was done he got a sharp rock and scraped off the moss and skin. The meat was hot and spicy – good - he ate it all. He looked up and standing there was Old Bear. "I see you got a fish. Where is my part? I shared with you, or have you forgotten?" "No," Weasel Tongue said, "I have not forgotten. Had you have been here, you would have gotten fish to eat, but you were not. I was hungry so I ate it, as you would have done. You never wanted me in your lodge, I was shown this, and you think I am a coward for protecting the girl I was in love with. The Sioux was enemy of the Crow. I should have been given a feather; what I got was two broken arms and cast off by everyone in my home camp. Now I must go. I have no bow no knife and no arrows - you should kill me because now I am dead anyway." Old Bear thought a long time, and then said, "Most of what you say is true but not all - you should never have tried to kill a guest in camp, it is not done. You knew that when the girl chose the Sioux over you it was over between her and you. We all knew that the Sioux, wolves, and eagles speak the same tongue, their horses too, so you knew the wolves were guarding Moon Boy - you are not stupid."

"It is also not true, that you leave with nothing, this knife," he put it on the robe, "is from Fast Fox. He said give it to you when you were ready- he asks you not to bother him or his new people or your bones will whiten in the sun forever. Two Dog gives this bow and arrows; he has more then he needs. Your mother sends the robe so you can sleep warm, and I give you this advice, go to a camp and be a Crow brave, hunt well, share your kills with others not so good at hunting. Forget Plum Leaf - by now she is with child with Moon Boy. Forget revenge and hate: they are poison and will kill you quicker then an arrow well placed. Hear me and live, we here don't all hate you, we just hate what you tried to do: you shamed us all. One more thing, your pinto mare is outside; I'll keep the colt because he is just in your way. If you are gentle you could have the milk; she would be glad to give it next sun. Don't use it all at one time or you will hit a tree a good bow shot away. You are sixteen snows now. Hear my words and you may be sixteen more, and if you chose not to hear, they will be like dust and be gone in the slow rain. Our people have a saying about when a brave goes out looking for trouble, trouble finds him first long before he is ready every time." Weasel Tongue said "thank you for my life. I was ready to go waste it." Old Bear said, "Full grown braves many times speak too fast and lightning comes first then the thunder, it is like letting a bobcat out of the net - he is much harder to put back in than to let out. So think before you speak."

"There is still yet a little more: keep clean. No one wants to be near someone who looks bad, smells bad, or acts stupid. Have patience. Be considerate of others' feelings and look wise even when you don't feel wise. Smile when you would rather frown and speak few words, but when you do talk let them have much meaning. Go now! I, Old Bear, have spoken."

Old Bear put a rope on the colt. He was big enough to get along by himself. Weasel Tongue got on the mare and turned to go, and Old Bear said "hobble her and tie her well for two or three suns or she will come back and you will walk." The mare sidestepped and looked back, then nickered to her colt, which made loud sounds in protest at being left behind. Weasel Tongue rode out of camp to the west and toward a new beginning, he hoped. He rode west along the rolling tumbling stream to where the path was at the water's edge. The water was shallow and he could look and see all the way to the bottom. He let the horse drink and saw the round yellow rocks of different sizes, some not even in the water. He put the horse on a rope tied her to a tree. He walked back to the water and drank and looked.

Weasel Tongue had a good idea of what he was looking at, for it was what the Sioux wanted so it must have a value. He picked up a big round one about the size of an eagle egg. It was heavy, too heavy for a plain rock; he held it up and the pale sunshine made it shine with a golden light. He did not know it, but what lay at his feet was wealth way beyond his wildest dreams. He got a few more, only the perfect ones - the ones he found that had no other rock still on. Weasel Tongue put them into a bag made from skin, put it on his mare then rode west looking for game for his night meal.

Brush and young trees blocked his view of the stream so he strung the bow and put an arrow to the string. He eased around the brush, and watering was a deer. His arrow went high and caught her behind the ear, breaking her neck - a lucky shot, for he had tried for a heart shot. Oh well, he had meat for three suns and he was hungry. A fire was made and soon a leg of venison was cooking on sticks over the fire. He turned it so more meat would cook. The skin was pegged and scraped too; he wanted the skin. He turned the leg again. He cut off the cooked part of and ate it. Good, very good. He set up drying racks too and put more fires to work. Then as strips of meat were cooking he ate more of the leg. Weasel Tongue sat and rested, turning the meat on his racks. He wanted water so he went to the stream to drink. He found a club and a round blue stone fixed to an ash stick two feet long, perfect for hand use, or throwing. Now he felt armed.

Many suns he went west, not always in a straight line but mostly west. The little mare was not fast but steady, and he knew he had covered much ground. When sun was high he stopped and milked the mare then he drank the rest on the ground and ate dry deer meat too. The horse was put on grass and he rested, and he realized that he was lost. He had followed the sun west and found nothing. Soon he must go back, for he was low on food too and had seen no game lately. He got his pack firm and turned north when he put the horse to a lope and headed for a tall hill. At the top he looked and saw nothing, so he turned east going at a fast trot. By sundown he was by the stream so he watered the horse, put her on grass, drank some milk and slept. He would see.

At first light he killed a spike bull elk grazing in a draw by the stream. This time his shot was good: one arrow one elk. He got a fire going and skinned the elk happily, for now he would eat meat again.

The hide was pegged and scraped and his meat was ready so Weasel Tongue ate elk steak then more.

"I could help you cut meat, I am very hungry and you have much." Weasel Tongue turned quickly and surveyed the situation. The stranger appeared to be friendly, and alone. Weasel Tongue answered, "Yes. I will get meat cooking for you; come and eat." Weasel Tongue, was startled by a voice so near. "I did not see you."

"I am Blue Owl. I am from a Crow camp not far away. My father was killed by a mean stallion. I live with my mother and I am a poor hunter so we are hungry most of the time. We should take this meat to my mother's lodge, for she can cook well, and you need a lodge because it will be cold soon."

They loaded all and went to Blue Owl's lodge, not far but Weasel Tongue would never have found it: a small camp - five lodges only in a hollow in a grove of trees. Blue Owl's lodge was not big but big enough for now, when they got to where the lodge stood an older woman came out and looked. Blue Owl said, "Mother, this is Weasel Tongue and he has elk meat, and will stay with us for a time. He will show me how to hunt."

"Good. I am West Wind and I will make you some garments and cook some of this elk. We will have stew for our night meal. Unload it and I will do the rest." Weasel Tongue asked, "Do you have pack horses?" "No? Could you borrow some?"

"I don't know we have few horses in this camp."

"Do you have lance and more arrows?"

"I have my father's lance but no arrows."

"Get it and some lashings too and your ax. Now let us hunt." They went north out of camp in a draw where there were thirty buffalo, some bedded down, and some grazing. There was good cover all the way so they got the weapons and slid down the hill. Weasel Tongue sneaked to within twenty feet from a two year old bull. He considered the lance but thought it risky and so aimed an arrow just behind the left front leg. The arrow struck true and sank in to the feathers. The bull jumped, looked, and saw nothing then fell. Weasel Tongue killed a cow who bellowed loudly before she fell which caused the others to all look now; this was when they were dangerous. Show yourself now and they may all come at you. Weasel Tongue motioned to Blue Owl not to move, for the buffalo were moving now. The last one to move close enough to the hunters was a slightly lame young bull. Weasel Tongue's arrow was well placed, and in no time, the bull was down. Weasel Tongue said "get the horses." then got his arrows and began to bleed the buffalos. Blue Owl said "look!" People were coming to help. Good! One had an old horse with pole drags. All were smiling; all would eat buffalo tonight.

Back in camp, cooking fires were blazing and the odor of hump ribs and roasts could be smelled far away, and it was good. Weasel Tongue asked, "Does anyone make arrows? We need some then; we will hunt more, we all need meat and I will help." Weasel Tongue and the others ate good elk stew, then West Wind cooked some buffalo liver and all were well fed for the first time in a long time. An old brave brought arrows, some good, some just past not too good.

"Does anyone make bows? Blue Owl's bow will not kill a buffalo or an elk because it is too weak. He needs one made of oak or ash and it should be longer too." Weasel Tongue told Blue Owl, "I don't think the buffalo went too far; we will go before first light, and get more if we can because everyone needs more meat."

Next morning they left and looking as the stars were fading they found the buffalo bedded down two miles up the slope; more must have joined them because there were sixty two now with sage and buck brush enough for getting near. Weasel Tongue handed Blue Owl the lance and said, "Stay close, and use this only if I get in trouble." An old bull was getting up - no good, too hard to kill and the meat was tough. They moved left and saw two young bulls and a cow. One bull had his left side exposed not ten feet away. Twang! The arrow went in past the feathers. He got up, blood starting out his nose, turned, then slumped and rolled over. The cow smelled the blood and so got up to look, and as she turned, the arrow tore through her lungs and she went down hard. The other young bull was hit high up and he bellowed, looking for anything to charge. It took three more arrows to get him down. Weasel Tongue got a good shot at a dry cow and put her down. Then the herd was running, and soon they would be long gone. "Get the arrows, and bleed them," ordered Weasel Tongue. He cleaned the arrows - one was broken, but the point was good; maybe the old brave could make a new shaft.

People were coming from camp to help butcher. For some reason, the herd turned back and lumbered past Weasel Tongue one more time, so he chanced a long shot. The arrow took a buffalo in running stride with the front leg forward and cut his heart and lungs, and he went down hard. Great shouts came from the people, and Weasel Tongue was a hero. Blue Owl said, "I know, get the arrow and bleed him." Weasel Tongue grinned and nodded. They got the meat back to camp and the two hunters ate elk stew and hump ribs until they could hold no more. The sun was just three hours old. West Wind told Weasel Tongue, "I will make a coat and boots out of that last hide." "Thank you mother I have none now." The old brave came bringing a bow and more arrows; he was given the point of the broken arrow, and said, "Yes, I will make a new shaft too." Meat was drying every place you looked - all due to Weasel Tongue. He could do no wrong! It was the first time in his life he felt good about himself. "Let us hunt," he told Blue Owl, "Elk will be coming down out of the high places to the low ground. Let us go see."

Weasel Tongue took the new bow and the best arrows; he let Blue Owl use his old one. "If you shoot an arrow go pick it up - arrows don't grow on trees, and I never made any." They rode to where he had killed the young elk and said, "Let us look – quiet! I hear sound -something is coming. He strung the bow and it felt good. The sound grew louder, and then they saw movement: a royal bull elk could be glimpsed through the underbrush. He was very angry as he polished his antlers on the brush and trees. He tilted his head, opened his mouth and bugled a high sound like a whistle. He was very large when he stood at attention, one foot raised, then, stomping and snorting, shook his head, fourteen points gleaming in the sun. Weasel Tongue fit an arrow. Twang! The arrow went out of sight behind the front leg. Twang! Another hit again and the bull fell.

Weasel excitedly called to Blue Owl, "Bring the horses!" He cut the bull's throat. "It's a good thing we got the drag logs; we better get his inwards out." They cut down on his heavy paunch so as there was not so much to lift onto the drag. So they took out all that was waste, and put the heart and liver on a green branch. "Now go. Take this to the stream and wash it and cool it then let us go to camp. Ahh! Knife handles," as he looked at the antlers, "take what you need," Weasel

67

Tongue said to the old brave. "And thank you Grand father for the bow - it works well."

West Wind Women was happy for more elk stew. "Yes that would be good I never get enough of that but we have heart and liver too. We could have that now if you are hungry."

"I could eat, go ask the old brave to come he may like some too." He came, and Blue Owl asked him, "How are you called?"

"I am Yellow Rock and thank you for asking me to eat. It has been a long time since I had enough to eat but now you two all have food we are grateful." West Wind Women called, "if anyone need elk meat for your cooking come now then I will dry the rest." They did come all smiling and got meat. Weasel Tongue was glad; he for once felt needed. "Yellow Rock, are there others in camp who could help us hunt? Help load the meat maybe or just come and do things to help."

"No maybe a boy but young, too young I think. I will go hunt."

"I have no horse. If you make arrows and maybe one better bow that would be enough, thank you."

After eating they rode north to see if the buffalo were still near. The herd was not in the same place, but not far either, so they studied their location and got as close as possible. Weasel Tongue wormed though the tall grass and brush until he was behind a small evergreen tree. He could have almost touched them, they were that near and all grazing toward his left so the left side was exposed to him. Two young bulls, a yearling bull, three cows and the old bull, a massive huge old thing, all looked as fat as butter. Weasel Tongue took five arrows out, handed them to Blue Owl, and signed to give them back to him, fast, but one at a time. He killed the young bulls fast - they just went down and then a fat cow. Now he put an arrow in the old bull - a heart shot. The bull bellowed, but could see nothing to charge so he tore up sod and went to his knees. Weasel Tongue saw the buffalo was down and then killed the other two cows as they were turning to leave. Blue Owl just looked, his mouth open, "You killed them all! I know, bleed them and get the arrows." By then the people were there from camp and all got to work. They had all the horses and drags in camp, and that was good because they needed them. Now at the next hungry snow time they will have food for all and new robes too.

Bald Eagle and two more came out of the blue, sat down and when Moon Boy welcomed them and got food. When they got finished, Eagle said "Weasel Tongue has found a new life. He is living with five lodges of Crow and is their only hunter. He killed much meat for them, all are old but for some very young. Their lodges are full of dry meat and fresh too; old Yellow Rock made him two good bows and many arrows, and a boy, Blue Owl, is helping too. He killed elk and buffalo. He feels needed now, and I don't think he will come to bother you or yours. Old Bear had a long talk with him; he heard his words. He no longer has hate and maybe even is sorry too. He stays in the lodge of the boy's mother so has shelter - just in time, for it snows there now and will be cold. I will watch. Fill your water skins and get wood in. Get Curly, Cubby, Pounce and Shadow to stand guard at all times; I don't know why but do it." Moon Boy got the skins and two wolves went too, asking, "What is it?"

"I don't know but Eagle is not wrong many times; snow is coming and wind too - we will see," Moon Boy said stoically.

"Curly, ask six very wise wolves to come to guard with you; Eagle is not sure but feels there is a need to stand guard at all times, or until she finds out what is bothering her. I feel Eagle can sense something we cannot, so be on guard for anything coming from any direction. Ask my father, Fast Fox and Skunk to come to my lodge, we will talk and maybe smoke too." When all were sitting on robes, Moon Boy told them what eagle had said, "she thinks some wolves should be on guard at all times because she is bothered by something, she don't know what, just a feeling. Snow will come soon then the wind, do any of you have a feeling too?" Fast Fox said, "Have you thought about Weasel Tongue?" "No," Eagle said, "he is with five lodges of Crow far south west and has a new life; he is their only hunter and feels needed, and even sorry for what he was about to do."

Six more wolves were on hand now, all large: Droop Ear was one; Slide Foot was another then Fast Kill, then Cold Nose. Also Slant Eye and Red Tongue, and all were Moon Boy's friends. Eagle said to be on guard at all times. She doesn't know why yet - she just has a feeling to be watchful. It is better to be careful and have no need then sleep much and get bit in the behind, and you know Eagle is right more often then not. A gritty, no good southeast wind was blowing, so full of moisture you could squeeze water out of it. A cold and damp wind is a no good wind, and suddenly it was snowing hard and in minutes, the brown hillsides were white. The nearby lodges had disappeared. Suddenly, a scream came on the wind. It was high-pitched and full of anguish. Four big wolves answered the call for help and were gone, then the wolves called for help and four more wolves were looking. They found the little girl and drug her to her mother's lodge; she was alive but barely.

The wolves were back. All came to Moon Boys lodge and wanted in; they came in and sat down by the door. All were snow covered. Pounce said "it is bad out there - you can see nothing, we found her with our noses only. She will live I think, but even a wolf could die in that snow - many old horses will die this night. Where are Cubby and Curly?"

"They are with Fast Fox, I think. It came too fast we had no warning. It was just here, and anyone on the edge of camp would not get back in time." There was a sound at the door. Curly and Cubby stumbled in all packed with snow sat down and said, "We were lost in camp. No one should go out, and not even you Moon Boy. You would not last at all. You must stay in; we will go if we have to, and no one else." The wind went down around midnight but it still snowed. Then as suddenly as it began, the snow also stopped, and all was quiet. Pounce said, "We had better get wood in. It will come again from the other way." Soon wood was put on the fire so they had light, then all returned to their wood pile. They dug the wood out from under the snow and took it in; Moon Boy got the snow off as best he could, and Plum Leaf helped too. Skunk and June Bug were doing the same and the wolves went to help Skunk. Tall Elk and Eagle Plume were getting wood, as were others. Moon Boy called, "Curly and Cubby come back," and they came, "Stay with me - I may need you – and maybe Pounce too." He came. "I am frightened. I don't know why but I am." Skunk came in and sat on a robe "I have seen many other snows but not like that one. Moon Boy, go get your cooking pot and fill it with snow, and as it melts, fill it again so it will be water to drink and cook with, and be fast, for I must get back to Rose Bud."

The other wolves had returned now, curled up and sleeping by the wall, and the cooking pot was full of snow. Curly came and sat down by his boss and said softly, "I am here: go to sleep. I will guard." Curly licked Moon Boys eyes gently as he did when he hurt from the bad fall off the clay bank mare. He sighed and went to sleep; after all, Moon Boy was just a boy who grew up too fast. Cubby came over and looked, "he will be fine. We will have to look after him for a long time yet I think." The she wolf had told stories about many things that happened but nothing like this it must be a first. It was darker outside than the inside of a buffalo's belly at midnight in a heavy fog, and with Moon Boy not seeing well, it was frightening to say the least.

As all bad things pass, the dark eventually gave way to the pale gray light of morning. Nothing looked as they remembered: the wood pile was a bigger looking hump of snow and some of the lodges were almost covered. Doorways had to be opened so people could get out. Wood must be taken inside or fires would go out then some might freeze and still more cooking had to be done. Teams were formed, some digging, others packing wood, still others breaking trail and it was hard work. Stronger men and boys went to the near wooded draws and got more wood for the fires; the women cooked for everyone. The wolves captured rabbits and ate some, then brought the rest for the cooking pots. If quarrels erupted the guilty were moved to other teams, for there must be no fighting - time was everything and very important. The wind may come back at anytime. When it did all things would come to a full stop, and there was even no time to go check on the horse herd. The stallions would take care of that. If you discovered something bad they would have to take care of it anyway, and as much snow as was on the ground, it would take all sun to get there and back.

Chapter 9

Bald Eagle and two other eagles sat in Moon Boy's presence. Moon Boy said, "I am glad to see you - I was worried for you, it was so bad the wolves got lost in camp." "Yes we found a place to set it out, nothing could move in that we see."

Suddenly, a snow cloud loomed far to the north, growing larger by the second. Moon Boy shouted to all, "Get inside quick or you may get lost!" Then they were gone. "Get into your lodges! The wind comes!" Then the wind was there. Wind was angry - it grabbed fist full of snow one after another, then arm loads of snow and flung them at all things, moving or not. It screamed and roared then moaned, then got its breath and caught more then came at all objects infuriated anew. It intended to crush all. Then bury all and go laughing to the southeast, thrilled by its own might, as if it shrieked "Stand before me if you can and I will destroy you!" It lasted for six hours more then lost interest and moved on to do its will on new victims elsewhere. It left the people in camp shaken and sad - three older women, one old brave and two children must now go rest on scaffolds. This is where they would sleep a very long time: forever.

In the timbered draws to the east, horses moved out single file to go feed on the exposed grass on the ridges where wind had swept it clear. Down in the bottoms and brush along cut banks, snow banks were moving, exploding into motion as more horses got up and shook themselves off, blew snow out of their nostrils, then stomped and lunged clear. In other places snow moved but no shapes appeared then stallions plunged in, kicking and snorting and the combined effort got more up and on their feet. Soon more action and horses came bursting out nickering and calling; some of the young came out with springs on their feet. This was going on wherever they took cover - some older horses were grazing on lush green grass by sparkling streams of pure waters, where snow can't go or wind either. Wolves and other meat eaters would eat their remains but they were finished with them anyway.

All told the loss was light, they had gone into the storm fat, and well haired, but forty-seven horses had been lost. The old king was one of them lost. He was eating grass mixed with wild strawberries on the bank of that stream just mentioned. You cannot see him, or can you? Close your eyes and look with your imagination, see him? I thought you could. Wolves never touched him and saw to it that nothing else did either. His golden speed would be remembered by Skunk, Tall Elk and Moon Boy, the only humans ever to ride him. His blinding speed would be passed on by his sons to other generations to come. The wind still is free - it moves the tall grass by the fence rows and gently turns the blades on the wind mill and the wind charger on your grand father's old farm. The same wind is ruffling the main and tail of the golden stallion, as it will forever.

In camp, the snow piles had been reversed by the wind. What was on the back side was now on the front side, blocking doors opening to the southeast. Wolves worked overtime getting lodge door skins open so people could get out and dig others out and so on. Snow on the wood pile had turned too, leaving the covered wood open so they could get wood to the lodges' fires. Curly, Cubby, Pounce and Shadow took thirty wolves, went to the horses and dug more out. Curly came back and said, "The old king and forty-six are sleeping forever. We may save more but it must be fast; some are in bad positions. We can't save many more but some. Wolves are working but we need help to save more, and the sun is near falling of the world's edge. You, Moon Boy should stay in camp, and I say this with respect if wind comes back you would have a hard time getting back. Help here. I will be back. Nothing will eat the golden stallion - we will see to that."

"Thank you my brother - you are wise and good."

Curly made it back to the horses quickly and helped recover a chestnut mare who had been buried in a gully with snow over eight feet deep, not far from where the great King lay. Then big cat came gliding up, and sniffed the old King, "Good. I will eat this one." Eighteen big prairie lobo wolves got up, and eighteen sets of fangs shown white in the starlight "Oh, I see. You will eat him."

"No one eats him, and if you try, your blood will run red as a river in spring time, and we will eat your heart, even if it is black. You may eat horse, but make sure it is dead or you will not see sun at first light, now take your ugly face and go. Bother us no more or you die just for the fun of it. You should eat old rabbit - he is more your style, but make sure he is old or he may eat you." Everyone thought this funny all laughed. Then Cubby and Shadow made the terrible sound, and big cat was gone, like an arrow leaves Skunk's bow not be seen again. You could say big cat was as welcome as three skunks quarreling over a radish in Tall Elk's lodge in hot time. For a hundred years or more the bones of the horse king were undisturbed; not a bone moved. The sign of the lobo pack was still there and no one wanted their wrath, and even though they were long gone and mostly forgotten, the sign was still there, it may be yet, I don't know. But I will not bother them, will you? I thought not.

At the time that light fades to gray light, Curly, Cubby, Pounce and Shadow went to Moon Boy who was not feeling well. The storm had unnerved, him making him unsure of himself. When the pack got there, he felt better and he ate some food that Plum Leaf had fixed for him. Moon Boy asked that Skunk be called, and when Skunk got there he was almost his old self again. "Skunk you have been in other big snows. How does this one compare to others you have seen?" "I have never seen others to compare it to this," as Fast Fox came in and sat, then remarked, "Or I either - we have big snows in the highlands too but always you could see a little. It took my breath and when I took air all I got was snow. I was lost and was leaning on my lodge and if Morning Light had not pulled me in I would be there yet."

Iron People and Taken Alive were there, and they shook their heads and looked wise, "we have been on the prairies a long time and our fathers and grand fathers here longer. Many story told and I cannot remember any like this one. I say hear Eagle every time she talks; no matter what she says - she saved us all." "Yes," said Curly, hear Eagle well; she knows things we do not, and feels more. My mother knew some but not when or how much." Tall Elk came in and sat "Ho!" he said, "are we having a counsel?"

"No, just praising Eagle for saving us all." Said Taken Alive. Tall Elk said, "I hear you, and you speak true. All you said is true; we put six of ours in trees this sun and with out Eagle we would have put many more. I say hear Eagle! Ho!"

"Ho!" All said it with much enthusiasm. Tall Elk stood in the lodge of Moon Boy and said, "My son, call Eagle - if she is near I would talk with her," and eagle was there. "Eagle, what of the buffalo and other game, how did they do in the snow just past?"

"The buffalo are fine - the others not as well, they lost many members."

"Thank you for saving us, or many would be gone in trees now." Eagle ruffled her feathers, "We were glad to help." Tall Elk asked, "Are the buffalo in small bunches or big? Are they near or far?"

"Mixed numbers - most little bunches on hillsides in the sun grazing, many went south. When you are ready I will show you."

"Good. I will know soon and then we will call you." Some of Moon Boy's followers were there awaiting Moon Boy's orders. He turned to them and said, "We go to the river with axes to get water. Give us your water skins we will fill yours too. Good. If sun is bright on sun coming, get your best horses and Golden Star; we will look for buffalo. Have ropes and drags too - thirty or more should go, more if they want to. Then we will all eat well again, for we must provide for the ones less fit to hunt." Eagle was asked to show the way, then fifty-two young Sioux and most of the pack with six eagles moved to get meat.

The snow was deep; they picked their way around large drifts and across draws and deep gullies. The wolf pack kept scouting the way in constant contact with eagles. The first buffalo seen were all old bulls and they were passed by. Just past mule deer draw they found a large bunch of cows, calves, and young bulls. Braves moved in under cover and killed forty or so, and the meat and skins were packed on drags. The pack, along with eagles, filled their plates and ate their fill before starting back; well they never filled plates but in a manner of speaking they did. They ate their meat raw - they liked it that way, and they filled up. It was cold now so they hurried and when they got to where the old bulls were three were killed. Not because they wanted the meat so much, but bull hides in winter made good robes and some of the tribe needed them. So they took the skins and the some of the best cuts and let the other meat eaters have food for a week, a way of helping the ones who needed help. Most of the hearts and livers went to camp where they cut them and put them in old skins. Then they were covered in coals, left alone to bake and in a few hours they would make very good eating.

When they got to camp, Moon Boy took a large piece of meat to his lodge and his braves brought liver and heart. They got a surprise, for Plum Leaf, Morning Light and Sweet Grass had the pot over a good blaze and they were just waiting for meat. Skunk and Rose Bud came in and Skunk began to cut meat. The braves went and got more meat to put behind the skin. Doves Tail was there, cutting liver and heart to wrap in old hide to be put in coals. Fast Fox was here now. He had something for Morning Light. "Is this, what you wanted?"

"Yes, I will put it in the pot. It will give it a good flavor." Skunk said "Oh my. I now can hardly wait to eat." Rose Bud smiled, then mused "he is this way every sun. I think his legs are hollow and maybe his head too." Tall Elk brought in snow to add to the cooking pot, and Rose Bud said, "if the snow is from our lodge making sure it is white not yellow, Skunk is not careful." Skunk was so kind and considerate of everyone's feelings he was hardly aware of that fact himself. When a hard job was at hand he just performed it to such a degree of excellence that all never expected anything but the best from him.

Plum Leaf was stirring the wonderful mixture when just a little spilled into the fire. Instantly a white cloud of steamy mist trimmed with blue rose above the cooking pot. In the mist a kindly face of one passed in long ago times appeared. The face began to speak, "Moon Boy and Plum Leaf, in the spring when warm winds move over the land, a child will be born to you. It will have the wisdom and the knowledge of the ages and will guide and advise our people in the troubled times to come. She will be called White Buffalo Calf Women and you, Skunk, will be her other father. You will teach and advise her in all things and will work with her mother, father, and grandparents in all things. She will sit in council of the bands at an early age all will hear her for only truth will she speak. This is a great responsibility you have been given. Perform it well as I know you can. Now eat your meal and prepare for your task; it will be hard but rewarding; I will come again when it is time."

The vision slowly faded and was gone, and all sat in awed silence for a time then Skunk said, "Let us eat. My strength is all but gone and we must plan. I thought that visions only happened to other people." Tall Elk whispered, "It does, only to very wise and good other people and that is you Skunk. We are proud to be near you." "Ho!" all said. Bowls were passed around and food put in them Skunk did his best to eat all, saying never had it been so good and others liked it too. Skunk was very content just to enjoy the ample food. Fast Fox was grinning so his face was just a display of teeth; his lips were stretched so they lost their color and his eyes were just points of mirth. He could not restrain himself any longer, and he leaped up and took Plum Leaf in his arms and danced around so others had to get out of the way or get stepped on. "I will be a grandfather, Grandfather Fast Fox and just think, Grandmother Morning Light, you will have to share your robes with a grandfather," he laughed long and loud. Tall Elk got the idea too and grabbed Sweet Grass. They too loped around the lodge making much commotion. Curly and Cubby told Pounce who had just came in "they have all gone crazy I think. They are doing this because Moon Boy will be a father." "I never did that," Curly said. "Yes you did!" Cubby said, "When you found out, you went out, sat on a cactus, and howled for a long time. Then we all pulled thorns the next sun and you were wondering why your butt was sore."

"I think pups and babies are like bull buffalo poop, if you wipe their noses too good they yip and whine and then the mothers think you are a bad sitter. You then have to go roll in grass to clean up a little then they do the same and don't know why. If you don't, they slobber all over you - I say what is worse? Baby people take longer to get ready for a hard time of noses, butts and skinned knees and also getting your ears gummed on. Pounce said, "I am the biggest so I will be the horse. Skunk will make her spurs just to see me jump." Cubby grinned and said, "I will get her a green switch too, so she has a change of tools to keep you going." Pounce said, "You are not that much smaller than I, maybe she could ride you too, uncle." Skunk said, "Spurs? That's a good idea. I will start working now and when she gets here I will have some made of gold. Sharp, too. Pounce just grinned, "She will be nice and try them on you first."

Skunk got up and went to his lodge, and brought back two flat rocks of sandstone. He had carved out a buffalo bull standing with head up and wind blowing and Curly's head looking at you and the carvings were good. He went back, got the little pot and some yellow gravel, and then he put the pot in the fire and built it up. Skunk put the sandstone so it was handy and poured the yellow gravel into the heating pot. Very soon the gravel melted and ran together. He mixed it and when all was melted and like water, he filled his molds and let it set. Skunk felt the gold and got another surprise. It was warm but not hot. Gold does not hold heat long. He turned the mold over, tapped it, and out came the golden buffalo and Curly's face - perfect in every way. Every line that was in the mold was on the gold. The buffalo was magnificent; the detail was professional. The face of Curly was inlaid on an oval piece of pure gold, and was so detailed that it stood out wherever it was viewed and world artists all over the world were given credit for its origin. If anyone had known the truth and said that the piece was the work of one Skunk Sioux craftsman, all would have said impossible. You and I know the truth, and that is all that really matters anyway; the works of art can still be seen, because they were never lost and hundreds of years later the name of Skunk was never known. The two molds were lost and broken over time. Skunk made others but never filled the two again.

Skunk told us in the beginning that he would make only a few and told us why. He had an idea what too many could mean, for he was very wise. All in the lodge looked long at the gold but had little to say- you might say words could not describe the spectacular beauty of the freshly minted gold pieces so grand in every way. Curly, Cubby, Pounce, and Shadow were called in too look also. Cubby said, "It looks like him, but why not me? I am better to look at." Pounce said, "Skunk will do me next and I am better to look at than any of you: I have class." Shadow asked what that meant; Pounce looked wise and said, "Fast Fox tell him what class means, you are wise." Fast Fox said, "Pounce has a bigger mouth and the bushier tail."

"See, I have class."

All smiled. Sometimes the smallest words can have the biggest meanings and because they cost so little it is good to use them a lot. It is better to make someone feel good than not. Pounce got Skunk to make a cast of him, and it looked fine but if Pounce had been dressed in a coat, his old coat would have been two small. The four big prairie lobo wolves got to like sleeping in Moon Boy's doorway, and he felt better with them being there. The door was crafted so they could push out whenever they needed to and sometimes they ran the guard to make sure no one was near. Two or three eagles sat in cottonwood trees on the edge of camp, as an early warning detail so all were safe, or reasonably so.

Chapter 10

Far to the southwest on the north slope of the black hills there stood the five lodges of Crow. They were nestled deep in their grove of birch, elm, plum and cherry, so thick one could not move through them fast. Snow had found them too but with their protection they were not hurt as other bands were. They lost one old horse but he was ready to go anyway, so no big loss. Weasel Tongue said to Yellow Rock, "I will go to my father to maybe trade something for two horses. I will take Blue Owl with me. I go now. We will be back as soon as we can."

By next sun, Weasel Tongue sat his mare in front of Two Pine's lodge, "Father I have brought you two deer for your fire. I have changed. I no longer want to kill the Sioux and am sorry I shamed you. We only have a few horses, and I would like to trade for two horses of yours. I would trade for lesser ones, of course. I hunt for the camp and need pack horses to bring in meat. See, my bow is good. Yellow Rock, an old brave, made this bow so I can kill meat. This is Blue Owl, and I live in his mother's lodge. Blue Owl can not make his arrows go where he sends them, so I kill the meat." Two Pines looked at the deer then at his son, "Come in my lodge; your mother has prepared food. We will eat some, and then you may take horses, for I have enough." They ate food, and his mother was overjoyed to see her two men back to acting like father and son once again.

Two Pines gave him six horses then gave him five more mares that would have young, "now you will have horses again." Weasel Tongue and Blue Owl took the eleven horses to camp. He called Yellow Rock, "now my friend; take this horse and ride with us when we hunt". Yellow Rock was well pleased "I have a bow and many arrows. When do we go, chief?" The use of that word mildly surprise Weasel Tongue, but he readily accepted the title. Chief was a good word to be known by, even if the lodges were few in number. He smiled – he couldn't help it – then answered, "Now if you like." They hobbled the new horses and put them on grass then rode to look for game, not too far from camp as the two horses were about spent.

Weasel Tongue's arrow took the spike bull elk just behind the left front leg; he bellowed and fell. Yellow Rock's shaft went a little high, but it would have killed him later. Weasel Tongue's arrow put him down. Yellow Rock's grin was not as impressive as it should have been. The years had removed most of his teeth, but he got his point across anyway. Six elk went to the far side of the meadow, and all stopped to look back - a far shot but he maybe could kill one more. But no, they had meat, why take more? Blue Owl said "I know bleed them and get the arrows."

"Yes. That's your job until you learn to shoot arrows better."

"Yes my chief, I hear you."

"Let us get the skins off and the meat ready for your mother's cooking pot."

"Good. I hear you, and then we eat elk and have warm elk leggings to keep out the cold." Blue Owl put a green branch though the hearts and livers then took them to the stream to clean. The meat was put on Blue Owl's horse and he walked home, leading the horse. When they got back to camp, all came to get a part of the kill for their supper fires. Weasel Tongue was having elk stew, well-seasoned and satisfying. But why should he not, he was the chief: not a very good one, but still the chief. Weasel Tongue wondered what Plum Leaf, would say if she knew he was a chief, not some stumbling brave, but a chief! He was someone and others looked up to him and this made him feel good. The new sun was mild. Snow was turning to water in some places; he took them north by east to the head of a wide wooded draw. He stopped his bay stud, because he smelled a buffalo bedding ground.

They rode up the side of the draw and looked over the trees into a clearing below. The buffalo were just standing, loafing and enjoying the sun. Weasel Tongue slid off his mount and slithered his way down to within easy bow shot. He signed to fan out and kill only young bulls and cows without calves. He signed to kill a few old bulls if time was allowed; he wanted a lodge for himself and would need lodge covers. Some three year olds were near, and he killed four of them; they never moved just fell. Only steps away, two yearlings smelled blood so he put them down. Yellow Rock killed some cows and calves. Weasel Tongue killed an old bull and then the herd began lumbering away but it didn't matter; Weasel Tongue's band had meat. Blue Owl was getting arrows and bleeding them. By then the people from camp arrived and the loading of meat and skins and choice parts was under way.

Old Yellow Rock was young again, dancing and talking at the same time. "Our chief wants a new lodge, so let us help him. He has helped us plenty, so dress the skin good and start lodge covers." When they got to camp, Old Bear was there. "I have learned that the lodges of chief Weasel Tongue have much food in them. I would join you. Now I see this is true, may I join your camp?" "Yes Old Bear. You are welcome. Set your lodge by me; you fed me now I will feed you. Now we will broil hump ribs and more. We have elk stew too; come and eat. Old Bear you are welcome." Weasel Tongue smiled inwardly at this opportunity to gain another loyal follower. So Old Bear ate and ate some more, "I am a poor hunter but I can fix hurts, so I will fix cuts, breaks, and other hurts." "Good. You can do that," said Weasel Tongue, enjoying his position more and more.

"Blue Owl, go get the horses and Yellow Rock's too. I want to find more buffalo, so if the snows come again we will have enough. I want a bigger lodge. I might go look for a wife too, so go tell Yellow Rock to get ready. It may get cold, so have a warm something on." They rode north by west at a long lope covering ground fast. They went over some low ground and found a good sized herd grazing on the slopes but there was not enough cover. "We need to get in front of them," said Weasel Tongue. So they went off the hill, crossed the draw up the other side, and got behind some cedars. They dismounted quietly and waited. Buffalo topped the crest and looked at the trees just standing there. Others came and pushed by.

Six or eight bulls and a four year old pawed the sod, bellowing, and began a royal fight. One older bull hooked a bull on his left. More pushed on; now they were close but not yet. The fighting pair spun, dirt flying from vicious hooves, and then ran right toward their cover. The bigger bull lunged at the other, pushing him away, and then stood still for a second, tossing his huge head as the second made a charge. The big bull was just right so he got an arrow in his heart. He was so near you could have got on his back and rode down the hill. He fell under the other bull who then just stood there confused. Others were looking now so he turned and got his arrow and he fell. Four younger bulls loped up to see why two of their numbers had just fallen over. They found out, as arrows from cover dropped them too. Two cows mounted a downed bull, a bad idea, and they joined the bulls on the ground. A huge monarch of a lead bull turned to push the cows back and took three arrows, two in the heart one in his wind. He fell and was bigger than the standing cows - taller I mean. He would have weighed nearly one ton. He was as fat as butter too. The young cows the bull pushed back now drew near the dead bulls. One cow, I don't know why, jumped over the big bull and got hung up and Weasel Tongue killed her and then two more. Yellow Rock said, "You do have a way of piling them up." Blue Owl said, "I know, get the arrows and bleed them. When do I get to shoot? All I get done is the messy work." "But you are good at it," Weasel Tongue said with a smile. The others were near now so all got to work.

When they got to camp, the fires were going under drying racks. Hump ribs were cooking and the meat was in cooking pots. A new lodge was up and everyone was helping too. "I am Hawk's Feather. I have heard of you, Chief Weasel Tongue. They say you hunt well. I know now this is truth. I could help you but it looks like you do well enough by yourself." "You are welcome here," said Weasel Tongue. "We kill from cover, because running them sometimes makes them bad to eat. We kill only the fat and young; the old and thin never feel our arrows - wolves eat them. I wanted that old bull. His hide was needed for my new lodge. He almost makes one cover himself, and his meat is a little tender, so he will feed us a long time."

Hawk Feather said, "Come and get to know my family. I have a girl just your age too and a good lodge keeper. You could do much worse, chief," Hawk Feather said. Weasel Tongue followed Hawk Feather to where his family was standing. "Chief, this is Night Shade, my girl child - fourteen years old." The girl looked up and smiled and she offered her hand. She was beautiful. She had long hair, a little wavy and the strangest color too. It was dark brown with a highlight of soft red running thought it all. Her eyes were soft and large. And stunningly, they were blue as early mist on a summer lake. Weasel Tongue was lost. If someone had asked his name, he would not have known. He could not walk straight or talk. He just said, "I'm building a lodge. Will you help keep it? Will you live there always?"

"Yes," she said. Weasel Tongue was so happy and he hugged Hawk Feather. "Wait!" grunted Hawk Feather, "You're supposed to hug Night Shade!"

"I will hug her for the rest of my life. Just now I am glad you came to our camp to live and brought her with you, and now we will be one happy family all our suns." Everyone worked on the new lodge so it went up fast and soon it stood tall and fine. It was well banked too, so no wind got in; the fire pit was dug and lined with rocks, and the fire was lighted and ready, so the young couple moved in.

No one paid much notice to the three Eagles who sat in nearby trees seeing everything with careful and thoughtful scrutiny. The people never saw two of them leave to catch the air currents and glide north by east out over the plains. Fast Fox and Moon Boy would know very soon that Weasel Tongue was in a new lodge with his young wife and that they had made Weasel Tongue chief of the camp. He was doing well, for he was a hunter and there was food for all. Bald Eagle was fast; she made short work out of flying; and she just glided along, not working at all. She dove down, picking up much speed then a few wing beats saw her high again only to swoop then glide more. The other Eagle worked to keep up and then just barely could manage it, so in less then three hours they were landing at Tall Elks camp on the Moreau River ready to give their report on Weasel Tongue and his camp of Crow. Tall Elk said, "Ho! Bald Eagle! We see you are back again with us. Are you hungry?"

"Yes, we have traveled non stop and had no time to eat or drink anything. We would eat and drink then tell you all." After they had finished with a quick meal of buffalo meat and water, Eagle said, "Weasel Tongue is chief of his camp of Crow. He hunts for all and they eat well. His arrows go where he sends them and he don't miss very often. Old Bear gave some advice on how to live, and he heard all his words. He has his own lodge and has taken a young wife and he is very happy now and will trouble you no more, I think." Moon Boy and Fast Fox were now hearing Bald Eagles words too and looked relieved, "we are glad for him; now we can live and work without fear of his coming out of hate to kill us." Fear and hate are ugly companions, and don't ride well together, for they kill your supper and make it lay like a great rock in your guts that don't go up or down and you can never rest. "I tell this softly," spoke Bald Eagle, "when hate is mixed with anything no matter how good or bad it is, it brings out the very worst in what it falls into. Then nothing good will ever come out of it."

Skunk was setting cross legged on a robe by Moon Boy's fire that was cozy and warm. He was working with a flat sandstone rock on another of his creations to be of gold. Near him sat Fast Fox looking into the fire, and Tall Elk was there also, as was Moon Boy. The mothers were on the other side of the fire talking with Rose Bud as what to eat for the evening meal, while Plum Leaf was doing something with a few of the beads taken from the white one. Curly, Cubby and Pounce were sleeping on their robes. Shadow had just come in, letting in a draft of cold air, and Cubby gave a short woof! "It is getting cold." "You are spoiled - you never minded the cold before," scolded Shadow.

"That's because I knew nothing of fire and its warmth."

"I think I will go dig a fire pit in the den and build a fire. Then you can singe your fur and make all sick, or just be in Moon Boys lodge and be warm." With that, Shadow retreated to a dark corner of the lodge.

Many suns later, Skunk put his carving of the sandstone down, and said, "will someone go and ask Looking Back Horse, Taken Alive, Iron People, Hump, Buffalo Tongue, Horse Dung, Runs Fast, Yellow Footed Dog and The Skunk You Can Not See and maybe Circle Eagle to come to this lodge of Moon Boy; I have words to say." In time all were in the lodge sitting on robes to hear the words of Skunk. "My friends, most of us here have ridden over this land in our youth and in older age together, and have seen much change. We now grow our own food from seeds which was never done before; our grand fathers only hunted meat and lived well. Now we have the wolf pack and eagles to help us; we will never be killed in our sleep as long they stay with us. Moon Boy brought them to us - in his short sight he sees far - no one ever before talked with wolves or horses either, or could see in the mind of big cat and now we can. We now can see into the minds of the lesser prairie folks too and ask them to not bother with our crops and we will give them some when it is ready, and they hear us. I knew when we were digging the hole for our cool place to store our food and we found the old one with the red stone that shot fire and the gold pieces with pictures on them. When we found all that and the sharp knives made of something we know nothing of, I sensed the world we knew and understood was coming to an end."

"Then on the Grand River, Pounce, Shadow and Droop Ear found the white man. He was bad - his thinking was part like that of Eagle Claw and big cat all mixed together. He only wanted to kill, but with a difference- he wanted our friend's fur coats, not for himself but the wealth they would gain him. He wanted to turn them to gold, and all he wished for was wealth. He wanted to have all that we have so he could trade it for things we know nothing of. We now have his thunder stick that kills five times as far as my best bow can send an arrow. I have looked long at it and cannot make one part of what it is made from. Knives are made of the same: they are hard and sharp and I can't understand them either, and if many of them come with thunder sticks we will have to kill them, but many of us will die too. We must know this. For our good, we will stay away from them but I don't think this will be good after many suns because some of us will want the things they have so badly that they will follow them and tell where the rest of us are hiding. It may be a long time before they come again, and it may not be, but I don't think so; we killed this one and put him deep in the ground so they will never find him."

"The vision we saw in this lodge in the mist was a warning. Plum Leaf will have White Buffalo Calf Women in the warm time. She will grow up fast and have much wisdom on what to do with the newcomers we must hear her even if she is too young to know. I feel they won't come too soon - I think it may be at least fifty seasons before they come in numbers too great for us to kill all. Pounce and I had the same vision: we saw many white ones gather on our lands, but they did not hunt and gather as we do, or eat the food they grow. So they had nothing to do, and they turned over the sod and planted crops not of this land. Then the wind came as it always does, and blew the crops and land away, and the white ones too. They only planted for gold; everything they gathered they sold. That is why they will never be happy on our lands, but they will come, many of them. They will be like many grasshoppers in a bad season. We will be pushed into small places of our own land with nothing to eat because the whites will kill all the buffalo for their skins, again to be sold for gold. They will kill too many too fast and then no one will haul the hides away and they will rot in the sun. The stink will be on the winds forever and the shame of it will be on mankind for a long time. Most of us will never see it because we will be gone into the next world to live as we always lived, but our great grandchildren will know and learn to live with it. In any tragedy some will live through it and change to survive, but many will die fighting. It that is the vision we saw, Pounce and I." Skunk finished speaking, sighed, and closed his eyes for awhile.

The fire crackled and sputtered and smoke drifted up to go out the smoke hole, and to be gone in the wind, without sound. The gathered people just sat and thought. Skunk said, "For now, I will live as I have always lived. I can't see them so they are not yet here. Now we should eat. Someone put the cooking pot on and built up the fire; I will get buffalo meat, and we will boil it. You women can add to that. Now I will ask you, Looking Back Horse, for your wisdom."

Looking Back Horse took a long deep breath and spoke in hushed, reverent tones, "I have lived on this land many years, and have seen much snow fall only to pile up in big drifts, then bitter cold so you could see your breath in the warmest of our lodges. Then the sick times came and many of our people had to go sleep in trees forever, but always baby came and replaced the ones lost. Now the white ones are coming and they want our wealth, cannot they see life is our wealth and the feel of a fast horse between their legs and the wind rushing by sweeping your long hair back is things. They already have it now themselves, why do they want ours? The only golden wealth we have is what was brought back from Fast Fox's streams in his high lands far to the southwest, and the only furs we have is a few beaver, mink and some otters. I think he is crazy and should be killed just as fast as we can, but how? He has thunder sticks that can kill many times an arrow flight, so we must trick him and get him near so our arrows can find him, this must be our plan."

Skunk said, "Thank you, Looking Back Horse, for your wisdom. As always you speak with a true tongue."

"Iron People, do you have any words of wisdom to speak to us?"

"Only this: I have lived on this land many years. I have seen many things come and go with much change. I now grow old; I do not see well and my bow arm is not strong and my legs are not fast either, but I think we should try to live with the ones coming first, and see what white man is all about. We should not judge all of them because of one man's greed. This is right. If we cannot live and trade together, then we fight. If we fight, many more of us will die than we kill. If we trade, then we bring out our poor things, not our best, or we will have only our poor things for us. Control the young braves, for they will charge the white man's thunder sticks to show how brave they are, and when it is over you will put them in trees and few of them will live. We have the bow and not much more to fight with. They have things we can't make or know how to use either; I think some sun we will have to walk their road with them, or die. No one spoke, and all remained quiet, for they had heard the truth and all knew it.

When Iron People was finished talking, no one spoke. There was nothing more to say; he had said it all. Buffalo Tongue slowly got to his feet and went out the door skin; in a short time he came back sat down on the robe looked at his friends then spoke. "I just now was outside. I took a long breath of air and smelled no thunder stick powder. I let my ears hear, and no white man sounds could I hear. I let my eyes look and saw no white man. It is about time to plant our new crops. So I say that if I cannot see, hear, or smell him he must not be here, so then why should I worry? Just maybe the next ones will not be as evil as the one that the wolves killed. Maybe the ones to come will not want our lands as we have so few furs and no yellow gravel either. My wisdom is to not love his goods too much, and use nothing of his we cannot make ourselves. In this way he cannot hold his power over us. We have lived well for many seasons doing as the Great Spirit has shown us; why should we change now just because of one bad white man? Some of us will be in the place where snows and cold can never go, and water is pure sparkling and cold forever and where the golden stallion crops green grass on the hill sides mixed with wild flowers and the breeze is always sweet when the white man again comes to our land.

We do not need to see our faces in the shiny things we found in his packs, or hear the boom of his thunder stick either; the twang of my bow string as it sends my arrow to its mark is good enough for me. Now let us not feel the stickers of the rose bush or the spines of the cactus, but let us smell flowers as they were meant to be. Be not so glum but smile more, what will be will be, we will ride that horse when he gets here, for now put your heads back and shout and laugh. Be happy for the sun is warm, the wind is soft, and life is good. I, Buffalo Tongue, have spoken." With this a great shout and much laughing came out of Moon Boy's lodge and life was good again.

Chapter 11

Two suns later a long line of Crow riders leading pack horses and twenty young mares to be covered by Golden Star and Golden Light rode into Tall Elk's and Moon Boy's camp on the Moreau River. Eagle had reported their activity almost before they left their camp. Then, last sun out, ten big lobo wolves under Pounce and Shadow flanked them in, one on one side, one on the other, while the rest remained in back except for one in front. This was how the wolves brought them in: an armed escort, if you will. Black Thunder was not with them because he had a bruised butt that made horse riding uncomfortable so he sent Tall Pine as leader of the group. Moon Boy's braves took the mares to a place out of the way and hobbled them, then put the stallions with them. The two braves had stayed to keep other less desirable stallions away, as Tall Elk's horse herd had many stallions.

Tall Elk and Fast Fox welcomed Tall Pine and the other crow riders and gave them a feast - the best that could be had, for Skunk was in charge of the cooking pots, and as usual he sampled each pot many times. He said he was making sure it was good enough but all knew he made sure he got his fair share and some of theirs as well. Skunk was also in charge of cleaning the pots, and it was good the camp dogs had a lot of buffalo insides to eat, as they got little pot leftovers. I would not say Skunk over did his eating, but he did eat enough for six. After they were finished eating, all rested except Skunk who was planning his next full feed. Nevertheless, Skunk was the most loved man in camp and if you needed anything he was first to give help no matter what it was. I wish I had a few friends like Skunk, don't you?

Next sun they took the bags to the seed lodge and filled them. They got instructions for each crop as to how to prepare the soil, and how to plant the seeds, and how to keep weeds out. They must keep all grass eaters out or they will eat the young crops and then there would be no crop for winter food. Weasel Tongue and his young wife Night Shade were along with the rest, as was Blue Owl and Old Bear, for a little outing and sight-seeing trip. Weasel Tongue shook hands with Moon Boy and said he was sorry, and that he was glad he had not fired his arrow, and then he saw Pounce and Shadow near him and gave a start, for in their eyes he saw his death. He knew death was near if he should harm Moon Boy in any way and even when Moon Boy told the wolves that he was safe, the glint of death was still there. The wolves watched his every move intently, not hiding their anger, their fangs gleaming white and Weasel Tongue knew fear. Pounce told his boss they wouldn't harm him as long as Weasel Tongue made no move to harm Moon Boy. "If he does, he will die quickly. Tell him that." and Moon Boy did.

The packs of seeds were loaded and tied in place and the Crow left the Sioux camp with Weasel Tongue along because with Pounce and Shadow feeling so suspiciously, it was not safe for the Crow to stay one moment longer. Moon Boy sat on the ground and asked Pounce and Shadow to sit with him, "Do not follow and kill him as I know you can; he was along with the rest, so he was a guest as they were. Give me your word you will not kill him." So they did and Weasel Tongue's life was saved once more.

"I think my son," surmised Tall Pine, "that you should never go closer than two hundred bowshots of those wolves again or they will kill you. Moon Boy has forgiven you but they have not. In their eyes you are a killer bound to kill their boss, and they need no excuse to see you dead. So hear me my son: I, Tall Pine, have spoken." Weasel Tongue dejectedly sat upon his horse and said with downcast eyes, "I thought it was over, my father, or I would not have come to shame you. I am sorry again."

"Yes, so am I. Let us put some distance between us and the wolves." On into the night they rode and when the dust settled down and the sound of the horses faded they were just gone. Pounce and Shadow, along with Curly and Cubby, looked long at their trail and deep sounds of hate came from them. Only the love for Moon Boy held them back or Weasel Tongue would never see another sunrise, or even have enough left of him to put in a tree. Weasel Tongue felt this and cold sweat was on him as he rode on into the night. "Father, we must stop. There is water is here, and my wife almost fell off her horse again. We must rest and the horses must rest too, and feed some. I don't think the wolves followed us; Moon Boy will not let them and they hear him. Even if they come, two hundred miles will make no difference anyway, so let us stop." Tall Pine agreed and they made camp.

Bald Eagle was relaxing, sitting in a tree right in the crow camp and no one paid her any attention. They spoke freely because the Lakota people had given them seed to plant and had not killed them when they could have. The Crow, however, still thought them untrustworthy and said as much. Had Moon Boy broken his neck in a fall or got hurt in any way the wolves would have pounced on Weasel Tongue and this would have been bad. Would the wolves be following the Crow even though Moon Boy instructed them not to? All felt uneasy about what might have happened. Weasel Tongue was a changed man, or was he? Eagle thought long and hard about this one. Eagle floated away and no one even saw her go.

She went to Moon Boy's lodge and Pounce and Shadow were there, so she told them what she had overheard. Pounce went to the she wolf and told her. She looked wise then spoke. "If you cut the stingers off the burr, its nature still is to stick you. Grandfather rattlesnake would still want to give you his poison if he lost his fangs. Weasel Tongue would have killed Moon Boy if he had not been stopped and maybe would again if given the chance: once evil always evil."

Two suns had gone by and Tall Pine and Black Thunder chose a long, mostly level flat piece of land near one of their streams to plant their first crop. This was a first ever: no Crow people had planted any food crop before, and so it was new to them and exciting as well. Tall Pine and Black Thunder along with other head men of the tribe marked out the long first rows, nearly a quarter mile long. The men and older boys got their axes and knives and begin to break sod. It was slow, hard work and completely new to them so a few tempers flared and workers were moved to different areas so work could continue smoothly. Tall Pine was the one chosen as the field boss. He then picked the people that most of the others got along with and would listen to. Then he made them overseers, but when you have fifty or so working for one goal it is amazing just how fast ground can be worked. Before that sun had gone to rest on the west side of the world, six full rows of corn had been planted, and eight rows of beans as well. When sun boy brought his torch again at first light, the vine crops would go in and make mother earth pregnant with new life to feed her children good food from her ample bosom. This was life and everyone was glad to see the fruits of their labors. All could hardly wait to see the first green plants come out of the ground, but wait they must because that's life: the calf doesn't grow to be bull buffalo in one sun either.

Seven deer came to look at their green meadow now marked with rows of bare ground with grass taken out. "What does this mean?" asked a young deer, "Are the ones that walk on two legs crazy?"

"Of course they are!" said a rabbit, "We always knew that they are too tall - they stand too close to the sun and it has taken their brains out and cooked them. Look! They worked all sun just to kill our grass, and for what, just to make ground open and bare."

"But they always have a reason," said a gopher, "I have watched them many times do strange things and always they have a reason."

"Why don't you all just wait and see." said Owl as he floated by on wings that made no sound, "He maybe has done you all a favor, and you just don't know it yet."

Deer looked up with scorn, "He didn't do my son a favor when his arrow took his life and he was gone from me not to ever come back; he does no one favors." Fox slid up quietly and said, "Deer, your memory is bad: don't you remember two winters past when you stood looking at the wonderland of snow on trees, and big cat was about to eat you and the man put his arrow in cat's heart and killed her or you would already be gone two years. Yet you say he does no one favors?"

"I had forgotten that. Fox you are right: maybe we should wait and see."

"You wait; I say he is crazy! He was trying to catch father one sun," said rabbit, his long ears twitching, "and he fell over a tree stump and hit his head on a rock. He was on all fours then - the smartest I ever saw him - but he was short too, not so close to the sun."

"Ho!" cackled a blue jay, "You all make too much noise! How is an honest bird to get any sleep with you all standing around jabbering! Don't you know when sun goes to the other world it's time to sleep? Now you rabbit, you say the tall ones are crazy and there you stand beside fox who has dined many times on your kinds' bones! You, gopher, don't you know that was owl that was just here, and he has eaten your kind as well as rabbit? I, at first light, must go find grasshopper or cricket to feed my young or they will never grow big enough to warn you of danger from the top of some tree. Now kindly go so I can sleep - some of us have to work next sun!"

Chapter 12

At first light, Tall Pine and his workers were back to work in the meadow, some digging, some pulling out grass roots and brush stems. Others counted out seeds and still others planted seeds of pumpkins and squash, and several others waited to take over the duties of those needing to rest. Tall Pine took his turn too because he was not lazy, and so the work went on smoothly. Black Thunder came out to look at the work; he was not real ambitious, so he never got off his horse, and he had mixed feelings about the crops that came from the one man he had set out to kill. Tall Elk was the one to defeat him; he had given the Crows the seed to plant when they could have killed them all. It was very confusing. It was midway to sun down and the work was on the lower slopes near the stream, when one of the sod breakers brought a very heavy rock to show Tall Pine and Weasel Tongue. It was of uneven shape and it looked like it was melted rock. When washed in the stream and held up to the sun it shone with a yellow glow: it was pure gold and was as big as two fists.

Weasel Tongue knew what it was, only much bigger than the ones he had, and Tall Pine suggested they give it to the Lakota Skunk so he could use it to make things. Weasel Tongue knew it would be a good thing to do after the good reception the Lakota camp had given them so it was agreed to give it to Skunk. At sundown the seeds were planted and the only thing that would help would be a soft slow rain, and that night they got it.

At the camp of Tall Elk, the spring planting was all but completed. The potatoes were not in yet but should have been, but it was agreed to put them on new ground. A good sized plot of land was now being worked and that took time, but as usual everyone was involved in the turning of new sod so the work was going well. In the wolf camp several new batches of pups were born and were causing problems for the single males. Pounce and Shadow had been sleeping at Moon Boy's lodge and Pounce was not himself. Moon Boy could see trouble was coming and asked, "What is bothering you my brother?"

"Weasel Tongue still lives and I feel he will come when we least expect it in order to harm you and take Plum Leaf back with him. Shadow feels the same, as does Droop Ears along with two or three more big lobos. We feel our paws are tied just waiting to see when he comes. I would like to go confront him but I know I would kill him quickly when I put eyes on him. He and big cat are the same: they are evil and always have been, just like Black Thunder who hates us all. It is because wolf and Lakota defeated him and he lost much face. He may come too but will bring no war party as no one will follow him to war against the Lakota under Tall Elk and you my brother." Shadow now spoke, "I feel as Pounce does-why give him the advantage of striking first?"

Eagle came to speak to the group. "Four eagles and I are watching him even now and he can't move without our knowing. So rest well; you are in good claws. Go to the sweat lodge and ask advice of the wise ones. See the she wolf and ask her what she thinks. My advice is to wait and see." Eagle spoke directly to Pounce, "Hear me Pounce. I know you hate Weasel Tongue and I know why. Hate is a bad companion because he doesn't ride well with you, he robs you of your wisdom, and advises you to make bad choices and do things you may later regret. Send him away or at least to the back of your mind. If you love Moon Boy as you say you do, and then don't shame him now. Weasel Tongue came to the Lakota camp as a guest as did the others, and it would be against Lakota law to seek him out and kill him." This was a long speech for Eagle, "I go now; ten more eagles come to join us; we will be enough."

Weasel Tongue sat in his lodge holding the huge hunk of raw gold in his lap, feeling its warmth and power. He did not know why but he knew it had value, much value. He was not alone; Old Bear and Blue

Owl sat with him, and Old Bear asked, "What will you do my chief? Give it away? Or keep it?"

"What would you do Old Bear, or you, Blue Owl?"

"We would keep it and give the Lakota your smaller ones. No one will know and you will have this one that makes you feel good."

"What would you have me do my wife?"

"Do as you all said you would do, or some sun they will see it and know. Then what will you say? A brave or chief without honor is not fit to be chief." She turned and left them is a sort of stunned silence. When the truth is spoken softly it has much power, and if you hear it not you are less then nothing.

Later, after Old Bear and Blue Owl had gone to their lodges, Weasel Tongue sat long on his robes then he looked at Night Shade. "You are right, my wife, as always. We said the Lakota Skunk should have the gold, and we all agreed to it, so he shall have it. I may find another, or I may not and maybe then I will have a golden rock like this one. A chief's word must be his law, or in his heart he can never lead or advise others in any way. I thank you; your wisdom is good, I am lucky to have you with me it was a good sun when you came to share my life."

In the Crow meadow, the morning sun was just up enough to see the rows of planted crops. Rabbit was standing up on his hind legs looking around to see what he could. "I told you the two legged ones were crazy. In sun just passed they found just a plain old yellow rock and they cleaned it in water, then held it up to the sun to see it the better and now they took turns holding it and rubbing it. Now they hummed to it, like one does when putting young to rest, and then they put a fine skin around it to hide it, or keep it warm. Now I ask you, is this the way rabbits would do?"

"No, rabbits like you would talk to it so much it would run away just to get some quiet time. I say, rabbit, you could talk the fleas off a fox and make them think it was their idea." With this, blue jay ruffled his feathers, looked disgusted and flew away. Fox walked up and sat down. "Rabbit," he said, "I like you as a friend or I would eat you, but you talk too much. Why are you sitting in the open like this? Owl or eagle could see you a mile and would eat you, and then I would miss you. Go to your burrow and rest; I will walk you home.

Buck deer walked up, "Just a minute fox, just a little minute. I think they are crazy too. I don't know if being too close to the sun has anything to do with it or not but far to the north and a little east others of their kind do the same. They find land they like and then they take out the grass and make the ground open, and then they put in seeds they do like, cover them and plants they like grow. Now after some time has passed the plants they like form more seeds that they eat. So why did they not just eat the seeds in the first place and save all that work? This is what I ask you fox."

"Deer, you mean they put seeds in the ground that they like? To make more seeds they like so they can eat them?"

"Yes. That is the very reason why they dug up the ground here-just wait and see."

"My, oh my! They are very clever or very crazy."

"Well they are not crazy. I can tell you that they do all kinds of amazing things, and they control fire-something I wish I could do. When it is cold, oh, so very cold, they stay warm." The buck shivered in spite of the day's warming sun.

Chapter 13

Tall Elk and Moon Boy was looking at the growing crops along the Moreau River also known as the Owl River, when three eagles came gliding in and sat down near Tall Elk. "Ho, my chief, you have visitors coming," said the son of Bald Eagle, looking important. "They are the Cheyenne: Antelope and Lone Bear, the two the Lakota saved from the bad white one that the pack killed and put in the ground by the Grand River." "Yes," said a young she eagle from the mountain clan. She had just joined to help scout and she continued her report, "They will be in your camp two hours after sun up, next sun. They are all well mounted and armed with bows and many arrows, and ten or so ride with them."

"Good. Do you remember how to talk to them, Bald Eagle's son?" Said Tall Elk.

"Yes. I can then tell them we will have food for them next sun and they will be welcome. Ho! We go now and they will know many things to tell us."

They arrived the next sun. A feast was awaiting them. All enjoyed the company of the Cheyenne group.

Next sun after all had eaten and drunk, Antelope spoke, "Our people the Cheyenne have learned of a people who come from far across the big water in very big canoes, many times bigger than the ones we use to cross lakes and rivers. Many of the big canoes sail as one, and bring many people at one time; they come to find yellow iron that they think we have. They also have thunder sticks and long knives, and they love this yellow iron so much that they kill each other over it. We fear for our safety but don't know what to do about it. "

"Is this yellow iron like our yellow gravel?" asked Tall Elk.

"I think it is the same, and so then they will look for us," replied Moon Boy nervously, "and I fear they will come soon."

"No, I don't think so," mused Lone Bear, "They are many suns south of here and would look in the mountains first. I think you are safe for now, but the Cheyenne are much closer to their march and are in their path."

"Will the Cheyenne speak of us and our yellow gravel?"

"No, they will not; the ones who come first are most crazy and our people know this, so they say nothing, but the sun will come when they will find us all. When we cut them you will see that their blood is red as ours. We are all humans and all blood is red."

"Yes this is so, but the buffalo's blood and the fox's blood is red too, as is snake and bird blood, yet they are different from us."

"Yes but you miss the point, Lone Bear: we are humans and can think. That makes us different, but Antelope knows that Curly, Cubby and Pounce and the rest of the pack thinks. We know this from our new friends, the Lakota - how is this?"

"I don't know all; your questions are too much for me to know. I do know that we know things now we never dreamed of before: who could have guessed that other life forms like wolves, big cats, horses and more had understanding more than just to stay out of our way when we mean to hunt them. Pounce said, "The buffalo is so big, that he does not fear little sticks shot at him, and when he feels them he is already dead, and don't care any more. Buffalo is not a fast thinker anyway, as is Eagle, horse, or the rest." The rest of the Cheyenne braves were still trying to see how the wolves could think and do things, and were confused to say the least.

"Come," said Antelope, "enough of this heavy thing. Let us go catch the big fish with rainbows on him in Fast Fox's streams in the mountains far to the south and west. Let us go now as soon as we can, for I am hungry now for them. Who from the Lakota band would stay and who would go?"

Tall Elk said, "I would stay to see to the weeding of the crops. Moon Boy would go if Plum Leaf was looked after, as she was showing child, but he knew she would be." Fast Fox would go, as that was his home band of Crow. Skunk said, "I go. I want to see the big fish and see the gold in the water." Ten of Moon Boy's braves would go to protect him, plus fifteen big lobos and six eagles would go. Pounce would stay to see to the guarding of the crops and camp, as no one was better than him to guard. Buffalo Tongue, Runs Fast and Horse Dung with six more would also go.

Next sun, twenty-two Lakota, twelve Cheyenne, fifteen wolves with Shadow and Cubby as captains rode south by west just to go fishing. The six eagles, some in front, one in the back and on each side, high up saw all. Nothing got past them, and the big lobos fanned out on all sides, so they were safe.

In the Crow camp, Tall Pine was resting on his back rest when a scout rode up to his lodge and told him a large bunch of Lakota and Cheyenne braves would soon be in camp. The wolf pack was along too, but not the wolf king Pounce, as he stood out from the rest, as did Little John in Robin Hood's outlaws because of his size and strength. Good. They did not need that with Weasel Tongue being in camp. Fast Fox rode up and slid off his horse to greet his old friend, "Ho I am glad to see you my friend! We and our friends the Cheyenne have come to eat the fish with rainbows on them and to see your crops; do they do well?"

"Yes; we will show you, but first we will eat." Tall Pine said. Moon Boy brought Skunk, and he and Tall Pine talked. Then Skunk told him he would like to see the fish with the rainbows on them in the water, and see the gold too, if he could. So he went fishing with the Crow youths. Then Weasel Tongue came to his father's lodge. Cubby and Shadow's lips rose instantly to show gleaming fangs, and deep sounds of hate came from them. Moon Boy sat down and told them he was safe but to watch closely as he knew they would. The wolf captain's eyes never left Weasel Tongue and even the eagles watched.

I think if I was Weasel Tongue I would have gone into my father's lodge, covered with a robe and stayed out of sight, but Weasel Tongue was not smart, in fact he was dumb. In his heart he still hated Moon Boy, and evil was there too, a fact that one sun would kill him. The wolves knew this, for somehow they could read his thoughts, and could smell the odor of his rage coming though his skin. He was just bad: it is like covering a piece of rotten meat with roses, you may hide it but not the smell.

Skunk had never had so much fun; he even caught some fish, one quite large. He looked closer and saw the gold in the water so he picked one or two pebbles just for the fun of it - not that he wanted - he already had a lot of it, so why not have more? Skunk knew some what about gold; he saw the greed of the white one at the Grand River and knew it had value because of the way the white one tried to buy back his life. So he knew a little about it, but he did not believe many other humans wanted it badly enough to kill for it.

The evening meal was a huge success with Skunk doing his best to out eat everyone, although Antelope ate more. Weasel Tongue was there but stayed close to his father and made sure he had no bow or knife handy. Either Cubby, Shadow, Little Bit or Red Tongue were always close to Weasel Tongue and were watching his every move. If that was not bad enough, Moon Boy's body guard watched too. Weasel Tongue could not lift a hand or they all would fall on him and kill him quickly; he knew that. He also knew that someday, somehow, he was going to kill Moon Boy and take Plum Leaf back, for she was Crow – his Crow. Weasel Tongue had not yet thought of a plan of how to kill Moon Boy. He was too well watched by wolves and body guards to make it an easy kill, so for now he just bid his time. A better chance would come along soon enough. In his heart, hate grew like an evil thing because he was evil. He just hid it well.

The next sun, Tall Pine and Black Thunder took their Lakota guests to see the crops that they were so proud of, and they should be, for they were the first the Crow had ever planted. They had not as many kinds as the Lakota, but the Crow were not given as many seeds. No potatoes, tomatoes, or peppers were given and only some kinds of corn and greens were given.

Rabbit and blue jay were watching. "See, more of the crazy two legged ones come," remarked rabbit, "and they are looking at the growing plants like they never saw anything grow before. The two legged one are too close to the sun, I tell you. Their brains are cooked."

"I hate to admit it rabbit, but you may be right this time," blue jay commented but you better go home - they have wolves with them, and you would hardly even make one bite for that big one." With that, rabbit was gone.

Night Shade was holding the deer skin object, looking at Weasel Tongue as the braves came back from seeing the crops. Skunk was talking to Moon Boy and saying how good the crops looked. "They should do well in this high country, with much rain and good soil."

"Yes, they should," Moon Boy said. Weasel Tongue again looked at the Lakota with eyes filled with hate; he could kill Moon Boy now but then he would be dead too, and that was not his plan. Skunk came near and Weasel Tongue took the deer skin and gave him the object, "This is for you - we agreed you should have it." Skunk opened it and saw the huge hunk of gold, and Weasel Tongue continued, "You can make many things with it." Skunk could see how he disliked giving it up, but said, "Thank you. I will." When he looked again at Weasel Tongue he saw the hate arrows come out his eyes at Moon Boy and knew death when he saw it. Shadow and Cubby saw too, as they all did. They immediately surrounded Weasel Tongue and watched closely, growls coming from deep in their throats, but he made no move so they let him live one more time.

Rainbow trout was the main food at the evening meal. Crow boys and young braves had fished all that sun and many fish were cooked and eaten hot from the fire. It was so good it vanished as if by magic. Shadow and Cubby sat by Moon Boy, and Cubby said, "He will kill you if he can. He hates you and wants to take Plum Leaf again. We saw it in his eyes and read his thoughts. If you make water this night, do not stand in the light of the fire or an arrow may find you. We will watch. When sun was at rest to the west of their world, all found their robes, for at first light the Lakota would start back to the Moreau River also known as Owl River. The pack spread out around the lodge that Moon Boy was in and slept in shifts, keeping guard all of the darkness. At first light, Weasel Tongue gave Skunk a package of skin tied up with rawhide strings and said, "Give this to Moon Boy to put in his shirt to keep it warm. At mid sun open it and look inside it."

Weasel Tongue left with an odd smile on his face.

As Skunk held it, a black spider came out of the folds, and then crawled back in again. Skunk scowled, then put it in the fire and as it burned, many black shiny black widow spiders scrambled out of the package and were burned to death. Shadow watched them burn and then said, "They are as bad as little grandfather rattlesnakes: black death." When they looked and saw that Weasel Tongue was gone, Skunk got the chunk of gold and went to Tall Pine's lodge. Weasel Tongue sat cross legged by the fire and gave a start at the sight of the angry Skunk.

Skunk threw the gold at his feet, "I take no gifts from a coward. If Moon Boy had put that skin in his shirt to keep it warm we would have put him in a tree by sun down." Then he told Tall Pine, "I am sorry, my brother, but the next time I see him I will kill him or the wolves will." He spat on the ground at Weasel Tongue's feet and stormed away.

Tall Pine looked long at his son. "Get your wife and any who ride with you and get out of my camp. You have shamed me and your mother for the last time; do not return or I may kill you. Take the yellow rock that you wanted so bad. Now go." When Weasel Tongue had gathered his followers, Tall Pine told them why he was sending his son away. If anyone wants to stay he may, but if he follows Weasel Tongue out of camp he may not come back. Hawk Feather, Blue Owl, Old Bear the mother of Blue Owl, and eleven more rode out of camp to follow Weasel Tongue, but Night Shade did not ride. "I will stay with the main camp, Weasel Tongue is crazy. He had me, but that was not good enough - he wants her, Plum Leaf - the wife of the Lakota, so now I don't want him." Tall Pine nodded, "So be it. We will help find a better mate for you, if you wish."

Yellow Rock got on his horse and rode to set by his chief, "I think him wrong in this but he needs me, so I go too." Hawk Feather took his horse out and came to set by Night Shade, "He is a wise chief when not evil and bad, but I cannot follow a coward, I stay." Tall Pine lifted up his arms, "Ho! It is done! Not any of them may return again." Tall Pine picked up the yellow rock which Weasel Tongue had left by the fire and gave it again to Skunk who was gathering his things, "Take it - all of us want you to have it - go in good health and come again when you want to. My heart is black and on the ground. Forgive me, I did not want my son to be a coward, and so my face is sad." With this he went into his lodge and closed the door skin.

Skunk and Moon Boy turned their horses and quietly rode north by a little east, away from the quiet camp of Tall Pine. Shadow and

Cubby fanned out the pack a half a mile on each side to see that no one hid in ambush, and the eagles flew high and low to watch everything in between. They did not push the horses; no one felt good about leaving the camp, and all were quiet, deep in their own thoughts. Skunk held up the big nugget and said, "The white one at the grand river would have given his arm for this. I think it has more value than a thousand skins and yet I feel no joy in it. My wealth is this good horse I am riding, you all, a full belly and my wife Rose Bud. I need nothing more or want it neither." At mid sun they stopped by water and ate food brought from the Crow camp. They let the horses graze and rest some, and Skunk put the nugget away in his bed robe, for he was tired of holding it. Shadow killed an old antelope so the wolves ate well; Red Tongue found a jack rabbit with a broken hind leg and Little Bit napped - he liked his sleep.

After a while, Moon Boy thought of Plum Leaf and her good smell and warm smile and was a little homesick, "Let us go, and go fast: I want to get home." He jumped up on Golden Star and kicked the big stud hard and flew to the north, the rest stringing out behind doing the best they could. Cubby ran on the left and Shadow ran in Curly's spot on the right and shouted to Moon Boy, "Slow down! No one can keep up with Star!" Moon Boy slowed down and soon the others had caught up, then on they rode at a long lope on into the afternoon. Two eagles flew back to look at the back trail and saw nothing, but all knew Weasel Tongue was coming and would be as mad as a stepped on snake. When and how many would come with him? Not too many; he had few followers and would get no more help from Tall Pine's band of Crow. His spider trick was a low down cowardly thing to do, and no one liked it.

Chapter 14

Old Bear looked long at Weasel Tongue then said, "I told you once hate and anger make poor riding companions. I thought you heard me. Now you lost your wife and your father too and you have little chance of killing the Lakota. No one wants to get killed by going with you, so no one will go I think. I would go if you were right but you are not - you go only for revenge and to your death. When you go from here I will sing your death song and you will hunt no more for us or for anyone because your bones will become white as they lay in the grass without honor. Do as you will; no one can stop you. I will remember all the good meat you gave us and I will be sad. The birds will pick you clean and your bones will turn white in the grass and not anyone will know that was you but go. Now your ears are covered and you cannot hear me."

"I hear you Old Bear, but everything I ever wanted was in that girl. Now I can only think of getting her back or my life is over anyway, and I may as well throw it away too." Old Bear looked at the ground, and then at the sky. He traced some shapes in the sand, and then rubbed them out. "You cannot win this time, Weasel Tongue, the girl is happy and with child and will not come back. Give it up - she is lost to you - don't go kill yourself for nothing, hear me and live to see better suns. Just one or two of those big brutes against you would be too many, but they are many. His guards watch always. Then it is so far to ride and the eagles fly light and dark. Moon Boy would know you were coming before you left and laugh as you crept from bush to rock. Stay with us. Ask your wife to come back and just say you went crazy for a short time." Old Bear got to his feet and brushed off the sand, "I go now back to our camp. In three suns I will ask Blue Owl's mother to live with me in your lodge; you will not need it because dead braves sleep under the sun." With this, Old Bear mounted his horse and without looking back, rode away.

Weasel Tongue sat a very long time, looking at nothing, hearing nothing, thinking of only Plum Leaf and how warm was her hand the time she touched his arm and how bright was her eyes when she looked at him, and how sweet was her voice when she asked him if he would like a bit of her food she had made. Then he thought of Moon Boy, he who had it all. A flood of hate and bitter bile came up his throat. It almost choked him. Moon Boy must die or he could not live, but first he must go to his lodge, for he had only his light rabbit bow and three arrows with him: no robe, no food, and a poor horse.

As he rode back to the small camp of Crow, he made up his mind to ask no one to come with him, for he was going alone. It was better that way, because then he would have no one on his conscious if he failed, and even he knew the odds were not in his favor. When Weasel Tongue got back to his lodge, Old Bear and Yellow Rock were seated before the door, "We see you have returned, our chief. You will not stay. Your mind is in a very big fog, and you see nothing yet. The fog is a poison that has robbed you of reason and will kill you. When you go against Moon Boy, you will have to face Pounce, the wolf king, along with Curly, Cubby and the rest of them. It is a task too large for a full war party and you are just one! Kill yourself now and we will put you in a tree then we will know were to put spring blooms."

Weasel Tongue sat silently with his friend for a long time, lost in his thoughts. He knew he owed them an explanation and was not quite sure of how to begin. "Now hear me, have you ever wanted something so badly that you could think of nothing else and then in a short time see it gone from you? When Moon Boy came to our camp I was glad to see them as everyone was. Fast Fox was a Crow come to get his family - we knew that - then Morning Light, the wife of Fast Fox came to stand by Fast Fox. Plum Leaf stood beside her. I saw the look that went from one to the other and it was like a lake of cold water washed over me suddenly, and I knew fear. Then I saw red and lifted my bow and the rest you know. I was shamed before the camp. Now I must do something or I cannot live in the way I should, or want to live. If you cannot see this, then my words are like mist of the morning soon gone and forgotten. I do not ask any of you to come with me as I will probably be killed; I cannot hide from them all. The wolves would be too many, and what of the eagles? They fly in dark and in light and they are many too. Even if I kill one or two, what of the rest? So you must not come for the good of our people, you must stay."

"It is a foolish thing you do, Weasel Tongue," said Old Bear, "but we understand. I only wish I could help, not to kill him but to help you in your mind; you don't need to die or him either. Plum Leaf made her choice and you should hear her words and let it pass like a spring rain. We need you with us, not dead. If you must go, then wait a moon or two - now they watch well, all of them, but later they will not."

"You speak with much wisdom Old Bear. Yellow Rock what are your words?"

"My words are much like Old Bears; what I try to see is why do you go at all? Nothing good can come of it: if you kill the Lakota he will be dead. Then the wolves will kill you and you will be dead too, and then Plum Leaf will have no one. Now what good has been done?"

Weasel Tongue did not go that sun or the next, then thirty suns past and he was still there. Night Shade came back with Hawk Feather and her father too. The spider thing past by and was almost forgotten. The crops were growing, Weasel Tongue killed meat for them all, and things were back to like they once were but one of them had not forgotten or forgiven. What Weasel Tongue did not know is that two eagles watched from far off and knew his thoughts. They knew him for what he was: an evil one who would never change. Skunk can bathe in the river many times but he is still a skunk and will stink like a skunk no matter what. Weasel Tongue was bad clear though only not too many knew of it. Weasel Tongue asked Yellow Rock to make him a new bow, very massive so as to send an arrow farther and faster than any ever before. He said he wanted to be able to hunt from farther off. He did not say what, but you know and I know. It was not prairie chickens he longed to kill.

Every sun or two, two eagles glided in from the northeast and caught the air currents, gliding north by east so Pounce and Moon Boy knew all thoughts, words, and deeds. Plum Leaf had her baby girl and they called her White Buffalo Calf Women. She was a joy to see, much loved by her parents and grand parents and the whole band. Skunk, her foster grandfather, doted on her most of all. Pounce, Curly, Cubby, and Shadow could not wait to be ridden like a horse and quarreled often to see who would be first to be ridden. Shadow cut her a green willow switch and Skunk made her a little pair of spurs. He did not use gold but carved them out of wood. He thought, "Works just as well but not as heavy."

He hid the gold deep in the cold storage cellar they had dug. With all the other lumps of gold and the big nugget, he had enough to start a bank, but Skunk knew nothing of banks or money either. What he did know was to keep it hidden out of sight, and what he did not know did not hurt him any. Not yet, anyway. They had only one thunder stick which was old when they got it, and very little powder left as they used most of it to start fires in very cold times and some of it got wet over time and some was lost. Skunk could make the best bows and had improved them so they were almost as good as guns anyway. Not true as we know but they were a simple people. A well placed arrow from a mighty bow with ragged edges could kill you just as dead as a flying lead ball and dead was still dead so what did it matter, and besides you can shoot arrows faster then load a thunder stick so what is best? There had been no wars for two or three years - the warring bands of raiders had learned their lessons well: don't mess with Tall Elk's Lakota if you want to live.

Two and a half miles southwest of the old camp, the grass was full of white bleached remains of the last Crow war party who had tried. The long hair of that Crow chief stayed on the long stick a long time and waved in the wind. The wolves and the eagles with the Lakota made the difference, because no one could get close without being seen and reported. If that was not bad enough, the eagles came at you from the top, slashing at you, tearing out your eyes, while the pack - now over fifty of them - cut your backsides and drove the horses mad. Try shooting an arrow with your horse bucking and rearing at the same time you are trying to dodge incoming arrows just to stay alive. I never tried but can I can see that it would be next to impossible. If you were friendly and rode in with right arm up, palm up and your bow not strung, you got more food to eat than you had in seven suns. If you got real lucky you could land warm robes and a different horse to ride away on, if you needed one, but if you tried to hurt one of them, you got the pole in the middle of camp where you were tied for two or three suns then given to the wolves. It was just to keep them in practice, and after that they drug you down by the river, covered you with rocks and that was that.

Far to the south and some west a lone brave came riding; he was carrying a new bow made by Yellow Rock his quiver was full of new arrows and a flint knife was in his belt. A single feather hung in front of his left ear, and his face was painted yellow and black. He sat on a fine bay stallion that pranced sideways from time to time. Weasel Tongue looked fine, with new foot gear on his feet, his head held high and a half smile on his lips: he was going to war with a song in his heart. He saw the eagle lift up out of the tall pine and go north, and he knew the second eagle was off to his right and following along. If he had been smart he would have turned around and went back, washed off the paint, hung up his bow and quiver on their pegs and asked his wife to forgive him. He then would have asked her to tell him the story about the old rabbit, who when she was a little girl told her where to find the best turnips and the sweet strawberry patches and just where to find the nice flowers for her hair.

Weasel Tongue was not smart; in fact, he was dumb. He had everything a young brave should want: a wife, a good horse, and friends. Then why was he casting his life away? He could not understand that himself. He had been seen first hand what the wolves could do and would do. Even now the eagles had reported that he was coming and was alone. He knew Plum Leaf had a baby, and knew she would never come back with him. Weasel Tongue stopped the stallion and sat, feeling the soft wind on his face, cool and sweet, full of sage and spring flower scent. There he had a feeling that life was too good to just give it up when he knew he would not win. He turned the stallion around, kicked him into a lope then a full gallop, and soon was out of sight. He was going home.

The second eagle was confused; the one she was following was going back the way he had come, and fast too. The others must know about this and fast. She flew north and soon saw them; wolves and riders with eagles high up. Bald eagle flew up to her and asked, "Why are you not following him?"

"He goes back, I saw that he wants to live - he gave up his revenge. He will never come this way again, I think." Moon Boy had mixed feelings; he wanted it over with once and for all, but was glad Weasel Tongue had chose life today by casting the evil one out of his body and seeing the light and just in time too. In another mile or so Pounce and Shadow would have cut him to rags, no matter what Moon Boy said.

Moon Boy announced, "Let us go kill two young buffalo - we will eat meat then go back. We should find them at the last water. Pounce, the baby likes to nap with you as her head rest; she says you are soft and comfortable." Pounce grinned from ear to ear, "She is wise, that one let us go then." The tension was gone now; Moon Boy had got his mind off killing because Pounce was hard to control some times.

When Weasel Tongue got back to the small Crow camp and his lodge, sun had almost disappeared over the edge of the world. The big bay stallion was lathered from ears to hoofs; Old Bear took charge of the horse. "I will rub him down and cool him out my chief." Night Shade came out of the lodge, "I see you are back - did you find hunting poor?"

"No, I found life better than death and I chose life and you, my wife. My revenge I gave up; it goes poorly with my food, only runs in a circle, and goes nowhere. We will talk of Moon Boy no more. Do you have food? I am very hungry. Come, Old Bear, let us eat in the light of the new sun. We will hunt, you and I. Yellow Rock and Blue Owl will go too - the four of us are enough -we need no more."

Chapter 15

Tall Elk came to the lodge of Moon Boy. Curly and Cubby were lying near fire and the baby was sitting on Curly, pulling Cubby by the tail. Pounce was pouting by the door flap, because the other two were getting all her attention. Pounce grumbled, "I am the best looking and she plays with my uncles more. Why is this?"

"She loves all of you," said Tall Elk, "I am her grandfather and she doesn't ride me but I saw her riding you not an hour past." Moon Boy called for Bald Eagle and her clan. "I would talk to her." Very soon Eagle was there. "Eagle," began Moon Boy, "In my dreams I have seen the white ones coming from the east, from far beyond the big rivers. They have new thunder sticks and always they look west. I would like for you and some of yours to go and see. Be careful, some of them have your people's feathers in their head gear. Watch them and see what they do and how many come. I know they come but I don't know when and we will need to be ready, for some of them are bad, others are not so bad, but they all will want our wealth. They all want the yellow iron, but it comes in many forms and one form is the fur that our friends have on their backs. For them to get this, our friends must die. I would kill them first but then some of us will die. I wish I knew what is best. We will have to talk with them first but we do not know their tongue and much meaning will be lost. If we are good to them then they will think us weak or stupid or both, so we must be firm and strong and not help them much."

Eagle climbed high and gave her long call; soon others of her kind were there. "Ten of us go. We will cover much land; we will see all. In

115

four suns two of us will be back, and then you will know all we know by that time. Eight of us will go deeper in their land to where they are; we will see how they live, what they do and how many of them are there. I think they are many. Then you will know. Feed us; our way is long and there will be little time to hunt. We will eat and then we will go." It was a long speech for eagle; she never wasted much time talking. Usually from her it was short, and to the point; only mankind said many words without meaning. He spoke many times just to hear his head rattle and feel important. When the eagles had ate and drank all they wanted, they lifted up and climbed west, and when high enough they turned east and floated on the air waves out of sight.

Two suns later, Weasel Tongue and his three braves rode to the woodlands to get a turkey or two if they could; they had much dry meat but wanted some roasted turkey or a young deer for a change. Blue Owl asked, "I thought you were going to kill the Lakota?"

"I was foolish, I would have to have three times the arrows I had just to get by the wolves, and then never miss a shot. Then the eagles, not to mention the body guard, or Moon Boy himself, I may just as well cut my own throat and be done with it and I did not feel like dying so I came back. I like the sun at first light and at sundown, I like to eat good food and feel the wind on my face. I have seen many things dead on the ground and I don't think they know anything."

"Why did you make the deadly black spider bundle?" asked Old Bear, "Had the spiders killed him, Skunk would have known for sure it was you, and then he would have come for you. Pounce the wolf king would have been in front and he is the most deadly killer wolf I have ever seen or heard of either, and yet I have heard he is as gentle as the first wind of spring to the baby, for she rides on his back and sleeps on his neck pulls his ears and pokes at his eyes and he does nothing but lick her hands. I don't think it wise to have that killer so close to her: he may forget himself sometime and tear her into with out thinking."

Yellow Rock remarked, "A wolf like that can't be trusted - why not get her ten grand father rattlesnakes as toys - that makes as much sense to me. I don't see how the Lakota got so powerful, as dumb as they are, letting a known killer sleep with a baby. Plum Leaf is a Crow too; she should know better." In an oak grove they found a large flock of turkeys: ten gobblers or so in sight. Each brave pulled his bow and let fly, two big birds fell: one miss and one wounded gobbler flopping around that Weasel Tongue's second arrow put down. Blue Owl missed again, but just then a gobbler ran up to look and Blue Owl's arrow took him down. "Good. Now that was a shot!" Blue Owl said, "Do I still get the arrows?"

"Yes that's your job, and you do it well, too," so Blue Owl got the arrows and the big turkeys after the rest had run off. When they got to camp Blue Owl's mother took charge of the birds, pulling the feathers, saving the best for arrow fletching, and then stuffing the inside with sage and other plants known to be good and put them to cooking over the fires.

On the fourth sun, two dots were seen coming from the east, then two eagles landed near Tall Elk, and asked for food and water. When they had rested the first eagle spoke. "We flew east by a little north for two suns and a little more, and found no movement of any kind." Now the second eagle spoke. "We went east what it would have been six or seven suns on horse. Eight more eagles go to the rising sun. They are many miles now; the wind is at their back and when we rest for a time we will ride the air to the east also. It will not be hard - sometimes we sleep a little but not much, for we may miss something. We are near big trees now with many lakes, and just your kind of people live there. They ride over the water in little wood horses that they push with long sticks, and they move smoothly over calm water. I don't think the horses eat grass, only water, because they always sit on the water."

The two eagles lifted up as light as a thought, soon to be dots again, and then were just no more. It is said that in the long ago times, a great rock hit our mother land, and made the big cuts in her sides then water came and healed the cuts by filling them with water. This formed the lakes but as you know you can hear anything: a rock that big would have killed a tree or maybe two. Tall Elk said, "He who said that drank too much juice from crushed wild grapes that were left too long in the sun." "I don't know," remarked Skunk, "it could have been so. I would not bet on it one way or the other - I have never seen a rock that big or one that fell out of the sky either, but I did see a flower grow out of rock and bloom too, which seems impossible but I know it to be true. I think mankind should talk less and think more, and when he says something he should mean it and not just say what others said, because they could be wrong. Just because he said it, others say it is true, and so a big windy becomes truth. When I see a rock that big hit our mother land then I will think about it again."

Fast Fox now spoke, "Many say I am wise. I don't know; the biggest thing I saw fall out of the sky was bird poop or hail, but hail is just water, hard water. I think he who said that may have been in the sun too long and cooked his brains. I have never seen a rock fall out of the sky, big or small, and I have lived thirty-four snows on our land. I think Skunk speaks true: we all say too much and know too little. He with a still mouth has a wise head." Pounce came by and baby rode with her little spurs on and was loping him along. Curly and Cubby were on either side with Shadow behind; all were grinning like they just found out they had teeth, and baby was laughing. She both hands full of his mane and hanging on.

Just then they were joined by eight more big lobos fanned out in front and to each side to make sure that grand father rattlesnake was not sunning himself in their path, as they did not want Pounce to spook. He would not have, but they loved to run with baby anyway. The grandfathers grinned, no power that they knew of was going to hurt baby with the twelve big wolves on guard and woe be to him who tried it. They were good baby sitters and loved it. Plum Leaf came out of the lodge and gave the wolf call, and the twelve big wolves turned as one and came back to the lodge, and it was quite a sight. "You wolves could run all sun, but White Buffalo Calf must eat! Bring her in; I have food for all." Pounce lay down so baby could get off, but baby did not want to: she wanted to ride more. Curly said, "You must eat, then we will ride after your nap. Your horse must rest: you rode him hard," Curly looked at Pounce and winked - he knew Pounce could run all sun and never tire, but baby did not.

"Come! Your mother is going to give us all food. And I am hungry- come now." White Buffalo Calf said, "Cubby, you need food to ride old Pounce. He is a big footed horse, and may cry if he gets too hungry." Pounce looked at Cubby not too friendly but smiled. He knew Cubby was joking and that he would never hurt his uncle anyway. So in they trooped to eat; the wolves were not very hungry because they had killed a buffalo calf with a broken leg that morning. The wolves would go though the motions anyway so baby would eat, then they would all nap or just make out they were.

It was nine suns before the eagles were back, and they ate and drank much then sat in the trees to rest and sleep. The trip was long and they were tired, but in the new sun Tall Elk would know all. In light of the new sun, eleven eagles landed before the lodges of Tall Elk. Moon Boy and Skunk, also Fast Fox as well as other Lakota men seated on robes to hear all. Bald Eagle the leader of the eagle clan, spoke first. "Tall Elk asked us to go far to the east, to see where the white ones lived and were and how many. After many suns we found them. They are many horse miles east, maybe forty or fifty - it is difficult to know because we go so fast and horse can only go maybe thirty or forty miles in one sun. We found them to be more than we could count.

They live in lodges made of wood and rock in different places, and they have animals they care for, and they grow crops as you do. Some live close together and do things for the ones that live out away. They are coming and going all the time and go nowhere. They are hard to understand - they talk too fast and sometimes they hit each other. They go in a lodge and drink bad smelling water and fall down. Now another of them comes and drags the down one off to a lodge like a cage and that one must stay there. He can't get out, but after two suns have passed they let him go again."

Golden Eagle now spoke. "Then others stand on a raised place and say. Let us go west and get the furs and gold away from the heathens. I think he means you. I think he is one of the bad ones - I will know him when he gets here and you must kill him quickly, or he will kill you all. So far no one wants to go so far but some are ready for your furs. They will trade you things you don't want like the stinking water or the funny hats or the things you look at to see yourself in. You have them now, from the first white one and they do you no good, for you know what you look like. Two of us will go back to the tall trees; they will get there first, and then we will tell you. You must not trade with them, at first they will give you their things, and then when you want more they will say no, now you must pay us. All your furs and yellow iron then you will have no more to give. So they will say, give us your young girls."

"No! We will never do this bad thing!" Tall Elk said with anger in his voice.

Eagle then said, "Some of you will, or try to. Then when you do, sing your death song for you and the young girls. Hear us eagles: some of us can still see the big cats with the long teeth in the long ago, and some can see the far ahead to the hard roads that go nowhere. The people of all colors, living together as one, in places that smell bad. Most of them do things they would rather not do, but they do them anyway to get things to trade for food and other things. I say to you, stay as you are now for as long as you can, for you won't like what is coming, but no one can stop it. Some of you will like living their way too, some of your great, great grand children will miss the old ways, but some will remember too and be sad."

It was a very long speech for golden eagle and he had said so much wisdom in so short a time that few could grasp it all, and needed time to think on it long, even then not many would understand it all. Some would never understand any of it, but that's life. The things we need most we cannot grasp, and the things we should not be concerned with we know very well.

Looking Back Horse now asked to speak, "I wish to thank the eagle clan for their friendship and long hard trip. I also want to thank our brothers the wolves, for without them and the eagle clan, I don't think we would be here now. Bald Eagle and hers have told us much; now we must act wisely, and when the time comes to deal with them make good deals and not love their things too much. We should take nothing from them we can't make ourselves, for if we do, soon our wealth will be as mist of the morning gone."

Skunk now spoke, "I have said this before, and now I say it again: I cannot see him so he must not be here. When I do see him I may worry more. Now I am making a stronger and better bow that will do as well as our thunder stick can and we can do it ourselves with no help from any of them. This is our plan, the plan we must use. I am not chief but I want some of you young people to help me make the bows and arrows. I want you to learn the gift of bow making so our people can long remain strong." Fifteen young men and a few girls came and pledged themselves to Skunk, to work sun and dark if he said to.

Some went to the hills to get tall pines without bends, for pine was known to be a light wood for arrow making. Some went to get oak solid grained oak to carve out massive bows from. Still others made the jagged edged arrow points, and the rest caught prairie chickens to borrow their feathers for fletching arrow shafts. Older men joined too and soon Skunk had an army of good help.

Tall Elk, Moon Boy and Fast Fox rode to the crop lands to see their pumpkins, squash and beans. The garden was beautiful, a mass of green many rows wide, a quarter mile long with a few golden flowers starting to show here and there. The corn too was good to see through it, tall and a few tassels beginning to show. They crossed the river to where the potatoes were and found the striped bugs. "This cannot be!" Tall Elk said and gave the call, and many people came, young and old, to pick of the bugs off and put them in bags. When the bugs were caught they would be killed or else they would go back to the potatoes and eat again, killing the food crop.

Chapter 16

Far, far to the east two brothers and two or three others sat in the shade sipping beer, a drink made from soaking barley and hops. The water was then put in kegs to age and ferment, after some time had past, the strong waters were put in mugs and drank. Too much and you went crazy, got sick, fouled yourself and did other things you would not have done otherwise. If not too much was drank at one time you could think better, talk louder, make more good talk then before, or so they thought. In this way, plans were made that would kill many, harm more and no real good would ever come from it. Some would find wealth in furs and some gold but would have to travel much farther then they thought and are gone longer, and others would be killed. The road to riches is a bumpy one and hard to travel. It has a many turns and dead ends in it and when you do find it, you may just have time to look up and see the arrow coming that will take your life.

Hans, one of the brothers, was talking through the mental haze brought on by a little too much beer. He had a broad face and looked at the world out of blue eyes set deep, and wide apart. He was big, standing six feet and then some, and just twenty years old. His hair was muddy yellow that needed trimming and he did not smell like the first breath of spring either but more like the barn yard and old sweat. He passed gas a lot too, and that did not help. "John?" he asked his brother, "do you think the red heathen savages have a lot of gold?"

"No, and I would not call them heathen either; they have lived out there a long time on just what they could make themselves, and have done well too. We will trade with them, but we will be fair too or I will not be part of it. You and the other mutton heads setting here can go it alone, but you four don't have four bits among you to buy trade goods with. What are you going to give them? An I. O. U. that would be as bad as they are here?! We do it my way or else my money stays in the bank!" John was big too, a little taller and broader, and was quick on his feet. When he spoke you had better hear him the first time because you may not have the second chance. His hair was darker and well kept; his eyes were blue and his face longer. Every thing about him was neat and clean, and he smelled better. He was good with his pistols too, and with knives as well, a fact some had found out the hard way. One could not learn and was now in the grave yard. John spoke again, "we will need riding horses and pack horses and a spare mount for each man, camp gear, bed rolls, guns, lead balls and powder. We will also need flour, bacon and coffee and if any man goes with hate for the red man in his heart I will send him home or in the ground, his choice. One will not spoil it for all! Hear me well, for I will not say it again, and Hans don't call the red man savages where I can hear it; we are more savage than he is. It is us who are going to his land for profit and his wealth - don't forget that."

Hans did not like big John talking to him that way; he was just repeating what other men said about the plains natives, but they needed his brother's leadership and money so he said nothing. "Do you hear me Hans?"

"Yes I hear!"

"Then act like you do."

"Pete, Jim, Bill! What do you say?" John asked gruffly.

"You John are the boss!"

"Then see to your horses and gear - we will go west in the spring, for it is too far for this year. Save your coins too, and stop drinking so much beer. If you know one or two more good men send them to see me, but not more than that. Work hard and build up your bodies - we need no lard asses along."

In the spring, six big men left the settlement and rode west toward the setting sun. The sixth man was Gus P. Gustafson; he was broad and thick and stood over six feet tall, and he had a thick shock of hair that stood up like a lion's main as yellow as a grain field in fall.

His eyes were light blue, like white ice and little lights flashed from them when he was unhappy. If you were wise, you stayed on his good side and made sure the little lights never came on. At such times he became very quiet, and then he was dangerous. He never mistreated animals and would not stand for others doing it; he should have stayed home making toys for kids in his shop because he was good at that. Gus was different in another way too: he carried a long bow made from a hickory tree and many arrows that he made himself. Guns make a lot of noise - too much thunder – and that tells anything with ears we come and we are different. With an arrow he can get camp meat quietly and not frighten the other game away. Gus never rode too close to Hans because his smell was bad and Hans was bad. Hans would be the root of many problems to come; he should have been left behind in the settlements, but he was big John's brother so no one said anything.

Bald Eagle, Golden Eagle, and an eagle far to the west were resting in tall trees when Bald Eagle saw movement to the east. It was a long line of horses and riders that came over a small rise moving west. "Let us go see the white ones coming with many things in their packs. All have thunder sticks but one has a bow and many arrows, and there are six of them. They have twenty-two horses. I go to tell Tall Elk. You stay and see if more come. If more come one of you come quick and tell all, but I think this is all this time. In that little stream are many fish - eat your fill and be ready to come quick if more white men come, I go now." Then she was gone.

In the camp of Tall Elk, Bald Eagle was telling all to the leaders Skunk with them, "Six white ones come with twenty-two horses, and have many things in their packs they would trade. Some you have now and can't use or make yourselves. They may have more - I did not see all. You said I was very wise in the big snow, and saved many of your lives, so hear me now. I say take forty wolves and fifty braves well armed, with club and ax. Take the best bows by Skunk, many arrows of the new kind, and catch them in their sleep. Disarm them and send them back on foot after you take what you want and burn the rest. Make them know we don't want them in our land, for any reason. To help them on their way let Cubby, Shadow and Pounce show them how to fly on foot, and maybe cut them a little so they run faster. Take their foot gear so they run on skin. Get ready and go now. I and some others will see all from up high, and we will advise you as you go."

For twelve suns Big John and the traders had labored though water ways and around the lakes of the tall timber country, and had found hoards of blood sucking bugs that came at them by day and made nights unbearable, but they were passed that now. They were out on the rolling flat lands where one could see for miles, and were looking for the first good night's sleep in days. After a good meal all found their bed rolls early and were sound a sleep in a short time. One or two of them should have stayed awake, but no one thought of that, and I am not sure it would have helped anyway. As the fires burned to fluffy ashes, the nightmare began: six big lobos on signal pounced on a man they had chosen to hold with fore left over to help any group needing help. Then the braves came and tied them, hand and foot apart from each other and the fires, and then their elbows were tied behind the backs making them unable to get free, left to lay there until sun comes again.

Antelope, the Cheyenne, knew the white tongue and was at the Lakota camp so he had come too, to speak for the Lakota. Big John and his men had lain all night on the ground without blankets. It was cold and uncomfortable as men ever get. "Tall Elk asked who is chief," Antelope said in the tongue of the white man and John said, "I am."

"Why are you in our lands?"

"To trade with you."

"No!" shouted Antelope, "To take from us, to steal you should say. We have no yellow iron or yellow gravel either, and our streams have no mink or otter and few beaver. We have only buffalo robes and you don't want them. So why are you here and don't say trade because we know better."

Pounce asked to speak, "I am Pounce the wolf king," and six mouths fell open - a wolf that could talk? "The white one who came a year ago wanted to by me from Tall Elk, not as a friend but for my skin, my fur, so the pack and I killed him, as we will you." Bald Eagle came and spoke, and again, six mouths fell open - an eagle too? We have been watching you come for suns and suns. We saw you leave your settlement. You should have stayed there. We saw the blood suckers eat you in the water country, and will again if we let you live. We tell the Lakota all that goes on; we are his eyes in the air, and we see all. Nothing happens that we don't know about."

Pounce said "we are his scouts on the ground; no one can sneak up on him." Eagle spoke again, "and you, Hans, you asked John do you think the savages have gold? As you sat drinking the bad water in the shade of the trees by your camp, I almost fell out of the tree laughing. We have no use for gold, and you don't either; it takes away what reason you have and leaves you dumber than the rope that holds you. If you live, thank John; he told you not to call the Lakota savages, and that you were more savages than they are. I will tell Tall Elk to kill most of you; you are too stupid to live. Big John will live, and maybe Gus because he is good and is kind."

Tall Elk asked Antelope to say "now we will look at your packs - we will take what we want the rest we will burn or destroy, and you leave here with nothing." So a pack was opened - it held trinkets and bobbles and things of no worth to the Lakota but did have some beads and string so they were saved, and the rest was to be burned. Tall Elk sent two braves to kill two buffalo. "Bring them here, for we will eat," and others he had build up the fires. "We will feed you and you may start back. We don't want you in our lands because you have nothing we want. So don't come again or you will die quickly. I will take what I want: your thunder sticks, lead, and powder. His bow and arrows stays. I will give you each a horse, one knife, one ax and your life. Be satisfied; my braves say kill you but I will let you live this time."

The six men were given six horses and told to go back. Big John looked at the packs long and hard and Tall Elk said, "Go now with your lives. Stay, and I will take them too; the rest of your things stay. Eagles will follow to see that you don't turn back. So too will the wolves; if you do turn back, your remains will stay as you fall and your bones will be white in our grass." Cubby and Shadow made their terrible sounds, and the six made tall tracks toward the rising sun, and were seen no more.

Tall Elk opened the packs and things that could be used were put in one pack: knives, axes, beads, wet stones, food, powder and other things of use. The rest was soon aflame under big clouds of smoke billowing skyward. Skunk took charge of the thunder sticks, big and small and the powder, lead balls and patches. He also took the bow and looked at it long, a new wood he thought. It felt good, and then he examined the arrows. The points were made of the same hard shiny iron the knives were made from. "I wonder how they make this," he mused.

Six unarmed, frightened men rode east on poor horses to get food, with only a knife and ax for each man's protection. Big John looked back to see eagles up high and to catch glimpses of running wolves on ridges and flats, and knew the Lakota were making sure that they kept going, for to stop was to die. John was too mad to die and he saw the smoke and knew the trade goods were going up in flames, along with his hard earned money too. Hans was so scared he wet his pants and was blubbering like a new born. "Do you think now Hans they are stupid? It is we that are dumb, we walked in their trap like sheep, and lost all. You and your gold and your furs - where are they now? The Lakota never had any gold! If there is gold it is far west of here in the Rockies. Now we must go back without our packs and no money, with wolves and eagles making sure we go, or we die! The next time I hear you drooling about gold you will be horse whipped!

Gus asked, "Do we go back?"

"Go back and do what? See that smoke? That is the trade goods burning - the new rubber toys make the smoke very black. Look behind you! The wolves follow us and eagles too."

"I lost my bow and many arrows."

"You can always make more but not if you are dead. We have knives."

"Yes we do - the cheap ones that will break the first time you try using them. 'Buy cheap; save money,' you said; now we are stuck with them - any more good plans?"

"Yes get more men and go teach them a lesson."

"Go against the talking wolves?" He was astonished at even considering the idea.

"Who plans better then we do?"

"Not me. I am done with that; if it was just the eagles it would still be too many. We must stop soon the horses are done up," Gus said, "But first we'll get off and walk. We will try to get to water then stop."

Curly, Cubby, and Pounce were unhappy because they did not like the outcome with the white men. Pounce said, "It is not over." "No, remarked Curly, "more white ones will come." Cubby said, "We must be ready to stop them; what do you suggest?"

"I say, get the wolf clan in one place and have a meeting of our minds, and maybe then we can form a plan. When do make a plan, we must execute it quickly! Call Sniff and her pack, Fatty and his, and Dusty Rose with hers. We will have over one hundred wolves, but ask only the full grown lobos - let the young stay back, unless they are wise, then let them come. Pounce you were very wise at a young age, just like Curly and I because we had much responsibility. We had to help mother since she had no other to help her. Curly could sense danger: before he could see, he felt it. Ask Bald Eagle and her clan to be there too. They can see them coming for miles and tell us when and how many come, and then we will know what is best to do." Pounce said.

"Where?" Cubby asked.

"Let us meet on the north bank of the Moreau River where the old Lakota camp was. Be there two suns from now at mid point to sun down. Let mother head the meeting."

"Good, we will all be there." Call Bald Eagle and her clan. Soon it was done.

Chapter 17

"I am known as the she wolf, and have been asked by my sons and the son of one of my she-wolves, Sniff, to hold a meeting of the wolf clan and also the eagle clan. We gather to plan how to help our Lakota friends live a life of their ways for as long as we can. In helping them we help ourselves, for if the white ones come and want furs, it is we they will find. For we are fur bearing, and there are one hundred and sixteen wolves now here with us. Also we are proud to have eighteen eagles with us who see from up high and can tell Moon Boy and Tall Elk what they see and how many come. We the wolves have helped stop them two times now: when we killed the first white one on the Grand River for trying to buy Pounce and Shadow to kill them for their furs, and now just four suns past when we stopped them again. We took all their trade goods and burned them, then sent them back with nothing. Bald Eagle and her clan saw them coming and planned the taking of their trade goods and sending them back. They are our eyes in the air, and we together are an unbeatable team. Now it will be harder, for they will know of us and our ways. For now, the white men know we can hear them, and understand what they say, and the eagles too."

"Now you have heard me speak. I, she wolf, now want to know some of your thoughts of how best to protect all of us and the Lakota who are our friends from the white ones who don't live off the land as we do but sell all for gold. Even if their young starve and their old die, they still will sell for gold all they produce and keep nothing for themselves. The white ones have no hearts, and would not act any different if they had much gold because they love it so much.

Pounce said, "We hear your words, Grandmother. When they come again - and they will - we kill them quickly and that will be that."

Bald Eagle spoke, "Four of us will go to the rising sun to the tall trees to watch every two suns. Four more can come to relieve the ones there, and in this way we will watch all. We must do this and we will live to raise our young as we always have. If we don't watch diligently, in a few seasons we will just be gone, all of us.

Sniff now spoke, "I and mine except Pounce, have not been near them as most of you have. I feel that if we kill them all as my son said, it will make them very angry and they will come, many of them, with thunder sticks, poisons like sick skunk has. They will come to put these poisons in our food and they will bring things to put in our way to catch us by our legs and necks to kill us. We cannot kill all of them. So we must take away the things they love so much, like what they turn into gold, their tame animals, and even the crops they grow. We could talk to the grasshopper people so they will eat all and to the blood sucker people who could make them want to go back and never come again. This we could do and then they would not look at us as their only enemies."

Curly got to his feet and walked to where his mother sat, looked wise, and spoke. "I am the son of this she wolf, first born and a male. I and my brother Cubby have been with the Lakota people longer then any one of the wolf people have, and we know them to be good. Now we should ask them to be here at this meeting with us to give us their advice on how to proceed for the good of all of us. Ask Tall Elk, Moon Boy, Fast Fox and One Skunk, for they are wise and most of the fighting will be done by them. We will fight too but in other ways and they can speak our tongue and eagles too so they will know what we say."

"Good," the she wolf agreed, "someone go and ask them and others too if they plan well." So it was done. Soon six or seven Lakota were there to help plan: Looking Back Horse, Iron People and Buffalo Tongue came too, for their wisdom was asked much. "Thank you, our brothers, for asking us to this meeting; we know it will not be easy this time to turn them back. They think we have wealth and they want our wealth at any cost. Fast Fox spoke again, "Listen to me, my friends, someone must watch that Weasel Tongue does not come; he is a greedy Crow from my band of Crow. I was a Crow, but now I am Lakota. He will bring the yellow gravel or yellow iron to trade, and then they will know we have it too, and this must not be. Let two eagles watch him light and dark if he starts let one eagle tell us. We will kill him then, as we should have a long time ago. The white men love gold; it makes them crazy. They think they should have it all no matter who owns it and will kill for it if not given to them. Then some of us will die as we cannot give them what we don't have. Even if we did trade with them, they would still want more."

Now Iron People said, "I saw in a vision many suns ago that there were different kind of men coming to this land who did not live off the land as we do but took from it and were angry when they got too little. The men coming only wanted wealth to go away with and not to stay, to our way they were evil and harmful, not only to us but to themselves as well. Many of them came, too many for us to live at peace with. So we fought them, but they fought unfairly with weapons we did not know or understand, then they told us now you must walk our road with us or die. I saw this and was sad. Now we found few places to hunt and gather our food. We must go to their lodges and trade for food, or do things for them we did not want to do, all for food and other things we needed. This I saw in a dream, but I will stand with you and fight to stop or slow them and pray my bow arm stays strong. This was my vision."

Skunk said "I cannot see them or smell them. I don't hear them coming so they are not near yet. I will not waste my time wondering when they may come but when they get here I will be ready. My bow is strong and I have many arrows with grandfather rattlesnake's medicine on them. It does not matter where my arrow hits them - they will be too sick to fight more and some will never fight again. I don't feel sorry for them at all; they should have stayed in their lands and not bothered ours. Our real wealth is our lives and our loved ones. They will not get mine, and if they try, then they better be ready to walk the long road." Skunk was a mild man and was thought of highly by everyone, but get on his bad side and he made big cat look like a kitten in comparison.

Bald Eagle asked four eagles to go east to the tall trees to watch for the first movement of the white men. This guard was to be changed every two suns or so, and three more were sent to watch Weasel Tongue's camp of Crow. He was not going to come and spoil anything by bringing gold to trade with the white ones. Curly, Cubby, Shadow, Pounce and Red Tongue and a few more had not been to play with baby for a sun or two so loped over to see if she wanted to ride on her big horse Pounce. She did, so they told Plum Leaf and were off to look at the crops or anything that looked good. White Buffalo Calf was not ready to quit riding yet, so after looking at the crops they went past the old camp grounds, up past the den and on up a wooded draw. They continued around a bend into the deep shade under the ash trees.

There, laying in the green cool shade, was a sleek tawny she big cat. Pounce knew in a heart beat they were in a little trouble, not because the eight couldn't make short work of any big cat, but because they had baby with them and no time to call more wolves to help get her out of the way.

Big cat looked at baby out of her yellow glittering eyes and smiled, her long fangs gleaming white. "Oh, thank you, Pounce. I see you have brought me a fat baby human to eat; how kind you are. I have long wondered how they taste and now I will know."

"I see, Sheila, you are as evil as ever. Is there no good in your kind? You know that before you harm her we eight lobos will be dead on the ground, and then the pack will hunt you until your death is long and painful." By now the seven had moved past Pounce and were ready to spring; Cubby and Shadow made their terrible snarled sounds and baby started to cry. "Do not cry; come, and set by this rock so I can move quickly. I will not let big cat hurt you." Pounce joined the others, "Now we are eight. Go, Sheila, and maybe you live this time." The big cat was going to leap over the wolves and grab the young one. Her idea was to go up into a tree and laugh at the stupid wolves, and then eat the baby. Pounce saw her mind and so leaped first, as the she cat leaped over the others and in the air; Pounce caught her soft belly with teeth and claw and opened it up. Out came some inwards and it threw her off balance at the same time. The big cat screamed a high pitched scream of pain and terror. She landed on her side and the other wolves cut her to bits. Pounce licked baby's face and Curly helped baby climb up on her big horse's back. "Come. There may be more - we go quickly. At the lodge, Moon Boy was told all and he thanked them all for bringing baby back safe, he then said, "You are more like Lakota than wolves so I make you Lakota forever."

Chapter 18

Weasel Tongue knew he was being watched when he came out of his lodge and saw an eagle in the tall pines. Then he saw another farther away and still another up behind his lodge. But why? Weasel Tongue thought to himself. For what reason? Also he was sure if he had done something to anger the Lakota he would have no chance to do differently, for one of them would go get the Lakota and the wolves and kill him. What did they not want him to do? It was making his head spin and he was worried for his life, because after his ride to kill Moon Boy, he had loved life more then ever and wanted to keep his. He knew that no one angered them three times and lived to brag about it. Any one of them was too many to fight, but all of them – impossible - he made up his mind not to go too far on any hunt, just far enough to get meat then back to his lodge.

Blue Owl and Old Bear came to stand near and Blue Owl asked, "Well chief, do we hunt meat this sun? And do we hunt near or far?"

"We hunt near; the eagles are with us again. That means I am being watched by the Lakota and I know not why. Soon one will fly north to tell all to Tall Elk and the wolves. I can't move without them seeing and reporting to them. It will be this way until I am not a threat to them for whatever reason. If I do anything they feel is bad for them, I may die. I have lived two times now after I did something bad to them. I fear the third time will be too many."

Old Bear had seen buffalo not far from camp, so they got their hunting gear ready. Blue Owl caught the horses and the three rode northwest out of camp. The eagles were along to watch, one high up, one off to the right, and the last behind low and to the left. Weasel Tongue wished they would go set on a hill or anything. He knew that the big one with the white head was the eagle that took the head dress off Black Thunder's head and cut him deep. That one you watched well, if you liked your eyesight. She could take your eyes faster than a lightning bolt could split a tree and Weasel Tongue liked to see far and near, so he watched the eagle closely.

They killed two buffalo and since it was near camp they would drag them to camp and let the women butcher them – now there were only two eagles - one had gone to report and they never even saw it go. The one that left was the white headed one, the chief of eagle scouts. Weasel Tongue believed and he was glad she was gone but the other two still were watching and he did not know why. Blue Owl and Old Bear had came and sat with Weasel Tongue. "The sun is not old and I will get the horses and Old Bear can get his fish net then we could go to the stream and catch fish.

"Good," Weasel Tongue said, "Fish would be good, let us go." Soon the three were at the stream, and they put the net in and let it sink. Then the two in the water pulled and the net had two fish in it, and soon they had enough fish. They cleaned the bigger ones and put the little ones back in the water to grow. As the other two put moss on them, Weasel Tongue went back in the water and found a fairly large rock with much yellow iron on it. He found two more with mostly yellow iron, not as good as the one the Lakota had, but good. He was excited now and found a round one of all yellow iron. He kept this one and put the others back in the water.

"What will you do with that? It is heavy and no good for anything," Old Bear grumbled.

Weasel Tongue said, "I like to look at it and it feels good, now let us go to camp and eat fish."

Far to the east, much farther than the many lakes and tall trees, the six white traders made it back to the settlements very angry and broke. They were starving, bug-bitten and sore. They rode on six used up horses that could barely put one foot ahead of the other. They had no furs, no gold or guns either, just their lives and were glad to have that much. Even Gus had lost his bow and arrows because they were caught in their sleep. After getting past the blood sucking bugs of the water lands, they had enjoyed the first good night's sleep in days until they found eight wolves to the man holding them in place, then the natives bound them hand and foot. Their blankets were taken and they had to lay on the cold damp earth till first light when a Cheyenne who had been with Oley Olson, the first pale skinned trader, spoke to them in their tongue. The scene replayed in their minds the entire time it took them to return.

When they got back, they went to an eating house and ordered food for they had nothing to eat, and were very hungry. "Feed them," John said, "I will pay." Gus sat with Big John and the others at a table nearby. They ate much food and drank a lot of coffee as large men will who had gone without for a long time.

"Now what, John, what will you do now?"

"Not go west again not for a long time anyway; what will you do Gus?"

"I will make tables, chairs, beds and toys as I did before and be a lot happier than riding a poor horse like I did coming back here."

"It was good you could make bows and arrows or we would have starved for sure. That's all that saved us," John mused. "That and knowing how to use them."

"We were lucky," Gus replied, "my points were bad, most of them, the best ones were the points we found and used again. The natives are better craftsmen than we are and Hans thinks them stupid? He just repeats what the men around the beer house say and they know nothing, just beer talk I want none of it."

Hans bred hogs, and he mated them for their best meat and quality. He sold them alive and also as sugar cured maple or hickory smoked hams and bacon. He always thought of the west. He would find other men to go. He would go north then west then come in from the north from a way they would not expect him to come. Hans wanted a shot at Pounce, the huge wolf that could think better, plan better, talk better then most men could. Ridiculous! Wolves should not talk, or think or plan either, but Pounce could and Hans was going to kill him, or die trying.

A new harvest time had come again and the Crow of Tall Pines band brought in their first crop ever, and it was a large one. The three old friends were resting in the shade of a stately pine tree, observing the gathering of the crop- rabbit was talking as was generally the case. Blue jay and fox just looked on as owl glided in on soft wings and sat in the low branches of the pine, "Don't you three have something better to do? The last time I looked in your burrow, rabbit, you had not made your bed with new ferns yet, and blue jay your nest is unsightly to say the least, and you, fox, could dig a bigger den.

"Well owl, you have no room to talk - all you have is that hollow tree and that takes very little house keeping, so why are you nagging at us?"

"To keep you on your toes, so you don't get lazy."

"Humph!" said rabbit, "You should talk, what do you do? I will tell you: you sleep most all sun long and hoot all dark time that is what you do. I was going to say, the two legged ones are not that crazy. I have eaten some of their crops and find them good to eat and they put the most of it away for cold time eating. We should do that too; we can learn from them and live better. Fox, go get one of the round orange things, a small one and eat it. You will find much to your liking and Jay, the plant that is tall and has long things that hang down has food on it. That you can eat: try some, it is good, and I will show you how to get at the food by pulling off the covering."

Chapter 19

In the Moreau River country far northeast, the Lakota were doing about the same thing. Their crop also was big, only they had more kinds of food to get in than did the Crow people, because they had been at it longer. The eagles still flew guard duty and watched for the coming of the white ones, all knew they would come but they knew not when.

Some watched Weasel Tongue's camp but sly they were and he never knew he was watched and after sometime had passed, and after no eagles were seen he grew bold again.

He was a coward and his hate for Moon Boy had never slackened. He was a father now but that made no difference to him. Weasel Tongue remembered the words of wise Old Bear when he said that hate, anger and revenge make poor riding companions; they rob you of your reason and tell you to do things you later regret just as you are dying. Weasel Tongue heeded those words once, but again grew to not care about that either, for in his heart his wisdom became less and his hate grew larger. Then one sun he was planning to kill again and he forgot the eagles, Pounce and his gang of killer wolves, and the Lakota. All he remembered was what his hate let him – the memory of seeing Plum Leaf walk away with Moon Boy. Soon, he would ride away from his good wife and son too. Did he see Bald Eagle setting low in the dense growth of a red cedar? No- Did he see Bald Eagle send an eagle to Pounce to tell him of Weasel Tongue's coming? No- He mounted his red bay stallion and rode hard to the northeast to his fate that was very near. Weasel Tongue made good time for ten miles or so then the stallion got his second wind and flew over the ground with long strides that ate ground like candy. Suddenly, between one stride and another, a wolf had his horse by his flanks. His screams were terrible to hear; he leaped high in the air, went over backwards and put Weasel Tongue on the ground hard, knocking the wind out of him. He now heard the growls of Shadow and Cubby too terrible to describe with words. His blood turned to water and he looked full in the face of Pounce.

"So, old coward, I see you have come at last to kill Moon Boy. Or me, who is first? You better start with me; I am very near, and so is your death. Did you not see Bald Eagle send the silent one to tell me of your coming? They never stopped watching you.

"Let me live, I will never come again, Pounce, I tell truth!"

"You don't know truth, Weasel Tongue. You are a lie yourself. But let me see, I will think on it. I have thought on it; you tried three times to kill Moon Boy, one time with an arrow, again with spiders and then you came to kill and went back we let you go- and now four times. Weasel Tongue grabbed his knife and Shadow broke his arm. Wincing, he got the knife in his other hand and Cubby broke his other arm.

"Now we are even - your teeth and my teeth - we will see." Pounce sat down and laughed, then up came his lips showing his long dripping fangs- when you are ready then...

"Pounce, no! It will be murder!"

"I know nothing of murder evil one. I know to kill a bad snake or a sick skunk when I see one, and you are more evil than either of them. Bite me in the ear, I may cry like a puppy," with this all laughed and rolled on the ground. Weasel Tongue turned white and wet with sweat. He messed himself then jumped at Pounce who killed him quickly. The bay stallion was bleeding at his flanks but not badly; he looked at Weasel Tongue then turned and started back to the Crow camp and the horse herd because it was done.

The next sun Old Bear, Blue Owl, and Yellow Rock saw the bay stallion with the other horses so they caught him and looked at his flanks. Old Bear said, "Wolves did this."

"Then why is he not dead?" asked Blue Owl.

"Our chief rode him to kill the Lakota, Moon Boy. We better go see." They knew what they would find, and the trail was plain to see marked with little blood drops and the tracks of the bay. When they found him and they just looked at each other and shook their heads. Pounce had been there and other wolves too. The braves saw he was messed and cleaned him the best they could put him in a robe and put him on a horse and took him home. Weasel Tongue was then put in a tree to rest and they were without a good hunter and friend, but that's life. Old Bear said he should have heard my words better, and then he would be with us and not in the tree. Now his son has no father and his wife no brave to care for her so we must do that too."

"Blue Owl you must learn to shoot better. I will make more arrows because you will use more than he did, and we must make Night Shade and her son feel better. It will be hard to do but we must do it. Old Bear, go set with her, hold the baby and do little things to make her talk and help her do things around the lodge. Blue Owl, take his good bow and arrows and go kill a young buffalo so we can eat buffalo soup." Yellow Rock said.

"What about the yellow iron chunks - do we put them with him?"

"No they will be his son's to have something from his father that he liked. Now someone must go tell his father, Tall Pine of his passing, and how he died and where his tree is. We should all go," so they did. Tall Pine stood with arms folded on his chest and looked out to nothing as he got the news, then went to his wife and put his arm around her and said, "Our son is dead, killed by wolves. We will go back with them and see the tree he is in and then we will talk to his son, our grandson and to his mother. If she wants to come live with us for a time she may, we leave that to her to say. Get ready; I will get the horses."

They found Night Shade in the lodge, feeding the baby who was hungrily eating from his mother, and enjoying every slurp. Tall Pine and his wife came and sat down on robes and observed the feeding of the baby, "He is a fine boy and you can be proud of him. I, Tall Pine, his grandfather, will show him how to be a Crow: brave, strong and true and not a coward, but know that we will help you in anyway we can and that you may come live with us if you need to or want to, I Tall Pine have spoken."

"Thank you I will remember your words, but my lodge is here and so are my friends. I will stay for now. Old Bear, Yellow Rock and Blue Owl will help me too and I will cook and do for them, but maybe we could have some of your crops if you can spare some."

"It will be done and you will have it in three suns from now." Tall Pine said. The baby had enough food and was given to his grandmother to help let air up by patting his back and that he done at once. Tall Pine got up and said, "We go now, but will return in three suns and bring much food for you and your friends to eat." Old Bear and the others came in and sat on robes. Old Bear was given the baby to hold. Yellow Rock got fire wood and Blue Owl brought a large piece of buffalo meat and cut it up for the cooking pot, saying, "He taught me well - now I can kill game for us all."

Pounce, Shadow, Cubby and the other wolves that had gone to stop Weasel Tongue came to Moon Boy's lodge. Tall Elk and Skunk and others were there also. "It is done," Pounce said, "Weasel Tongue came to kill you Moon Boy and me too if he could so we killed him. He will come no more." Bald Eagle and others came and told how the body of the dead Crow was put in a tree to rest forever by his friends. Eagle held the long flint knife in her talons that she gave to Fast Fox. This is yours; you gave it to him to use and he will need it no more, so I give it to you."

"Thank you eagle, I will use it better than to kill our people." Baby came and set on Pounce's back. "Ride, Pounce, ride!"

"But my paw is hurt. I stepped on some grass on the way here."

"Poor Pounce," Baby said, and kissed the huge paw, "Now it will be better." Cubby covered his eyes and said, "The son of my sister is as big a joker as he is a killer." Then he rolled on the ground and laughed long. The first look Pounce gave Cubby was not good to see, then he smiled and told baby that after she ate her food they would go for a ride and she could hold Cubby by his tail to show the very best way to go and that he would do it or else. All knew what that meant.

After baby had her food, Pounce took her for a ride but he did not go alone. Twenty or more lobos went also, as it was known the big cat clan wanted revenge, for the she cat they had killed was well liked by her people. Since baby was the reason for Sheila's death, they would kill her if they could. Cubby was there, as was Curly, Shadow, Red Tongue, Sly, Little Bit and others known to have long fangs and much size and terrible power in a fight. Eagles were along too, high and low, looking for hiding spots the big cats could hide in or under, so all in all the ride was safe enough.

Most of the crop was safely gathered, but not the potatoes: they would stay in the ground for a time, only eating potatoes were eaten. The new potato cave was not ready yet. It was much larger and deeper then the first cave and it was made about the same way, dug in the steep bank of the river. It had been dug high enough so water would not get in but with overhead enough to give it strength. It had uprights of poles and braces to help hold the weight of the earth above. The floor of the new cave was different too: much old grass was cut, and dry sand added to it to keep it dry and cool. Skunk was in charge of the digging so all things had to be just so, or you did it over again. All expected to find more old remains of men from the long ago times but none were found and no gold either, a fact that made everyone glad.

The new cave would have one more thing different too; it would hold not only potatoes but also pumpkins and squash as well. Wolves helped too, not only in digging but also now as guards to keep out grandfather rattlesnakes and other prairie pests who may want to live in its cool dark depths. A door had to be built too, one that could be opened and shut tightly so you could go in and out to get what you needed and not freeze what was inside. Skunk thought on this long. It would be big enough to get through, and made of strong ash poles lashed together with rawhide and covered on two sides with old buffalo hide to make it almost airtight. Tall Elk, Moon Boy, Buffalo Tongue, Iron People, Taken Alive and more came to see and much praise was given Skunk and his helpers for a job well done.

The wolves were not left out either, for twenty or so had worked as hard on the cave as the Lakota had, digging and pulling out soil then as guards until the door was made. Now it was ready to put the big crop in, but that would wait, because the ground was the best place to keep the potatoes in so the skins would harden and keep longer. There was no reason to watch the Crow camp with Weasel Tongue gone, but eagles still watched the east. The white ones had not come back yet, but all knew they would. More likely in the spring, but they watched anyway, not every sun but enough to stay on top of it. Skunk played with his bows, always trying to send an arrow farther and faster and hitting what he shot at. He had twenty young helpers too who were learning bow making under him, some like Wind In His Hair and Big Legs were learning fast and soon would be as good as Skunk himself.

It was time to hunt winter meat. The fall hunt would start at first light; seven groups of hunters would go seven different ways so as not to take too many buffalo out of any one herd. Twenty braves traveled with each group, with pack horses along to bring back the meat and skins for robe making and other needed things for the people. Then the drying and smoking of the meat could begin, with the women doing most of that work with help from the young ones as fire tenders and fetchers. Other groups were building the wood piles up for winter use so just about every one had a job to do.

The eagles took word from one hunter group to another so not too much meat was taken at one time, or the camp tenders could not keep up. After two suns of hunting a big meal was planned with Skunk in charge of that and everyone would take a sun or two off and just enjoy. All except the wolves and eagles who watched all the time for raiders who could show up anytime, and no one wanted that. War did not go well and spoiled one's meals, and someone might get killed. There was nobody on the prairie who did not know that the Lakota and their wolves and eagles could not be caught with their pants down, so to speak, because of them talking in each other's tongue. Air or ground made no difference. They could speak with thoughts only or open conversation near or far, and to all things: horse, people, big cats, owls no one was left out, but if the wolves were your friends you had not a worry or care in the world. If they were against you, don't pack your bag just get and that may not be fast enough. Did I hear some one say, the plain tribes were just dumb savages? Well then you have not studied your history very well, they had better thinkers than we do now or just as good.

Winter came again, with its entire splendor: cold crisp winds, a thick covering of snow upon the land, then it would warm a little, and frost formed on all things. Trees, grass and brush glittered like diamond dust had been sprinkled over all things, then sun came out and the evergreens looked like glittering gems. Tiny blue and white frost lights were every place one looked; it was so beautiful it took your breath away. Smoke curled out of every lodge and paths were made from lodge to lodge by people bringing good things to eat. The sound of laughing could be heard all over camp because life was good. The men played the dice game and smoked their pipes and spoke of brave things they had done. The women talked of cooking and baby talk. Young ones played with puppy or chased each other, rolling in the snow.

Curly, Cubby and Pounce came to Moon Boy's lodge to be lazy and sleep by the door, but baby would have none of that; she rolled on them, pulled their ears and begged for a ride. It was to cold to be out in the snow for her so they just made excuses as to why they could not ride with her: Pounce had a bone in his paw, Curly saw two things at one time and Cubby was still thinking. Pounce got to his feet, stretched, told baby, "Have your mother find something warm for you to put on, and after you eat, we will maybe go look and see what we can see. Come you two lazy wolves let us see if big cat has been here." Cubby and Curly were only too glad to go; Cubby had not thought of a reason why he could not ride with baby yet, and this was as good an excuse as any.

Wind Runner, a young antelope, was nervous. He thought he saw wolves out of the corner of his eye on a ridge far away, and then he saw nothing - they were just not there. Not that he was afraid; he could outrun any wolf he had ever seen, he thought, but he had never seen run Pounce before, and then they were there. Wind Runner was fast, very fast, and had fed well and felt good. This run would be fun, and he would show this stupid wolf a thing or two in running and dodging. Then he saw the lead wolf was Pounce, that terrible wolf king known for his killing ways, then he did not feel so good, but too late now - he would have to run for his life. The flat that lay ahead was long and smooth, evenly covered with snow. Wind Runner ran, each stride long and sure. His sharp hooves cut to solid footing and he flew without wings. He was warming up now and felt good, so he looked back and Pounce was ten yards back also running smoothly. Wind Runner ran faster. The snow dust billowed out behind like a cloud of white, and he gained a little, but still there was Pounce six yards back and to his left; he had gained some. It was time to trick the wolf. He cut right then hard left and put on a burst of speed that was blinding. Pounce was left in the dust then Wind Runner looked again and Pounce was only four yards back. How had he done that? Wind Runner opened up to full speed - that was very fast, but Pounce was still there, red tongue out to the side of his mouth and enjoying every leap. Wind Runner could go no faster and Pounce was getting closer. Now Pounce was beside him and knocked him down. It was over and Wind Runner had lost, "Get it over Pounce," he gasped, "I am your food."

"No," Pounce said, "I am not hungry just now. I just wanted to see you run, and it was fun, but know that I am faster and could catch you anytime I want to. Go now and enjoy your life."

Wind Runner got to his feet and shook off the snow still clinging to his coat, "I have always heard, Pounce, that you are a killer, but I see now you are not. I thank you for my life and yes, I will use it wisely."

"Go then, before the others get here."

"But we are here Pounce. We saw and we feel you are bigger than we thought. It was a good run and the pronghorn ran well but you can run much better than Wind Runner. Come let us go play with baby, she will be ready, so they did, and she was ready. Nine more wolves joined them just in case the big cats were watching and three were too few, not to fight the cat but someone had to protect baby from harm and twelve was a nice round number. If you added up their combined weight it would be over fifteen hundred pounds of fighting wolves, you want to try that? Not me, I pass. My mother never had any dumb kids.

They took baby over hills of white but stayed away from cedar draws so as not to chance where the cats lurked, so they looked at the horse herd and baby even petted one or more of them. The afternoon was mild for cold time and baby enjoyed all of it, but it was time to take her back. Her little nose was cold, and the wolves caught a few jack rabbits for the cooking pot and themselves too. All said and done it was a good sun to run and play. Pounce, Curly and Cubby took three rabbits into Plum Leaf to cook and the rest the other nine ate. The three big lobos lay on their robes near the door flap resting. All were tired, but when Cubby sleepily remarked to Curly how the son of their sister had ran down Wind Runner the fast antelope and then let him go unharmed, was that great or what? Moon Boy over heard the comment and wanted to know all about it, so they told him. That was good of Pounce Moon Boy had told him. Pounce said, "That Curly and Cubby had much room for their teeth." They all knew that it meant that the two uncles had big mouths. Moon Boy also told him that he was proud of him, and with that he went to sleep.

For the next two suns, Pounce, Curly and Cubby stayed around Moon Boy's lodge, and they played with baby and relaxed. Now it was time to hunt meat again. They stopped by the wolf head quarters and had a short meeting with the she wolf; she, after all, was still the brains of the pack. She asked them to maybe pick something for her, if it was handy, as she had hurt her left hind leg leaping up to catch a sage hen. Red Tongue, Sly, Little Bit and ten or so others went too, not because they were hungry but for something to do and they liked to run anyway. They went past cedar draw, west, and ran into a small bunch of buffalo.

The buffalo ran on, seeing the wolves approaching. That was good: get them hot; they tasted better that way. Buffalo were running in a pattern to get away from their pursuers, crossing back and forth in front of each other, adding to the confusion and sending up much snow dust. They were in a long line; the younger and faster buffalo in the lead, the older slower in the back. Pounce and Red Tongue turned the leaders to the right, running them in a curved formation, bringing them back to their starting point. An old bull and this year's calf were last in line because both had bad feet. The old bull had fathered many calves and had eaten many young onions and much green grass and saw springs come and go. Now he was angry. He was tired of running and his feet hurt. So he whirled on the nearest wolf, bellowing out his rage, but his bad leg failed him and he went down hard.

Shadow got him by his nose and pulled his head back, and Pounce opened the big vain in his neck letting out his life in the snow. Grass was his food and now he was food, and the calf was next. The she wolf would get part of him. Curly and Cubby removed a hind quarter of the calf and put it to one side, because this was for mother to eat. The bull was large so there was plenty of meat to go around. All ate their fill and there was plenty of meat left over for the lesser meat eaters too: badgers and coyotes would come. Skunk was sleeping so would miss out on the meat but eagle and magpie would be here soon, but not likely the weasel, because weasels liked blood and not meat so much. Pounce, Curly, and Cubby took turns carrying the calf leg back to the she wolf who received it with much pride and many thanks to her sons and grandson.

"Think nothing of it," Curly said, "You did it for us many times."

"Yes," Cubby remarked, "And we will help you anytime you need it."

Chapter 20

Hans finished doing hog chores early and had gone to see his brother at the mill. He needed more screenings and waste grain that John had to get rid of anyway. "Bring your horse and cart out back and I will help you load up some moldy corn and oats as well as screenings for your hogs. You should give me a ham as much grain as I gave you Hans."

"I will, and I want to have a barn dance too, maybe. I keep thinking of the west and gold and furs John. Just a little gold and we could retire and do just what we want to."

John looked a long time at Hans then said, "I am doing what I want now, and I thought you were doing the same. We know nothing of furs. I would buy the good furs at a bad time and bad furs at a good time and soon we would have nothing, and as for gold it is way up in hill country. I don't think the natives have any at all, but go if you want to. I know you want a shot at that big wolf who outsmarted us all. He will be the death of you if you go with revenge the only reason for going. You have a lot of time to think about it; it's quite awhile until spring. But remember to tell the men going with you that gold we found no hint of, and the furs would be just wolf and coyote, no mink or beaver or otter either. Timber is not there - only along the rivers so building log houses or a fort will be hard too. The Lakota are well organized and don't want to trade, they are much smarter than anyone thought and can see a bad deal a long way off. You must think of them as being as smart as we are or you will fail. Maybe there is something they want but what that is I don't know and it maybe too costly to trade. And one more thing, they have got teamed up with wolves and eagles too; how, I don't know but you do know wolf pelt will not be a fur you can trade for and who knows what else. Think on it, Hans, before you go and think about what you are leaving behind - it may be more than you will gain."

Winter went by a day at a time and Hans's hair got longer on his face and head. He also smelled bad too. He spent more time at the beer house and less with his hogs and they began to suffer. Big John walked in on him setting on a bench, sipping beer. John took the mug and threw it out the door. Hans started to protest, and John told him to shut up or he would beat him and drag him in the snow, but he was coming anyway and that was that. The two brothers marched to the barber shop, well, one marched and the other staggered, but they got there anyway. "Now get out of them filthy rags!" and John pushed him into that tub that was steaming in the back room, waiting for him. John told him to take out what money he had because the rags were getting burned. "Now get at it or I will help you." John threw a bar of soap in the water and told him to use it up.

When he was clean again and in the new clothes, he was barbered then John took him to the eating house. "Now we will eat. I will talk you will hear me, and you had better hear me good. I will not tell you again. I have sent men to feed your hogs and women to clean your house, build a good fire and warm up the house so you can get a good night's sleep in a clean bed - something you have not had this year yet. When I found you, you were dirtier than your hogs and smelled bad too. Now in the morning get the hogs on the gain again then I want one smoked and ready for the table as payment for what I did for you. Then in the spring we will go west again, not to trade but to talk and find out what they need or want. Then we will go on west to the mountains in the time we have left. Now read up on gold digging so we know how it is done and done right, then we will see. Now we will go to your house and you will go to bed and rest. We have much to do, and if I find you again as I did today I will shoot you and that will be that."

When Hans got out of bed the next day he found a full meal on his table, hot and good. An old woman had it ready for him, thanks to big John's thoughtful ways. When Hans was finished eating and had thanked the kind old lady, he went to his hog yard and was shocked. He had no idea he had been so slack, for the hogs looked bad. Well, he would fix that starting now. Hans sorted the hogs and put them in their proper places for feeding, butchering and breeding. He cleaned pens and bedded them. Two or three were ready to kill, so they were soon hanging in the cooler. They would be smoked soon and he had orders to fill and then one for John. In the next few days ten or so sows had pigs, all big litters, so Hans was off and running again. Maybe the west thing was a pipe dream but he did want to go and look and see for the adventure of it, if nothing else.

So they planned, he and John, and studied on gold digging, what to look for, the equipment needed while the long days of winter slid by, like a snake sliding over a log. Before they were ready, spring was at hand and they were not ready to start. Good people had to be found to look after Han's and John's operation. They were both going too well to just leave the operation by itself. So they looked, interviewed, and found a farmer with two strong sons who could also do math. It was found that they had much grain on the farm that they did not have a use for, so they became part owners in the hog operation and also at the mill. For a week Hans and John showed them what must be done and how to do it. Now they were ready to go west. Five men would go and help in anything that needed. They loaded up the equipment and personal gear on pack horses and started west by a little north to miss some of the many lakes known to have too many blood sucking bugs.

By the end of the first day's riding, an eagle was seen sitting in a tall tree, and they knew that it was started then. By the next sundown they all will know of our coming. Hans studied the situation and two seconds later blurted out, "I could kill that one with my long gun and they would not know."

"Stupid one," John said, "what about the one over in that tree or the one high up and to your left? Can you kill them all? Not by your old tin type you can't. If you start that killing business talk I go back now, and you go on by your own self. I told you if we do nothing to try to hurt them they may be friendly. It's our only chance to get anything we came after. Now smile and wave at them, let them know we know why they are here, we must be open and friendly, or we will fail. Forget

153

about Pounce too; do not think about a shot at him. By now he can probably shoot one of the guns they got from us and maybe better than you can, what do you say to that?"

"I say humph! I can out shoot any old wolf!"

All smiled, for it was a joke and Hans missed it like a blind man throwing horseshoes. All knew that in order to shoot well, one must close one eye and aim, and Pounce never learned to close one eye. Ha! I got you too, humor goes a long way: it smoothes out the bumps on many a long trail.

By sun down the next day, Tall Elk, the Lakota, the wolf pack, all of them knew the white ones were coming again. Would it ever end? No, it would take many years but the high plains the Lakota knew and loved would one day be settled with farms, schools, towns and cattle ranches. It is called civilization and no one can stop progress; you just learn to live with it, or die being stupid.

Bald Eagle and two more sat with Tall Elk and Pounce, along with others of the pack and the rest of the camp as the eagle told of the white ones coming. "They have no trade goods that we could see," eagle was saying, "just their camping gear. I think they want to just talk. Maybe we had better do the same, or until we find out what it is they want. Pounce, try to control yourself; I know you would like to kill the big faced one with the deep set blue eyes with yellow hair that hangs down, but try not to. We can't kill them all, anyway. If they do something stupid then we will see. There are seven of them in all; all are well armed with thunder sticks and long knives of the hard shiny kind. They have pack horses loaded with gear we know nothing about but it looks like digging tools. Maybe they dig for food - we are not sure - but I don't think so."

"I feel they are after something more than that. We have heard them use the term GOLD, whatever that is, many times." Eagle finished speaking, and Skunk looked at Tall Elk and shook his head. What he feared was now happening: he said when they found the gold in the digging of the storage cave to keep it hidden, because it would make trouble for us some time. Then Eagle added more, "Five of them we have never seen. One of them is the leader of last time, and three of them have bows with arrows. One bow is as thick as a tree limb and that one aims like a thunder stick and shoots a short arrow very hard and fast. I saw it kill a deer a very long ways away, but it made no sound. That one is very dangerous to us and must be watched close. It will be a moon before they get here, because they look at all stream beds and river gravel, like they lost something they want back. When they see a rock yellow in color they all look at it long then they see it is only sand stone and drop it like it was nothing. I think they have been in the sun too long and have gone mad - I don't know."

Big John was saying, "Hans, you know I think we are all crazy. There is no hint of color in any place we looked and we looked at every gravel bed so far along the way." Hans was thinking. "We have not come far enough yet John. We are not to the Lakota yet and we may have to go beyond that point to find gold. You know gold is where you find it. That's what the book said." It was late in the day and the seven men were in the flat land past the many lakes, out where sleeping was better, and no more blood sucking bugs. An arrow from the bow killed a buffalo calf, and water was at hand so they made camp and cooked a good meal with meat the main part of the meal. Grass was plentiful so the horses fed well too; after all, their well being was important for travel as well as the success of their goal.

John asked the other five men, "What do you boys think?"

"Well, John, as you said we have not come that far yet," Andy said as he spread his big hands to the fire to get its warmth, not any of us know what to think about eagles that can talk to men or wolves either, and this Pounce who sent you boys back the first time. What kind of a wolf must he be?"

"Well, he is big, the biggest I have ever seen. Maybe one hundred and eighty pounds or more, and when he looks at you, it makes you wish that you were far away. His eyes look through you like knives, and you feel small and cold then he tells you in plain talk what will happen to you the next time his friends or him are bothered by you. Then he laughs, yes he laughs, and it sounds like thin ice breaking on a cold day and you know he could kill as quickly as a wink. Then there are the others, maybe seventy or eighty more wolves talking and smiling and you understand every word and most of what is said is how they mean to kill you slow. Even worse if you bother the Lakota or other friend they have, and you have to guess who the other friends are.

Peter Burke, the small man of the group, had little blue eyes that missed nothing; all his movements were quick and sure and he was the best shot of the seven. Pete said, "If anyone here has a plan to take a shot at that Pounce count me out, or all you will see is me sucking wind and that not longer then a tenth of a second or so. If he is only a tenth as smart as you say I want to be his friend for life. Hell, he could dig the gold, sack it, hand it to us, and not break out in a sweat, if he wanted to. Bob Jackson, the older man, said, "I second Pete's plan. I may not be that fast but I will be back east and no time lost; you boys had better not think of Pounce or you will be short handed.

At first light the seven white ones broke camp, and rode west, not bothering to clean up their mess. Shortly after four eagles came in with cupped wings to find good meat left to rot so they helped them selves and ate meat. This mistake Pounce would know about soon and the Lakota too, for good food was never left, a law all knew and never dared break. Jared Leff rode beside John this morning. Jared was a smaller man with quick light brown eyes set behind a high slightly hooked nose above a mouth always ready to laugh at any humor at all. His skin was pale and his long hair caught behind his head with strip of raw hide forming a tail. Jared had one of the long bow and arrows, a good hunter and a fair shot with gun or bow. Jared was eager to give you a helping hand and quick to use his fists or knife if you double crossed him; in other words he was a better friend than foe.

He wanted to meet Pounce. He had heard so much about this big lobo. I am not sure Pounce was eager to meet him but Pounce could like you if things were right and you were not a threat to him or ones he protected. "How far to the place you met the Lakota and wolves John?"

"Not far now. I think we will see them soon when we don't expect it, and when we do don't do anything stupid or we will not go any further but stay here dead on the ground or go back with nothing." Big John spoke grimly and his eyes continually paced the horizon. The sun was high and a little past mid point to where it would fall off the edge of the world. The seven rode to a well watered draw and got down to water the riding stock and themselves. John stooped to drink, then looked up and full into the face of Pounce and fifty or so big lobo wolves.

"Well John, we meet again. I see that idiot Hans is with you. I would have thought you would leave him back, because he would like to kill me you know, but he will not. He will die if he makes a single move too quickly."

Moon Boy and thirty Lakota braves stood up with bows at half cock on two sides of the seven. They were unseen, and then they were all around them. The Cheyenne, Antelope was with the Lakota, for he knew of the white one's tongue and would speak for both sides. Pounce knew all tongues but talking with thoughts and signs and feelings - with some words too - was his long suit. It is hard to explain but when Pounce talked you understood every word and thought perfectly, just as John did a minute ago when he looked full into Pounce's eyes, and he could not have explained it then or now but he knew.

Moon Boy said, "I am sub chief of the Lakota. What are you here for? We sent you back twelve moons ago and we told you then we would not trade with you for furs from our friends' backs. We burned your goods and kept only what we could use and we learned how to shoot your guns and found our arrows best for us because we can make them ourselves. Your guns we cannot make one part for, and we know nothing of the powder that makes the thunder stick boom. We want nothing from you and we give you nothing of ours. So why are you here? Do you want to die? If you do, we can do it now quick." Antelope put the words in the white tongue.

Two eagles came in and sat down. "Skunk and Tall Elk want to talk to the white ones. Bring them to camp but tie them first." John and the others were tied on their horses guns were put in charge of Moon Boy and his braves and all started for camp. "Well," Jared said, "now we will see how they live."

"Yes, just before they kill us all," remarked Pete.

"I don't think they will or it would be done by now. Keep your mouths shut," said a terse John.

At the Sioux camp all killing tools were laid out and studied. The cross bow was looked at by all. It was decided that first they would eat then they would ask how it worked. A meal was spread out, fit for a king and John, Jared, Bob and the rest never saw such food or expected to find it here. Buffalo stew over boiled potatoes with corn, beans, corn cakes with honey and all done with style that put an eastern café to shame.

When all had eaten his fill, Skunk asked them, "why they had come again to the home land of the Lakota. All the wealth we have is our food, our horses and ourselves. There are no furs and we would not take them if there was; it would mean killing our friends and we don't kill friends. If you killed them we would kill you so nothing would be gained. The eagles said you have digging tools with you; what will you dig, food? I think you will find little buffalo stew in the ground or corn cakes either, or do you just enjoy digging in the dirt to see grass roots. Or did you come all this way to make us laugh at how stupid you can be? Or may be you wanted to eat good food just one time before you die, I don't know. But this I do know: we are tired of seeing you come and bothering us. Now one of our young will look at you, she is wise beyond her years and she will tell us all why you are here." Antelope put all this in the white tongue, it was a lot and took some time to do, but it was done and done well.

Plum Leaf brought baby, and Pounce, Curly, Cubby, and Shadow went to get her and baby got on Pounce's back. She rode to where the white ones sat with a little smile on her face. Pounce went to John and lifted his lips just enough to show a white gleam of teeth. Not something I would care to see. Baby looked at John, and then said, "He is mostly good, but he wants to find the yellow gravel so he can be the head of all things and be rich." Pounce told John what baby said and asked if that was true.

"Yes, but how did she know?"

"She is very wise," Pounce said. Hans was next - he shook like a leaf in a wind, what of him? Baby looked at Hans a long time then said, "This one is bad through and through. He wants your skin, Pounce because you are smarter than he is, and he wants the gold too but for different reasons. He wants to control all things, even his brother." Hans jumped like a bee stung him, "She lies!" he said, and started to get up. John and Jared pulled him back down and he sat like a man about to be hung, which was not too far from the truth either. Jared was next, and Pounce took baby to him. What of this one?

Baby looked at him and smiled. "This one is good. He would like gold too but if he finds no gold he will not be unhappy. He wanted the ride to a new land to see what he could see, and he would talk to you. He feels that you would be interesting to talk to and he is curious about how we live and our way of life. When more of them come I hope they are like him, for it will be better for us all." Pounce smiled then said, "I will talk to him then and maybe all will." Pete Burke was next - baby looked at him only a little, "He is only a little wanting gold but he wants only what he finds himself, and not what is someone else's. His mind is clear and he is fair."

The other three of the seven were grouped together as one. All had come west to gain wealth, one kind or another because they thought it easer than working a regular job doing this or that. It wasn't that they were lazy but they were not ambitious either. So they went along just to be doing something and thought if the other men who were greedier found gold then they would get part of it. They also knew that they would never go on their own. They never thought about the gold belonging to the natives; if you were not part of the so called civilized world they thought you had no right to it at all. So just take it, and if they put up a fuss shoot them and be done with it. Who would even care?

Now here they sat being judged by a child setting on the back of a huge lobo wolf who was smarter by far than they were, and would ever be and if she ruled not in their favor they may be killed. Now if that makes sense to you, let's trade places: I am ready.

Pounce began to speak, his eyes flashing in the light of the fire. "So it is gold you came for, is it? Did it dawn on you that even if there was gold here that it would just be yours for the taking? That we would just give it to you? Because you wanted it after we found it, dug it and made skin bags for it, then sacked it up nice and good and you come along and said I will take that now, and we just give it up? What world did you say you came from? Not this one - now I am getting unhappy with all of you so you had better start making sense quick or I, Pounce, will kill you where you sit. As the seven sat there in the Lakota camp on the Moreau River, beads of cold sweat began to form on foreheads and down back sides as they looked in the eyes of Pounce and others. The good meal they had just eaten did not feel as well as it had a short time ago."

Big John was thinking of his mill and how nice it would be to smell the dust again and Hans could see in his mind's eye the hog lots and hear the pigs eating. Jared could feel his long bow in his hand and he could see a deer standing in bow range and he could almost taste how good deer meat was when cooked outside in the open air. All the others had thoughts too; how could this happen to them? Were they not young, strong, and smart? How a bunch of wolves and some dumb Lakota could outsmart them in every way from sundown- or were they dumb? Slowly it came to them, that if anyone was dumb it was not the wolves or the Lakota, it was them, and from that time on they thought of them as equals or better, because they were, if they got the chance to prove it. "Well," Pounce said irritably, "I am waiting. Has the cat got your tongues?"

Now let us pause for just a second, I said Pounce could speak in all tongues. He can; the power of thought is so strong and when mixed with signs and actions with some words you could make yourself understood to anyone no matter where you were. Pounce had a powerful mind, and so when Pounce looked full at you with his clear intense eyes you knew exactly what he said and meant.

Big John and Jared were talking to each other; "May we speak? It will take many words to say all we have to say, and will take much time."

"Yes," Pounce said, "We will hear you." Skunk, Tall Elk, Moon Boy, Fast Fox and many more were there to hear too, as was Bald Eagle and ten more eagles. John began first. He said, "We were wrong to believe that you the Lakota were dumb, and by that I mean you knew nothing of gold." Antelope the Cheyenne put this in the Lakota tongue, but Pounce knew at once what was said as did the eagles.

"Gold," John continued, "has a recognized value all over the world, known by men everywhere you go, and can be used to by anything you want or need anywhere.

"The world is not just in your country or ours. You come forty suns to the east past the tall trees and many lakes, but the world goes beyond that. It is maybe two hundred more suns more until you come to the big water that you cannot see over. There, other men live different from us; they have black skins, and some have yellow skins. But they all know of gold and its value, and you could by anything with it you want or need. The world goes west to over the tall mountains until you come again to the big waters."

Here Bald Eagle asked to speak, "Yes. What he said is truth. Some of us have flown past the tall mountains far to the west and came to the big waters. I rested for two suns then I went out over it. I could not see land in front or back and I was very afraid; I was lost I did not know where land was. I almost never got back, and when I did I was too tired to hunt. My son hunted for me, and I lived, but I will never try to cross it again."

One of the young she eagles asked to speak, and Pounce gave her a nod, she spook thus- "My mother's brother and I flew north up over tall trees and tall mountainous to were there was mostly snow on the ground. We went more to the north and the air was cold and more snow. We caught some white rabbits to eat. We were not tired so we went more and found white bears with large feet, black eyes, and noses. A big wind was blowing so we caught its drift and come south again, but the point is the world never stopped going north. We did and came back. Bald Eagle spoke again and said, "I have not gone far to the south but others I know have, and told me that far to the south is another big water. By it is a forest all green and tangled with under growth so dense that only little long tailed men can live there, and it is warm all the year around and is called a jungle. So the world must be very big. As for me, I think I will stay here and live as I like helping my friends the wolves and Lakota and stay away from places I know nothing about."

"Now," said Pounce, "What do we do with you? Why did you not stay in your country? Has it gotten too small for you to stay there and work at what you know best? There is no gold here, but there is gold in the mountains far to the west we have heard, but there is one thing bad about that: other people live in that place who may not want you to dig. Some of you will be killed and some of them too, have you thought about that? Then you will tell others of your find and they will come, many of them, and the people who should have it will be killed if they get in the way. Hans is not going with you. If we let you go I am going to kill him. He is as evil as the first one who came who wanted to buy me, Curly and Cubby for our fur from Tall Elk. He never thought if we wanted to die or not, he just wanted our fur to sell for gold. Hans is like that so he will die. If we let him live he will come again to hunt me and I can't always see him first. His thunder stick kills from a long way off.

Skunk, Fast Fox and Tall Elk, along with the she wolf and Sniff Pounce's mother were concerned with the decision made by Pounce to kill Hans. Not that he should be spared - he was lazy and mean minded and had said he would kill Pounce or die trying. So why should Pounce take that chance and let him live? Bald Eagle joined the conversation, "I have been in contact with eagles and hawks in the settlements and they say that if Hans makes a move to come west I will know of it in a sun and a half. So Pounce should be safe but we should make him think if he tries again he is gone at once. Killed I mean, at once with no questions asked. Hans will just be gone, end of story." So Hans's death sentence was lifted and he would go back with the others a free man, and he knew better that to try again.

Pounce went and sat down with the seven white men and spoke these words, "We have had a talk and the others have talked in your favor. I see their wisdom is good, so not anyone will be killed. I would talk with you Jared about things I am not sure about. I would ask you what you will do with your wealth if you find some, is there something you want or need? Or are you just looking? Skunk wants to know about the bow on the stick and how it works; he is always making bows."

"Yes," Jared said, "We will show him. Now I would like to know why do you help the Lakota and scout, fight, and protect them?"

"Because of Moon Boy. We are his eyes and ears. He is almost without sight and we saved him when he was lost in a snow storm a long time ago. My grandmother's sons, Curly and Cubby, have looked out for him ever since, and now I do too. We all love him and now his baby too. She rides me I am her horse. We care for her in every way, and no one will hurt her as long as we are near. Let me try to explain something to you: I, Curly, Cubby, Shadow, Red Tongue, Sly and ten or so more are wolves with all the feelings of wolves but we are like Lakota too. We speak the same tongue, we think like Lakota and we have more cunning than other wolves. I can out think anyone who comes to bother us. I see through their plans to harm us, but I have no little voice telling me that's wrong. The Lakota have a conscious, I don't. I would have killed Hans quicker then a fly bothering me and thought nothing about it at all. I can see in others' minds and know what they are thinking; I know Hans is bad. He would kill all of you - his brother John too - for gold and blame us for it."

Tall Elk, Moon Boy, Skunk, Looking Back Horse, the eagles and other wolves with more cunning in figuring out problems than others came and sat with the white adventurers. "Now John, we would like to know what you would do with gold if you had it. I, Fast Fox, know were there is more gold then you seven could carry away, and we could gather it with all of us helping in three suns working together, but we want part of it. You would have to turn it into money and put it in one of the places you call banks for us. We would all be partners and we would take out enough for the good of the people when we needed to. We did not know how big the world was. We still don't but we have a better idea now than we did before. Before we were not concerned about what other parts of the world were doing; now I think we had better start. So we will help you in your search for gold as long as you are fair and honest with us. Forget how we helped you and your bones with turn white without honor in the grass. Skunk, will you show him the things called charms you made?"

Skunk got up and went to his lodge, then came and sat down again. "I carved this out of soft sandstone, then melted some yellow gravel and put it in the molds. Now I have these," and showed the golden charm he made. John's breath went out as the sun touched the virgin gold, and shot golden fire in all directions. All looked long at the charms, and John asked breathlessly, "Do you have more?"

"No. I only made the two and then I put a little more of the yellow gravel away in a place only I know of."

"The only problem I see is that the gold is on other people's homelands but they are friends of ours. We did not kill them in battle when we could have and then we gave them seeds to plant a crop so they may help gather it up. We will ride two or three suns to get there. We may take you when we come to agree on how we should share the gold and what you plan to do with yours. But first," Skunk said, "Show me the bow on the stick, and how it works. I wish to know." Andy Anderson, the one that used the crossbow, got the bow and arrows, and he showed Skunk a lever where the string fit that was attached to the trigger on the under side. He then put his feet on the bow in the middle of the stick and pulled with two hands and put the string behind the lever and said, "Now it is cocked."

He now put an arrow in a groove up against the string. "Now you point it like a thunder stick and aim at what you are shooting at, and pull this trigger. He pointed at the lever on the bottom side. He then put the arrow though a grass-filled buffalo hide a long ways away. The arrow struck the target. Skunk took out an arrow and looked at it; the point was of the hard shiny medal like the thunder sticks were made of, and again he could not make any like it. Skunk reached for the weapon, "May I shoot it?"

"Yes, but be careful hit what you are aiming at."

So Skunk cocked it, put the arrow in place and put the arrow though the target. "Did you make this?"

"No," Andy said, "I traded for it. I do not have the parts to make one myself; I used money to buy it."

"So this is what you use gold for?"

"Yes, but that is only one of many things we trade for. There are many people in the place we come from, each one of them doing something and they get money for what they do. With this money they trade for things they need: food, clothes, anything that they need to live, and it is called working. Here, all of you work for the common good of all, and it may be a better way. When you plant your crops all of you do it old, young and middle age, and each of you do a part and you do it well and fast. Where we come from, a man his wife and their young ones plant the crops and care for them, then they sell their crops for money to buy things others make that they want or think they need. If we find gold it is a short cut to making money, only we hope to find more than we could earn working a job. We may find nothing, and if we find nothing, we may have come all this way to get no return for our time and then we may not be able to live well. It is a gamble - we don't know that we will find anything. It is hard to explain, and I think I like your way better."

Skunk thought a long time, and then said, "If all of you came at the same time, then we would have to try and stop you, or you would destroy us and our way of life and many would die on both sides, do you want that?"

"No we don't want that."

Tall Elk spoke, "There are things you have that we could use, but we don't need them. Our wisdom says that if we can't make the things we need ourselves they are bad for us. Your thunder sticks kills a buffalo quick, but when he dies with a lance or arrow, he is just as dead and feeds us the same. Pounce and the wolf pack have not spoken, or the eagles either, and they have good thinkers too, and all of us have not spoke. You will make a camp by the water. We will keep your killing tools and your horses; we will feed you and you will not look at our women. If you look at our women, the one who does will lose his male parts quick; we will be watching.

Get your camping gear and go down by the water and rest. Make your fires small - we don't want them to get away. Someone will bring meat. Be very careful; the wolves will guard you and if you try to leave they will kill you. Jared was talking to John, "I don't know if we are better off now or not; but I do know that charm made by Skunk is the best I ever saw. He is a craftsman of high quality and the gold was pure."

Hans was scared: he thought he would be killed by Pounce and his boys, but then he was given his life back and now they were disarmed, setting by the river not knowing what to expect. "I think we should wait until full dark, and then slip out of here and get some horses and go." John looked at him and asked, "Then what will we eat? Grass or mice? Or just not eat at all. On that bluff above the river sets two eagles, another is in that tree to our right and another is high and to our left just floating on air currents and I see three wolves and here comes Pounce. I knew Hans you were dumb but I did not think you stupid too. You wanted to be here and now we are just set and keep your mouth shut." Pounce was over by the river bend and then he was standing in front of Hans, how had he done that? "I see you would like to go. I read your mind; your mind is easy to read, because there is so little to read, it is easy."

Pounce said to Jared, "That rock by the water to your left is as far as you go that way. The tree to your right with the white branch is as far that way. You may look for gold in between, but I don't think you will find any; it is far away in the high hills, not here. I don't understand your motives for risking coming here. You came from a place where you had your work and a place to live. You had food to eat, but you

165

wanted our things; I think you are lazy. We don't come and bother you and yet here you are. Again you want our gold and you are bothering us. We killed the first one who came because he wanted my fur and my life. We sent you back two times hard. We could have killed you and should have, but we were sorry for you."

"If we help you, more will come and try to kill us for our wealth. You love gold, but we have no use for it. We live to help each other and you live to help only yourselves, to have wealth and I see now that you will never have enough to satisfy you. All you want is more; you will always want more. I am a wolf and think like a wolf but sometimes I am a Lakota, a human and am sorry for ones as stupid as you seven are, and would help you find happiness if it would end there but I think it will not. We will be asked to make a choice soon on your fate, how should I, or we if you will, vote as wolves? Or Lakota, but I tell you this I am tired of you and your greed and don't wish to see you more. The next time we will find you it will easy to make up our minds," and with that, Pounce turned to go and was just gone.

Andy said, "How did he do that? He was standing here talking to us and then he was not, did he evaporate or what?"

"I don't know," John said, "but I wish I was at the mill eating grain dust - I understand that."

Chapter 21

For five suns, the white men were left alone in their camp, as uneasy as a bunch of long tailed cats in a room full of rocking chairs on a hard wood floor. On the morning of the sixth sun, Tall Elk and the leaders of the Lakota camp along with the wolf pack and eagles came to see them. Tall Elk said, "Some of us have gone to get some gold for you. We will never tell you where, so don't ask. They should be back in twenty suns or so, but for now you will work for us tending crops, working with young horses, getting wood for the fires or anything we say. The same laws are still in place: you will not look at our women, and he that does will lose his man parts with this." Tall Elk took out his flint knife, "I have taken out the seeds of many a horse with this, you should be little different. When you have the gold you will be given your horses, your camp gear, and food, one bow with arrows, your knives, and your lives. We keep the rest. If you get greedy and try to find more gold, you will be killed in your sleep or along the way and you will never know we are near. You will have no warning at all. The vote was very close, and it was Pounce that saved you, or you would now be dead. So don't forget to thank him; he is your friend, the one called Jared made up his mind, I think he likes him."

"Now get your knives and come. We will work with crops this sun." The white ones worked well with the people and for three suns, crops were weeded, then they rested and ate a lot of good food cooked by Skunk, his way. For the next four or five suns some worked with horses and others got wood in for the cooking fires and the days slid by like winds of the morning and were gone. Then on the twenty-first sun, the gold diggers rode into camp on dusty damp horses with loaded pack horses in tow, packing much gold.

Tall Elk called a counsel and the white ones along with leaders of the camp, wolves and eagles sat and watched as the gold was put on robes, and what a pile of shimmering, golden beauty it made. It came to camp in eight buffalo skin bags, each bag around fifteen to twenty pounds. It was put in thirty smaller skin bags. John, Jared, Andy and Pete sat and just looked. Hans started to leap up and grab at the bags but Pounce and Shadow pushed him down hard, "Sit, and don't touch or you will be in no shape to enjoy any of it."

"Tall Elk, Skunk, and the rest of us will say who goes back to your country and how much goes with you, or did you think we would just give it all to you? If you thought that, then you are crazy as two flies fighting over ten dead buffalo after a snow storm. We will say how much goes with you and what you must do to get that, so set there and shut up. If you grab again, I will break your arm. If you think I can't, just try me. After that I will break your neck then there will be just six of you. Hans was too furious to think; his gold lust was making him lose control of his better judgment, and he lunged at Pounce who broke his left arm with a snapping sound that could be heard all over camp. "Want to try for your neck? I am ready."

John grabbed Hans who was writhing in pain and hissed in his ear, "You idiot! Set still and shut up! There is more gold in front of us than half the world has ever seen in one place before, and we are doing business with people fifty times smarter then I thought. We know nothing; it took almost thirty days to get it here and that means it could be as much as twelve hundred miles in any direction or under your fat ass - we don't know, and they hold all the cards including our guns. Now you want to fight with a huge lobo wolf which has a college degree in cunning, savagery and thinking with a common sense minor, remember that you have not gotten out of first grade yet. If you blow this one, I pass. Then you deserve to sleep with your hogs; I will help you no more. So think, man, don't do any more stupid things!" John said all this while helping Hans rig up a make shift sling for his arm which was quickly swelling and turning red.

It was now time to get down to business. Tall Elk, Fast Fox, Skunk, and others known for their wisdom along with Pounce, the she wolf,

Curly, Cubby and more, with Bald Eagle and her clan - all sat with the seven gold hunters. Hans was not comfortable. His left arm was splinted by Skunk, but pained him as sat to hear the terms of the gold bargain. Tall Elk began to speak, "We have much wealth in front of us; none of us know for sure how much it is, but you saw what it did to one of you seven. It drove him crazy and now he has a broken arm. He is lucky, it could have been his neck, and maybe it should have been. But," Tall Elk went on to say, "I know this- if you go back waving this gold like a scalp on a stick, and telling all you see of this gold you will have three out of every four men flogging horses to get here quick to find gold that you have no idea where it came from."

"We never told you and will not ever tell you the location of the gold, and then many will come and many will kill to find out and some will die on both sides, you too. Do you want that? No I thought not, so you must use many brains: go about selling it carefully, only one of you should do that, maybe John or Jared. Do it slowly and in more then one place as not to get noticed."

"Now our part in all this," Skunk now spoke, "I want twenty-five bows on a stick with ten times ten arrows for each bow with the hard points. I want a pot to melt balls for the thunder sticks we have and ten new thunder sticks with much powder to make thunder sticks boom. I want ten new cooking pots and twenty bags of salt for flavor and some pepper too. I want bags of the bean that turns water black when boiled in pots with some white sweet snow that doesn't melt to make it taste better. We want thirty skinning knives of the hard kind, not the kind that breaks like the first you brought: no good, that kind. The women want colored bead to work art with, and we also want sticks with the yellow red something on the one ends that makes fire jump when rubbed on a stone."

Now Tall Elk spoke, "Do not bring any stinking water that makes men sick and throws up good food. It makes him lay on his back and makes sounds like a sick coyote or we will kill you quick. We don't want that. Bring some tobacco to smoke in our pipes and robes of many colors, like you have on your sleeping bags, many of them, and the hard things to melt that makes balls for the thunder sticks. I will send you ten bags of gold for the things we want, and you will get more gold when you bring us our things. Be very careful; we will be watching, if you do us bad you get no more gold and you may die as well. Bring no more new men or all will be gone, including you."

Pounce and Shadow were talking, and asked to speak. "We have heard all you said we think it is good to get the things you need, but we think ten bags is too much gold. Five would be about right. Gold is much wealth and five bags is much value and we should make some of them stay with us until the others bring back what we want, or they may not bring us anything. We say keep Hans and Andy. Shadow and I will watch them very good, and if they try to go they know what will happen to them." Tall Elk thought this idea was good, and so sent braves to get their horses and gear and camp goods. Jared had his bow and arrows to get meat for their night camps and five bags of gold were put in old buffalo robes and tied tight and put on horses. Tall Elk said, "Now go quick and get what we want." They did and were soon out of sight.

Bald Eagle came and said, "I and four more will go and watch them gather the goods and will report to you every five or six suns." Pounce and Shadow stood and smiled at Hans, "Now we are brothers, we four. You cannot move without us knowing." Five eagles went with the others to watch the leaving party of men. "I will ask other wolves to help us watch you so know you are well cared for." Hans looked in to the unblinking yellow green piercing eyes of Pounce and knew fear, for he saw no mercy only dislike, hate and knew they would be watched, oh so well. Then he saw Sly, Red Tongue, Little Bit, Long Fang, and Kills Quick and knew for sure just how well they would be watched and Hans had no choice but to do as he was told, every time.

So the suns slid by like slow snakes over rocky ground, with the two white men working crops, pulling wood and doing what ever Pounce said. At the end of forty-seven suns an eagle came at first light to report that a long pack train was on its way. So the next sun, the two white men along with thirty-eight Lakota braves, twenty-five big rangy lobo wolves and eagles were going east to help bring in the pack train. They found them crossing the land of many lakes, and with the help of the Lakota and wolves and eagles flying high surveillance the pace was speeded up and better time was made.

Fifteen lobos fanned out in front with five on the right and five more on the far left; the other five trotted along in the back. Who would bother them? Not me, I say let them go and be glad they were not stopping. An old she bear with a cub was going to be grouchy but when she saw what she up against, she and the cub climbed a tall tree and got out of the way and sat there until all had gone by. She smelled the ham and other good food but the risk was too much - she would eat fish. In a sun or so they had passed the many lakes country and were out on the flat lands, away from the most of the blood sucking bugs. One could finally sleep without getting eaten up, making everyone more agreeable and better to get along with.

In the next suns, Hans rode up front with John there being enough help to move the pack train along nicely, "John did you sell all the gold?" "No. I just sold three bags and that came to near fifty thousand big ones. I then spent around twenty-three thousand to get what they wanted, and we still have more than a king's ransom in our account at the bank, plus the two bags I have in the bank's vault. How did you get along Hans?"

"That Pounce is a slave driver! He made us work in their crops and pull in wood and if a young girl walked by we had to shut our eyes and look at the ground, then he would poke me with a stick he had in his mouth and laugh then say if I was a good white one, I could talk to her maybe, but since I am bad, I can't even look at her."

"Did anyone say where the gold came from?"

"Yes. Some said to the far north in white bear land where snow is always on the ground. Others said to the far south in the jungle and little men with long tails knew where to look, but you had to give them bird eggs with honey or they just sat and laughed at you. Others said to the northwest where trees were hidden by rain. What story do you think is right, John?"

His brother just looked at him, "They have been pulling your leg, you big dummy. None of the above are correct and we will never find out. They will never tell the truth. If we get out with our skins we had better be satisfied; we already have more than I thought we would get. We have enough money to last a long time if we don't get stupid and get ourselves killed by that big wolf."

171

They at last were at the Grand River, with the sun still an hour old, before it went to rest in the west. All the horses were tired and hungry, so they were unpacked and put to water and grass. Camp was made, cooking fires crackled, buffalo ribs hissed and fat dripped in the fire. The men were hungry as the horses, for it had been a long sun. It was almost done, and next sun would see them at home camp. They would unpack and store things away. Pounce was glaring at the white men, as was Shadow, Curly and Cubby, "No we have not forgotten - it was here, where some of your kind tried to buy us from Tall Elk for our skins our furs. It was here where he wanted to take our lives and throw them away, like it was his right to do, with no thought of us. Moon Boy went to Pounce and sat by him, "Now Pounce, the other one was evil. The ones here don't want furs, they want gold."

Pounce licked Moon Boy's eyes, "You cannot see well again, your eyes are cloudy; don't you see? Gold and furs are both money. We have no place to spend money so we can't use it, but they can. The things in the packs were bought with gold we know how to get and they don't, if they did we would see them no more or see many of them at one time. Then they would try to kill us and we would kill them, now tell me what good is that? What they don't know is I myself could kill a hundred of them and they would never know I was near; all they would see is the dead on the ground and twenty of the pack could do that good. The first one that came was evil, we all know that if he had been better to his men they may have helped him more, not that it would have helped him any, for we had him cold, but Hans is bad. That's why they keep coming back - he is lazy, and he doesn't want to work. He wants to pick it off the ground or have us do it for him, and I will not help him."

Hans was very hungry, and the first hump rib he ate was so good he wanted more, so the second was as good as the first, but then he saw Pounce glaring at him out of his flat, cold, and unforgiving eyes and he knew fear again. Hans could understand every thought and word Pounce said and the good food he had just consumed now felt like a rock in his guts, and he wanted to run, but run where? And with the others feeling the same way he would not get two steps. John and Jared saw too, and understood. John shook his head and watched a lady bug climbing a grass blade; he had been that close to getting back with enough wealth to travel the world and see things, but no, Hans had spoiled that as well.

Jared said to John, "I will try to help. Say nothing to the others - they may not know how bad it is." Jared went to Pounce and Moon Boy. "May I sit and talk?"

"Yes, I see your mind is clear and your heart is good. I will hear your words- Hans is like one of your cubs or like one of our little boys: his body grew faster than his mind or brain did: he cannot see the landscape, he only sees a buffalo cow and her calf and thinks of food for him. He don't see how the cow loves her calf and would gladly die to protect it, or how the morning loves the soft breeze that touches the blooms of the flowers so bees can find them. He don't know why a meadow lark lifts her face to the sky and sings to all the world her joy of just being alive on this earth a free being. He can't see the forest for the trees, and doesn't know why you dislike him. He knows why he hates you: it is because you are smarter than he is. He sees you as dumb animal, a wolf, and you outthink him every way there is and he doesn't like it." Pounce heard all this quietly, and then listened more intently as Jared went on.

"The rest of us will see that he never comes by himself, and we won't bring him so this should be the last time you have to put up with him. Someday maybe his mind will catch up with his body so he can think like a full grown man, and not like a newborn. I don't know - some never grow up and stay little all their lives. We will just have to wait and see, but I wish you would not judge us all bad. For one, we will not harm you or yours in any way or the Lakota. It is better that we go back saying good things than to all die out here on the grass, because sometime they will know and come looking for revenge." Jared finished, and after a while, Moon Boy spoke. "At that time there would be a war, and some always die in a war. I say this not as a threat but a fact, hear my words as a friend - we will all be better off if you do."

Pounce looked at Moon Boy a long time. "We hear your words and they have much wisdom. We will wait and see the things we asked for. We will see if you forgot anything, and if you did it will go bad for you, and you will go again to get what you did not get the first time. Some of you will stay here. You will have only a short time to get back and if you run out of time some of you with us won't be. I respect you,

173

Jared, for your goodness and your understanding, but I lack what the people have: a conscience. I don't care if I kill you or not. I think I would not enjoy killing you, though, but don't stake your life on it. As for Hans, he is like the animals. I would kill him quicker then a bug on my paw. Now eat more meat if you want; at first light we go to the big camp and then we will see what we will see."

At first light the wolves had the horses up close and packs were put on and snugged in place. The long line went slowly, going south to the main camp and just past midpoint to the time sun would fall off the edge of the world to the west, the Moreau River breaks were in sight. A very good sight to all, but the white men were worried that they may have not gotten everything and would have to rush back and get more.

Then in a short time, they were at home camp among the hustle and bustle of a large camp. Wives, friends, and children all glad to see they were back came out to greet them. Packs were taken off horses and tired dusty horses rolled in the grass and moved out to water and to graze. All of the camps were present: wolves, eagles, and the people. The first to be laid out were twenty-five cross bows with twenty-five hundred iron-tipped short arrows which would need to be sharpened some. Wet stones were laid out, and John took an arrow and rubbed the point on the stone, "This is how you do that." Hammers came out next, then anvils. "The points will bend if it hits a rock," he got a hammer and tapped the point with the hammer, "this is how you straighten it again. They will get red rust on the iron. I would put buffalo grease on them once in awhile."

Now, the new thunder sticks were brought out in their cases with little barrels of gun powder, balls, patches and flints all so powder horns could be filled out of the barrels. Skinning knives long and sharp, came out, one hundred of them. "I got you more than you asked for; they will come in handy," John said. Then he pulled out twenty bags of coffee beans, with thirty bags of white sugar, tobacco, many matches also salt and pepper in bags fifty of each.

Next the blankets were unpacked. "They are not made out of skins like your buffalo robes, but are made out of wool that comes from a sheep. A sheep is an animal that is as big as a buffalo calf that is three moons old. The wool is like hair, only all kinked up. The wool is cut off the sheep one time a year, then is combed out and twisted together to make long rope like threads, then it is weaved together, looking like a skin. It now is colored with plant juice and other things giving it all the colors you see. The wool coming off the sheep is white to light gray, but some are black to a brown in color. The clothing is very warm and many other garments are made from it, and it's called homespun. Many white men, women, and young too have clothes made from it. You can clean it in water and hang it up to dry, but sometimes it gets smaller and you pull on it so it keeps its shape. It is very hard to explain."

Big John smiled for some reason as he continued, "The idea came from people over the big water which came here in big boats called ships and they brought the sheep with them too. All you see in front of you is knowledge from people all over the world over many years of trying to make life better. No one people or one man did it and you are not alone as the only people in the world. There are many and one day they will come here to make homes, and you will have to get along with them or die. You could kill the first few who come but it will not end there, they will just keep coming. The goods we brought to you here are new to you, but they will not last - they will wear out, and you will want more. You don't know how to make these things yet, so you will trade again, and still again. So when you use things you cannot make yourself, your old ways are dying. Its called progress: you or I cannot change it either, but it is coming."

John's eyes got a far away look, "You never farmed but other people did, so you planted crops for food, like the ones on the big river, and now you know how to grow food. Do you know how to make guns or thunder sticks? No you don't; can you make the hard shiny knives? No, you can't but you want them, so you trade us gold for them. If you had sheep, Skunk could do it because he is very wise, and Pounce can see how to do things he is smarter than many I know. Be glad they are with you, but they can't make iron or steel and this is what the knives and thunder sticks are made from. You can't make glass either but that is what the beads your women do art work. A tree bends in the wind, or it would break off and be gone. You had better learn to bend too or you as a people will be just as gone, and one more thing you had better know truth too, when you hear it spoken." It was a long speech by John but he said it well and all who heard it knew it for the truth. The new cooking pots were brought out and put in a row, each pot having herbs and spices in them for making food better, ten in all.

Bars of lead were brought out and new melting pots to double as gold melting pots as well, bags of caps and gloves of different sizes came out, needle and thread and things that could be used by a group of people, so all in all everything that was asked for and more was in the packs. Tall Elk, Skunk, Fast Fox, Looking Back Horse and Pounce, Bald Eagle and others of standing all said the packs were in order, as to what was asked for and the white men had done well.

John and Jared, their shirt buttons popping, walked around saying how the cost of the goods brought was close to the gold sent in value and they should have more gold for all they did and that- "Stop!" Bald Eagle yelled. "Just a little minute, just a damned little minute John! Before you get too deep in your little lie, know that I and two more eagles were fifteen hundred feet above you and a little to your right when you told your brother Hans how you sold three bags of gold for around fifty thousand big ones and how you spent around twenty three thousand for the goods, and they still had twenty thousand plus left over. And you still have two bags of gold in the bank vault not sold," at this point eagles voice got kind of high, for she was angry, "Remember I can hear at more than five thousand feet perfectly well in any direction. You want to be fair, and then be fair! Don't lie, and not to me in anyway. That is what you said to Hans in confidence so I think it is true. I also think you should have more gold so you can travel some. We will need more things from time to time and we will call on you at that time, so you should be paid as our partners. I say we should give you three more bags of our gold. That would give you around fifteen thousand each. Now I ask you John, how long would it take you to make that much at your mill, or you Hans with your hog lot? Not two moons, much more time than that. So tell truth, how long? I am ready to hear truth."

"Maybe four years," John mumbled, "maybe more."

"And you Hans?" The shrill edge to Eagle's voice was fading.

"Two times that long, if I don't drink too much," said Hans, looking at the ground.

Tall Elk said, "At first light you seven will start back, and you will have your pack horses, your three bags of gold, your camp gear, your bows and arrows and your lives. Everything else we keep. We will need your digging tools to get more gold just in case we run short; it will be in many places and where only we know so don't ask. Tell no one - we don't want to kill, so say nothing to anyone about the gold. If a big rush comes, our agreement is over and you get nothing more. If no one comes, you get more next time as partners should."

Before light the seven were got out of their beds and helped pack their gear, and the pack horses were tied in line and three tightly rolled heavy bundles were put in place. The bow men had their bows and jerky was given each rider. Pounce went up to Jared and John and smiled, "Ride easy my friends." Then he looked at Hans and there was no smile, only a flat cold eyed glare, and he lifted his lips so just a hint of fangs showed. He said nothing, but Hans knew and understood; no words were needed. Seven eagles floated slowly past, low down and to the right and reminded the men, "We watch, as always, if there is danger we will tell you, but go fast and put miles behind you. When you pack gold it has a voice of its own and screams to the world it is near; even the worms want some. So they did and miles fell behind like fat horses in a race for the roses. The unloaded pack horses made good time at the stiff trot and then the lope. After a while, they let them walk for a time then back to the rolling lope. When the blue shadows ran to the east they grazed and walked but always moving east. At sun down Andy killed a deer with the cross bow and they made fast camp. They ate the deer and the horses grazed then they went east again. They stopped at a seep of water, rested some then continued east, but they had covered much ground that sun.

At the Sioux camp the gold was put away in different places that were known to few people. Tall Elk and Skunk were saying that a gold gathering ride was needed to get enough before too many knew of its value and made it hard to gather and the sooner the better. Pounce would go and some of the more active wolves as well. Bald Eagle was called back with three of her best, and the others stayed to keep the white men from coming back to look for more gold. The she wolf would be in charge of camp security with the rest of the pack. They would form a net a mouse could not get past. Twenty or thirty riders would go to dig and pan for gold. They wanted to get in and out again fast as not to get too much notice. They would call on the Crow camp too, and explain the reason and they would send a lot of goods to them. The gold runners would not find out where the gold was at so would not bother them at all. Horses were gathered for packing and riding and braves picked to go; all wanted to, but some had to stay back to guard camp with the wolves and eagles too. They would leave with morning light armed with cross bows and some thunder sticks along with Skunk's best bows and arrows.

Skunk had trained twenty braves with the guns and cross bows, just in case, with a long knife to each man. I don't think I will bother them, will you? I thought not. Moon Boy was not feeling well so he was not going. He was running at his bottom end and could not set a horse comfortably so he would practice with the war gear. He would have three or six of the young wolves as his eyes then he could shoot as well as anyone. They were ready for anything night or light, and they would get better. They were different from other tribes - they fought as one and had a good leader to set up rules to follow.

Pounce had three of his big burley sons along; he had mated with a big she of the northern pack and he was training them well. They were gentle and kind to baby and Moon Boy, but that's where it ended: mess with them and you could see death quick. Slayer could jump on the back of a running buffalo, break his neck, jump on another do it again, and eat his fill before they stopped kicking, but all Pounce had to do was lay an ear flat and they were like lambs - no one messed with the old man - his word was law.

Loafer was very large, all bone, muscle, and gristle with little fat and had the stride of his uncle Ling Lang. His was the bounding gate of the mule deer and his snarl was terrible to hear like his uncle Cubby and his first cousin Shadow. He could turn your blood to ice water. He was tall and long and one hundred and fifty two pounds and ran on Pounces right just a little back. I don't know if he was faster then his father Pounce, but on the long trail it would have been close. His face from his ears down was almost black, and black ran a line all the way to his up turned tail. A thin gray eyebrow was above each eye and his eyes were yellow, light brown in color; his fangs were long and snow white. The rest of him was gray edged with black, with some tan color on his under side.

Frost was smaller than his brothers, but much quicker. He could be way over there and be in your face the next instant - how could he do that? And fast, Frost could outrun his shadow without so much as a whisper. He never made a sound in running or killing, was almost white with blue gray markings, and ran on Pounce's left. If you were on Pounce's left, Frost told you about it, and if you stayed there you got slashed hard. Pounce was proud of his boys, and should have brought them all but left four to help watch the camp. Pounce told them to hear the she wolf every time, for she was their great grandmother. If they did not, they would hear about it when he got back. Two of them were to stay near baby at all times light or night. Big cat was a never ending threat and would kill baby if he could. Pounce's was a big litter of seven sons and a little she; her name was Blue Night, she was as small as the others were large, but she was growing and soon would be a wolf to reckon with.

Grandfather rattlesnake, a five and a half foot long prairie rattlesnake, was too near where baby played, so Bald Eagle's son slid out of the blue and got a hold of him just behind his head and four inches back with his talons and air lifted him some five or six miles south of camp. He then dumped him five hundred feet to the ground below, aiming at some cactus but missed and the big snake lit in some grass and right near a young rabbit. The snake struck and it took the rest of that sun to get him down. Eagle was not fond of snakes, but snakes were not fond of air rides either. The rabbit was not fond of snakes or eagles but somebody must lose and snake had food for two moons or more. Eagle got some target practice in so I guess it worked out.

Chapter 22

The gold seekers had left camp and were moving at a slow pace south west. Thirty-nine Lakota riders, twenty-seven members of the wolf guard and ten eagles with Bald Eagle as point guard leader, thirty pack horses packing camp gear and equipment for digging, panning and washing out the wealth they hoped to get. Skunk was riding golden star, as his pinto stud had a split hoof and Moon Boy was staying back so he took him. Tall Elk and the young men who would do most of the heavy work with Fast Fox were up front. Pounce and his sons Shadow, Red Tongue and Little Bit were in the far up front guard in touch with Bald Eagle and two other eagles. Other wolves were on the two sides and the rear. All were heavily armed with cross bows, thunder sticks, and bows by Skunk with a few lances for good measure. Long knives gleamed on every brave's belt; it looked like a war party but it was meant to look that way. Bald Eagle flew in and told that water was ahead but they would have to speed up some, so they did. The miles slid back and soon they could see the green of the draw and an hour before dusk, camp fires were going and hump steaks were dripping fat.

The aroma of good food cooking was all around the camp site. At first light all were gone - just a little smoke curled up out of put out fires could be seen and soon it was gone. The horses wanted to run so they put miles behind them. They were on the big flats now, and moving fast, the blue of the hill country was plain to see and they turned south a little to come to where the Crow camp of Tall Pine was. Fast Fox was in the lead and moving faster; he was going home to his country the hill lands, and soon they were there. Arms were lifted in greetings all around, and Tall Pine was standing there. "Ho my friends; we saw you coming and have caught fish with many colors on backs as a treat for you."

"Good. Very good. We have brought many gifts for you."

Packs were opened and blankets of many colors were given, long knives, coffee, and salt were given out. Beads and other art work things were also given as well. Tall Elk asked Tall Pine if he wanted thunder sticks too and if he did he would get some for him when they traded again. "Yes we would try some, are they good for hunting?" asked Tall Pine.

"Yes, but they make much sound and are slow to load. Arrows are faster, but the thunder stick kills far away, if you can make them shoot where you want them to."

"What of the bows on sticks?"

"They send short arrows with hard points made of iron very fast, but we cannot make them I am going to make arrows our way short but with our points. I will try when we go to our country but now we have come again to get more gold to trade with. We will never tell them where the gold is, to keep you safe - or many of them will come and we will have to fight again and we don't want that. Or you either." The food was ready so they ate much rainbow fish and other good food known to the Crow people. When the meal was over Tall Elk got some toe- back- oh and they smoked.

"Did you get this too?" asked Tall Pine.

"Yes."

"Can you get us some?"

"I think so, we will see. Tell us what you would want. It will be awhile, they think it is very far, and we meant it that way so they won't come looking. Tell your people to say nothing to any one."

"We have gold ready for you. Much gold."

"We will look at first light."

The next light, food was eaten and bags of gold were brought out, many of them. The Lakota had to borrow some pack horses as they did not bring enough. Raw gold is heavy, too heavy. So pack horses were brought in and all was loaded. Tall Elk said, "Tell us what you want, and when we have it, eagles will come and tell you then you can come and get it; we will help." Horses were tied two by two and the long line started.

Rabbit and blue jay were watching, and rabbit whiskers twitched as he spoke, "They come again and they take much yellow gravel - do they eat it?"

"I don't know, rabbit," blue jay mused, "but I am glad they go, see how they look around they don't trust anything, not even their horses."

"I think they are crazy. Like I said they stand too high up - their brains are cooked by the sun." Blue jay looked at his old friend rabbit and said, "You say that all the time. I'm starting to think you may be right rabbit; maybe we should move. Let us talk to fox and owl and then we will see."

"Yes, then we will see - now let us eat, they do grow good food."

Tall Elk, Skunk, and Fast Fox rode side by side as they loped through the long sun, stopping only to water the horses and themselves and rest a little. Tall Elk asked, "Eagle, what do you see?"

"I have made wide swings far to the sides and nothing is moving. Other eagles are far to the front and nothing; our tail guard just got here and no one is coming from behind. Pounce and his guard came and sat down. "We can see nothing. No one has passed this way in a long time, and I think we worry for nothing." Tall Elk looked at Fast Fox. "Pounce is right - we worry too much but we have so much more wealth than we ever had before and we must remember that it is not all ours. Much of it we will use to buy goods for the Crow people and Tall Pine's band."

"We also know how the white ones love gold and would kill every one here - wolves and eagles too - just to have it. So we must be careful and not be caught sleeping: we must get to the Moreau River and our camp. Repack the gold to smaller bags and put it where no one can find it then. Get John and tell him what we want and give him more gold to get the things with. Now water is not far, so let us go and make camp. Get some meat and we will have a talk on what must be done.

Pounce is there anything that you want? Or that the pack could use? If so, think about it as we ride - you are the best guards so you and yours will be in charge. Now let us go." The party soon drew near to the wooded draw. There was good water and grass, and plenty of dry wood and branches for fires. Two of the new sticks with red and yellow on one end were used: dry grass and twigs were gathered and crushed, and then a fire stick was rubbed on a stone. Fire jumped out and caught the grass and twigs and they had fire quick.

The two young buffalo were eaten almost completely by the time all had eaten. The pack would finish, and there would be not much left over. Pounce got up and said, "I think some many colored robes when the young ones come would be good. We will lay them on them and cover them to keep them warm. I don't think a thunder stick would be good for me: remember I never learned to close one eye when aiming." All smiled, but Shadow laughed longest, "I can see you loading it Pounce, you would get so excited you would swallow your balls." Now all laughed, and even Pounce smiled. Tall Elk wiped his eyes then said, "Yes you can have them - just say how many you need."

"Maybe twenty would be enough; I maybe could use one but I cannot use much of what they have or any of us, for we are wolves and to have things we would have to carry them, and that would slow us down. We don't need weapons. We ourselves are weapons as we will be forever but we help you because we want to, not because we have to; no one could make us do anything. We love Moon Boy and I love baby but I could not say why. I just do."

At first light the packs were tied in place, and the long line was put in a lone lope, and if a horse lagged he was cut with a lash of buffalo gut, dried and braided to around six feet in length. This generally got the sleep and the fog out of the horse's brain then he was good for the rest of the sun. Eagles flew, and Pounce with his guard prowled and looked in all directions and if you thought to surprise them, think again. Your chances of that would be better if you would jump from a butte to the sun's sister, moon, and ride all night then be back at your lodge to eat food and tend crops all sun.

Tall Elk and the riders loped and trotted; walked a little then galloped toward their home camp on the Moreau River, packing more gold than that anybody in that part of the world would probably ever see again. They looked so innocent that no one would have given them a second glance; they looked just like a group of warriors coming back from a raid, only there was no one to see. So they moved forward at a brisk pace, dust billowing up behind them and lesser animals just getting out of the way, and so they rode into camp with the sun still two hands to falling off the world on wet dusty horses. Quickly they unpacked the horses and turned them free to roll, and also to go to water and graze. The gold was left in a heap in front of Tall Elk's lodge and robes were placed over it then all went to their lodges to rest until morning.

Far to the south west in the small Crow camp of the late Weasel Tongue, Night Shade was teaching her son to walk. Blue Owl had moved in with her and was helping with the walking of little Weasel Tongue. Blue Owl was now the chief of the little camp; he had learned much from his former friend, but was not the hunter the former was or planner either. Yellow Rock and Old Bear had stayed to help and the three of them had got by with the older men making most of the decisions. Old Bear had moved in South Wind's lodge and the two of them helped with Yellow Rock to take care of the little grandson of Tall Pine, the main chief of the Crow. They had helped gather some of the gold to send back with the Lakota to trade for things they wanted. Blue Owl was to have a thunder stick in return for his band's part in gathering the gold. He could hardly wait - now he would kill buffalo with little effort - he was a dreamer and a little lazy as well. It took work and planning to be a hunter and he knew that. He thought too simply to realize that hunting buffalo was more than point, boom, and buffalo fell dead. And there would be no arrows to retrieve!

Blue Owl had found some large chunks of gold, and secretly covered them up. If the Lakota could trade for thunder sticks, why not him? A bad plan was forming in his little mind; he would cut the Sioux out and get the glory himself, and all would say that Blue Owl was great, and they would probably make him head chief of all the Crow bands. So he dreamed on; he got his horse and rode to where the gold was and with much labor got the gold out, washed it off and packed it on his horse. He did not know that a southern eagle was watching and had told Bald Eagle what a dumb Crow had done, or that Bald Eagle and two more had flown to the little camp to watch and listen to all. Blue Owl rode to his lodge, and laboriously took the root of all evil inside the lodge and informed Night Shade to not bother with it, because soon he, Blue Owl, would be chief of the southern Crow. He also said that he would have many wives and if she was not careful he might just send her away.

She snorted disdainfully at him, "Because you have some yellow rocks that are too heavy to carry? You should take it all to Tall Pine at once! And for this you will be chief? You would be chief of what, all the dumb Crows in the world?" By now she was pretty well shouting in a near fury. Old Bear and Yellow Rock came running, "What is all this noise about?"

"He thinks because he has some yellow rocks, the people will make him chief of all Crows."

Old Bear said, "Blue Owl, Tall Pine is not chief because he has yellow rocks. He is chief because he is wise, good and thinks of the people first. What does a yellow rock have to do with that? If you take this gold to where the Lakota trade, the white fools will find us, and many of them will come in a short time and take our gold and our lives too. We are safe because they don't know where we live. We must never tell them, so take this gold to Tall Pine, or keep it. But don't do a stupid thing like going around the Lakota."

Blue Owl knew truth when he heard it, but was very angry to have his dream lost. He had seen himself on a great horse with many eagle plumes flying in the wind, and many crow warriors ready to go anywhere, and do any thing he, Blue Owl, said. It was a hard dream to give up. He had other problems he knew nothing about, much graver then he knew - Bald Eagle had heard enough to send her flying to see Pounce and tell him another Crow would have to be killed. She and hers could probably do it but Pounce could do it better and faster. Bald Eagle could take his eyes then he would run screaming and fall into things and maybe fall off a high place and die, or she could use her talons and beak and let out his life that way, but no, she decided, let Pounce do it.

When he was told of Blue Owl's doings, Pounce lifted his lips and a low snarl came out of his deep chest too horrible to describe with words. His eyes slanted down to slits with yellow green fire shooting out like lightning bolts and Slayer, Loafer and Frost got up and moved out of the way just in case their father exploded in a violent eruption that would burn them to a crisp. Pounce bellowed a howl that shook the ground and made a flock of black birds leave their tree in sudden motion in all directions two full miles away. He told Shadow, Red Tongue, Long Fang, Kills Quick, Sly, and five more known for their cunning to get ready to come with him. He asked Cubby and Curly to go and be with Moon Boy and his family. They would take ten more wolves and be on guard. They would be back but did not know just how long it would take. Five eagles would fly the air guard. One minute they were standing ready to go and then they were just not there; they were gone.

Pounce was in the lead, Loafer on his right, running low, neck outstretched, and covering ground with no effort at all. Frost ran on his left, silent as always. Slayer ran on his left, head up in a bounding gate, and Ice ran to the right of Loafer, big and burley and almost black in color, except for tan front paws and tan eye brows. His fur was long and silky and ruffled in the wind like long grass in a wind. Iron Eyes ran on Pounces right hind quarter, his eyes were intense - always moving. They were golden brown in color with a black center, and he saw everything at a glance. He never had to look the second time. He was large, maybe not as big as Loafer but big. Iron Eyes was all gray with darker gray to trim. He had white on his underside with a black tip on his tail.

Flash was on Pounce's left hind quarter. He was small when compared to his brothers but if he liked you he was friendly and kind, but he had some thing against you, go find a tall tree, climb it and stay there. Pokey, the seventh son, ran right behind Pounce and in the middle. He saw his six brothers and father at a glance, and had a low bark that he used seldom because it meant "a flying horse is about to land on you." Maybe that's why he was always so quiet; I haven't seen any flying horses lately, have you? Pokey would rather one of his brothers or father would kill the game. He liked to eat but hunting was work and he was a bit lazy, not that he could not hunt, just that he rather someone else did it for him.

If Blue Owl had of known they were coming he would not have taken the time to bake a cake; he would have climbed the tall pine behind his lodge and stayed there, but it would have done him little good, Pounce just would have got two beavers and forced them to cut down the tree, or else, and all knew what that meant. You did it quick and lived or he killed you and got some other beaver who wanted to live but in the end the tree would come tumbling down. Blue Owl was in a short time going to answer to Pounce. That was that.

The southern eagle that started all this was not even of the Bald Eagle clan, and had overheard him in his day dream telling his wife Night Shade how he would be a big chief with the gold he now had. He would go to the white traders himself and get all the goods for the people. They would be so glad that he would be made head chief of all Crows. Tall Pine would be just out, and he Blue Owl would ride a great horse, and have many eagle feathers and many warriors under his command. The southern eagle thought this a joke, and flew to tell Bald Eagle who flew to the camp of Blue Owl and overheard enough to go to Pounce and tell him. Now it was anything but funny, because Pounce and his killer pack was about to turn a daydream, into a nightmare. Blue Owl, because he could not help bragging and thinking bad thoughts, probably would not survive, unless Pounce would see him no real threat and let him live but, if he was stupid his blood would be spilled in the lodge quickly.

Blue Owl had by this time forgot his daydream and making Night Shade sad by saying he would have so many wives he would get rid of her just as soon as he was head chief if she was not good. Pounce was getting closer and closer to Blue Owl's lodge with every bound of his mighty body and he was getting very angry thinking that a nobody like Blue Owl could threaten the Lakota people and the wolves and eagles too, by just talking and being overheard by an eagle not even of the clan. It was light out and Pounce and his sons had run all night.

Old Bear and Yellow Rock had come to have a pipe with Blue Owl, and were sitting in front of the lodge. A burst of motion and eighteen big lobo wolves had them backed against the wall with six other eagles because Bald Eagle had joined them in their night flight.

Shadow and Loafer grabbed Blue Owl and slammed him on the ground hard in front of Pounce, who was sitting to judge him. Blue

Owl's pipe went flying and he screamed in pure fright, "NO! He pleaded, don't kill me; I have done nothing!"

"You lie and you are a great coward. You have done plenty, as I will tell you." Pounce snarled angrily.

Bald Eagle spoke, "You told your mate how with all your gold, you would pass the Lakota and deal with the white eyes yourself and get all the things. Then they would make you chief of all Crow. You are not fit to be chief of the worms."

Now Pounce spoke, "Yes I am Pounce. I killed Weasel Tongue as I will probably kill you for bragging and being stupid. How did you plan to get rid of the LAKOTA, not to mention us wolves and eagles? Stupid one, you are too dumb to live, and you would send your wife away? She is the best thing that ever happened to you. You not fit to wipe her nose. As close to chief as you will get is to hold his horse, maybe. NOW get all this gold you speak of in front of me, NOW! Be quick." And three big lobos helped him be quick.

Blue Owl staggered out, carrying the gold, show us, and it was uncovered. Pounce continued on, "This is worth dying for? A pile of yellow rocks you cannot even carry. You will carry it all the way to the Lakota camp on the Moreau River and give it to them all of it, and every time you go to slow we will cut you a little so your blood runs. Old Bear get your horses; the woman can stay, it would be too hard on the small one, but you two will go. Get three - he will walk - leave your bows but get your knives and fire starting tools. One horse will carry all I say. Pack the gold in two packs; one stupid will carry the other the horse will. Now stupid one, when you get done you will never want to see gold again. You will hate the sound of it, but you will say it many times in the suns to come, and if you live it will be because I say you can. This is what I do to anybody who goes against me."

"Now pick up your gold, and start walking," said Pounce. Old Bear put the other on the horse so their trail began. Before sun had reached the top of the world Blue Owl had fallen two or three times and his legs had been cut by the fangs of the pack. He was crying and tired and had no water and had said gold twenty times or more. About midway to sundown, two of the wolves killed a buffalo cow by water, and all drank and Old Bear made fire and meat was cooked. All rested and sleep was enjoyed by some while others watched. Yellow Rock made a water skin, and hump ribs were taken along. At the end of eight suns, stupid one staggered into Tall Elk's camp and gladly gave the gold to Tall Elk and Skunk. "Take it. I don't want it anymore." An old bow was given and Pounce said, "Take your life; get on the horse and go but bother us never again, or I will take your life. Do not play chief again: you are not a chief and be grateful to your wife; she is good, too good for you."

The Crow turned their horses to the southwest and rode away, glad, oh so glad to be going. Pounce that terrible wolf had given him his life back, and had taught him a lesson too- that greed never stops when it get a hold on you, and robs you of your reason and takes away all the good things in life and leaves you with nothing. Blue Owl was going back to his wife, his feet cut to rags, but he could heal up again. "Don't call me chief; I am not, one of you can be chief - it almost got me killed. I hate all yellow things now. I would eat grasshoppers now, before I would see yellow. Bah! I am done with it. Now let us go home." They kicked their old soup bones up to a lope and soon were gone out of sight.

When Pounce and his guard were gone to see about the outlaw Crow Blue Owl, people were busy at Tall Elk's camp. Tall Elk, Skunk, Fast Fox and Moon Boy with Moon Boy's young braves went to the new potatoes cave with the new digging tools used for gold digging. They dug a deep hole in the center to put the new gold in. Then they returned to Tall Elks lodge, spread out new blankets and put the gold just acquired on them, and the heap of glittering, shimmering gold was breathtaking. The purity of it was shocking. Gold was put in bags depending on its size from large to dust and filled fifty-six bags that weighed around fifteen to twenty pounds per bag. Skunk and some of his helpers put in a floor and side walls then lined it with buffalo robes. The new bags were placed inside and covered with robes and dry sand. The old grass was put over that. Last, the potatoes were placed in and no one could have said it was disturbed at all; they called it the glory hole and it contained a fortune that was mind boggling.

Chapter 23

Thirty-two days later, seven big dusty, bearded men rode into the settlement on tired horses. They were leading a long string of trail weary pack horses, dusty and lean with no fat on them and were turned out to grass and water. "Well boys, we got back with all our hair and a hell of a lot richer then we were when we started, so it worked out. We will go to the bank and get this gold in the vault, get some new duds go to the barber shop and clean up some then go eat. I could eat a horse." John said, "But keep your mouth shut if this gets out of hand - a rush will start that no one could stop and we lose. I want more, do you understand? I hold you all responsible, and don't get drunk, not any of you can hold his drink or you will answer to me. We don't even know where to go look, so just play dumb and that will not be too hard for most of you, now let's go."

New clothes were bought and they all went to the barbers where all had a hot bath and were combed and trimmed. They went to the eating house changed men. Many heads turned and some wanted to talk, or start conversations as to where they had been and what did they see. "A lot of windy grass many snakes and not much more, now we would like to eat and drink coffee we can talk later," Stated a suspicious John.

Over at the bank Mr. Bodkins lifted his heavy brows and asked John and Jared, "Where did you get this gold? I would sure like to know."

"Well I should have made a map, but we had no paper, but maybe I can find it again, I think. You go ten days west, turn north and go eight days, then three more days northwest. You have to get there on the first day of the month at eleven in the morning. If it is cloudy a big pink bull moose will appear on a hill. If he thinks you need gold bad, he will lift his tail and shake his head. Then you hold the bags and he will shit them full, or as much as he thinks you need. Then he just goes away, no more to be, but he will be back next month on the first. That why it takes so long to get it. Once it was clear, not a cloud in the sky: no clouds, no pink moose." John smiled wryly, knowing he had gotten his point across.

Mr. Bodkins threw a crumpled piece of paper in the trash he was writing on and said, "Humph."

"Now do you want the gold or no?" It was weighed out and much money was counted to John; some he put in his account the rest was for the men. In his office at the mill, John gave each man his part of the money, and advised them to open accounts at the bank, "Or you will lose it and if anyone asks you where you got it, say 'go ask Mr. Bodkins at the bank - he knows' but stay near, I think we will go again soon for more gold. I think they gave most of the goods to other tribes and will want more."

Fore ten days work at the hog lot and mill was in full swing: many hams and bacons were smoked, some fry meat such as chops and side pork also. The eating house needed a lot as seven of the biggest eaters were in three times a day and had money to spend, lots of money. At the mill the story was the same. Much floor was milled and orders of five hundred to a thousand pounds were common, because people were stocking up. They had good help. The farmer and his sons stayed on and worked two jobs. John stepped out of his house and Bald Eagle was there with one on each side and two eagles up high up, watching that no harm came to their boss.

Eagle said, "I have things we want you to bring, and there are many of them. We want more coffee, sugar, salt, and pepper many of them. Thunder sticks and all it takes to make them work, bows on sticks with many arrows and also iron arrow points. We will make some shafts too, and bring many colored robes of wool for the pack wants some. Everything you brought first only more, anything you think we could use, bring. Oh yes much to back oh and fire sticks to light fires with - they are faster. If you do well and fast we will give you ten bags of gold

- that is much of what you call wealth, but if you are slow the bags may be less. We go now. I don't like your settlement; I will be watching, and so will other eagles so make no mistakes, bring no new men and you did well when you told your story to the man in bank. Now he knows nothing, probably about the same as he always knew. We will meet you when you pass the land of many lakes and help bring you in; we are watching so we will know when to help. Did that surprise you when I knew of the bank man writing down how to get to the gold? I can hear fifteen thousand feet in any direction and see almost that good, some thing for you to remember."

The seven met at the eating house, where much food was consumed all were given lists of what to buy. Some had to go to other settlements. Hardware stores, gun shops and clothing stores were high on the lists. Food stores being next the other goods were anywhere they could be found, and the piles grew fast and merchants smiled with broad smiles as much money changed hands. The men buying were the best thing that ever happened to this community and they were proud to be serving them. Little did they know that some of the iron points and lead balls would find white skins to puncture in days to come, but that never bothered them. They were selling and taking money in, and that was very important. It is just about like now and forever will be as mankind doesn't change much. Horses were got in and packs put in place, and loaded. They left at midnight when the rest slept as to get ahead start on anyone fowling, at first light they were just not there, gone and that's the way they planned it.

At first light the horses were put to a long lope and that was kept until midday, then they grazed along the packs in place but moving west. It rained some and washed the trail clean so the two men banker Bodkins sent to shadow them got lost, and rode in confusion then went back and reported in and got relieved of their duty with no pay. The banker got his fat bay upon which he rode to church and he made it six miles, the horse threw a shoe and he had to be lead back. No one got a loan or the time of day for two or three days. Bodkins would fix the scales so they read a little light, but he must be careful: if John caught him at it he would get the ax by John and his boss. Life was not fair. He skimmed some on the last weighing, but the little sliver of wood slid out and he fumbled so much, he all most lost all he gained, and when John took out his knife and split a hair, banker went to the outhouse and tried to regain his composure.

Pounce, Loafer, Frost, and Ice along with others had come to play with baby and take her for a ride. Ten or sixteen always went too; big cat was never too far away and when the other big she was killed, all other cats wanted revenge. They wanted baby to die because she was why the big she was killed. It was an eye for an eye sort of a thing, so the wolves always went with enough to bluff the cats out, and the cats were never smart enough to bring more cats. Baby had changed mounts and was riding Loafer, patting his long silky hair and talking to him, "Loafer, you sure are pretty nice big horse but your back is boney and bumpy. You should get fatter so I can ride faster and my butt will feel softer, but baby still love you." Loafer smiled, and Frost covered his eyes with two paws and snorted then laughed, "Loafer you should get fat, but you are pretty two times: pretty homely and pretty apt to stay that way." Pounce started to pull his ear back, thought better of it and smiled, as they all did, after all it was in good fun.

They all loved baby and she loved them; they loped over to where Skunk was working on some short arrows for the cross bows, "We have arrows but I wanted to try to make some just in case we ever need to I know how. Three or four of his helpers were also helping. Tall Elk and Moon Boy walked over and baby went to her grandfather who picked her up, "I was riding Pounce but he got tired, so I rode Loafer. You know, grandfather, Pounce is getting old and needs to rest." Pounce covered his eyes with a huge paw and looked away as all smiled. They all knew Pounce could run all sun with her on his back and be fresh as a rose at the end of the sun just past. Ice looked at his father and smiled, "Yes, and his back is fat and not bumpy like Loafers. Could I have a ride too father?"

"No. Not unless horses fly and I don't think that will happen. You should carry me: I carried you plenty when you were a pup. You were lazy, you know."

"Yes but I was good at it."

A dot was coming from the east: fast, high up and all could see it was an eagle. She dove like a thunder bolt and flew in lightly on cupped wings so quietly you would have thought Frost had sprouted wings. It was Golden Girl, a young golden eagle who was with Bald

Eagle, and she spoke quickly, "They come again, a long line of pack horses carrying many goods. They are the same white ones as before and are now in the land of many lakes. Bald Eagle sent me to tell you as I can fly very fast. Remember, you told them you and the wolf pack would come and help. What do I tell her?" Tall Elk asked her if she was hungry. "Yes, I could eat. I did not stop to hunt." So food was brought to her and she ate. Tall Elk said, "Tell Bald Eagle we come soon and will see her on the flat land west of the many lakes."

"Pounce, ask Curly and Cubby and maybe thirty more to come too. Pick a guard to watch camp. Maybe your grandmother can be in charge. I, Tall Elk, will go and maybe forty or so more can go. Who wants to; do you go, Moon Boy?"

"Yes, father, I go, and many of the braves who go with me can go too, and anyone more who wishes to."

"Good. Get horses and war gear. You never know; it's better to have them and not need them than to need them and not have them. Skunk will you come and carry a thunder stick? Or will you use a crossbow with your new arrows?" Skunk said, "I will bring Blue Jay, and he will carry one of my bows." Tall Elk said, "I will ask Eagle Plume to come - he can carry one of your good bows, Skunk." Fast Fox said, "My son and I will come; we carry bows by Skunk, for there is none better and none more quiet. You don't tell the world you are near by breaking their ears with the big boom." Tall Elk looked at Moon Boy. "Moon Boy, ask some eagles to watch camp and get us if they need."

"It is done, father, and eagles fly with us too. All is ready: let us go," and they went.

Moon Boy was up on the bay with white forelegs halfway up, with Curly on his right and Cubby on his left and Shadow up front. It was good to ride with old friends again. "Yes, old fat horse - watch where you put your feet," warned a grinning Curly. The horse snorted and tossed his head, "I remember, old wolf, the sun when you took me from Bird's Wing. You were not pretty then, and you have gotten no prettier." Cubby laughed, "I see you two are still at it; the only one who is good to look at is me and I don't brag like you three do."

"Humph," Moon Boy said, "is that why your hair around your nose is getting white Cubby? Or have you been in the flower sack again?" Sly spoke from behind the bay's right hind quarter, saying, "Now boys, be nice! We all know how glad we all are to be running together again. But watch closely; old grandfather rattlesnake is coming up fast on your right and is as mean as ever. So don't spook, bay; he will miss you but will sing," and so he did, then he was behind them.

They were on the south hills of the Grand and in the valley below a large herd of elk grazed peacefully. Skunk's mouth watered but it was too early to stop so they rode through them. Big bulls, six points or more and young bulls too, grazed beside many cows and calves and yearlings. Skunk looked at Moon Boy, "When this is over let us get some for the cooking pots."

"Yes Skunk, we will do that; you make the best elk stew I ever ate."

"Yes it is good," Skunk mused, "Very good." Much meat was at hand: buffalo, elk, and dear. Old lord grizzly was there too, although few in numbers. That was good: one of him was too many so they rode east, eagles high up and watching, and Pounce and his guard on all sides. Curly, Cubby, Shadow, and Sly were with Moon Boy as it should be. The crossbow was slow, so Moon Boy carried his bow by Skunk and a crossbow for far shooting. He could do that just as long as his eyes were near, but if his eyes were not there he could not even see the thing he was shooting at, a vexing problem, and not good to say the least. He wondered why he had such a problem - he for sure never asked for it.

For two or three suns they rode then Bald Eagle was there, saying. "They are five miles more, make camp and cook food; they will be here when sun is low. The horses are tired and the packs are heavy. They come slow, but will be here soon, I think." Slayer ran up to a dry buffalo cow, jumped on her back and broke her neck. Others were running so he jumped on another and broke the neck the same way, and then he killed one more young bull. "Now pull them to the fire and get the hump ribs cooking!" Skunk spoke with all the intensity of a newly awakened appetite. Skunk and Blue Jay skinned the buffalo and tanned the hides. Steaks were cooking as were other good parts on more than twenty fires, and when a piece of meat was done to someone's liking, it was eaten and more was put on. The first of the pack horses were in and packs taken off. The dusty tired horse watered and grazing while the men were eating more meat, so then more was put on. In time, all were eating and the buffalo was nearly gone, so they ate more.

Bald Eagle sat down, ate meat, and then said, "Men are following."

Tall Elk and the others looked only mildly surprised. "How many come?"

"Two, maybe three, are as far back as nearly four miles or so."

"Let us go call on them, and see what they say. They want to find out where the gold is." said Pounce. Then Pounce, twenty wolves, and ten Lakota went back. They found them around their fire, three of them talking loudly about how they would fix the seven white men. Get the gold, they said and go to other places and to hell with the banker. The Lakota and the wolves took them easily: stripped them bare and hung them upside down by their feet. "So you want our gold, do you? What you get is a whipping!" Pounce said with his teeth showing. Switches were cut and used long and hard. The men screamed and threatened then begged and then cried. "Now you can hang here until you are dead or the wolves cut you down." Everything they had of value was taken. Pounce looked them in the face - theirs were, of course, upside down - Pounce said, "So you want gold, do you? Why don't you go dig the gold yourself then." "No!" shouted one of the men, "A huge wolf that talked? How could this be?" Pounce continued, "And you say to hell with your boss? I say to hell with you then."

Shadow came face to face with them and let go with his hideous horrible growls and two of the three passed out, the other messed himself. Instead of going onto the ground, the mess ran over his head and face. He screamed long and hard then sucked in air and the mess too. Pounce got wood and built up the fire then he put all their clothes except their britches and watched them burn. He got a long stick, put it in the fire, and when it was burning well, he took the end that was not burning in his teeth and singed off their beards and mustaches, and told them, "Now you look better."

In the morning, the three were cut down after they had hung all night and Pounce told them, "This is the least that happens to anyone that tries to take from us. When you get back to your settlement, and if you get back, tell the banker to be watching for a wolf track by his door. If he finds one, tell him to get out of town fast, anywhere as long as it is far. If we come for him, he will get what you three got and he may not be as lucky to live as you did, now go and go fast."

After the three would be spies had stumbled to the east as fast as they could on bare feet with just their pants. They kept looking back to see the talking wolves, and kept bumping into trees, rocks, and logs. They ran, always looking backwards, and kept banging their toes on any thing that was handy. Pounce and his boys loped to night camp to find their friends gone on west. Shadow killed a deer so they ate it - just enough to go around, barely, but enough. An eagle set down and said, "The three men you sent to the east travel as if you were right behind them with burning sticks in your mouths, and from the look of their faces that's what you did."

"Yes," said Pounce, "I did singe them a little just to get their attention. It may keep them from harm later."

"They are very hungry; they eat even grasshoppers and one has a sharp rock he found with which he cuts the skin of snakes. One found some fire sticks and so they have a fire. They cook snakes and frogs, and choke on them when they eat. They found a large flat rock and set on two poles, it has a cup to it they have built a fire on it and carry it with them as they go. One of them is good at throwing rocks." The other rear guard eagle flew in and said, "The one that throws rocks hit a young tom turkey with a lucky throw and they are roasting the turkey now."

Pounce and his guard loped west on the trail left by the pack train, and came up to them around mid morning, making good time. The horses were pushed to about all they were capable of doing so when they come up on a trickle of water, the horses drank deep and were pushed on the west bank and let graze but always west. Pounce and two of his sons came up to Jared and walked along with him. Jared had a grass stem in his mouth and was chewing on it.

"Are you hungry Jared?"

"No."

"Then why are you eating grass?"

"I am not really eating it; I just like the flavor it has and it helps me think some times."

"Over by the tall hills near the Crow camp of Tall Pine, a rabbit lives; he thinks all two legged ones are crazy. He says you are too tall and your brains are too close to the sun and the sun cooked them. So that's why you are all crazy - is he right?"

Jared gave a short laugh, "No, he is just talking because he likes the sound of his voice. There are lots of men like that. What about a horse? He is tall, and he is not crazy, and eagles spend much time high up. They are not crazy either, but rabbit is short; he would probably like to be tall, but he is still short. Why don't you eat rabbit?"

"No. Then his friend blue jay would be by himself and rabbit is too small - not big enough to fill me up so he can live, unless I am old, cannot hunt, and starving."

"I was told you ran down Wind Runner, a very fast antelope and when you caught him you let him live. Are you kind, Pounce?"

"I don't know. I like to run and he is fast so we ran. I was not hungry and I kind of like him so I told him to enjoy his life. Is he?"

"Yes, I think he is a father many times by now."

"This is Loafer, my son; he is as fast as I am but not as big yet. But someday he will be, and this is Frost: he is quick, very quick, and also my son. He is quiet - when he runs, he makes no sound. We are wolves but we don't kill for the fun of it. We kill when we are hungry or our pups and mate are hungry. We have some wolves that just kill; we run them out of our grounds."

Pounce said, "I see Hans is still with you, don't you know he is bad? His mind is cloudy and he will some sun get you all killed. He has not yet because he is a coward and scared of you. If he could he would take all of our gold, and yours too. He would like to know where we go to find it; he never will, but if he thought he could, he would tell all men. They would come, many of them, and tear our country in two. Then many would die and probably more of you than us. I could kill a hundred myself and they would never know I was near - all they would see would be the dead on the ground. There are many in the pack that could kill as many as I could. I should have killed Hans that one day, but you talked me out of it, so Hans still lives."

Jared asked Pounce, "How can you know so many things that others don't?"

"Because I see with thoughts - not many can."

"I see you can, but you are a wolf; you have never been far from this land and yet you know things some of us don't. How can this be? I do not understand."

"Many talk to us. The eagles tell us and they have gone far into your lands, and they hear all you say and then they tell us. They know most of your thoughts they then sort out what is truth and what is not and we know from them and our own knowledge all you know. We see your greed, why you want our wealth, and what you will do with it. Most is bad even for you, but we want some of your things. We can't go and trade with most of you, so we send you who can. It is quite simple when you think about it, but you love life and you know we can take life. Even where you go you cannot get away from me. I will find you and kill you even in your beds where you feel safe, so you need to do what we want or die."

"It is too deep for me, so I will do as you say within reason of course, and we will get along."

"Good. See that you and all of you do."

"I will tell big John and the others. It is clearer now that I know."

Chapter 24

The three spies got back to the settlements and told the banker all. He was so angry he turned red and jumped around the room, but gave them their money and when he was told about the wolf track by his door he was cold all over. He knew he had gone one step too far on a path he knew nothing about and knew deep fear for his life and his job and his spot under the sun.

The day was almost gone and when the pack train came to water they made camp. The horses were tired and so were the men. They did all that is done at camp: ate food, rested and told stories of faraway places. They were close to the Grand River, just a sun or so, then on to the big camp then they could go back men of wealth and wealth meant power. Loafer went to Pounce, "Father the one called Hans still has his killing tools." He is thinking bad thoughts and will try to kill you and me with new sun. Pounce went to Tall Elk and Moon Boy, "You must get their killing tools now because Hans will try to kill us at first light then we will kill all. So go to John, and take them away from that snake Hans."

Tall Elk got other Lakota, approached the astonished white men, took all their guns and knives, and told John why. He got Hans up and slapped him hard. "So you were going to kill Pounce at first light, were you, and get us all killed, stupid one!" John hit Hans with a fist again.

Hans looked out from puffy black eyes. "How did you know? I told no one."

John bound him hand and foot. "You will finish this ride over your horse head down, tied like a side of beef." Two suns later they came to the home camp; Hans still head down over the horse. John took him down and untied him, "Now Pounce and his boys will take you to water to clean yourself. You stink more than any of my hogs do." Hans said "my hogs, don't you mean?"

"You lost them. They are my hogs now."

"Dry clothes - I need dry clothes," whined a bedraggled Hans.

"Put them on wet or go without. You nearly got us all killed and we are not even close to being out of it yet."

When Pounce brought him back, Hans was tied again, and all the goods were looked at. All were satisfied; it was fair. Ten bags of gold were given to John, who asked, "Is this all for this year or will you need more?"

"We don't know. If we need more we will tell you," Tall Elk replied. Hans was put over his horse head down, and Pounce and Loafer went to him to talk. Hans' face was without color, and Pounce told him, "If we see you more, you die on sight." Loafer snarled in agreement. John and his men got their guns back, all but Hans who was upside down on his horse. They started on the long back trail, five good men one bad one - Hans would never see the Moreau River country again, and should not, for he bit the hand that fed him and lost all.

Golden Girl, a young golden eagle and two more soared high into the cerulean blue sky of the early morning. They were winging their way to the southwest to find the camp of Tall Pine, the Crow chief. They were going to tell him the white ones' goods had arrived to Tall Elk's camp and that he wanted them to join him this sun. Eagle said, "Just as soon as you get your pack horses and braves ready." Tall Pine got the message around mid point to when the sun would fall off the edge of the world. He had gold loaded and was loping on his way to the camp of Tall Elk on the Moreau River to get the goods he needed, or thought he needed. The horses were well rested and well fed and made the ground slide beneath their pounding hooves. The ground shook and dust spiraled up in billowing clouds and all other smaller prairie dwellers ran for cover or just got out of the way, with the sun three hands above the horizon.

They disturbed a very large diamond backed rattler in his quest for a young prairie dog out for his last stroll on earth, but thanks to the pounding hooves and blinding dust clouds he was saved from the fangs and death and would live to be a grandfather prairie dog. The snake proved not so lucky, as he was cut and bruised. He got dirt in his mouth, went hungry, and was very angry. Golden Girl had flown to find her mother's brother who was sailing over the high peaks and tall pines of the black hills cutting wide circles in the blue. She found uncle Thunder Roller grumpy as always.

"What are you doing? Have you found a young he yet? And built a nest under some rock overhang? I know several good places. Have you raised eaglets yet?"

"No not yet. I have been scouting for some Lakota on the Moreau River and just brought a message to Tall Pine, the Crow war leader." He said, "Humph! All of them are a miserable breed!" He snapped his beak. "Landlocked and dumb, they are always trying to trap me with a dead stale rabbit in a stick pile. I am supposed to go near enough so they can grab my legs and pull out my tail feathers. If they love them so much why don't they grow their own and leave my feathers alone?" With that said, uncle Thunder Roller, swooped at a morning dove and amid a poof of gray feathers was gone.

Golden Girl banked left, found an air current, and floated out over the plains in time to see the young prairie dog escape the big rattler. Those horses not only had they spoiled his meal but cut his side and broke some ribs too. He was bleeding now and flies would put their eggs into his flesh. He would be lucky if did not have some little maggots growing in him that would probably take his life. All he was doing was trying to eliminate one of the diggers; the horses were always breaking their legs in a prairie dog hole and staggering around on three legs or died and this was their thanks.

Rattlesnake was looking for some dust to roll around in, to coat his wound and maybe keep away flies from putting in their eggs when he was grabbed just behind his head and in his coils by an eagle that lifted him up then way up then higher still. Now the ground was so far below it looked like a blur and he was carried higher. Golden Girl had extra long wings and much lift power; she had climbed to two thousand feet and it was getting cold. Snake was scared, never had he gone away from hot the ground and the way he liked it. He thought he was losing his mind - he just went through a cloud, something no rattlesnake should do. Golden Girl grew tired of the game, so she just turned loose. Now snake was falling back though the cloud with the ground rushing at him and getting warmer again; he saw the cactus coming then he was in darkness. Flies were all over him but he did not know it, and later a skunk ate him - he did not know that either. After Golden Girl dropped snake, she and the others reported that the Crow were on their way. Tall Elk asked when, and they told him maybe late next sun or the next. She would look when sun was back, now she would find a perch and sleep.

Chapter 25

John and the traders made good time too; Jared rode next to John and asked, "When do you put Hans up again?" Hans was complaining and making much noise, and I can't say I blame him. I would not like riding like that or you either.

Sullenly, John replied, "Why did he have to be so stupid and try to kill Pounce and almost cost us everything? He did that once before, and they burned my goods. He said buy cheap and make more money, so I did. The knives must have been made of clay - they broke in our hands."

"You got any idea how much is in the ten bags?" Jared's eyes were brightly shining.

"Over a hundred thousand or more and that's just the tip of the iceberg. I think they have much more, and we can be rich as we want to be and I will take only the best." Jared gasped quietly and shook his head in disbelief. When they stopped to make coffee, John untied Hans and said, "You can never come west again, and if you try, I will kill you myself. Your trying to kill Pounce was the single dumbest thing you ever did. You're so stupid that you could not clear more than two thousand a year even if you were smart and Hans, you are not smart. We have over a hundred thousand in the bags; more than you could get in five hundred years with the hogs. If you even say the word gold, as soon as I hear of it I will come and kill you if a rush starts. We are done, then and can get no more, if we are lucky enough to live."

"They could put us in jail for running guns to the natives; did you know that? Well they can, so you keep your mouth shut or you are dead, do you hear me Hans?"

"Yes, I hear."

"Then see that you do." Hans got on his horse and rode the right way. John rode by him, "There are six eagles watching and there may be more. If you see one, look at the ground and don't even look around, or it's over your horse again, upside down. And one more thing: if you try to send someone to kill Pounce I will get word to him and he can kill you. This killing shit is over for you. You are lucky to be alive and so are us all. The Lakota are so much smarter than we think that if I was to make a guess as to where they find the gold I would not know where to begin. Pounce knows but you may as well sit on the moon if you think he will tell. He knows if a rush begins, he and his family will be shot at too and many will die, but he will be terrible and will kill many before he is stopped. His sons will be worse, all seven of them, and don't drink a lot of beer. You know how you tongue wags when you get too much.

At night camp John told them, "Make a list of what you spent on the goods. This will be given back first, and then I will sell enough gold to pay each of us money. Put it in your accounts at the bank and you can draw on that; don't carry it around. Or if they ask you where you got it, tell them my uncle left it to me, or tell them to ask the banker because he knows. Of course he doesn't or he would not have sent the three men to shadow us. He would love to know. He tries to shave and skim a little gold but he is so clumsy he gives it away, then I just look at him and clear my nose, then he is all thumbs again.

Tall Pine and the Crow rode into Tall Elk's camp the next sun, about mid point to sundown. Much food was prepared Skunk's way and coffee pots were bubbling over the low fires with tin cups and sugar to sweeten the black drink. Thunder sticks and crossbows were in plenty too with Skunk's helpers to demonstrate how to use them and safety was shown. They were told that guns and crossbows have one thing in common; they don't think and would kill a friend or child as fast as a wild animal. And that they must be kept away from children as they don't think and safety should be first.

Coffee, sugar, salt, pepper and tobacco was put in their pile, cooking pots, coffee pots, tin cups, arrow points, knives, fire sticks, gun powder, powder horns, caps, gloves, blankets and hammers mixing spoons, forks and other things were piled up too. Gold was unloaded and put to one side like it was nothing. The Crow packed all their goods; Tall Pine carried a thunder stick balls, patches and a powder horn as did others, and some carried crossbows. They were eager to start back so they did. Fast Fox, Tall Elk, Moon Boy, and Skunk put down blankets and spread them then the gold was dumped out. It was not as much as last time but enough. Gold was sized, sorted, and sacked again and twenty-six bags with the old bags used. A new hiding place was already prepared under a rock ledge. Brush and flat rocks were used to seal it, and a rat's nest was arranged in front. Blue Owl's gold was there first and now this filled it.

Tall Elk asked Pounce to pick out the blankets that he and his mate wanted, and they would be taken to the wolf den or he could take them himself. Twelve big blankets were chosen and six of Moon Boy's braves carried them for Pounce. They were happy to do this, as Pounce was one of them. If you recall, Tall Elk was a Lakota, and had made Pounce a member of the Lakota for life. It was an unusual arrangement but so were the times.

Chapter 26

John, Jared, Hans and the others kept the unloaded horses moving fast. Five of the more trusted horses carried the gold, two bags per horse. It was a light load so it would not slow them down. Much better time was made going back then coming west, but they knew the way and had no loads to carry. Thirty-five days later they were back in the settlements, and they wanted to be there in the morning so the bank would be open. Seven armed men, dusty and bearded, stomped in and banker Bodkins gave a start. He looked like he wanted to run but got a hold of himself. Ten bags were put on the counter, five were put in the vault to join the other bags and five were to be turned into money.

Two tellers came to help weigh the gold and count out the cash, and all were very nervous. No one had ever seen this much gold before. Bodkins looked like he wanted to cry, and when John took out his knife and cleaned his nails, drops of sweat formed on his forehead. It took all morning to do, but in time all seven men each deposited sixteen thousand seven hundred and ninety-two dollars in their own personal accounts and were more wealthy than Bodkins himself. John kept a larger share, but he was boss. As they were going out the door John turned to the banker, "I say Mr. Bodkins, you look like you need a little exercise. Get your garden rake and rake the ground smooth by your doorway, for someday you may see a very large track, one you must not overlook. It will be big about as big as a dinner plate, like a king's foot print and it will be a king's too. It will be Pounce's track."

"Oh, by the way he is a lobo wolf that is smarter than you, and a hundred eighty pounds of hell on earth. If you find a track there, don't pack. You will not have time; just go, and go fast anywhere as long as it is far. Have a nice day Mr. Bodkins." Some boys were looking at the horses so John gave them a five dollar gold piece take the horses and said, "Turn them into my pasture, rub them down and put the gear in my barn. Water them and come see me, and we will give you another coin just like the one you have, but be sure to do a good job." All their faces were gone; all you could see was teeth as they hurried the horses away.

John and the men stopped at the barber shop and had tubs of hot water filled. They went shopping and got new duds all around. After their baths they all went to the eating house and the owner was so glad to see them he got eight of his best chairs and put them by his biggest table, his table, and had a new table cloth put on it. "BRING COFFEE," he told his help, "And be quick about it; we have wealthy eaters." John looked at him a long time, "Slow down Bob, we are just people and hungry to boot. Your help don't have to jump just because we come in. I won't have it. We would like some of your biggest T-bones and all the fixings please. Oh, and maybe some cookies with the coffee if you find the time; that would be nice. The boys tending the horses came in and John told Hans give them a five dollar gold piece and the owner Bob he said give them some cookies and milk too.

In good time the meal was put on the table, and what a meal it was. The T-bones hardly fit on the platters and all the fixings were spilling off the edges of the plates onto Bob's new tablecloth. Bob didn't care; he'd make enough money off these men to buy fourteen more tablecloths. After all were finished eating, more coffee was poured. John leaned back in his chair and enjoyed a brand new cigar. "Now boys, you have more money than you would have made odd jobbing in twenty years. You can work for me if you want to. I think we will go again before too long and I want you all close. Tall Elk doesn't want new faces and Hans will never go again, so I need one or two good men who can keep their mouths shut. It was Hans hair brained idea in the first place so he still gets a share, no questions asked, is that clear?" All agreed. "Now Bob, how about the bill?"

"Well let's see." Bob fumbled, "Two dollars a T- Bone, three more for the fixings comes to, oh, - "

"And the boys' cookies," John said.

"-oh yes. It would be twenty-two dollars," Bob was strangely nervous, but maintained his composure in summing up the biggest bill for one meal that he had ever seen. John gave him thirty dollars. "Now our morning meal is paid too - don't forget Bob." Some men came in and asked, "What did you see this time, John?"

"Oh I don't know - more grass, more snakes a lot of miles on horseback. Oh yes, we got some fishing in, caught some nice catfish in one of the rivers, but can't remember the name of the river. Something up north I think."

"But John, where did all the money come from?"

"The people liked catfish and paid a lot for them." John stood up abruptly. "Good day gents. Some of us have to work for a living, and we have to go to work. You boys that want to work for me get your working duds on and come to the mill in the morning after we eat. We will find something for you to do; there is always something to do. If you are asked, make up a story but put no truth in it. I don't want them to get ideas, or the rush is on and then we are done and Tall Elk's people too."

They walked by the banker's house and found Bodkins raking by his step, making the ground smooth. "Give me a twenty Hans," John put the coin in the dirt by the step and said, "Well look at that Bodkins, a twenty dollar gold coin by your step! How did you do that? Can you show us how?"

"That big wolf will get me." He put the coin in his pocket. "I must have lost this." He thought about it for a couple minutes then said, "No. You put it there." He tossed the coin to John.

"You should not have sent the men to shadow us. It's your doing and now you will pay, but Pounce may never come for you. It is a long way just to kill a skunk, and you stink. It's your greed for gold that got you into this, and don't try the sliver of wood again either. Or we will see your boss and you will eat the stick and I hope you are hungry. You have lived a long time on the earth Bodkins and you know that cheating and stealing is the same thing but you tried to do both today. It's your greed that is bad, and you being a banker, dealing with other

211

people's money all day long should shame you into being honest. Never mess with my money or I with finish you, and you will be lucky to be able to clean the floor, or dump waste cans. I have been lucky but I worked hard too and was in much danger. Now Hans and I can go see the world if we want to. Here you are, looking back to see, never knowing if Pounce is coming or not, and what if a big dog runs here? Will you know? No you won't. Not for sure. You may run for nothing, all because of greed for something that belongs to someone else. Learn Bodkins, learn from this and you will be a lot happier man when it is over." John said. "Help me!" cried Bodkins remorsefully. John said nothing for a long time and then said, "We will try. I don't know how, but you must stop wanting what is not yours, and do it now."

John continued speaking as he and Hans continued on. "I am going to have to help those people out there adjust to the coming of the white settler, and you know they will need help. Land is eighty dollars a quarter here now, three hundred and twenty dollars a section, but out there it is free. You know they will go where it is free no matter how dangerous it is and if the tribes fight to keep their hunting grounds many will die. They will fight and here we are running supplies to them. At first, I thought it was for hunting but it is much bigger than that. We must help but how, I haven't figured it out yet. It is too big for just me or us, and that big horse herd needs grass and so will the cow herd. That land will grow crops and they will farm it, but horses eat crops, and so do cattle but you herd cattle, they never look to see what the horses are doing or the buffalo either so the buffalo will have to be controlled to but how?"

"You know how, John? The buffalo will have to be killed - most of them anyway." Hans said thoughtfully.

"And what about the antelope? They don't eat much grass so they will live but the big horses herd will have to be in fences. You could never fence the buffalo or the Lakota either so the Lakota will have to change; the buffalo will have to die. I wish I had never thought of this I will not sleep well tonight," John said.

"We must buy land here before it is too late. We must buy tomorrow if some is for sale and have enough so we could have some of them come here and live." Hans said thoughtfully.

"It is a good idea, Hans. We will do it. I feel better already. Now let's go and see the hog lot and the mill. Thank God it is not tomorrow - we have some time yet, but we must act tomorrow and buy land. We can get in a block of land, so we could if we have to have some of them live here with us.

The seven of them had breakfast at the eating house. After eating, John and Hans outlined the plan of buying land before it got too expensive. John first asked if any or all of them wanted to work for him. No one had any objections so all of them said yes. "Now," John asked, "who would want to invest some of their money in a land company to buy land as a group?" Everyone thought this was a good idea too, so tentative plains were discussed and outlined.

Bob came out of the kitchen drying his hands on a flower sack, all smiles. John scowled at him. "The breakfast is paid for, Bob, don't forget, so get that shit eating grin off your face. Now that we are on that, we are not going to pay you every time we eat anymore. Get a sheet of paper and write each man's name on it; a sheet per man, and put on it what that man ate, and the cost. After the meal he will check it and if it is what he ate, he will sign it. Then every seven days we will pay. At dinner we will begin. This meal I paid for, as you know last night. Bob don't get to charging too much or we may eat at home. We eat here because it is convenient and none of us like to cook but know that we surely could. Oh, and two dollars was too much for a T-Bone. You got paid for the entire beef; now let's have a nice roast beef for dinner - we already paid for it. Get to cooking Bob." John mussed Bob's hair and pounded his back, as they were old friends.

"Jared and I will go to the land office and check listings. You boys work around the lots and the mill. We will see you at supper." At the land office, there were ten sections not quite in a block, but close enough for sale with three more nearby also for sale. Six sections were for sale a mile away with four sections that connected owned by a man who had died. The office attorney told them that the son, the only relative, would sell for eight hundred dollars cash for the four sections. "Sold," John said, "draw up the papers, and when all is done I will give him a bank draft for the eight hundred dollars." John and Jared rode out and looked at the ten sections, and found them flat to rolling with some patches of timber that were good. They would need to fix up the house that was there and the dry deadwood for fires would keep them warm. They would take it all.

When they got back the others were just going to the eating house. Over supper John told them about the land and its capabilities and how in time they would have something they all could be proud of. Jared said, "We looked at most all of it; it will take some work, but this way we are working for ourselves and not somebody we hardly know. I am going with John and Hans on this and my name will be on the title deed with theirs." The other four said, "Count us in," so John suggested that all of them put five thousand in a new land account to buy land with. When the land was bought they would need equipment to work the land, like mowers, racks, buckers for haying and other tools as were needed. This could be bought with funds that were left over after the land was bought. In two week's time the twenty-three sections were in the seven's names, and they were all land owners. They were wealthy to boot and the bags of gold in the vault were not used yet.

So the Moreau River Land Company was formed, named after the general area where the gold that funded the operation was procured. Tall Elk and the Lakota people were to be included as well and in the future if need be. Especially if enough settlers came in and made it impossible for the natives to continue their free roaming way of life on the vast prairies as they had done in the past. This was still many years in the coming but John and the land company had made arrangements for the Lakota people to have a safe place to live when the time came. Now boundary lines were marked out and land for crops marked, carpenters hired to build and improve housing on their holdings. They began to build shelters for livestock and the pens to hold them. A large horse barn was built and a buying trip was made to the eastern settlements to buy work horses, wagons, some dairy stock and a herd of range cattle with bulls to grow beef for themselves and to sell to others. They had hogs, so a few chickens and sheep were added to round out the barnyard. Mowers hummed and rakes clattered and hay piled up like magic for winter feed for the livestock. A trip was planned to go west with a light pack train for their friends the Lakota.

On a warm fall sun, Golden Girl and Bald Eagle flew in on soft wings and sat down by Tall Elk's lodge and told them that the white ones were coming again with a pack train lightly loaded and would be there in a few suns.

Chapter 27

"How, my friends!" was the greeting John gave as he John, Jared and Andy rode in, "We have brought you some things you may need." Bags of coffee, sugar, salt, fire sticks and tobacco and other items were unloaded from the horses. "We have come to say many words to you. We hope your ears are uncovered and you hear much wisdom in what we say. The prairies you live on are very large, but the white people that are coming are many, and each family of them will want enough land to live on and grow crops, and have livestock.

They don't live together like the Lakota do and each will want their house to live in, and the land they will want will be a half mile in a block or a mile square, more if they can get it. They will be close enough to help each other but not all the time. They will fence their crops with anything to keep out horses or buffalo. If you try to be friendly they will think badly of you and shoot their guns at you and some of you will die. Then you will kill them. They die easy, then many of them will be together for a short time and if you ride your horses near they will kill you, even boys; they won't understand."

John continued on, "They are very frightened so they don't think they just want you to fall on the ground so you can't hurt them more. If Pounce kills them they will send for help more men with big thunder sticks to kill you back. They will need water, so they will live by the springs, streams, and rivers. They won't want you to get water - they are afraid of you, so they will shoot at you again. I don't think they will come soon, but they will come. They will get a paper that says this ground is mine. They can do that because they are a citizen of

217

the territory, and you are not. In time there will be farms, towns, and ranches all around you. Many of you will be gone to sleep in trees, but they don't like that either. Some sun they will want you to put your dead in the ground and cover them up. The change we talk about will take maybe fifty years or more, but it may come sooner. We have used some of the gold to buy land, and when that bad time comes some of you can live with us and be safe, because we say you can be there and they can't hurt you. You will work with us in growing food as you do here There are no buffalo so the meat you eat will be cattle; it's like buffalo but not so wild. We cut the bulls or some of them so they get big, and we eat hogs and sheep too. We also eat chickens, turkeys and some wild game too but they are not many. But to help you, you must help us. We need to buy more land and work it, and make a place for you to live with us or near us. There will be a place for Pounce and his too, and the eagles can come and go as they like and help us if they want to. We will be one big family working together for the good of all. Now I ask you the Lakota to send more gold with us to buy land our way. It's the only way it will work, as we will need a lot of land to take care of everybody and keep us all safe. The white man has rules to follow and we know of them. You let us take care of that part. We must go back east soon to get the land we will need, before it is all bought up. It takes much gold to live the white way. Help us and we will save you." John said.

John paused for a minute and then said, "When we are gone, go to the place were you find the gold and get more before it is all found. To do what we speak of will take much gold so to have plenty will be good. Send maybe ten bags or more; you can't use it, and we can. We are your only white friends you have, I think so trust us."

Tall Elk looked around at the faces of his people and looked at Pounce and his. "I don't like walking the white man's road much, but the other way is maybe worse. Let us ask baby. The vision said she would be wise in the white man's way beyond her years." White Buffalo Calf was asked what she thought. "The white men who are here now are good and trying to help us live. I say trust them - do you see others trying to help? No. I don't either; give them what they want and go get more. Skunk, make better arrows; we must protect ourselves. We should get much meat and dry it. Pounce you and your sons go find other good places to camp so we could get out of sight if we need to. Give them gold and eagles can watch from high up to see that no one bothers them. Pounce, you and twenty good wolves go with them to guard them. They carry much wealth to help us live. I have spoken my words. Do as they ask, and do it now."

Fifteen bags of gold were loaded on the horses, and John marveled at the wisdom of a child and her grasp of the situation at hand. He and the men started with their armed escort at once. They would go to other settlements and open accounts in bigger banks dressed as wealthy men, for indeed they were wealthy men. They would buy much timbered land, a better place in which the Lakota and the wolves to settle. They would need wood for building and fire wood.

Jared asked John, "How much land is too much?"

John thought a long time then said, "I don't think you can have too much land. Remember they are not making more land but new people are coming every day. If we feel we have more than we need we can sell some for much more than we paid, and we pay for it with gold we did not have to dig; it is all free. No one ever had a better deal, so don't complain. Hans, a hair brain, for once had a good idea, and he is as dumb as a box of rocks."

Banker Bodkins had grown bold again, for no big wolf track had been found by his steps so he lost his fear. He knew John and two men had taken a light pack train west. He also knew it was loaded with coffee, sugar, salt, pepper and other items, he all so knew they would be bringing back gold. Bodkins wanted that gold. His greed got the best of him again, so he found five of the lowest order of men he could find and sent them to highjack the train on its way back with orders to kill the three men and bring the gold to him. He then would cancel what they owed at the bank plus give them some gold - a good plan, he thought, but he forgot two or three points. First, the men were as greedy as he was. Second, not only were they dumb, but they were stupid as well, and they had no leader. They could not find a plan that made sense, so they came to agree that one of them would have deer blood on him and be laying in the trail like he was hurt.

When the three men got there and jumped off to help, they would be shot dead.

What they did not know was that Golden Girl had seen them coming three suns before and almost fell out of the tree laughing as they past under her, fighting on the best way to do it. When she told them in night camp about it, Pounce and Frost figured it out. So when the time came and one was on the ground with deer blood on him, two evil men on one side two on the other all - watching front. They should have been watching behind them. Twelve big lobos had them quickly and no sound was heard. John and the others got off their horses and asked the man on the ground, "Have you been fighting with deer again?"

"Don't shoot! You may hit me!" No sound.

"Who are you talking to, the trees? I did not know trees shoot, what would you call them, sling shot trees? Or blow hard trees, or what?" John slapped the man hard then he was tied and the wolves brought out the other four who were slapped then tied hand and foot. The first one was untied and told to take off his clothes, all of them. Ropes were gotten from their horses and he was hung by his feet upside down. "So you want our gold, do you? "What you get is a whipping, a good whipping! Who sent you?"

"We sent ourselves, you hillbillies!"

Three green ash sticks were cut and the whipping began. The man jumped, screamed and cursed, and then he cried, begged and red lines were on his back, butt and sides. "No, I will tell all. Stop!" Tears, snot, and spit ran together and fell from his weak chin. "Bodkins made us do it! He wants the gold, and he said to kill you three, throw you in the water and he would cancel our notes at the bank."

"How kind of him. How much was your loan? Two dollars or ten? No one would give you more; you are not worth that. Well, what can you tell me? Who will be next to feel the sticks? Who pointed his gun at me? You, fat boy?"

"No not me!"

"You lie. You came to steal, kill and you all are guilty. Get their horses; we will see how they like riding upside down."

"What of their guns?"

"Get them. They will all be primed so shoot into the trees to get them unloaded. They may have a good knife or two that we could use in butchering. The rest let the rust have - throw them in the lake." John thought for a moment while the five men were put over the horses. "When we get back, you will go to jail for robbery and plotting murder. I will bring charges."

Chapter 28

They went to the bank first, and the other four men were there to help. They went in and when Bodkins saw them he turned completely white. John looked straight at him and said, "Yes, your five men are outside over the horses. They told how you hired them to kill us and bring the gold to you, and you would cancel their loans." Bodkins boss, the head banker named Darrel Burke, said "is that right Bodkins? You will go to prison too; the banking world can not tolerate a thief and would be murderer in a bank. Get the law." So they all were put under arrest and taken away. The head banker and three tellers weighed out eight bags of gold and seven bags went to the vault. A few hundred dollars were kept out for each man as eating money. The rest was put in the Moreau River Land Company to buy more land. It amounted to nearly two hundred thousand dollars in all. Head banker Darrel Burke commented, "This is more capital than most small banks ever see. I am extremely grateful. You chose our bank and I will help you in anyway I can with your banking needs. John, I will name my first son after you. Is that all right?" John laughed a hearty laugh, something he had not done for quite awhile, and said, "Sure!"

After the banking was done they went to Bob's for a meal. "What do you have to eat, Bob? We could eat a horse."

"Well, horse is not on the menu but we could fix up some beef and the fixings, if you want."

"Well go do it, Bob, and quit talking about it, and bring some coffee." Then he turned to his partners and said, "Jared and I will go north to the timber country tomorrow and find what is for sale up there for timber and open land. I hope to find a large track of land well watered with timber and open land. It needs to be a good place for Tall Elk and his Lakota to settle on and run cattle for their use and farm crops too." After the meal they went to the jail and asked if they could talk to Bodkins. "Well Bodkins, you did it; now you lost your job and your house and for what? Your greed got you into this grave - why did you not hear me? The men you sent were the very bottom of the barrel too. We had fifteen bags of gold along and you would never have seen them again. They would be halfway to anywhere and you would be still out. The eagles found them and Pounce caught them, and then we whipped them. They told us what you tried to do. They were ready to kill us from cover. You told them you would cancel their loan too, with our money, and also to try killing us: that was murder. I don't think you will ever be a free man again Bodkins, I think you are here for life."

In a week Pounce and his sons and the others were back at home camp. They were well fed as Frost could kill anything from deer to buffalo; he was so quiet they never knew he was near and then they were dead. Twenty-five wolves can eat a lot. The eagles were back in one sun but they had no hills to go over either, and Golden Girl could cover much ground fast with her long wings. She just floated – all the other eagles had to pump to keep up. She never worked at it hard; she was just good at it, so she was looking over the plains to the south and east. The Cheyenne were due to come soon, so she was looking, but so far nothing, but she was not tired; she never got too tired. She could sleep at two thousand feet, wake up and be miles away. She then saw them: a small group of horsemen, and sure enough they were the Cheyenne coming with Antelope in front. They would be at Tall Elk's camp in two suns or three, so she turned north and Tall Elk knew in a short time. He said, "Good. We will not go until they get here then. Thank you Golden Girl - it is good, you have done well. Are you hungry?"

"Yes, I could eat meat. Now I will go to my tree by the river and sleep. If you need me just call. When she got there she found some noisy crows were building a nest on her perch. Indignantly, she brushed the nest away and shooed away the crows. No crows were going to build a nest on her perch. The nerve of some birds. Golden Girl was just in the mood for a little nap and was drifting to sleep when the crows came back. "Well what have you done now, you big over stuffed dummy of an eagle! You broke my nest and now I will have to rebuild it." Startled, Golden Girl replied, "Not on my perch you won't. What nerve! Just as I was napping, too. Go build your nest on buffalo dung but not on my perch and besides you are too noisy. I would never get any sleep with you twerps around. Now go away; I want to nap!

"Squawk!" screamed the she crow, "Do you claim all the trees?"

"No not yet, but I will if you don't stop bothering me."

The crows knew better than to bother eagle more and could see that if they stayed longer eagle may come after them, and they knew of her speed so they went to find a tree down the river away.

Antelope, the Cheyenne, and some of his friends including Slow Bear were on their way north to the Moreau River country to visit Tall Elk, Skunk, Fast Fox and Moon Boy and others of the Lakota. Antelope as you recall, was with the first white fur trader and the first white man the Lakota had ever seen. He had tried to buy Pounce, Curly, Cubby and Shadow for their fur and had been killed for his mistake, as you don't sell friends to be killed for their fur. Now Antelope was troubled as he rode along, for his news was not the best for any of the free roaming tribes. His news was that white settlers were slowly moving up the rivers in the far south and west, into the hunting grounds of the Comanche and Kiowa people, and had brought the terrible white man's disease, cholera, with them. The Comanche warriors had come in contact with the disease from raiding the settlers and pushing them back down river. When they return, they had taken the cholera back to their home camps. As a result, the tribes had lost much of their strength and many people died, young and old.

Buffalo Hump the war chief of the Comanche had the disease but recovered from it, but was very weak for a long time and did not feel well enough to raid, so the push for free lands had begun anew, and adventurous settlers were pushing west to build new homes anywhere it was available and would include the hunting grounds of all the tribes.

225

Antelope loved the free roaming way of life and that was why he was troubled; he also knew it would be a long time in completely reaching all the lands. As he rode along and looked at the sea of grass, waving in the soft sweet breeze he knew why they wanted to build homes there. Antelope was sorry that their ways of life were so different because he knew they could never live in harmony side by side. One, a hunter and gatherer, the other, a build a home and stay put, fence it and keep all others out type of society. Both had their advantages, but he liked his way better. They probably liked their way the best or they would do it another way.

As they topped a ridge his thoughts were changed instantly because Pounce was suddenly there: a tall majestic king of wolves in the prime of his life and three of his stout sons stood proudly beside him. Just behind him stood Shadow; and together they were five of the most vicious killer wolves the world had ever produced to this date, but in this case, five of the best friends you could ever have. "Greetings Pounce. How kind of you to come and bring us in to your camp. Is it close? I hope so. The crow baits we ride are leg weary and tired. We have come far."

"Yes, it is not far and food is already cooked by Skunk so you know it will be good."

"I cannot tell you how hungry we are. The trail has been long and I have difficult news to tell."

When all were sitting on soft robes, food was presented to each. The Cheyenne were served first. The containers must have had holes in the bottoms because they emptied so quickly, and so they were refilled quickly, and in some cases two or three times. Pounce and the boys even had some, all though they mostly liked theirs uncooked, but in this case they put on their dinner jackets and dined with a passion. (Not really but in this case it sounds better) When all had eaten their fill, coffee with sugar and then tobacco were offered.

Antelope spoke, "Far to the south and west the whites are moving up the rivers into Comanche and Kiowa hunting grounds and have brought the killer disease, cholera, with them. You know the white man's shitting disease. Many died, young and old among the Comanche and Kiowa so they killed more whites and then more warriors got sick and died. More died from cholera than guns, but we feel they will be coming to make homes other places too. Maybe even here, we don't know when or how long it will take but when they come their numbers will be like grasshoppers in a dry summer. They will have thunder sticks and you won't have enough arrows to stop them all. You won't even have enough thunder sticks either - we know you have some. They will be like a swarm of bees – too many to kill." Then he continued. "This black sweet water is good, but you can't grow it or make it or the tobacco either. What you can't make for yourself, you must get from the white man. We know you give him gold for the things you want, will he still bring you all this when your gold is gone?"

"I don't know, but I think he will. They came and explained it to us; we can't go and buy, but they can. They are buying land now so when the white settlers come we will have a place to go and live." Tall Elk said. Antelope thought long then said, "Then some of you better go soon and live there, and be part of that world; what would happen if they get killed? Who would say 'yes that is our agreement you can live in this place.' We know in order to live with them we will have to change or die, and it is better to change than die. If you are dead you can never come back and be a human again. If you change and don't like it, just be as you were - no harm done."

"The words of Antelope ring true in my ears" said Tall Elk. "I know him to be a good man, and I have thought of this also many times. When we get back from the Crow lands, I think some of us should go to the other lands and learn how to live as the white ones live. We will tend the animals he keeps for food and sells for money. We will even get clothes like he puts on to work in, and we must cut our hair so we look like him. Our hair would grow long again if we want, and we will learn his tongue so we can talk to others of his kind. We will NOT FORGET WE ARE LAKOTA! We are Lakota and will always be. The Great One who watches over us all knows we must change or die. If we die, what is the reason that we now live? Why did we gain all our traditions and learn how to be as good as our words? I tell you, it's not just to die and be no more, but also to better ourselves and our children's lives. The words I speak now make me sad, and my heart is on the ground, but if this is the price we must pay to live then pay it gladly and maybe in the suns to come it will be better for all of us. I hope so."

When sun boy brought his torch back to the land of the Lakota, fifty pack horses were standing ready to start. Some carried gifts for the Crow, others carried digging tools, and others just stood. Thirty big lobos were sitting or talking but all were ready; eight eagles, some in the air others sitting on anything but all ready. Ten Cheyenne and forty Lakota were on horses looking at bows, cross bows or thunder sticks, talking, laughing, patting horse necks or silky backs, just waiting. Then Tall Elk, Fast Fox, Skunk and Moon Boy and Antelope came out of lodges, all with bows by Skunk and mounted horses. Now ninety-five horses, thirty wolves, eight eagles were in motion.

It was beautiful to see all the colors, tails and manes flying in the breeze, and the sound like thunder far off. Prairie dogs, weasels, skunks, snakes and birds all looked for a place to hide. The ground was damp so not a lot of dust was in the air. The horses mostly set the pace; they were all from wild stock and the long swinging gallop was easy to hold. A rock a mile ahead was soon just a dot on the back trail. They could do this most all sun, with nothing to eat but the distance and nothing to drink but the wind. They ran, heads up, ears pointed, nostrils flared, and if they needed to blow, as of one they slowed to a swinging trot or a fast walk. Men just sat talking, joking and dozing once in a while. The horses knew where they were going - just point them once, and unless you changed the course they would keep to it.

When they came to water they watered themselves, grabbed a few mouthfuls of grass, made horse apples and let water go. Then as one they found that long gallop and were just gone, not there anymore.

I sometimes wish I could have lived then, and maybe I did. The words I write maybe are just remembering other days. I am with them now, or my spirit is. Is yours? I can see the color, smell the grass, feel the motion, I see the ground go by like silk sliding over marble, smooth, and soft, and I am not here anymore, I am gone. (Come with me reader, if just for a second see the blue of the far hills, hear the song of the meadow lark clear and far away, leave your pain and troubles behind and be free.)

A well watered ash draw was on their left, so the horses just went in and watered themselves as they had done all sun. The men got stiffly down and since it was nearly sundown, or where the sun fell off the world in the west, they made camp. Nothing fancy, just made small fires and ate dry meat. They got their sleeping robes and sat by the fires and talked or smoked pipes. The horses watered again and went to feeding on the lush prairie blue stem a grass that all liked.

Frost killed an old cow buffalo not far away and the eagles ate meat with the wolves. Pounce was good friends with the eagles; they even pulled the hide off a hind quarter and let the eagles eat first. Pounce and the rest then ate and when they were finished and not a lot of buffalo was left, but they were not fussy and ate the insides as well as the red meat along with some of the bones. After they had eaten they fanned out and ringed the night camp. Others used the water too: big cat, old lord grizzly and old renegade wolves too mean and ugly to be in any pack of wolves, so they ran by themselves. They were tolerated just as long as they watered and left. Big cat they had no use for at all. So he left quickly and spent the night in a tree. He was sputtering and hissing to himself the entire night.

The grizzly was a different matter: he was too big and powerful to mess with much, so he was just warned to drink and move on or else. "Or else what," asked one meanly.

"Or we will come at you as one then you can rot here on the ground. Your choice but you will not bother horse or man." Bear knew he could easily hold his own with four or five of the big lobos, but not thirty. Nope, he would pass. He could smell gunpowder with humans too. He had little to do with that because it bothered him. He had heard where it was; death was there too, and he was not willing to find out. He knew also that his bluff was called. He knew of Pounce and his seven sons too - never had there been wolves like that in one place before and they helped humans too. Grizzly looked at the buffalo, then at Pounce who just looked back, and then the white of fangs of Pounce showed, and he thought better of that to. So he lumbered away fast, and as he looked, he saw wolves on all sides. Then he saw Frost, Pounce's big left hand son, and knew fear, cold fear.

Frost had killed a massive old buffalo bull by just splitting his spine, and he was dead long before he hit the ground. Now Loafer, Pounce's right hand son, was at his nose smiling at him. The bear growled and stopped, and Loafer took his cue. "Frost has been teaching me to be quick; I can rip out your guts and see what you ate for the last three suns and be back in camp before you fall dead on the ground. Want to find out?"

"No. I pass." Frost was way over there, and now he was on the grizzly's back. "His neck is smaller than that big bull's was. I think I can kill him quicker then you can, Loafer."

"No," old bear said, "I just wanted to get a drink."

"Then go, old Grizzly, and be nicer. Loafer and I are never more than ten steps from each other and we know your smell. Now we can find you and finish our contest." Frost was on his back, and then he was gone. Grizzly had good ears, but he never heard him land or as he went though the hillside brush, never a twig snapped or a branch moved. He was like smoke, and Grizzly hoped he never saw him again.

At first light they were ready to go, so they did. Golden Girl, Bald Eagle, and Ruffles, Bald Eagle's son, had gone on to Tall Pine's Crow camp to inform him Lakota and Cheyenne guests would join him at the night meal. Fifty-five of them would come and they would be hungry. Fish with many colored sides would be good if they could find that many. If not, anything would do; they were not fussy. They had many words to say so Ruffles told them to have their ears uncovered. Tall Pine got the words from the eagle, and asked men to get nets and go the deeper pools and catch fish. So they mounted and the horses lined out as before at that ground eating pace they set themselves, racing over the long flat lands. They galloped onward, the blue of the black hills showing now on the horizon.

Tall Elk turned a little to come to where Tall Pine's camp was. It was dryer here so a dust cloud billowed up behind, marking their way. It looked like many warriors on the move. About mid morning the horses slowed to blow and came up to a stream with enough water to water the stock. The grass was poor so they did not stop long. Up a few miles, a draw was grassy with a trickle of water so they stopped and watered again. The horses rested and grazed a little, and then in a little bit, the eagles were back and said the grass was better in ten miles or so. They galloped again, and when they got there all stopped for a short rest. Meat was eaten and the horses grazed on better grass. So they started and went faster if they were going to get there by sundown.

Rabbit saw them coming and told fox and blue jay "They are back again with many wolves; I am going to my home. Fox, get to your den - blue jay can watch and see what they do."

Tall Elk and Tall Pine greeted each other warmly. Horses were put on grass, and the gifts were given: salt coffee, sugar, gun powder, and lead for making balls and other things too. The meal was ready so they ate much fish and other good things as well. When the meal was over, Tall Pine asked, "What is this news the eagles spoke of?"

"Antelope, our Cheyenne friend, has brought the news we are concerned about. Far to the south and west in the lands of the Comanche and Kiowa, the white settlers are moving up the rivers and building homes. They have brought with them a sickness, the white man's shitting sickness, and many have died in the Comanche and Kiowa camps, old and young. Some live, but more die. We fear the settlers may come to other places too, even to our lands. It won't be soon, we think, but they will come. Our white friends who bring us goods are buying land so some of us can go there and live. We will have to change and walk his road but that is better than just die. We give them some gold but it takes much to by land. You could send some of your young men to go with our young men, so they can teach us who how we must do things. We would help you get more gold; some we would like to take back with us to buy the place we need and more goods for all of us. Some you should put away that only a few know of the hiding place. No one knows where we got the gold, so you are safe and no one will know."

Tall Pine said, "We have gold to send with you; it's as much as you need, and we have put some away too. We will put more away; you can help find some if you want to but there is no need. We to have been thinking and will put more away and get more for you. We must stay friends and learn together. As for the young men, we will see. They could come later, and they must say yes or no."

Chapter 29

Sun boy was back with his torch and the pale golden light was everywhere you looked: it was fresh, clean and people were airing out sleeping robes and other garments by hanging them on branches so they smelled better. Tall Elk, Fast Fox, Skunk, and others of the Lakota and Cheyenne were standing by horses ready to go dig and wash out gold. Tall Pine and his workers were ready so they went to where the gold was found. A mile or so upstream, the water ran over rocks and gravel, then into pools. They put the horses on grass and went in the water. "All along here," Tall Pine said. Skunk could stand it no longer; he took a shovel and filled it with sand and gravel off the bottom, put it in a gold pan and swirled it around as he was shown. As the sand washed out, he picked a few rocks from the bottom and he saw that he had yellow gold in the pan.

Skunk just looked; he could not believe what he saw: others were getting gold now and bags were filling all along the stream. Someone gave him a bag so he put his gold in and got another shovel full. When it was washed out there was more gold than the first. He took out some dirt from the bank - just dirt - and washed it. Gold! It had gold, and more of it. Fat Legs and Wind In His Hair got Skunk's digging tools, filled the pan, and washed it. Skunk looked at it his bag; it was almost full now. Fat Legs dug a hole in the shallow water and found three egg sized round gold nuggets, and when he washed out the sand, Skunk's bag was full.

Tall Pine walked over to where Skunk sat, "Well Skunk, we filled all the bags we have along. Have you seen enough?"

"Yes, I have. There is enough wealth here to buy half the world and have some left over. Let us take it to camp and eat. Then we will load up and go, but I say this: when the whites find this, there will not be even a tree standing, so get a lot and hide it good in many places, and the fewer that know the better. Never tell Blue Owl - he cannot be trusted - he would sell out for a fire stick or less. Have your people make many bags to fill with gold. Fill them and make more."

"How many did we fill this sun Tall Pine?"

"Fifty or more I think." Skunk said, "I think this is an accident in nature. I think men have looked all their lives and never got near what we found this sun. We use it for the good of our people, not just ourselves - that makes it good. But it must be gathered fast before some white man finds it or you will get no more. This much of anything is not found too many times in ones life, so get enough. Then more so our people can have a good life." It was good they were only a mile or so from camp as the cargo was heavy and they had not brought the pack horses. No one thought they would gather so much in so short a time. A meal was waiting for them so they made a list of wanted things that was given to Tall Elk for the next time the runners brought goods, and it was a long one. Most of the digging tools were left with Tall Pine, as he would be using them. The pack horses were gathered and gold was packed. The Lakota were taking the gold gathered that sun, and Tall Pine and his workers would go back and get more.

Rabbit and blue jay were watching, "They get ready to go again, and taking more of the heavy yellow rocks too. I wonder what they do with them," said blue jay. "I don't know," mused rabbit, "but the world may tip over if all the weight is put in one place, and we may have to sleep up side down. I told you they were crazy; now this proves it."

"You may be right rabbit, but you seldom are, you know."

Fifty pack horses were loaded, two bags to each horse, and were tied two by two in a line so they could not stray. The riders flanked them and the pack of deadly lobos fanned out on two sides and eagles flew air guard. The horses, as before, picked their own pace and that was the long swinging gallop that they could hold for many miles. They were lightly loaded so very little stress was on them, and as the time slid by, so did the miles. At midpoint to sundown no water was found so they kept going. Ten miles more and a thunderstorm had just passed and water was running in little rivers into bigger ones, so they stopped and took on water. It was cool, cold water with wet green grass in it - a banquet if you happened to be a horse and nice if you were not. After a time they were moving again, slower than before, but they were still moving briskly. It was too early to stop, so they started again at a long lope, then back to a trot and finally settled down to a fast walk.

The horses had spent themselves and needed to rest and graze some. Bald Eagle stopped and said that a good night camp was six or so miles more. So they got the stock moving again with much complaining and snorts of protest, a big bay stud said to Frost who was near, "That little fat one that smells like a skunk should carry the yellow rocks. I am ready for a nap."

"Humph! You are always ready to nap, even when you are napping. You are a little lazy, you know."

"How about you, Frost, you can carry too, you know."

"I am keeping you safe. Big cat would love to have a chunk of your fat rump and eat it as you watch. Night camp is only a few miles up over that ridge then you can sleep or eat or anything that makes you happy."

"Frost, could you tell me a story? Then I could nap well."

"A story!? I don't know any story, you big dummy; besides, what if old lord Grizzly decides to show up? He would like to eat you too."

"Grizzly? That makes me want to climb a tree. I hate even his smell - will Loafer be with you?"

"Yes. He is most always near and Ice too: you are safe, now just do your job, and do it well. It is not that heavy and you are strong. I think you could handle old bear all by yourself - should we find out?"

"No. I will let you boys do that." And soon they were in night camp. Pounce looked at Frost and Loafer, "Go," he said, "four of them." A small group of buffalo got smaller by the number four in less time than it takes to tell you. Skunk and Fat legs with the help of Wind In His Hair skinned three out and had hump ribs ready to cook as soon as fires got going, and that was done in a short time. All were hungry; it had been a long sun. Drying racks were set up and meat was drying for the next sun's march.

The bay stud was loafing, napping and standing on three legs, and then changing legs. Frost jumped on his back and lay down, "All right horse, I am ready for my story now."

"Frost you are too quiet. I thought you were big cat. I just about jumped out of my skin, and now I don't think I can sleep at all!" Frost was snoring. "How can I explain this? Now I am babysitting a wolf, the quietest killer wolf ever, next to his father Pounce. Do I hum to him or what?" The horse pulled one ear back Frost was still snoring so he did too.

Loafer stood looking up at Frost. "Well, are you going to help guard camp or sleep on the bay's back all night?"

"I don't know; his back is soft and warm, and I am lazy. If you need me, just call. I will be there fast."

"Well my son needs a new name, maybe Frosty the horse wolf, or Frosty the horse flake, or Frosty the horse snow wolf." Pounce laughed long, his funny bone was tickled.

"I am doing my job, father. I am guarding the bay - he is of value to me. He is my new bed and good friend, but I have had my nap so I will guard the camp now. Is there anything out there that needs killing quick? Maybe something Loafer can't handle, like an old mouse or something."

"Funny," Loafer said, "Very funny. Remember small brother, you may be quick and silent but in a long run, say a hundred mile run, I would get there first." Ice and Slayer came to stand near, "Is this a family debate? If so, don't forget Pokey, he can see all with one look. We are all good at something and father is best in all things and he trained us all to be better than the rest put together."

The next sun they were back in home camp with more wealth than the world had ever heard of. It was dumped out, sized, sorted and put in bags again. Seventy bags were put away. Thirty bags of gold were to go east with the young men when Tall Elk decided who were to be chosen. Bald Eagle, Golden Girl and three more were to go to tell John to get the goods for the Crow and to get work clothes for twenty young men who would work for him and learn the white man's ways.

Chapter 30

John, Jared, and Andy had been busy the last three weeks. They had ridden north and east of the settlements and found land no one had been interested in because it was far removed from the settlements. The land was flat to rolling with much grass and it was well watered with streams of clear running water. There were timber lands with hardwood ash, oak, hickory, maple, black walnut, spruce and pine and huge elms. There were berry bushes: blueberry, blackberry, raspberry, plum and grape vines hanging everywhere - a dream come true. Wild life too: black bear, deer, moose, turkeys, wood grouse and more. The streams were alive with beavers, fish, mink, otter, and marsh rats. So they bought two hundred and fifty three sections more or less in a block - dirt cheap - as low as one hundred dollars a section. When all the paperwork was finished, it took a briefcase to carry it all in. Darrel Burke and his legal staff went over it, then filed the Moreau River Land Company legal papers and notarized the lot of them. Darrel then put the legal documents in the safe. The completed land buy was less than twenty five thousand dollars so they had done well.

John, Jared and Andy came out of their house early to go to Bob's to eat and Bald Eagle, Golden Girl and three more eagles were waiting for them. Golden Girl said, "This is a list of things they need. They will meet you where the tall trees are just before the lakes start. They are bringing much wealth - thirty bags of gold. Also, twenty young men will come and work for you and learn your ways. They will cut their hair and you need to get them work clothes, so they will learn your tongue and be like you. Then after time has passed, others will come and the first will go back, not all; some will help the new ones but at some time all will know how you live. Tall Elk is very smart. He knows you speak true and with a straight tongue. Get the things I told you. When you start they will start. We go now; I don't like your settlements," and they were gone.

"Thirty bags of gold. Can you believe that? We will have twenty good men to help mark and set ownership lines. And," Jared said, "I think we should fence our lands too, or the farmlands for sure."

"Yes we agree. Now let us go to Bob's and eat. Then we will get their goods and twenty outfits of clothes and hats with cutting tools to cut their hair so they look like we do. Bob, we will have twenty workers to work for us soon. They will not speak our language in the beginning but will learn to. You must treat them good. In the beginning I will order for them; if you treat them badly we will all stop eating here quick. Then I will get a cook and you will see us no more, so be careful Bob. I will only tell you once; you go to them first every time. You seat them at your best tables with new tablecloths and you give them refills if they want, no questions asked. I will pay but don't charge too much or I quit. Do you understand Bob? I want pie three times a week and lots of them; get more help if you need to. But don't mess up! Tell other people to be nice too. No bullshit; do you hear Bob?"

"Yes I hear John, do you think I am a baby?"

"No, but you are not real smart either. Now Bob hear me and hear me well: if you do badly with our new men I will build an eating house over in that open place. Don't try to block me, Bob. I bought it two days ago. Remember when we were kids, Bob? We made a pact to get along forever. I have, now you do the same. You can buy beef from us, and hogs too and I think many chickens too. You could have fried chicken on Sundays and everybody would be here. You could be rich and famous, but mess up with my men and I will do it and I don't want to. I have enough with the land management: we have two hundred and seventy-six sections of land and I will buy more. When I am done the land company will be the biggest around because of Hans' hair brained idea and our good luck."

It took a little more than a week to get the list together. It was an easy one: just coffee, sugar, salt, pepper, beads, thread, needles, blankets, knives, wet stones, gloves, some bags of flower and fish hooks, some gun powder, fire sticks for starting fires quick, two iron arrow points and rasps and files for shaping wood. John, as an afterthought put some dried fruits in and tins of tobacco, a few hammers and some saws. Ten cooking pots and long spoons for mixing, a few this and that's. They were ready to load up and start, so they did. At midnight they were gone. They left when the rest were sleeping as to not get any notice. John and three of the men, not Hans: he would never go again. They were just not there when the sun came up they were miles west of the settlements. When the sun was up they stopped for a short break, made coffee ate some canned beans and hard bread and were moving west again.

Golden Girl was catching some high air currents and floating eastward when she saw movement and saw that it was the supply pack train going west so she swooped down and made sure. She then went west and told the Lakota to get the twenty men ready and the gold loaded as the supply pack train was coming. There were some long faces around camp as mothers and fathers helped get gear ready; it was like going on a long war trail but less dangerous. No one was thinking of killing, for they would be learning a new way to live and would be gone three or four moons or more. All took bows by Skunk and a full quiver of arrows, their knives, but no feathers or paint; they were going to look like white men or as near to that as they could. Antelope, the Cheyenne, had been teaching them some white man talk and some could make themselves understood now in that tongue, not good but better than nothing.

Fifteen horses would carry the gold, two bags to the horse. The twenty young Lakota put their gear on their spare mounts and seven wolves would go, seven being the wolf round number of completeness. Pounce would send Frost, Loafer, Ice and Red Tongue, Sly and Little Bit and Shadow. He needed some of them but would send word to Sniff and Fatty to send some of theirs so he could train them. Pounce knew that Frost and Loafer could kill most grizzly before they knew how badly off they were but black bears were new to him so all seven would go to watch the men. Golden Girl and three more eagles would go also; Golden Girl was the fast one and would carry word back to the main camp if it was needed. Pounce told them all not to eat the white man's tame animals as that was one reason for going in the first place: to learn how to live the white way. "Ask John; he will feed you, and maybe they eat their own animals sometimes." So the twenty would be white men and twenty more to bring the pack train back got to horse and were gone, just not there anymore, and the other Lakota went about living as they always had, for riding of was part of life. Those would were fortunate enough to return to camp were simply more fortunate than those who didn't make it back; that's just the way it went.

So four watched from up high, seven watched on the land, forty led the way and set the pace, and fifteen did all the work. (Sounds about normal to me, how about you?) In the saddle packs there was enough gold to buy the settlements, give them away and never miss the pocket change. If the world would have just known it, they would have taken it no matter the cost, because men the world around love gold. And I don't know why: you can't eat it, wear it for clothing, and it will not keep you warm in a storm. Of itself, it is worthless. But mankind has been killing over it since someone threw the first rock, and that was not yesterday.

The sound that came from the three hundred hooves pounding the damp sod was like thunder in the far away, then over the hill they poured like a splash of color: bays, whites, brown and whites, black and whites, tans all mixed with manes and tails flying. It was a breathtaking sight that caught your eye and held it. All lesser prairie folks just got out of the way or got stepped on. Then after the whirlwind of color and motion had passed to quiet again, a meadowlark tuned up and sang his song. The wind made the tall grass hum like a harp and more birds sang and it was sweet and lovely, and it was the prairie again.

Long fingers of shadow danced in front of them to the east, and the horses were wondering if they would stop soon. They wanted water, grass and rest. A shimmering pond of water was by some trees, so they just stopped. The men could run more if it pleased them - the horses were taking a break. Dry sticks, old grass, last year's forgotten leaves were gathered and soon ten or so fires were going. Frost and Loafer brought a few buffalo near camp and Frost killed a dry cow and a yearling bull so quickly they never knew they were in danger. The men skinned them out and since they knew buffalo was not going to be had for some time, were going to enjoy eating hump steaks until they could eat no more. Eagles got the hearts; the wolves got the rest of the parts no one wanted and some of the red meat. The hides were tanned and set to go at first light, and fires were built up again and strips of meat were dried for next sun's eating.

The horses fed on the grass until they had enough then stood on three legs and dozed, or stretched out and slept. Wolves guarded the camp and eagles sat in trees also guarding; the safety of the sleeping man was never in question. A young grizzly got the smell of meat at the same time as the scent of wolves and men. He was not afraid but he was not stupid either; he knew of Frost and his killing ways. Loafer, Ice and Shadow were there too so he just went away, his skin tingling. He did not want his neck broken, and the word was out that Frost was as bad as Pounce his father, only meaner. Nothing was near so the men and horses slept like babies. Then the sun was getting ready for another run across the sky and light was coming back to the land. Young men broke camp, loaded the horses and started east. The land where the camp was remained unchanged but for some piles of used grass left by the horses and used meat left by the others. As the sun rose, the men blinked the sleep out of their eyes and the light got more intense. They were many miles east, more eastward than any had dreamed of going.

Chapter 31

The circuit judge was in the settlements hearing the charges against the six men who were involved in the attempted hold up and murder of the five men. Bodkins was found guilty for setting up the high jacking attempt, but since no crime was committed he was given two years probation and told by the judge he must find gainful employment or go back to jail. Banker Burke was asked if Bodkins could do odd jobs around the bank and grounds. Yes, that could be arranged, but he was not to handle money or banking matters in any form, or he would be discharged and would go back to jail. The five would be robbers were tried next, and about the same deal was given them: work or they go back and finish their time. They asked if their guns and horses would be given back. The judge told them that if they touched or even looked at a firearm, they would be in violation of their probation and they would go back and finish their terms. Then he glared viciously at them and said, "As for your burned property, they should have thrown you five in too and we would have all been better of." His gavel banged - next case. Then as an after thought, he pointed his finger at them and said, "You have two weeks to find honest work or go back to jail," and the gavel banged again.

Six suns later the east bound pack train rode into the tall trees to find the west bound one there, so the twenty Lakota started the pack train west, and the twenty who would learn the white ways got their hair cut by John and Jared and were given clothes to wear. After much trading back and forth, all twenty had a good fit, and were given some lessons in talking the white tongue. It was slow at first but went along well as the Lakota men knew they must learn and Antelope had got them started. John's men were introduced to Frost and Loafer and the other five wolves and the eagles too, because they all would be working as one for the good of all. The wolves were asked not to kill tame livestock, and Frost said they knew that - Pounce had made that point clear.

Five days later the horses stood in front of the bank and gold were being counted and put in different accounts. Fat Legs, the Lakota, got the largest amount. Twenty bags went to the vault and the seven white men all got some; the rest went to the Moreau River Land Co. to buy equipment and livestock. Banker Darrel L. Burke remarked John, "Where in the hell is all this gold coming from?" John said, "I don't really know, but if I did I don't think I would stand on a housetop and tell the world or it would start a stampede I could not handle. You are not getting ideas like Bodkins, are you Darrel?"

"No I am not."

"I will see to it that you get a bonus before we are done, but don't get greedy either." John asked the men, old and new if they were hungry and yes was the reply by all. "Then let's go to Bob's and eat." Frost and Loafer were edgy when Bob came to seat the men; Bob did a double take, and then just plain stared in disbelief. "Now hold it Bob," said John, "The wolves are part of the bunch, and they like their food not cooked so bring them meat and fat with some bones on platters and some water."

Loafer looked at Bob, "I can read your mind: you think we are dangerous. We are not if we like you; you will never have better friends. We like leftovers too just put salt and pepper on them. We are here to guard our friends from harm. You need not fear us, but hurt our friends and we will kill you quickly." Bob had to sit down - talking wolves? That was unheard of. John noticed his expression and said, "Get the food, Bob. We are hungry: beef and all the trimmings, pie, and coffee. Get the lead out now, some of us work for a living." When the meal was done, Bob got a dollar a plate and no charge for the wolves; their food was mostly going out the back door anyway, and all thought that was fair.

John and Jared got digging tools and took the new men up to the north lands. The others put the horses on grass and got to work on the big ranch yard and out buildings. A survey crew had found the outside edge of the land and drove stake markers. John told them to cut posts and set them where the stakes were: big posts, a corner post and two brace posts. He told them that up here would be the home main camp some day. At mid afternoon John told the men to leave the tools and they would go back to the ranch yard and go eat at Bob's. In the morning they would get a team of horses and a wagon then go to the hardware and get push/pull saws, some tamping bars, tilling spades, and punch augers, then the Lakota men with Jared as foreman could set the border markers. They would take camp gear and food and not come in until the job was done. A large stand of trees that grew too thick was found, mostly oak, that they would thin out and use for posts. They grew straight up so little trimming was needed and stood twenty feet or more high. The men were told to get gloves and coats as it might turn chilly, and if the wind came up they would be uncomfortable. John told Andy to pick a helper and buy a kitchen range to do some cooking on and install it at the ranch. John was getting tired of stopping everything just to eat, so they would do some of the cooking. "Jared, when you boys are done, cut a load of fire wood to cook with; we will need wood soon anyway." Frost killed a deer with a broken leg so the wolves had plenty on which to munch while they got used to the feel of the large ranch yard.

"Come on, boys! Let's go give Bob some thing to do! We will stop and get your coats and gloves and chaps too; it will be that much less to do in the morning." "At the clothing store, John said, "Here are our new men: get them what they need. I will pay; put it down to the land company. Bring out coats, gloves and chaps and anything else they need. Don't ask questions, just do it. Look them over - they work for us. Now off to Bobs." In a couple of minutes they were there. "Bob get us thick steaks and the fixings, then pie. Be careful, Bob, I am getting a kitchen range but I don't want to use it much. Put the table leavings in a box; the wolves can have them. Bring coffee, and be quick about it." Bob brought out a fine meal, and was told so. He wanted a dollar and a half a plate and got two, call it a tip. "That was good, Bob, keep up the good work."

245

The hardware was open so they went in and found six saws, some wire, and the other equipment they needed also, like some staples and hammers. As an afterthought they got six fencing pliers. "You got a team and wagon we could rent then we can take the equipment with us now?"

"Yes," said the happy shopkeeper.

So John bought the wagon and horses too and paid cash for all of it. "We will use the team and wagon anyway; the horses are not the best – he must have been starving them. Feed them hay and just a little oats. We will take four teams and wagons in the morning and bring them back full of firewood. We for sure are going to need that." The sun was just up when twenty-one men were bouncing north to do some hard honest work. It is said cutting wood warms you two times: once when you cut it and once when you burn it, and believe me, that is a true saying. Six teams of two were formed with one man to push and one to pull so the blade would not bind. The saws were sharp and in five or six times the tree was down.

Twenty trees were down by each team then they were pulled out to the wagons and cut into three posts; that made sixty posts - times six - that is three hundred and sixty posts. They were put on two wagons in order to mark boundary lines and six men were going to cut wood with two wagons. In the stand were dead trees just fine for firewood so they got teams and ropes and pulled them out. The men took their axes, trimmed off small branches, cut the rest into two feet pieces, and loaded them. By afternoon, the wagons were full, so they hitched the teams up and took the wood to the ranch. The wagons were unloaded, new teams put on and they went back, where they found the rest of the men making camp. John had sent beef sandwiches and pies from Bob's, so they made coffee and ate. Frost and Loafer killed an old deer so they ate well also. Frost, Loafer, and Shadow had seen a strange animal, tall and big with shovels on its head and standing in the water, his nose bent and it was eating green weeds in water. "When it looks at you it blows water out its nose and there are many of them," said Loafer. Jared laughed, "You saw a moose, a big deer."

"Are they good to eat?"

"Yes, but only the big ones with shovels on their heads. The others are cows and will have calves, and not till it get cold or the meat will spoil. Next morning the teams had snaked out much wood, so they cut it and took it to the ranch, John asked, "how are the lines coming?" Fat Legs said "About done, maybe next sun."

"Bring bigger logs and longer for the fireplace."

"We do that now. O. K. boss man, we do." Fat legs said. John had a sack of food from Bob's so they changed teams again and went north, by near sundown the two wagons were full and when the other boys got there fires were going, and coffee was bubbling. Food from Bob's was disappearing fast down hungry throats. Frost found a moose, a young bull with a broken leg and he asked to kill it. John told he could, so he did. Jared said, "Get a team and pull it out here; the Lakota boys skinned it, and Jared cut some steaks to fry in the skillet, "His leg was just broke too. I wonder how that happened." Frost smiled, "Unlucky I guess," and winked at Loafer. The eagles ate the heart and other parts they liked. The Lakota boys cooked meat their way, and the wolves looked like bowling balls with tails and Jared smiled to himself. He knew of course but said nothing.

A big black bear smelled the meat. He smelled wolves and men too and cared not for either. They always ran when he came. So he stood up, growled his bad sound, and walked into camp. The horses spooked and the bear laughed, same as always. A wolf stood in his way and then another. "Who invited you to breakfast, bear? We did not! Now go or die - your choice. I am Frost and I kill grizzlies ten times the bear you are."

"And I am Loafer, Frosts brother, and I kill quickly too."

"Ha! Big winds!" Loafer darted under the bear and opened his guts so they all fell to the ground. He screamed as Frost broke his neck and soon the Lakota boys had another bear skin to tan. "Well, get him skinned then tan him," Jared said. "In the morning we can cut two more wagons loads of wood then go to the ranch. We are done here."

"I am glad we are friends, Frost, and you too, Loafer. That bear would have gotten me fast but you boys killed him before he knew he was dead. How did you do that?" asked Jared.

"Father showed us. He is much faster then we are. Pounce could kill many times and you would never see him, just the dead. Be glad he likes you or you would not see morning and he is miles away." Jared shivered a little and never doubted it for a minute. Seeing is believing, and he had seen enough. He said, "Pounce is my friend and I am glad with every bone in my body." In the morning the black bear was still there. He was not black now, just a pile of bad meat, fatty and bad tasting. The eagles ate some then went to eat moose; the wolves never looked at all.

The men broke camp, got the teams ready and moved to a new spot. There was still plenty of wood there but so was the bear and no one wanted to look at him. Golden Girl went to the home camp on the Moreau River. Pounce would want to know about the black bear and his sons. She wanted to tell him not to worry about black bears - his sons had learned well from their father. They had enjoyed killing him. The deer and moose were just meat, but the bear was bad: he was a big mouth and a bully to boot so they killed him and enjoyed it. Pounce smiled when he heard the news. "I will tell their mother; she worry a little, and now she can feel better, and soon they will be back. They like buffalo too much to stay away long, or perhaps we will go see them - it is not that far."

With all six saws cutting, the other two wagons were full in a hurry and they started back to the ranch yard. The fireplace wood was this time longer and bigger wood for better heat this winter.

Wilber Anderson was a big man: over six feet tall, thick in the chest, much power in his arms and hands, a hard worker when he wanted to be but he had a mean streak in him. He had a good gun and was a good shot; by this I say he could mostly hit what he shot at. He could shoot and kill a big Tom Turkey by just waiting for the turkey to get in the right place then kill it. Or a deer, a moose - it did not matter but then when it was time to get the meat and use it, that was when his enthusiasm quit and many times he just left it to spoil or gave it away, if someone was near. He liked to think he was a good hunter, but he was not, for hunters take care of the game they kill; Wilber just liked to kill. He liked to see the thing he shot stagger and fall or bleed, and then get up to get away so he could shoot it again. He knew John and of the land John was putting together, but what he could not see is where the money was coming from.

Then he heard that the gold came from out west someplace. He knew of Bodkin's plot and the men he hired to highjack and kill the men and bring the gold to Bodkins, and how a few wolves had caught the robbers. But the part that he could not understand was that the wolves could talk and reason like men, smart men. He had been at Bob's when John brought his new men in to eat, and the wolves had come too. He heard the wolf, Frost, tell Bob he could read his mind and not to fear them, and that they were just wolves. So Wilbur thought that if he killed one of the wolves he would not go to jail. So he, the hunter, would hunt wolves.

He would have to be very careful: oh, so very smooth. It should look like accident or John and Jared would come after him, an accident like he would be protecting some cows and shot the wrong wolves, an honest mistake. No one would blame him for that. He was at Bob's drinking coffee with some of the local boys when Wilber said, "You know, I think I will go hunting soon and I am going to hunt wolves, maybe in the woods north of here." One of them was after brownie points with John went and found him and told the story to John. All of the settlement now knew of the unusual wolves who worked with John and the men. So John, Jared and Andy looked up Wilber and just point blank told him, "We have seen some of your kills you just left to rot. We don't want you hunting on our land at all, and as for the wolf hunting, you would not know what wolves were wild or the ones that work for us - so just don't hunt wolves at all on our holdings or near us. If you do, one of two things will happen: one, Frost or Loafer will kill you quickly and I will put no flowers on you. Second, I will kill you personally and you still get no flowers, and should we fail there are many more in the pack out west that will not fail. So if I were you I would hang up your gun and find work, not with us, I don't want you on the place. I don't like you; you are a bad hunter and are mean as well, and I will not tell you again."

Wilber was angry. He hated John so. Why had he said anything at Bob's? Now they all knew of his plans. Ah! They were just a bunch of old gossips down at Bob's. Wilber thought of the rest of the pack, something he had never before considered. It was getting complicated - he knew if he was smart he should just leave. Go to another settlement and start over. He was done here with the land company calling all the shots and everyone kissing up to them for handouts, but he was not smart. He had barely enough money to eat on but he was going to kill Frost and maybe the other two as well, or die trying. Where have we heard that before?

Frost and Loafer were moving around they could not set still; no position was comfortable Ice was watching them and said, "Did you two set on an ant pile? You can't set still." Frost then said, "I want to run west for a time why don't the three of us go see father and maybe Shadow too. Lets go tell John and the Lakota what we are doing, I think they can do with out us and ask Shadow if he is coming we are running at night as not to be seen, so the eagles can catch up they don't fly at night much." John thought it was a good idea but asked that some stayed as they were moving cattle in and wolves were good help, so Shadow would stay and go next time.

Wilber took his horse and went west a day or so. He found cover he liked and put his horse on grass and just waited. The moon was full and he had good light. He saw movement - it was three of the big wolves that were John's help; now he could get even and kill at the same time. Wilber took good aim and waited until the distance was just right, then shot. It should have taken Ice in the head but at that crucial moment, Ice looked down and the bullet that should have killed him just creased his skull. He went down like a dropped sack of flour. Wilber got up triumphantly, "I killed the brute! What a shot! And in the moon light too!" That's all the time he got - Frost and Loafer had him before he got loaded again and Loafer spilled his guts out while Frost took out his jugular, and Wilber was history. Ice was just getting up- he would have a scar on his head but not much more except for one of his ears was nicked a little. Frost and Loafer dug a grave in the soft soil at the bottom of the depression and pulled Wilber in then got his gun and put it in too, and by this time Ice came and helped cover up the grave, smooth it, get a branch and cover up their tracks. Frost and Loafer licked Ice's head and he was as good as new, well almost.

An hour later, the three brothers were gliding along in the light of the full moon with that stride all wolves have and all other wished they had: long, smooth, without effort and they covered miles like a cloud shadow on a windy day. Five days later, John and the boys came out of Bob's after putting a large heard of cattle on the north range. The four wolves were herding the cattle on grass - not much of a job - they were hungry and tired so they fed and rested. A horse came up and stood with theirs. John spoke quietly, "Wilber had that horse when he left. Well bring him. The saddle has been on him quite a long time; we will rub him down and put him with ours."

Golden Girl said, "I will go look. In a short time she was back, "He shot one of our wolves but not badly. The other two killed him and put him in the ground; there is much dry blood, then three tracks go west. I will go see," and was gone. John looked at the men, "Well I told him not to mess around or he would die and no flowers either." The fields to be were fenced and six one-bottomed plows were hauled in with breaking bottoms on them. Twelve big teams stood ready to plow and twelve young men stood by to walk behind the walking plows. Their shifts were one hour then they would change teams and walkers, so no one got too tired. They waited for Golden Girl's report. Then she was there. "Ice was creased on his head by a bullet; it knocked him out, and he is fine and eating buffalo. I should have gone too I would have seen him in cover and stopped his shot. I go next time." John looked relieved and said, "We will not tell anybody of Wilber getting killed; he is just gone, and not many care anyway. We will keep his horse and saddle. We can use them and if one of his relatives comes they can have the horse and saddle. We are sorry but that's all we know: nothing. He is just not here, and we don't know where he went, and we don't care. He is a big boy and maybe he is off hunting."

John asked Golden Girl if she would ask the wolf boys to come back and help so the other four could go back and maybe bring others too. They were good help, the best. The eagle looked wise, "I will go and ask, but Pounce will say yes or no - he needs them too and he loves his sons and one almost got killed by one of yours. If Ice would have gotten killed, Pounce would have came and it would have been terrible; there has never been a wolf like Pounce and all would pay with much blood, but he is fair, so we will see. I will have to watch better and I need more eagles for that, and that Bald Eagle will say yes or no. It is very complicated. You must help too. All must be safe for us all; there can be no more mistakes."

With that Golden Girl was gone. The other eagles came and said they would watch well. They asked if there were others as bad as

Wilber. "Not that I know of, but how can anybody know for sure what is in the mind? We can - we know if we find any, you must get rid of them quick. Send Hans away someplace; Pounce doesn't trust him. Send him and Jared to go get many more cattle, all he cows with no seeds. You will need much beef, maybe a hundred. Pounce will come this time and many wise ones and you will have to be here because you are boss. Tell Hans to be very nice and have his mind clear or Pounce will know. Send them now, this sun, so they get back when Pounce is here, and it will help. But Shadow should be here and one more - the other two must go help bring cattle, so Pounce knows you need them all then it will be good."

Chapter 32

On the morning of the next sun, Golden Eagle, Bald Eagle and five more eagles came to the fields where the fall plowing for next season crops was in progress. John was starting the first furrows so they would be straight. Six teams and six plows were turning six black ribbons of sod over, each team driven by a Lakota man. The field was a half mile long and when they got back; a full mile would be turned over. Then six new teams would be hitched to the plows and a new driver would start down the field, giving the first time to rest. Bald Eagle said, "I have looked at the lands the Lakota people live in the future it is good. Golden Girl will have the eagles she needs, Pounce and twenty old wise wolves are coming to look too. I think his sons will help you, but be fair to them. He was very angry one of your kind tried to kill one of his sons. If Ice had been killed many of you would be dead now. No one messes with Pounce, no one. Pounce has no conscience, he don't even know what that means so he would just kill until he was satisfied and Ice was avenged. That could be many and you may never see him at all, just the dead. You think Frost and Loafer are bad, Pounce trained them and he is the best killer of them all, and quick Frost is slow compared to his father."

Hans, Jared and Andy and some of the men and two wolves were buying big steers, as many as they could find. Bob would need some and local people wanted some, but the wolves needed them to eat, as there were no buffalo. They would be skinned and cut up and the skin made into leather. Three suns later ninety-five big cattle were in the pens, four were soon in the coolers and the rest on grass. Bob got four sides taken in and some was cooked and the rest the wolves would get. In due time Pounce and the boys and the wise ones were there; they rested and ate beef and went up to the woods to see the place the Lakota would someday call home all hoped it was in the future a long time. Pounce and the others were gone three suns. They ate an old moose and were well pleased; the gold was well spent.

Twenty older wolves, Red Tongue, Little Bit and Sly would start back when it got dark. Shadow would stay for a time yet. Pounce would go with them past the danger point then come back to help and get the feel of the new country. Three eagles would fly and watch that no ambush was planned, no more chances like that could be taken. So when it got dark they were just not there, vanished.

Six fields were fenced and soon the fall plowing was done. The soil was rich black, all loam, and promised to grow good crops. The disks that had been hauled in were hitched up to four large horses. The disks were set to cut and started down the field, cutting the sod up to finer pieces so it would mellow over winter. It was hard work pulling the disk, so one or two rounds was about all you could ask for out of four horses without changing them, so sixteen draft horses were brought to the fields to wait their turn to pull the disks over the turned sod. It was slow but gratifying to see the smooth soil being readied for spring planting. Corn, oats, wheat and barley would be the main crops.

Gus Gustafson, as you recall, went west the first time. He was the carpenter and was working full time now for the Moreau River Land Company. He and his crew, with some Lakota, built a long low chicken barn. The barn had a southern front to let in light. The chicken flock had grown too. Many hens brought in big bunches of chicks of every color that were mostly grown now and young roosters sounded off on all corners of the ranch yard, a most pleasant sound. They were now building bins to store the crops in as there was no market to sell wheat, oats, or any grain, yet that would come later. Maybe some to local demand, but mostly they would use it themselves to put pounds on livestock; it was a new country. The land office had contacted John and informed him of more land just to the west and north of their present holdings, for sale. So John, Jared and some of the Lakota rode and looked it over. It fit nicely with what they had, so it was decided to buy it.

The new land was timbered and rolling. Good to grow crops at some later time. A hundred and eighty sections or 115,200 acres of prime land, all dirt cheap some as low as $100.00 a section. Fat Legs said, "Well, John do you think we have enough land now? Or do we need more?"

"I don't know boys. It is indeed a big chunk, but remember: they are done making land, but they are still making people. And at some time, good people will want to buy a farm and we can sell them land and not lose money." When the paperwork was done and the money paid, it came to twenty-seven thousand dollars and came out of the land company's expenditure fund that was still over three hundred thousand dollars yet. And land was on the tax roll now that would not have been, without Hans hair brained idea of going west in the first place to get rich, and they were wealthy men now all of them including the Lakota. They all were enjoying it, and would for a long time. The settlement was doing well too and had grown, there was money spent buying supplies that would not have been spent all because of the gold

Pounce was back so he and Frost, Loafer, Slayer and Shadow and a few more helped get the bulls in plus twenty of the big butcher steers. The bulls would be kept around the ranch, so as not to prevent the cows from calving year around. Some of the cows had calved now, but as long as it was good weather they would stay out with the main herd. Pounce was impressed, "You have done well. We will have a place to live as we should when the settlers come to our homelands on the Moreau River country. Tall Elk, his wives and other leaders and their families plan to come and look at the land too; it maybe in the spring. They would like to find campsites with good water and wood supplies." John asked Pounce if they had gotten more gold and if they needed any goods before cold weather set in. "Yes, Golden Girl will bring a list soon, and yes more gold was gathered but it is harder to find so easily now, you must dig deeper but it is still there. I think we will have enough to keep going, as long as no one finds it then we will have to quit, I think."

Pounce asked John if they could go to the place called Bob's. Frost and Loafer had told him about it, and he wanted to see how food was fixed in a place where you ate it and others brought it to you. So John and most of the crew and Pounce and the wolf boys would go, as they came in, Bob did a double take. Pounce was the last thing he expected to see, because he stood out in any crowd. Bob, this is Pounce. He is wolf king and wanted to see how we ate with some one other than ourselves cooking the food, so get to cooking.

"Bob, I mostly eat my food uncooked but now I will have you cook for me," Pounce spoke so clearly that all in the place shook down to their boots. Pounce looked at his sons and said, "My sons, you perhaps are already acquainted with them, I think."

"Yes, I do know them but we don't get too many wolves in here that can speak so well or know so much."

"Oh, Frost and Loafer have been here and they speak well, and they know many things and can read your mind as I can. We will have beef and all the trimmings then pie. I would like water; coffee is too hot. May I suggest Bob, that anyone coming to call should do it by the front door? If they should come in the dark we will be there quick, and then they won't be at all. Now can we eat? I am hungry." When they were finished John paid and all left.

Bob went to the back, threw up and then shook for an hour; he was no good for the rest of the day. Bob knew now how Bodkins felt: to look into Pounce's eyes was like looking into another world, one he never expected to see, or go in to. And you better believe he would never go calling at the ranch at night without a brass band in full swing and off key; he was convinced. Then all the eaters had gone, a few coffee drinkers just stirred coffee - they had so much to talk about they did not know where to begin. "He knows where to find the gold, want to ask him?"

"Not me - I don't have many hairs left on my head and they all stood up and went down my collar to hide. I am out of here!" and they all left. Bob and his help cleaned the dinning room, washed all the dishes, washed the tables and when it was done he had a cup of coffee and just sat. Bob was a strong minded man, so he went through the dinner meal in his mind and considered Pounce's words. What did he mean? Was he warning Bob? Or just stating a fact not to go to the ranch after dark? He had no reason to go before, but now he sure was not. When Pounce looked at you, his eyes made you feel naked, and never before had Bob felt small. The chills started again as his stomach lurched once more. How could a wolf talk and make so much understanding go from him to you? When he looked at you death was looking and you knew Pounce could deliver it to anyone at all, whenever he so chose. Bob wanted to talk to John, but how? He did not know where he went.

An older employee, a pie baker, came out of the kitchen and spoke to Bob in a heavy Swedish accent. "That wolf, he sure is big boss you think? And he likes you too."

"Likes me? He threatened me."

"Oh no boss Bob, he just was talking about a bear or big cat and what he would do if he was in dark. I sure don't want to be bear. Ha - he eat me quick. Now I go make pies," and she patted Bob's hand. "You got a good friend boss, you no worry. He takes good care of you, you betcha," she said. Bob felt so good he had a piece of pie and more coffee. The old lady had made it clear to him and now his talk with John could wait. What a lucky day when the boys had formed the Moreau River Land Company and bought land then brought in workers. Bob knew they were Lakota Indians but they fit in and worked hard and were well liked and that's all that mattered anyway.

That afternoon Golden Girl and four other eagles found John and Andy working in the ranch yard building large gates to hold livestock in. Golden Girl greeted John, "The Crow are building things out of wood. They have much wood but few tools so they would like you to send push/pull saws, twenty of them, many iron pins to hold the wood in place, thirty hammers, files to keep the saws sharp, more digging tools, picks, more pans to wash gold with, more boom powder to make the thunder sticks say boom, a tool to smooth wood, fire sticks - many of them - then coffee, sweet white powder, salt, pepper, flour, cloth to make clothes, with all materials needed to do this, buttons too and ribbons also, the gray bars to make balls for thunder sticks, blankets too. The Lakota want the same but not the digging tools. Oh yes, much tobacco and soap to clean with."

"The Crow will send much gold. Go buy land - some of their young men come to learn your ways like the Sioux. I will tell you when, then cut their hair and make them look like white men. We will guard the train, some wolves too. We will go fast, and you will have much gold." John told Fat Legs to get a hundred pack horses and that may not be enough. Others were told to get five wagons and teams and meet in town we will buy the stores out again and they did. Most everything they found in the settlement may be not quite enough but almost. Pounce and Shadow and four wolves were going to guard; the eagles would start and ten more wolves would meet them on the trail, and more Lakota so the others could get the fall work done at the ranch, they were ready to start so they did.

A hundred or so loaded pack horses came through the settlement, manes and tails flying, clattering hooves sending up spurts of dust. Every horse was linked together with ropes and lashings and every horse was going west. Eagles flew overhead to guard from the air while wolves flanked them on the ground and many mounted armed men urged them to greater speed as they sought the horizon. It was sight that turned many a head from the loafers and onlookers. Even banker Burke got up from his desk to see what was the commotion, and he, like the others tried to see what the packs might contain. In a short time they were gone, just not in sight any more. The dust settled and the sound faded to nothing and all wondered at what had passed by and how it might concern them at some point down the road. Bob saw his best eating crowd would be gone for a time and cut back on his menu as not to cook more than he could sell. The store keepers made orders to fill empty shelves but that was good: they had made money and were pleased as they should have been. The wealth from the gold was spread around again. Daylight was fading and the pack train was miles west but they kept going until good water and grass were found, then they stopped as horses had to water and feed or could not continue as they should. The men also needed to eat as did the guard and air guard.

Golden Girl and two more eagles flew to get ten wolves then started east to guard the train, and Lakota men to come so the others could go back to do fall work at the ranch. Then on to the camp of Tall Pine's Crow to get the young men going east to work as white men do and learn their ways and bring gold to buy more land so they to could live in peace and not fight and die. It was a big undertaking for John and the other six men to hold and maintain the growing ranch and its holdings. It was clearly stated that in case of their dying that certain sections of land would be deeded to the Lakota people of the

Moreau River breaks and to Fat Legs as chief administrator, as he had a sizable account at the bank and had more clout than the others. Then to others as he would appoint to succeed him, so the paper work was signed and notarized and became legal and binding, and Fat Legs was put on the governing board of the Moreau River Land Company, a title he could not say two months before.

Ten young Crow with ten pack horses set out for the Moreau River camp of Sioux, each horse carried two bags of gold to fund the way of a band of Crow to live at some time in the future, as white men or as close as possible. At midpoint to sundown Golden Girl and two other eagles came and sat down. The Crow boys stopped to talk and let the horses blow. Golden Girl spoke to the young men, "We will fly air guard for you; up a mile or so, one of your kind is riding, leading a horse that we think is carrying gold. He is Blue Owl, and you should ride up to him and kill him. We think he will try to sell the gold to bad white men. If he sells, everyone will be here fast, and your homeland will be overrun by greedy white men, and your people will be killed. Go and catch up, we will see if they are near the bad white men. Kill him and put the gold with yours and hide his remains and turn his horses loose. They are not good; go quick."

"We will look." The Crow soon overtook Blue Owl, who did have gold. "Where are you going, Blue Owl?"

"I go to meet white men to sell my gold."

"Tall Pine told us not to do that or many will come and our people will die. What will you gain, trinkets and beads? They will not give you money; they will kill you and take the gold. You must not do this. The eagles came and reported, "Three bad men come. We heard them say 'find him and kill him take the gold after we make him talk, then we come back and get it all.'"

"Stupid one, see what you have done? You put us all in trouble," then Golden Girl said, "Do it quick. There is no time." Bob Tail killed Blue Owl quickly with a well placed arrow. Golden Girl continued, "Now hide him and put the gold with yours. See he has none on him." So they pushed a bank over him and put brush on that. "Now go north - we will chase the horses off, and then we will get their attention later.

We will catch up - stay out of their sight but keep going and go fast."
The eagles drove the horses east by some south. The horses were poor
and already tired but they made it five or six miles from where Blue
Owl was hidden. The eagles then flew to see what the white men were
doing. They found them discussing, "We should have seen him by now
- he said meet him on the flats, and we are here. I see nothing but
some eagles flying and fighting. I never saw that before, look at that!
One dives at the other two then the other two dive at him. Look; now
they are on the ground over there east aways - let go see. We can look
for the Crow too at the same time."

So the three rode back the way they came, and when they arrived,
there was nothing to see. "No water out here. I am out I am going back;
you two can do what you want to," one grunted, and he rode east. The
other two sat and looked but no rider, "Oh hell, I thought it was too
good to be true, let's leave or we will have to go by ourselves." Eagles
were high up and saw it all: the three going east, the two poor horses
just over the hill and where the stupid Crow was hidden.

"One of you remain here. We will go west then north and tell
them the danger is past for now, or until someone tells their plans
again. After a bit come to us and we will guard them." Golden Girl
sat down and Bob Tail and the young Crow stopped. "They go east; it
was very close - Blue Owl was going to spill the whole story of the gold
- they never saw the poor horses, just us fighting in the air. We are safe
for now. Come, water is in that draw over that hill. We can rest; your
horses need water and grass anyway. I wonder how many more whites
Blue Owl told of the gold. I am wondering if still others look for him.
Because we carry so much gold and are few, we should hurry and not
ride in plain sight but ride when darkness hides us. If others look they
will not find us. Let the horses' water and graze until moonrise then
we can put more distance from them. Blue Owl's bags are much heavy;
he has more gold in a bag then we do. He was greedy - they would
have killed him quick then took the gold – and then told many more.
Many men would have rushed to find where it was at, and then Tall
Pine's camp would have been lost, because of one man's greed. No, I
am not sorry I had Bob Tail kill him, even if he was one of us. He
was going to sell us out. I think we should say nothing of his death to
anyone no one will miss him long; he was no good. He thought only

of himself, and he is better off gone and nobody will find him. The old horses will go back to their camp then it will be forgotten. Now let us eat dry meat and rest.

When moon was high they rode northeast to the Lakota camp on the Moreau River, and by afternoon of the next sun they were there. Golden Girl had told them they were coming so the Lakota were waiting for them, "Our horses should rest some then we are ready to go and work as white men do. We bring gold to buy land and pay for the goods too." "Yes," Tall Elk said, "We are glad to see you. Now we will eat, and when you are ready we will start and go to bring in the train. The ten guard wolves have gone already to meet the train, and the others will go back to the ranch to work and guard."

Chapter 33

In the first light, ten young Crow men with ten pack horses carrying gold, and thirty Lakota men to bring the train in with two pack horses each carrying four bags of gold started east to meet the westbound pack train bringing goods back for the two tribes. It was a fine sun for traveling, cool yet warm with just a light wind, trying to make up its mind from which way to blow. The men felt better too, because now forty well armed men were there to guard the gold and all of them now knew the wealth it was. They could buy anything at all with it and men around the world would do anything for it, including killing for it. Golden Girl with five eagles were out in front on two sides providing air guarding so the chance of ambush was slim, just the way they liked it. The horses were fresh and moved out well; good time was made and the miles slid by quickly. The Grand River was behind them and they rode east. At mid point to sundown the horses were watered and grazed some, and Bright Eyes, a young eagle glided in and said a good campsite with water was just a head so they went the ten miles or so and made camp.

Buffalo were near so an old dry cow was the night meal. Soon hump ribs and other cuts were sizzling over ten fires. Eagles ate the heart and other parts they liked, not cooked - their choice. Horses grazed and rolled while men got their sleeping robes, and before long all were sleeping. A pair of coyotes slipped in and helped themselves to leftover bones and meat scraps, some fat from the buffalo insides and other parts no one wanted. The eagles watched but since they were not a threat, said nothing. It would be theirs at first light anyway so why bother? The wolves were not with them so they got away with it, and then first light was turning the clouds pink. Soon, breakfast fires crackled, cooking strips of buffalo meat that popped and sputtered. The smell of cooking meat with fresh sage and some salt and pepper brought out a flavor hard to describe with just words. Meat was cooked and rolled in the fresh tanned buffalo hide, then more so when it was time to go, not much buffalo was left and that would be gone before long, eaten by the lesser meat eaters because you never just left food to rot.

Before the sun was fully up they were miles east. The horses set the pace - that long rocking gallop they could hold to most all day, unless they were pushed, and then it was hard on them. When it was time to blow, the horses knew it, broke stride, and walked a mile or so. Then as of one mind they just put it in gear by themselves and galloped again. Golden Girl and two of her guard were miles east looking to see if anything was different; changed color patterns made a spot look different, and just small things like a piece of paper or some dropped food would alert the eagles. They would see it and know something or someone had been there. They were near the place were tall timber stands and back in a ways there was movement back in the trees, a black swish, then more. A black horse was there, a bay, then two other shapes. Then a man stood up and looked out then three more all looked but they could see nothing. Golden Girl told another eagle to go and tell the train to stop, and the eagle turned and went back to the gold train and did so. "Golden Girl said stop and wait. You should get bunched up. There are many men twenty miles away and are waiting for something. She thinks they wait for us." Golden Girl went wide around the back side and saw it clearly, an ambush in the waiting. She veered left again and said, "I am going to find the others; we need wolves and more men."

They were coming, some forty miles away so she did what she did best: flew fast and landed by John soon after. "An ambush some forty miles west; the gold train is twenty miles west of them but it is stopped and waiting. How many wolves are here?"

"Pounce and fifteen others are here."

"Good can they go back with me to deal with the ambush."

"Yes, but leave me three and the eagles I have with me. I will come as fast as we can." Pounce with twelve more ran, spread out low to the ground, missing nothing, making no sounds. They covered thirty-five miles in what seemed like minutes. "Slow down and catch your wind. Let me go look to see how many they are," said Golden Girl. She lifted up to around six hundred feet and talked to her eagles. Have they moved?"

"No, they just wait."

"How many?"

"Six on this side, four on the other."

"Go start the train, and tell them to come slow. Stay in sight; they will all watch." Then Pounce was there, with six on this side and four on the other, "We take the six first." Pounce spread the wolves out and all jumped at once. They had them. Six eagles sat on six men's necks, hooked beak open above six faces, "Just move or make a sound and you will have no eyes." Five wolves stayed to help. The other four were brought over and put with the first six.

John and six of the men jumped off their lathered horses and tied the robbers hand and foot. "Well just look- two of our old friends from the first time. Do you like jail that much? Or is it the whippings you like? Now you get both. Go get their guns and put them in a pile over here and unload them." The two first robbers now knew what to expect and were cringing noticeably. "Get the pants and shirts off the two here and hang them up by their feet just so their heads clear the ground. Go get seven whipping sticks. Now two at a time - start whipping." The two greeted their teeth, but soon were screaming and begging to stop. John said, "Stop. You want gold, you have to earn it and not by stealing it. Who put you up to this, who is boss? Tell me now or we start again."

"Bodkins. He said we would do it better this time."

"Well did you?"

"No we did not." The other eight were given the same as the first two, and then left hanging until the gold train continued east. Twenty Lakota that had brought the train east now took the supply train home to the west. John told them, "Get their guns and powder and take them with you. They are yours now. Use them well. Four eagles will go to air guard you." The ten Crow got hair cuts and new clothes. The ten robbers were taken down and put over their horses, face down. Ten wolves went with them and the gold train went east, ten Crow men stronger. They would work at the ranch and learn the white ways.

Pounce and his sons with more wolves went east to help work. Golden Girl and her four stayed with the gold train. So the shift was made and all were happy except for the ten over the horses upside down, but what could they expect? They messed with the bull and got the horn and were going to jail to boot. John went over to the ten, "How long can you live without food and water? It is ten or twelve days to jail for you; you were going to kill and rob us, why should I feed you at all? What did you plan for the ones of us that lived? I am waiting."

"We were going to take care of you."

"You were going to kill us and you wanted no one to know. Then you were taking the gold and running, and I'll bet that Bodkins was not getting any of it you mean. You did not plan anything for us but only to kill, so expect nothing at all from us, only to die. Untie their feet. Now get on the horses, but don't drop your ropes - put them around your necks - if you lose them Pounce will kill you quick. No more talk; I am in a hurry." So they rode fast; they had work to do. Ten days later they were in front of the bank, "Go get the law: they tried to rob us. Put them in jail; I will bring charges. Darrel cash out ten bags, the rest put in the vault. We will count it out soon and I will put it in accounts for my men. I want ten thousand dollars in cash. The rest goes to the Land Company account. We will be buying more land and equipment. Hurry please - we are hungry."

The amount to be put away in the Land Company account was huge, and when it was all put away and filed, Darrel Burke washed his face and said, "We are the richest bank around all because of John and the Moreau River Land Company. We can be proud." Bob saw them coming and made room for all to sit. "Bob, these are our new men. Take good care of them and now feed us with the best you got. We are hungry. Jared, go get Bodkins, and take Pounce; they are old friends."

Minutes later, a shaking Bodkins was there. He sat, sweating, until the group finished their meal. John spoke tersely, "I have some men over at the jail that just can't wait to see you: why don't we go talk to them?"

"I am too busy. I just don't have the time now; I work for the bank"

"Yes you do, Bodkins, you may have lots of time - all your time. Come, let's go and he took him by the arm."

"They lie!" He said.

"Lie about what? Bodkins, we have not seen them yet."

Bodkins turned red then white. "Oh no!" He screamed, "Oh no!"

"You did it to yourself again. You sent men to kill and rob, and you are the boss. Now you must pay. Put him in with them. They are good friends so they all must face the charge of attempted murder and robbery. Bodkins, this is the second time; the first you got probation as no crime was committed and you were told to find work. Burke gave you a job, but you got greedy and tried again. You found men dumber than you: if one of them got killed, you would have been hung. I bought your house from the bank this morning. Your notes were past due and now you have no place to go." He thought for a moment, and then said, "Let him out. Now get your horse and what you can carry in bags and leave the settlement. If you should try and come back I will press charges and you will sit in jail the full time. This is a good place to live. We don't need men like you spoiling it by being dishonest. You must be gone by sundown and don't come back. Maybe I should ask Pounce, Frost and Loafer to go with you. Then I know for sure you will never come again because they know just where to find soft soil to put you in and no one would ever find you. If you keep bothering us I will see to it that you are just gone."

Bodkins looked sick, "What about my pay from the bank? I can't get it until tomorrow."

"Then you lost it." John asked Fat Legs and two more go get his horse ready and bring it to his house. He took Bodkins' arm and he and more of his men marched him home the last time. "Now put in bags just what you need. No more, it is mine now anyway. The rest we will burn. Get food and camp gear, clothes, a blanket or two, simple tools, matches whatever else, but get a move on. This is more than you planned for us. We were to be shot down. The gold you would never have seen, or them either." Bodkins cried softly. He opened a hidden

Jack F. Reich

box and took out a small bag of coins he pushed into the bag. "You are hard on a man, John."

"You say that again, Bodkins, and you are going to leave with a broken arm. If you had your way, a lot of my men would be dead. I should kill you but I am giving you a chance to start over. Now get on that horse and go. Eagles will follow and watch then the wolves will finish the job." The brown horse did not want to leave the barn. He had to be kicked and hit to go but in the end he loped out of the settlement east and was gone.

Hay was needed at the ranch so twelve young men, Crow and Lakota, got the hay racks and hitched teams and got pitch forks and started hauling hay. Four big racks and eight horses made the stacks grow like weeds after a rain and they got in three loads a day. The hay was to feed the barn stock and bulls. The stacks were put in convenient places as not to carry it too far, and far enough apart to prevent losing them all to fires started by lightning.

Ten more men went to cut wood out of the stands of timber, dry hard wood mostly, and the push/pull saws got dull quickly. They got sharpened and got dull again, but in the end much wood was hauled in and stacked by the house and bunk house. Pounce and Slayer with five other wolves had gone back to the Moreau River to be with the main pack, as they were not needed at the ranch. Frost, Loafer and ten other big prairie lobos had stayed to do work at the ranch. Watching the cattle was one of their jobs as the timber wolves had taken a hungry interest in the calves being born. Frost had a talk with one of them who showed fight and the timber lobo said he would eat them if he wanted to, when he wanted to.

One day, Frost took care of him, and that was that. Frost and two others drug him back in the timber where he could be found and left the wolf sign, leave the cattle be or die as he did. Black Bears wanted the big cows and the calves too until Frost and Loafer killed two more of them and showed them their mistake in that thinking. They were so easy to kill that the wolf pups could handle that job. So the bears left them alone too after that; it was not healthy or wise either to bother the cattle as long as the eagles and prairie wolves guarded them and if they even smelled them they went the other way.

Chapter 34

John, Jared, and Andy took all the Crow and Lakota young men to Bob's for a meal, and when all were finished eating John said, "You are all doing very well. Most of you can speak the white man's tongue well, some very well. Now it is time to learn about money. Money is what the white man works for. His work is called a job and most times a man is paid every thirty days or one month. If you agree on three dollars a day, then in a month's time you will get ninety dollars, or three times thirty. If you are skilled at what you do, you may get five dollars a day or one hundred and fifty dollars a month but you must be very good at what you do to get that."

"Now out of that you buy your food, clothes, and what you need to live on for thirty days; if you go over that you must get a loan that you must pay back out of your next pay. These are rules that we all live by, and now you must learn to know money. This is a silver dollar," and he showed them, "This is a five dollar gold piece. This is a ten dollar gold peace and this is a double eagle or twenty dollars, and this is a fifty dollar gold piece. There is paper money too; it will tell you how much it is on the bill. If you go to a store and buy something for fifty cents, and you pay with a silver dollar you get fifty cents back as change because one dollar is one hundred pennies, and you just spent fifty of them, so you get fifty back. You must learn to count and well or you will get short changed, which is stealing, and it will happen if you don't count with them. Most people are honest, but some are not. There is smaller money too; under the silver dollar is a fifty cent piece. It is worth fifty pennies, or half of a dollar. Then, a quarter; it is twenty-five pennies, or one quarter of a dollar. It takes four of them to equal one dollar. Then this dime, or ten pennies - you must have ten of them to make one dollar. And this is a nickel: five pennies. Twenty of them make one dollar." Lastly, he showed them a penny. "This is a penny: it takes one hundred of them to make one dollar. Bob gets a nickel for a cup of coffee, or five pennies, so count out five pennies, or one nickel to pay him. Use your little money for this, not a fifty dollar gold piece, or it will take all day to count out your change. Bob's not as smart as you are; this is where you will get short changed if you don't count with him."

John told the native youth, "Soon I will go to the bank, maybe even today, and I will set up accounts for each of you. You will have your own money but first you must learn to make your mark on paper. This is how the banker knows what account to take the money out of and to keep their books and records straight. Then they will not take it out of someone else's account. So each of you pick a name to go by and we will show you how to put it on paper. Then when you need money for something the land company doesn't provide, all you have to do is go get out it of your account." John told the Crow boys that there was more land for sale north and west of their holdings and to get the horses in and in the morning they would ride up and look at it. If they could use it, the Moreau River Land Company would buy it and graze cattle on it, and when Tall Pine's people got ready to move it would be theirs to live on. "Bring your bed rolls and bows. We could be out two or three days to look the country over. Jared, you and the rest of the boys pick a hill by the house and dig a root cellar back in the hill far enough so it doesn't freeze, then the carpenters can build walls and roof it. We will cover it with soil. In the spring we will plant a big vegetable garden and grow a lot of our own food or Bob will have it all"

At first light John, Andy and Gus with the Crow workers rode north and west past their holdings, to an unspoiled land of deep timber lands of hard wood and pine, elm, and spruce. The trees were watered by clear streams of running water. Beaver dams had fish of a kind not known by John or the others. A vast land filled with wildlife of all kinds: deer, moose, elk and some buffalo who liked wooded lands, game birds too: turkey, quail, and grouse. High hills and valleys with flat land by the water are just perfect for growing food for an entire camp. The land was also rolling hills of grass and land suitable for farming and home building, a paradise come true. Frost, Loafer and three more wolves had came along were playing in the water and catching fish for their meal. Bob Tail, one of the Crow boys, killed a deer and a turkey and soon meat was cooking.

Golden Girl caught a fat rabbit and was enjoying it as she sat in a tall pine. She saw him: a very large black bear coming up fast on Frost's left side. She screeched, "Frost! Bear on your left!" He jumped out on the bank as the bear hit the water. The bear roared, "Stupid eagle! Who said you could spoil my fun in killing of a wolf. I would have enjoyed seeing him bleed." Frost said, "How are you going to enjoy anything when you are dead in a minute."

"And who are you?"

"He is Frost and I am Loafer. We are the sons of Pounce and if you would just touch us, he would make your death an all sun thing and your death would be a long time coming. Any of us here could kill you fast but we will take our sweet time in doing it so you can remember all the bad things you have done. If you want to live, lie down in the water on your back, wave your feet in the air and sing Yankee Doodle Dandy off key three times."

John and Andy were grinning like schoolboys, but Bob Tail and others were putting wicked, jagged arrows to strings - the kind that cut your insides to rags and just one would kill you because they had a lethal poison on them made from plant poison and human leavings. When it became infected, you were a goner. The bear was about to scream out that he was Bruno, the killer bear, but the name Pounce caused the words to freeze in his mouth and he knew great fear. Here were two of his sons, his left hand son and his right hand son all in their world had heard of them and they meant death was near. "Why eagle, did you not tell me?" The great bear moaned. "You never asked, old foul breath, and I would not have told you if you had. I want to watch you bleed and die slow. You only kill the young wolves, the ones you dig out of dens. You are a coward and I am enjoying this." If eagles can smile, she was.

Frost jumped on his back and snapped off his ear and then he jumped back onto the bank. He then spit it at him so fast the bear could not see him move. Bruno looked at his ear in the water and felt the blood running down his face. How did that song go again? Loafer rolled over and laughed and the bear looked at him in amazement, then Loafer was under him and cut a long slash in his belly then back to where he was so fast that no one could follow it. Nothing, then a red wormlike thing fell out of his belly, then another. "What's the matter, bear, are you losing your guts?" Loafer taunted. Bruno looked, saw his insides coming out, and knew he was as good as dead.

"I was not always bad - I pulled a deer out of the mud once."

"Yes," Golden Girl said, "You did, then you ate her and she was not dead."

"How did you know that?"

"We know many things. And remember that mother rabbit who said 'eat me and let my young go,' - so you did then you ate them too. You were even bad to your mother: you bit her taps. Frost pulled out the rest and Bruno was bleeding badly now. A nap, a little rest and he slept a very long time. The Crow boys took his skin and tanned it but he spoiled their camp so they pulled him away, as not to look at the cowardly thing. Andy looked at John and shook his head, "I have heard of greased lightning but now I have seen it. I never expected that today though; he moved too fast to see. How could anything move like that? He could kill anything before they knew they were dead."

"I don't know," Gus said, "Just be glad he is one of us and likes us or we could be just as dead as that bear. John said "Amen, now let us all eat - I am hungry. I worked up an appetite just watching the wolf boys do all the work." So they ate roast turkey and boiled deer with the biscuits and jam they brought from Bob's. No one had much more to say about the killing of Bruno the black bear, but all knew that with a hundred like Pounce and his sons, they could take over the world and hold it but who would want to? They had this wonderful land and the money to buy it, thanks to good friends and luck.

They rode back to the land office and bought it all, dirt cheap. It would be a beautiful home for Tall Pine's Crow when they needed it. For now the white men would use it; no one wanted it so far away from the settlements. And no one had a vision that land would go up in value but it did many times over, and besides, who had a gold mine? Not anyone else they knew of, just them. The land was bought and paid for by The Moreau River Land Company and Jim T. Short was made the administrator, better known as Short Tail, a Crow native. He was put on the board of the Moreau River Land Company as member. The cost of the purchase was fifty-two thousand dollars and was around two hundred and thirty sections of land, more or less. Some of the sections in the woods only brought from twenty-five to fifty dollars a section. The flat and rolling land suitable for farming brought up to two hundred dollars a section and was still dirt cheap. John asked Golden Girl to maybe take one or two eagles and go to Tall Pine's camp but leave some eagles to air guard at the ranch as they could never watch it all now because it had grown so big.

"Tell Tall Pine that land where they could be safe was bought, and one of the Crow, Short Tail had his name on the papers to prove ownership," so that was done. "Ask Tall Pine send more gold; have it well guarded and tell them to travel mostly in the dark so no one sees them from a long way. Stop and see Tall Elk and have him send gold too because a lot of money is needed to buy enough land for us all to live on and live as we wish. When the train starts some of us will come and help bring it in. If the bad white men ever find out where it is, they will be like grasshoppers in a bad dry time and that will be the finish of the gold and you too. Ask Pounce to take many wolves to help too; he knows what to do. If Tall Elk or Tall Pine need anything send a list, and we will bring it like before."

Chapter 35

In the lodge of Night Shade sat Yellow Rock and Old Bear spoke quietly to Night Shade, "Blue Owl has been gone almost a moon, and two suns past the two poor horses came back with his saddle pad still on and dragging the reins all broke and short. We will go and try to find him. You have meat and the crop Tall Pine brought you. We will take a horse for Blue Owl to ride, and a robe to cover him. We go soon. I have a new bow and many arrows, as does Old Bear. We should be back soon - I feel he is not far away. So they got on their horses and rode northeast leading the other horse. There was no need to try to look for tracks because too much time had passed for that so they just rode watching the ground. It maybe he dropped something. It was past mid point to where the sun falls off the earth to the west when Old Bear found the sage brush not in the place in which it grew, but pulled up and piled. When it was removed they found a bank of dirt pushed over something and under that they found Blue Owl.

They just looked at each other. Yellow Rock said to Old Bear, "We should leave him here. He is going to be hard to move."

"I know Yellow Rock, but we have it to do." The remains were pulled out and put on the robe, rolled up and tied. The horse was not in favor of any of this. Old Bear sighed, "It is good the wind is in our face and not at our back."

"Yes it is good. Now let us go back fast. I don't want to do this. There was no gold or his bow either; someone killed him and took all his things. It doesn't matter now who killed him. Let us get him in a tree as quick as we can - he is no rose you know." About midnight they were back, and they watered the horses and put them on grass. Then they went to the lodge of Night Shade. It was cold in the wind and they were glad to be inside.

Night Shade looked up anxiously, "Did you find him?"

"Yes we will put him away next sun."

"I will build up the fire and warm food."

"Good. We are hungry. It is done. He would not hear us or his chief and now he is dead. I told him not to go. West Wind, Blue Owl's mother sat and looked at her hands, "I knew he was gone; I felt it. Now I am alone."

"No mother, we are here and we will help you."

"What is this yellow rock that makes men crazy?" Her eyes sparkled in the firelight. "It is evil!"

"No, mother, the gold is not. We get many things from the pack train we trade gold for. It is what man becomes when he has lost his self control to greed – that is what is evil." So they took Blue Owl to a place in the timber were there were many rocks, found a groove in the ground, put him in it and covered the grave with rocks. He was in too much dishonor to place high in a tree.

Golden Girl and Bald Eagle, along with two other eagles were outside Tall Pine's lodge, waiting for him to come out. They knew he would come at first light. Golden Girl spoke, "John has bought much land for you to live on when that time comes, but much gold is needed and he will buy more. He asks you to start a pack train carrying gold and stop at Tall Elk's camp too, for more gold. He said if you need goods tell us, and then we will tell him. He said travel mostly in the dark so you can't be seen from far; bad men have tried to ambush the trains before. Pounce and some of his sons thirty or so other wolves will be here soon to guard the gold and we will see all from the air, so you should be safe."

Tall Pine asked, "How many bags should we send? We have dug much and we found a new place where there is much gold. We can send one hundred bags - is that enough?"

"Yes we think so."

"Have John send coffee and the sweet powder white and brown, salt, pepper, fire sticks, tobacco - much of it - and beads and things to do art work with and blankets, wood smoothing things, ten push/pull saws and any things he thinks we would like to try." He spoke to some men, "Get twenty five pack horses and put four bags of gold on each. Cover them with robes then twenty of you go to Tall Elk's with them. He will send gold too. Be well armed and watch well. Pounce is here now - he will help guard, and eagles will be seeing all from high up. Go quick and bring back the goods we asked for." The horses were loaded; the twenty men got their bows and guns or maybe cross bows. The wolves were on all sides eagles flew and they started, they soon were out of sight, just gone.

Pounce, Ice and Slayer were out front, running as point guards with other wolves out on both sides covering a wide sweep of ground. Bald Eagle was flying way out in the lead, crossing back and forth and in constant contact with Pounce on the ground. "We see nothing moving over the ground for a few suns," Pounce told eagle, "What do you see?"

"I am looking at the rivers and lakes to see if some one is hiding by the shoreline, and I have found nothing yet. Golden Girl is east and north, where danger could be likely and so far has seen no groups of riders coming or going, or just doing anything out of the ordinary. One eagle is watching from behind us, no one is following, and we have a guard way west too and nothing, so I think we are safe so far."

"We should rest the horses soon," Buffalo Lance, the Crow leader said, "Then travel some after dark; no one would think of that." So Bald Eagle looked for water and found a place to water not far where they stopped and rested and let the horses graze. There were buffalo by the water so Slayer and Ice killed a dry cow and all ate. Then the fires were put out and they stayed until moonrise, and then went north by east through the night. At that part of the night when the moon was far west they made camp again and rested until full light. The wolves had ringed the camp all night long and not even a mouse got though without being seen. They would be in Tall Elk's home by sundown, and soon they were. A meal was ready for them as Bald Eagle flew and told them they were coming. Skunk helped with that so all were well fed. Golden Girl had taken word to John that they were at Tall

Elk's camp with much gold and gave him the list of both camps. They would meet somewhere by the tall timber again. This time it would be well scouted with no chance to set up an ambush. Ambushes were no fun for anyone because when your life was in danger, unexpected things happen.

John, Jared, and Andy went shopping with some of the workers. They took five wagons and bought out the stores again, much to the delight of the storekeepers who made money every time they came in with such large orders. Bob saw them and groaned to himself - that meant that a lot of his best customers would be out of the settlement for two weeks or more with the pack train. Bob had just bought beef and pork from the land company and it was hard to keep it good; he must turn it quickly or he lost it to spoilage and out the back door was out of his pocket. Bob had overheard Gus talking about working on a big kitchen at the ranch so that cooking could be done, which was not good news for Bob either. At the hardware John bought all the push/pull saws they had, and the shopkeeper commented, "Must be making a lot of wood." John just grinned, "Beavers are hard to find, and then you got to keep them working. It's not easy to do, so I get saws." Well if you ask a dumb question you get a dumb answer almost every time. "Some friends of mine use a lot of wood to stay warm so I am just helping them. I know where to get wood and they don't so I get it for them." He got nails, too, of different sizes; he knew they were building something and could use more; he looked at this and that and got what he thought they might use.

The pack horses were rounded up and all the riggings were readied, and the goods sorted and laced in place, all ready to go. Frost and Loafer with ten other wolves were eager to start; they loved adventure and an excuse to run. Golden Girl was as good a scout as Bald Eagle and the eagles with her were learning as well, so as soon as it was light enough she was flying, looking for anything not as it should be. The packs were on horses, the men well armed so they got started and thundered out on the trail. Bob was getting breakfast started and watched them go as did others.

Two miles west of the settlement an eagle found a tall tree and sat high up, out of sight, and ate a young rabbit that was too dumb to stay in cover. The eagle kept a wary eye and watched the back trail while he enjoyed his lunch. He heard voices long before he saw the forms of men on horses moving through the faraway trees.

"It is too soon, Harry, unless we want coffee, sugar and salt."

"We don't want only what the other horses are carrying. When we hit them, kill two horses and the rest will run for cover, and then you boys get whatever is so valuable. Then go north to the hideout and stay there." Only six of them - there must be more on their way, or they are too stupid to live, so he just sat in the tree and waited. Swoop was just about go to his aunt Bald Eagle and tell her about the six men who were plotting taking gold from the train when seven hard looking men came riding, and one of them demanded, "Where is Harry? I told him to wait and not get too close or they will know we are following. If he spoils this I will shoot him myself."

"Murphy! I stopped at that jail and talked to one of them who tried to rob the train the last time, and he has cuts on his backside that they gave him by tying him upside down and whipping him with tree switches. Wolves caught them, talking wolves and said, 'If you move or make a sound we will kill you,' - that's what he said."

Murphy exploded, "Talking wolves! Am I working with grown men or kindergarten kids? Wolves are just big dogs; you kick them out of the way. Now let's go find Harry - he had better be nearby, too, or he'd better get out of here - I won't have him messing up my plans." Swoop found Bald Eagle and John resting the horses, "Men come from behind: thirteen of them. Murphy is the leader of all, and Harry leads six who will kill two horses carrying gold and when you go for cover he will get the gold and go to their hideout. Murphy is a bad and dangerous man; he will kill some of us. He hates all - even the ones who ride with him, and he just wants our wealth."

Frost said, "Pounce is coming; can you fly and ask him to come and bring ten others with him? Maybe we should put him in the ground, this Murphy, but it would be better if Pounce were here."

"I don't know how far back they are, but I fly now and Pounce can start on his way here to us. Then we will talk about it." Swoop was gone, "Now let us go, but have two eagles watch them - not too near - just watch: he may shoot at you if you are too near." The pack train moved along well. An eagle came and told them the robbers had made camp in a hollow and would stay until the other train was closer. Their plan was to then try to pass them to set up their ambush. John said, "All we can do now is keep moving like we know nothing of them and when the time arrives to set our own ambush, we will." Swoop was back, "Pounce is coming with others and I feel sorry for the killer Murphy. He will find out the hard way to mess with a wolf far smarter than he. Harry too - the rest are sheep; they just follow.

The horses had to rest and feed as did the men and wolves too but always, a guard was watching. Two suns later Pounce and the others were there and he was angry. "We will go back and scout them. I want to look at the one who thinks we are dogs that can be kicked out of the way." The thirteen men were coming slow, staying back some ten miles or so but they talked loudly. Murphy was telling them what to expect if one of them did not follow his orders. To the word, he was big, ugly and mean as well.

All day they traveled making good time. Bald Eagle and two more watched the raiders, and after they went into camp and were sleeping, Pounce and the wolves pinned them down. John and the men put them to sleep again with clubs. They were bound hand and foot then over the horses upside down and taken to camp and dumped in a pile. "Now you can sleep. In the morning you will find out how robbers are taken care of when they mess with us." After breakfast and all had eaten except for the bad men, the train started west but not the wolves and three eagles. Pounce and his sons sat by Murphy with other wolves, "Well Murphy," Pounce said, "Do you still think wolves are just dogs that you kick out of your way? Then start kicking, why don't you? Or that we can't talk or be smart or have feelings - has the cat got your tongue? Or you, Harry, kill two horses and when we run you would get the gold and go to your hideout north a ways."

"No!" Murphy screamed, "You can't talk! You are not humans!"

"And neither are you or your men, Murphy. You are killers and thieves, and a bully of men to boot. We overheard you telling your men to kill us and leave us lay."

"Who said that?"

"I did," Swoop said, "I talk also. I was in the big tree eating my breakfast when Harry was talking. You are so dumb it is a pity to kill you but we must, for you will never quit. So you will die." Pounce went to find a spot to dig and all the wolves dug. Soon a long trench was dug. Pounce said, "Now cut Murphy free." So it was done. "Get a club and defend yourself." The wolves cornered him but he fought well, and two wolves had bruises to show for it but in the end he was in the trench. Harry got the same chance and was soon beside Murphy, because he was a leader too. Pounce looked at the rest of the robbers, "Now you others - do you live or die?"

"We would like to live."

"Then cover them and smooth it down with tree branches then go, but not to the settlements. If we see you again you know what will happen to you. Now get your bed rolls and walk north; you can say two of you were killed by wolves - this is true, but keep the rest of the story to yourselves. No one would believe you anyway. Now go!" And they did. After all was done and the eleven men went north, Pounce, Loafer and Frost and the other wolves and eagles went west and caught up with the pack train and went back to their places and guarded. Pounce and sons took point guard and eagles flew air guard but most of the danger was passed for now and would be until they took over the gold. They knew danger was always near and their situation could change and would.

Golden Girl came in and said the gold train was only twenty miles west so the change of trains would take place this sun and soon. All the guards, wolf and eagle, scouted the ground well for anyone planning a holdup but found nothing. At mid afternoon the switch of trains was made; the goods and supply pack train went on west and the gold train went east with all the best guards and experienced eagles going with it as guards. Bald Eagle, Swoop, Golden Girl and five more eagles covered the land so completely that a small mouse could not move without being detected and no bunch of men, no matter how well concealed, and could not remain hidden.

Pounce, Frost, Loafer, Shadow, Red Tongue, Slayer, Ice, and Sees Far and more were spread out on the land, looking, and in constant contact with the air guard. No hiding place, no matter how small, was overlooked. The men all rode with heads up, guns out and loaded, and missing nothing. Five young workers were out front with bows and arrows ready, acting as decoys. They were seeing if any traps or snares were set which was not likely as the wolves had checked that as they went through, but they were taking no chances. Five more looked for camp places with bows strung and arrows set. They would have to stop soon: the horses had to rest and graze no matter the need to travel or the value of the cargo. Now the eagles worked over time because when they stopped the danger increased. Fires were started and food was cooking; it had been a hard day, and all must eat. The horses were watered and horses were hobbled with their packs on in groups of five. Pounce and the first guards ate first so they could guard while all could eat and rest.

The eagles and owls were never what you could call close friends but they had some things in common: both ate meat, both were birds of flight, but owls have the gift of night vision. Bald Eagle knew the value of the gold train they were guarding and what it would do in making a place safe for all her friends: human, wolves and her kind eagles too. So she asked the owls if they would watch for bad men in the night when her eyesight was not at its best. She didn't want anyone trying to harm her friends and she would return the favor, many times over. Soon, six owls were sitting in trees or flying over and around the camp on silent wings, watching all that moved. Pounce knew that eagles had spoken to the owls and smiled. Now he could get a little rest, not much but a little.

In the morning all had rested with nothing going bad over night, so they got started again much as the day before. So they traveled for seven days until the next day they would be in the settlement. Before the day was half gone, they stopped early at a very defendable campsite and had a meal. They would rest the horses and themselves and planned to be at the bank before noon as the gold was a heavy responsibility and meant so much to so many people. It was for their new homes in a new land. Before light the eagles, owls, and also Pounce and his boys were out scouting the trail and along either side; they found nothing about which to be alarmed. So they loaded up and got going. They were miles away from their camp grounds before the sun was up.

Around mid morning, twenty five loaded pack horses stood in front of the bank and thirty young men carried in the bags of gold and put them on the tables. Some was to be turned into cash and recorded on ledger sheets; some would be put in the vault in bags to be weighed later. Banker Darrel Burke came out of his office shook John's hand and started his employees to weighing and counting out gold; John told him he had around a million and a half dollars in gold - far more than any time before. "I want five hundred thousand to go to the Moreau River Land Company account as I will buy more land and equipment soon. Put three thousand in each of my new men's accounts; they have all signed signature cards and can put their names on paper. I want six thousand in the accounts belonging to the first seven members of the company. Put the rest in the vault - I will come in soon and we will take care of it then."

"Darrel I need to hire two full time bookkeepers to do ranch records - it is more than I want to do. I just don't have time to do it all. If you can recommend someone, send them to see me."

"Yes, I know some good help for you and I will have them see you. Oh, by the way, John, did you see some rough looking men out on the trail?"

"Yes we did - ten or so went walking north in a hurry with just bed rolls; the other two, Murphy and Harry, I think they were called, were hard to convince so Pounce and his boys showed them a shortcut out of the country. I think they took it. I have not seen them since but I was busy. They may show up again but I can't use them, they wanted way too much money and they had no skills, just greed. Oh yes, Darrel, put five thousand dollars in a sack. I want it to be in gold coin for spending money. I will give the boys some; they have all worked hard and their lives were in danger some of the time."

Darrell looked at him in slight amazement, "I don't know, John, could I have a job? You pay well."

"No you are lazy, and you don't like sleeping out on the ground and eating food that is not quite cooked." They both laughed. John went outside and waved to the men, "Let's go see Bob. I could eat a horse. The walk was short and quick. "Bob get to cooking; we all will have steaks, the fixings and also pie. Pounce you and yours come too; you worked harder than most of us did." Bob had seen them coming and got tables fixed and he also had coffee poured. Bob had set out loaves of hot bread and butter with jam too; he knew they had done without on the trail and were hungry. He fixed platters of food for the wolves too. It was left over food and fat with meat scraps; things he was going to throw out anyway, but the wolves liked them.

John got the sack of coins out. "Bob, forty of us had dinner," and gave him four twenty dollar gold pieces. "And this is for the wolves." John gave him a ten dollar gold piece. He gave all the men coins to put in their pockets go to the store and get a treat. "Oh yes, I put money in your accounts at the bank. You can draw on it if you need something we don't provide. It is your pay for working hard and doing a good job."

After awhile, all the men were reassembled at the ranch headquarters. John began giving the orders and said, "Now let's get to work. Go get the horses rubbed down and turned out. Then go find something to do. Break up the men in pairs, clean the barns, chicken house, get wood boxes filled and anything that needs doing. You should be able to do the basic necessities around the ranch without me telling you to do these things every time, so pay close attention, because I don't like repeating myself."

In the morning John rang the bell, a signal all knew and would come to a meeting being called by John or one of the other members of the company directors. When most of the men who worked for the ranch were on hand, John told them the reason for the meeting was that they needed to go and buy grain and other supplies from the settlements east of them. "Get ten wagons ready to go: grease the wheels, clean the boxes out, get tarps to cover them and camping gear for two or three days and shovels for loading. Get ten, four teams of horses in and check the pulling gear, Jared is the cellar dug and Gus is the building done?"

Gus said, "Yes it is ready to store things without them freezing."

"Then we will go when all is ready. Five of you ride horses and I will go with two or three more. We will get more stock too if we can find some. Pounce, you should go and some others too. You can help drive the stock. Frost, you and Loafer and maybe six more wolves go up in the north woods and have a talk with your wild relatives. Tell them not to bother the cattle or else. Make it clear to them what will happen if they don't. Golden Girl will you and two more go with the wagons? Have some go with Frost and Loafer so they don't get surprised. Jared, you and Andy get the survey crew to work on marking our new land out. I will go now to the land office and see if other land joining ours can be bought. Gus, would you go build a three room house by the big house? I am going to hire two cooks, a man and a wife preferably. Hire Bob and the pie baker; we are used to them.

Fat Legs said with tongue in cheek, "No he would poison us then for sure!"

"But we can't always go to Bob's to eat - it takes too much time. You other boys go up and get more wood for the cook stove if any wagons and teams are left. You can use the older ones – it's not far and the fires will be going most of the day and night too; we are many to feed."

At first light they left to travel to the next settlement; it was around fifty miles or so, really not that far but the teams were big and heavy and could not cover the ground like lighter horses. The trail was good most of the way but it still took time to cover the miles. They had covered a little better than half of the way, thirty miles or so; not bad for big horses but slow in comparison to lighter stock. A good spot to camp was at hand so they made camp and ate mostly what they had brought along from Bob's. At the first gray streaks light in the east, the teams were in place and they started driving into the settlement. They planned to be there before noon.

John and two of the men went on ahead to check on grain supplies and who had it for sale, and if any one had livestock or other supplies. They stopped at the eating house, had food and asked questions, yes there was men selling grain so that was the next stop. John bought eight wagons of corn, oats and wheat then they went and bought two wagons at the wagon yard. At the stable he found eight big horses with harnesses and bought them too. The horses were harnessed and they picked up the new wagons and at the general store bought supplies, canned goods, flower, twenty sacks of potatoes, salt pepper, sugar, and whatever it took to make meals, along with supplies for baking too.

When loaded and covered with tarps, the sides of the wagons were pushing out, so he got them braced with ropes and then finished loading grain. As an afterthought, he took one wagon to the hardware and filled it with saws, nails, and other things they might need for repairs on the way home, or materials just needed at the ranch. The last wagon he filled with oats. When all was loaded and covered, John left them stand and took the men to eat and have food packed to take back with them. Then he started back. The wagons were heavy now and the horses had to work. At the edge of the settlement was a stock yard. John found some young cows and twenty big steers so they bargained and John bought them cheap, as they had to be fed hay.

John asked the men, "say do you know someone who can cook? A man and wife maybe? If you do happen to know of a nice couple, send them to see me at the next settlement west. Just ask for John of The Moreau River Land Company and they will tell them where I can be found." John and two of the men rode in and put the cows together with the steers then pushed them all out the gate. The riders headed them down the back trail leading to the ranch some fifty miles west. The loaded wagons were moving now but slowly. It was going to be a long way back to the ranch. The cattle had been too long in the pens and wanted to run, so they did. The men just kept them going west, and after a mile or so they went to grazing.

When they were out of sight of the stockyards, Pounce and the wolves were suddenly all around them: they just appeared out of thin air, so to speak. Golden Girl was overhead with two more eagles to her left and right. "No one is on this trail in front or back for many miles," Golden Girl reported, "And if they are we will let you know quick so Pounce can hide." It was understood that Pounce and the wolves should stay out of sight then no questions would be asked and no answers needed. The lead teams were passing the grazing cattle so John rode up beside Jim Short and sat his horse, just watching the big horses work. "How is it going?"

"Slow, but good enough. We knew that." Jim P. Short said with a smile and pointed to the third wagon, "I think this is the heaviest load."

"Yes, I think so too. It's one of the wheat wagons but the corn wagons are heavy too. Give them a lick on the hind end just to keep them from going to sleep on us." The incline they were starting up was not that steep but it was long and switched back and forth over the ridges making it seem longer than the mile or so it actually was. John felt sorry for the horses but they were young and in good condition. It was hard to stop going up so they would stop when the land leveled out and they were not that far out of the settlement, maybe ten miles at the most. The five riders and Pounce and his wolves had taken the cattle over the hill to water, only eighty-seven cows with the twenty steers.

It was not as many as he had hoped to buy but all that were for sale at the time. They were not totally beef cattle, either, but leaned toward the dairy end - just barnyard stock every color that cows came in and then some. It was still beef anyway, and if they grew out the beef was just as good, just not as much quantity as the heavy breeds.

The last of the wagons were over the hills and the settlement was out of sight. A little stream just wandered along so they all crossed and made camp. "Boss," a worker said, "Maybe we should change the teams around and put the big horses on the heavy loaded wagons."

"Good idea," John replied. "In the morning we will do just that." John had thought of doing it anyway but he was a good boss and let the boys think it was their idea. It made all feel better and no harm done. Pounce smiled to himself. Yes, John was a good boss but more than that, he was kind. He thought of others first every time. Teams were each given a good feed of grain and hitched up and the bigger horses were pulling the heavy loads. Before the sun was up, they were out on the trail west. Pounce and the wolves with the outriders had the cattle moving and out of sight. They would take them ten miles then let them graze until the wagons caught up. By mid morning, the wagons caught up and were held up by their drivers to let the horses feed and rest some. Then were again moving west, the ranch not that far now but everything depended on the horses to keep going, so their welfare was the most important part of the trip.

By mid afternoon the wagons came to where the cattle drivers had camp set up by good water, and fires were going and deer roasting. It was a long day and now the horses were ready to stop water, roll, and graze. The ranch would be reached before noon if all went well and John hoped their luck held. He learned another thing: not to load so heavy, and take two wagons next time. It was too hard on the horses.

Just before noon the wagons pulled in at the ranch yard and unloading had begun. Two loads of wheat went to the mill and some corn to be turned into flower and corn meal; they had a lot of big orders to fill. Most of the food supplies were unloaded to the root cellar and the grain put into the bins. The cattle were taken to the north range and put with the big herd. The steers needed to put on pounds as they were light and had stood in the pens too long without enough feed so nothing was ready to butcher.

John said, "Let's go see Bob. I am tired of eating out of a can. I want to see what the gossip is." Pounce and some of the wolves were going back to the Moreau River country after it got dark so he would go. Frost and Loafer had not made contact with the wild wolves so would stay longer, but Pounce did not need them that badly so would take other wolves and leave Shadow with two or three more to work with John.

John and twenty or so of the workers, along with Pounce, Shadow, Frost and Loafer walked into Bob's and found banker Darrel Burke eating. Darrel got up and shook hands with John. "Sit down, sit down; take a load off" the banker said. "How was your trip?"

"Slow; we loaded too heavy; I should have taken more wagons but we made it fine." Pounce looked at a table on the far side of the room with four men at it then looked again. The men spoke in low voices but Pounce and his sons and Shadow knew everything they said. His ears went flat and his lips lifted ever so little. John noticed and asked Pounce, "Something the matter?"

"Yes. The four men and a few more outside are going to rob the bank as soon as it is night tonight. We read their minds and can hear them talk. They think it will be easy - they will have horses out back, down a ways, then two of them will ride fast west and have bags of old rags that the law will mistake for the stolen money. The Sheriff will chase them while the others will get the money and go east at a slow pace, so no one will go after them, or so they think. When the first two get caught and it is realized that they have no money, they will say 'joke – ha!' Then they will go east and share with the others. They don't know of the gold in your vault. They only want the coins and paper money that they can get easily. We should eat, and then I will show you how to catch them and put them in your little rooms with bars. Right now they see us and wonder what wolves are doing in here, but they know nothing of us. I could kill them all quick but Bob would have to clean his floors so I will not.

It was a simple plan, but made by simple men and should have worked. It probably would have worked, because no one had robbed the bank before so nothing was ever done to prevent it. How could they know that Pounce and his sons and Shadow could not only read their minds but hear them talk and plan too? They could not understand why wolves would be in an eating house at all, but they were not from this settlement and did not know of the Moreau River Land Company or the protection given it through the native people and their plans of someday living here. They were smart enough to know that to say something would only draw attention to them and they could not have that so they just looked and said nothing.

Banker Darrel Burke had mixed feelings about asking a wolf anything. He did trust John's judgment and knew that Pounce had gotten him out of more than one bad spot in the past, so he asked, "So what is best to do?"

"Leave some money out so they can find it, like if you forgot to put away. Two of them will come going fast to the west, but just let them go - they will have sacks of rags and will make much sound. The rest will go into the bank the back way and find the money. Have the law hiding deep inside the bank and two men of yours light lamps and catch them. We wolves and John's men will get the one or two men with the horses, and you will get your money back. They will be in the barred rooms so you can ask where they got the idea of robbing the bank from. We already know now, but let them tell you."

When it was over and seven men were in jail, banker Burke asked Pounce if there was something he could do for him. "No, said Pounce, "you have nothing we want or need. Our job is to help John and the native workers stay safe so they can make homes for us all when we need them. Pounce said, "In the morning, some of us go back to the Moreau River. You don't need us all and eagles don't see well at dark time and we are not in that big a hurry. They will tell us if anyone is hiding to harm us. We will ask Golden Girl to have two come with us, then if Tall Elk needs more supplies, they can tell you when they get back."

Burke remarked to John, "Maybe we should go over to the jail and talk to the men with Pounce along and try to figure out why they tried to rob this bank and who put them up to it." John said, "Fine with me if Pounce wants to, but Darrel you had better fix your doors and make it harder to break in: they just walked in, so to speak." A minute later, they were at the jail. The robbers were seedy looking men, wearing terribly worn clothes. Dirt creased every wrinkle in their hands, necks and faces. They needed a bath, and the jail stunk because of them. Darrel confronted them, "Who is boss here and why our bank?"

"Don't say nothing!" A man in a red flannel shirt with stains and holes in it warned the other men. "This man is a rich snake, and he's out to make it worse for us!" He scowled through his broken teeth and rough beard.

"On the contrary," said Darrel, "I was going to make it easier on anyone who offered me any good information, and you just lost your chance, so shut up and sit down." The man, still scowling, grudgingly took his seat.

One of the men wearing boots without heels spat on the floor and stood up. "Bodkins told us it was full of money and as easy to get in as a hen house. I don't think he likes you much."

"Bodkins, aye. And just where is he now, this Bodkins?"

"Two settlements east." He looked up and implored, "So you gonna make it easier for me now, right?"

"We'll see. So you just took Bodkins' word on that? You should have known that the gold doesn't stay here – it's shipped to the mint to make more coins. The wealth is on paper, not kept here at this bank. You don't look that dumb to me but now you are caught as a bank robber and gained nothing but time in jail." Darrel turned to leave, but a short fat man with a scar on his face blurted out, "How did you know? We told nobody."

"Yes you did. You told the people at the eating house and I heard you. I told John and he got the others," Pounce said. "No!" The man said, "A wolf that talks? A wolf that talks and hears? We were caught by a talking wolf? Not possible!"

Pounce continued. "Bodkins should have told you it was me and my sons that ran him out of this settlement - we were going to kill him – and now I see that we should have."

Now John said to the men in the cell, "You did not commit any crime because you never even got to rob anything. If the bank doesn't press charges for breaking in, you could go without jail time, but under one condition: you go find Bodkins and tell him if anyone ever comes again to this settlement to do anything under his order again, we will come and get him. No matter where he goes or how far it is, his death will be long in coming. With me and my men, the wolves and eagles to guard this bank and this community, no one is going to get it done. You don't all go - some of you will work for me, or stay in jail. It's your choice but if you don't do as we say, you will be in this jail a very long time. So make up your minds quickly because my offer is now or never. I have thirty-six men working for us now and if you try to run, you will be back in jail fast or dead on the ground."

Pounce said, "I and the other wolves will see to it that you work hard."

John thought hard for a minute. "You did two things you should not have done: one, you listened to Bodkins, and two, you went in after our money. Work Bodkins over good so he remembers, then tell him what we said then get back quickly. Now, you who calls himself boss and two more go and find Bodkins. The other five can work for us. If you want to stay in jail you can. But if you don't want to work and decide stay put here, this is where you will stay a long time. You are here and you get no second chance."

Chapter 36

At first light Pounce, Shadow and ten big prairie lobo wolves were just waiting for enough light so the two eagles Golden Girl was sending could see well enough to scout the trail ahead. Pounce was as quick and fast as any wolf ever gets but was not fast enough to dodge a bullet from ambush like the one that almost killed his son Ice. An eagle was back and gave the all clear; they were standing or sitting, just waiting and then they were not. They were gone, just vanished without a sound, like cloud shadows: if you blink, you never see anything. At full light they were miles west, they ran past the sun's midpoint, never slowing. They were tireless and moved with that stride all wished they had, but none could match. As dusk neared, the eagles who were waiting for them sat in a tall tree eating a luckless rabbit.

"Do you run in dark time Pounce?"

"Yes."

"We thought so; we went far west and found no man things with thunder sticks to harm you."

They ran though the night and around dawn came to a clearing where a deer was watching a pair of coyotes playing so intently, I doubt if she ever saw Pounce. The wolves ate the large deer to the last bite. In the wild some always become food for others. It's not bad – it's just life. If you became careless, you were food for some other animal. We are no different from the wolves: if you live, some other something must die - that's how life works.

Pounce and Shadow wanted to see Moon Boy but more than that, they loved baby. The other ten just wanted to get back to the prairie and hunt buffalo. So after a short rest they ran again. Pounce had an uneasy feeling all was not as it should be at home camp. Shadow had a feeling too, not that something was wrong, but that things were going to change in some way. Three suns later they had passed the tall trees and were on the big flats. A herd of buffalo became fewer by one, and after eating and resting they just were gone. Two nights later Pounce and Shadow pushed in the door flap at Moon Boy's lodge. Inside was warm and cozy, so they found robes and were sleeping; they were home.

In the morning Moon Boy got up, got the fire going, and discovered Pounce and Shadow sleeping on robes. "Ho, my friends I see you are back!"

"Yes, how is it with you?"

"I am fine. I will call my father and Fast Fox also Skunk, then you can tell us of the new lands." When they were seated with others of the band Skunk came in and quietly sat down. Skunk was too quiet, so Fast Fox asked him, "Is something wrong, Skunk?"

"Yes. Taken Alive is not better this sun. He wants no food or drink and is very weak; I fear he will cross over soon. The medicine man is doing his best and has been for the past five suns. Looking Back Horse came in and sat, and I have been with Taken Alive. He said that I should go and hear the words of Pounce and Shadow. I don't think I will ever go east but some of you must go. He also said that we must remember these words – 'live with him if you can, walk his road if you must, fight him and many will die on two sides and you will walk his road anyway.' I know that many of the young men will fight, I would have too. Our way of life is hard to give up but he is too many and his weapons are strong and strange to us. I am sad to say the words but I feel they are truth."

Pounce and Shadow now spoke, "The new lands John has gotten with the gold is good land but is much different than the land here. There are plants that grow there that don't grow here and more of them. There are not as many rocks and the grasses grow taller there. Here we have few trees there are many trees, hard wood mostly. Skunk can make bows with all of them if he wants."

Skunk looked up, "With my friend going I am sad, and I cannot help him. If I could I would make a bow to kill what is killing him, but

I can't see his death. He has no shape or color but I know he is near. I wish he would go away, but I know he will not go until Taken Alive goes with him. I feel like crying but my tears would shame him and I would never do that. Speak, Pounce, we cannot change what is coming; it will happen to us all. Now my heart is black and on the ground but it will get better and I will make more bows and more arrows."

Shadow spoke, "The white man come and go all the time, not to put food away to eat in cold time, but for wealth to put in a lodge called a bank. That is what gold is: wealth. They all put it away like prairie dogs storing grass to eat in cold times, and some of you will like it there, but many of you will not. I am a wolf as is Pounce. I will not like it there but I like the warmth of Moon Boy's lodge when it is cold so we have changed. We can't make fire but you can and if we want to sleep warm we come to your fire. I am not good with words and thoughts, but through Moon Boy now we can speak to you all so we are friends. In the old wolf ways I would never come near you; now we do, so we have changed much. You will have to change much too. If I never saw humans again, I would remember the warmth of the fire that I could not make and be colder for it."

Pounce spoke, "In the new lands you cannot hunt as you do here. There are no buffalo and other wild game is few. You can kill them, but not many, or you will kill them all. John has bought cattle that are like buffalo but not as wild; they will be your meat. In the new land, you can have crops and they will grow better than here; the ground is better and they get more rain. You had better get all the gold you can now because there is no gold in the new land to find and when you need something you must trade it for money that equals the same as gold. They have a drink some of them use: never use it or you will get crazy and when you start, you can't stop, and all your money will be gone, all this and more you must learn. The Moreau Land Company with John as head man has much land to white man's thinking, but to you it will be small. You will have to live with it or die, and be very glad you have a friend like John - he cares about you as a people."

Two suns had gone by and Taken Alive was resting in a tree. He would never go anywhere again, and he would stay in the country he loved.

295

Eagles were going east to join Golden Girl. They asked Tall Elk "are there goods you need?"

"Yes I will need some goods. We shall see what we need" Said Tall Elk. Then he turned to his people and said, "Go to Tall Pine's Crow camp and have him bring much gold and put it many places. In a short time, men will come and find the gold in the streams, and then they will take it all and leave you nothing. Go at first light – Moon Boy will guide you. Take many people, women and bigger children and many braves, many pack horses. Make it look like you are just looking at the land and hunting. Ask Bald Eagle to watch from the air and some wolves to scout on all sides. Take many bags to carry the gold in. If the Crow need things send three eagles to tell us, we will tell John."

In the lodge of Moon Boy, baby was showing Pounce, Curly, and Cubby and Shadow her new doll Rose Bud had just given her. Tall Elk and Skunk had come in, and Fast Fox was there also. Moon Boy said that his father had asked Bald Eagle if she would go tell the Crow camp and that we are coming in a large group to get more gold and put it away at our camp and that he should do the same. "The eagles fear greedy white men are going to discover the gold in his streams, then many will come at one time and some will be killed. He will have to move his camp and we still need more land in the east that must be bought with gold. We leave when all are ready; the young men are getting the horses now. Do you go Skunk?"

"No. Pounce and I will watch the camp and maybe his sons. I still mourn the passing of my dear friend but you go - I know the importance of the trip." Cubby, Curly and Shadow would be in charge of the wolf guard. They would ask twenty other wolves to go, and six eagles would fly air guard. Two had gone to tell Tall Pine to get ready and why they were coming. Looking Back Horse and Skunk were in charge of the camp. When all were ready and on horseback, a hundred and twenty Lakota followed Tall Elk out of camp they did not thunder out as they sometimes did but rode in an orderly way. If someone was watching from a long way off, it would look like a group that was out just for the fun of it, just what they wanted it to look like. There were many of them, too many to mess with. All had weapons too, even the ten year olds. An arrow from a child's bow could hurt as much as from one of Skunk's bow.

If they did have wealth along, why would they just ride, singing and joking as if it was something they did every day? The gray slinking shadows that were out a half mile on all sides could have been wolves looking for a food pack to fall, not scouts on guard. Who would have thought that the eagles, seeing all from way up, were reporting anything they saw to the riders? It was a good plan. Above all, they had no wealth yet that would be worth taking, so why bother? Attempting to rob from the Lakota would be risky too, with that many well armed riders. Now on the way back that would be different, for they would be carrying enough gold to buy small towns and never miss the pocket change.

It took four suns traveling that should have taken two, but there were many of them and they had women and children along, but at the end of the fourth day, the leaders were having coffee at Tall Pine's lodge and hearing the news. White men were seen riding out on the southern plains riding west and making contact with the tribes giving gifts to the head chiefs and trying to make friends. They were asking about furs and other things of value so all knew that white men were coming. Much sooner than they thought - it would not take fifty seasons before they were in the northern hills poking around in the streams and you know what they will find.

When the light of the morning was turning everything golden, there was much activity in the camp of Tall Pine the Crow leader.

Rabbit was standing on a tree stump, "They are back again," he remarked to fox and blue jay, "And many of them this time and wolves too, but the big terrible one is not." Owl floated in on silent wings and sat down on a branch, "Rabbit you are getting fat? You have eaten too much of their corn. Why they don't eat you, I will never know. I would have eaten you long ago, but your voice makes me sleepy so I can nap when you talk and talk so much and say nothing. Now I have grown to like you as a friend. You should be more careful. You have got as crazy as you say they are and eagles are here too - they could eat you also."

"I know, but I am very tough they know that, they would rather eat a boiled owl like you are; you would be better to eat than me so I am safe. I must go now; in my burrow is a young bunny with cute soft ears. She is putting new ferns on our bed. She came to live with me just this sun. Soon I will be telling bedtime story to my sons, and I will tell them about you, Owl, and then they will sleep all night long."

"I know rabbit you have helped me sleep for a long time now. You are good at it." Rabbit was gone; he headed back to his burrow. He was telling his little bunny about his friends, the owl and fox, and she cooed to him, "How wise you must be to have friends like that, husband."

"Yes I know, but I am not tall. The sun has not cooked my brains so I am not crazy like the two legged ones are."

Chapter 37

Tall Elk was looking at the size of the piled sacks of yellow gravel in Tall Pine's lodge. "We would help you find more."

"Thank you but there is a lot in one place that we have found so we dig it in the dark time - no one sees us. We just clean it in the water, let it dry and sack it. We have much more in many places far from this camp. If the greedy ones come and find it in our streams we will move to where it is hidden. Can you trust your people?"

"Yes."

"I hope so; they know if the white ones find out we will have to quit and that will be the end of all the goods they like. We need more gloves and more digging tools and more of all goods they brought before. We like the beans that make water black and the sweet snow. More tobacco too, much more. We have brought many bags to put it in."

"Good. We need them. You have many with you this time."

"Yes, so anyone who sees us from far will just think that we are out for the joy of riding and not know we carry much wealth that we will have hidden with the young ones too. We will go then as soon as we pack. I will ask eagles to fly with our needs to the east. It is far, even for them to go - we are lucky to have their help - it saves much time." They packed up much wealth and rode north by some east, and ten or so more young Crow went with them to go join Sharp Tail, now known as Jim P. Sharp so that others could come back. Two eagles were flying east so big John could get a supply train started west. He was asked to buy more lands and much gold was coming to buy it with. Also, more Crow were coming so others could come back to teach how the

299

white men lived to others would be ready so when the time came to go east.

As before, Curly, Cubby and Shadow flanked them on two sides half mile out and four eagles rode the air currents high above. They were taking much wealth with them, just what dollar amount it was they did not know as the Lakota or the Crow never understood that part of it until they had been east for awhile, but they did trust John. Half of the gold they were bringing would go east to pay for the goods and buy more land. The rest would be put in a new place even now being made ready. It took four suns to get back to the Moreau River and in ten days time, four of them had gone to rest in trees, three old and a small girl. The three were very old and just went to sleep; the small girl's death was a tragedy: she stepped too near old grand father rattlesnake while he was taking a nap. She was bitten high up in her body and he gave her more venom than she could take. Life on the prairie was not always kind, and in this case it was harsh and quick. She was too small, and died despite Skunk's best efforts to save her.

Eighty bags of gold were put away in the new hiding place and forty bags were loaded on the best pack horses and started east. Pounce and thirty older wolves were guiding; the fourteen new Crow were driving the twenty pack horses. There were four eagles flying air guard and the gold never stopped moving east. As an afterthought, twenty Lakota went to help show the way and keep the packers going. As the pack train was about to cross the Grand River, an unusual event was taking place so they stopped to observe.

Two Coyotes were in hot pursuit of a large jack rabbit who was at his wit's end. The jackrabbit jumped high and managed to land on a branch of a cotton wood tree that ran parallel to the ground some ten or so feet up. "What are you doing up there?" asked a coyote, "Rabbits are not supposed to sit in trees - you are not playing by the rules: you run then we catch you and eat you. That's how the game is played."

"Now wait just a minute, just a little minute! Who said you boys should win every time? What book did you find that in? Rabbits love life just as much as you. Now you are going to stay hungry today, but I can eat leaves and stay alive up here for much longer that you can stay alive down there waiting for me."

"No! That's not fair! Now jump down here so we can finish the game."

"The game is over and you lost, coyotes, now go or..." Pounce said as he looked at the coyotes. Their looks changed to mortal fear and the coyotes forgot about the rabbit.

"I will play too," Pounce said, "I will be judge on this."

When the two turned to look and saw Pounce not twenty feet away, no more thought was given to the rabbit in the tree; they were just gone and getting there as fast as they could go - they may be running yet. Pounce simply turned and left. "Well rabbit, I know now why you have four feet, but you about used up your luck," remarked eagle as he sat on a branch higher up. "Now jump down, enjoy your life, and don't worry about the coyotes - they will run to full dark or more. A look at Pounce that close will keep them going for a long time." With that he laughed long. "You should have seen the look on that coyote's face when he saw Pounce! Don't stand where he was, or your feet will get soiled." With that said, eagle was gone, still laughing to fly air guard for the eastbound pack train.

John and Jared with two more of the original seven men had the supply train moving west. Eight Crow and four Lakota men were going back to their home camps to teach others the ways of the white man as planned. John hated to see them go back; they were good help and friends as well.

All were not going back to the original Lakota camp. Jim P. Sharp and Fat Legs would return to the ranch to help show the new men how to work and what was expected of them and if this group was as good as the first it would work out fine. Ten days later at the tall trees, the two pack trains changed with the supplies going west the gold going east. The new workers got hair cuts and their new clothes were fitted with much swapping around to get the best fit. They had fun putting on the clothes and there was good humored joking, but the danger had increased many times over. Pounce went back with the supplies - they were important to a large number of people. Frost and Loafer could see to it that the gold train was safe, especially now that they had the eleven or so owls to watch at night and the eagles at daylight.

Ten days later, John and company were at the bank. More land had came up for sale to so John put a large amount in the Land Company expansion fund and more in the two tribes' name under Jim P. Sharps' name and T. L. Legs' names. The rest went in the bank's vault, except the cash he held back to pay the men working for the ranch. "Now let's go see if Bob has anything to eat," said John. Bob had seen them ride in and had gotten ready; he also knew that Frost and Loafer, the two big sons of Pounce, would come in too and told any strangers not to do anything stupid or chain lightning would be sitting on them.

John said, "My new workers they don't speak our tongue yet so the rest of us will help them. We just got in and are hungry." In good time a meal was eaten and pie was served. The young Crow had never seen pie before and thought it fine. John asked Bob, "How much do you want this time?"

"I don't really know, John; when you come with more people than we some days see all day, its hard to put a price on it. Give me what you think its worth - and we need more beef and pork too: hams, and bacon and all the eggs you can spare as soon as you can." So John put three twenty gold pieces on the table and told Bob, "If we pay you, then you pay us when we bring you beef, pork, and eggs. You pay for them when you get them from now on. You pay what I ask or we quit bringing them at all; now that's fair, Bob, and you know it. The chickens eat grain to make eggs that we get in wagons pulled by four big horses - a four day round trip. Horse power and man power, would make it worth around thirty dollars a beef, fifteen a hog - more if the hams and bacon are smoked. Four dollars a basket of eggs, now how much do you want?"

When they got to the ranch, John told Andy, "Take fifteen men, more if you think you need them, all the good wagons with four horse teams and get more grain. You should get them ready - we go in the morning. I will go to and buy more stock. Six of our new men on horse back and four old ones will come too. We can change off - I will get more wagons and teams too if we can get them. I am going to find us two or three cooks, too: Bob has gotten too greedy. Gus, go and get two more cook stoves and set them up in the kitchen. Hans, take Bob some smoked hams, bacon and a butchered beef. Make him pay out of his till - he knows the new rules, and take eggs too if we have them. Jim, take the rest of the new Crow boys and cut more firewood teach them to speak our tongue. We may have to make two trips. Snow balls may hit us in the ass soon and we need plenty of grain. The new calves will have to be gotten in and weaned; when we get done with that too, they will need some grain. Put tarps and camp gear in the wagons and start off to get the teams in now and pair them up. Oh yes, Hans, put two big steers in the cooler. Bob needs beef and we will as well. The rest of you fill in where you are needed; make sure the chickens have feed and water and that the barns are cleaned. Those wooden posts will rot much slower if we keep the manure off them at the ground."

Light was in the east and the day was coming so twelve wagons with forty eight horses pulling were going east at a fast trot. John and ten young native workers on horseback and two big prairie lobos were looking for breakfast, not a common sight but what was common? The teams were walking now but they were too large to go too fast for long. At mid day they watered and rested - some let them graze then were moving again. At sundown, camp was made. They had made good time and would be in the settlement before noon maybe. In the morning when the wagons were started John and some of the older help who could speak well rode on in and had breakfast got lunch for the others and bought wagons and teams of big draft horses at the stable or livery barns.

A fat, jolly looking short man came and asked if John was the one looking for a cook to cook for a lot of men on a ranch. "Yes, I am that man," John answered. "Good. I and my wife like to cook. Where is the place?"

"It's about fifty miles west by the last settlement. You want the job?"

"Ya, you betcha. How many do we cook for?"

"Around forty or so. Meet us at the general store and you can get the supplies you need. Fat Legs you and some of the boys get the teams and new wagons, bring one to the store, and take the other three and load oats. By that time the others should be pulling in and you can load them too. Load the corn and wheat wagons a little less as they are heavier. Send two men with the supply wagon to help load, and get a move on boys. Do you have a team and wagon to haul your things in?" he asked the man. "Yes. We are loaded up now." said the man. "Then let us go to the store." John said, "Hold it. I will pay you a hundred dollars a month; is that going to be enough?" Those kind of wages in those days was a windfall for anyone.

"Ya, very good. We do it." The wife was as jolly as her husband looked. Both of their eyes's sparkled with happiness. They got so many things to cook and cook with John was afraid one wagon would not haul it all but it did.

Albert and Hilda Schultz were the kind of people every one loved almost from the first words spoken. They were just good people, and if they could cook everyone was going to be fat as oxen in two week's time. The grain was loaded and the wagons standing in line. Food that had been packed at the eating house was given out and the long line got under way. John and six men stopped at the stockyards and bought all the good cattle that were for sale, and once again he got them cheap because hay had to be brought in to feed them. A few he got free, just to get them out of the yard: old and thin, but healthy enough. They may not make it all the way west so the wolves could just have them.

Two miles out Frost and Loafer and the other two wolves just came out of thin air. They were not there, and then they were. "How do they do that?" Fat Legs asked John. "I don't know - have not figured it out yet myself but be glad they are on our side or we would never have a chance. We would be wolf soup in less time than it takes to talk about it. John took them to the Schultz's wagon, "Frost, Loafer these are our new cooks Albert and Hilda. "How do you do," Frost said with a full curtsy. "Well, my oh my," Hilda said, "Talking wolves? Do you talk all the time?"

"No," Loafer said, "My brother is the noisy one. I am shy and quiet most of the time. But I like pie. Can you make pie?"

"Well my goodness, yes I can and I will make you all you want."

The cattle were a sorry lot, underfed, thin and from every blood line you could think of with dairy showing the most but they were beef and would grow out if given time. There was one good bull with them that they would save. There were another one hundred and twenty-one cows and twelve, three or four year old steers. None of them had enough feed to look good and were hungry, so they drove them two or three miles and let them graze. One of the eagles came and told John a group of riders were up the trail some and looked liked they were just watching for them to come and do them harm. John told the teamsters to put the wagons in a block, and by then the other eagles had come. "We will hit them from the air."

"And we will explode their horses," Frost said, "All you have to do is get their guns and tie them." In a short time, eight riders came dashing up. "We will take the wagons; get out of our way and maybe you'll live." Four screaming eagles dove at their heads and four wolves cut the horses undersides; John just tied them hand and foot, "And what was that you wanted again? Our what? Oh well. We will take your guns and horses and you can just lay here and think about it, and in a day or two someone may come along and let you go. If they don't, I guess that's your bad luck. I will not lose any sleep over it." It was cold, or cool anyway, depending on how you looked at it. Way to cool to lie on the ground tied up for my liking, but if you get involved in robbery you take your chances of being mighty uncomfortable.

The lead wagons lumbered around and started up the long grade all uphill for better than a mile, where it would level off only to descend to good water were camp would be made. As the last wagon got under way, the big burly bearded man, who was the boss, said, "What are you going to do with us? You can't just leave us - we will freeze. It is cold just laying here like this." John looked at him and snorted, "Maybe you boys should have thought about that before you planned to hijack our freight wagons. We never asked you to, and you did it because you are too lazy to work as other men do. So now you will just lay here until someone turns you lose. Do a lot of thinking and be glad some of you are not dead and change your ways. It doesn't look like to me robbery is a good business to be in, too risky."

They got the cattle moving; all looked better with some grass in them. As they moved out of sight over the hill, John and two of his men rode back to find the robbers still tied, bellowing like buffalos and thrashing around on the ground. "About time you cut us free. We thought you were leaving us!"

"We are leaving you, but I thought you should know that there are wild wolves in the vicinity that you will call in with all your noise; maybe you should be a little quieter." With that said, John and the others put their horses in a lope and were gone out of sight up the hill.

"Have any of you got a knife?"

"Yes, in my boot they did not look there."

"Turn around - maybe I can get it in my teeth and cut us free. No, the rope is over the handle. Maybe I can work the knots lose with my teeth. Everyone try - we got to do something or we will get too cold. First one knot slacked, then two, and they kept working. One man's hands were free. He went to the man that had the knife in his boot, got it soon all were free. "Let's get out of here, it's not that far to the settlement, and I don't want grain. The wagons all were loaded with grain."

Chapter 38

At first light the wagons were moving, after a cool night the day was going to be warm. "They are gone - untied the knots with their teeth," Golden Girl reported. "Good. I hope they learned from it but more than likely they did not. I think they will get other horses and come after the ones you took. We will watch and see. If they do we will know and stop them again. You have their killing tools too, that will slow them down, but they may come anyway."

Traveling was slow but the loads were heavy and big horses don't go fast but they were strong and in good condition so the miles just slid by. Cloud Walker, a young Crow, was interested in cooking and food preparation, so spent his time with Albert and Hilda, talking of ways to make food better. Hilda was a good teacher and soon his English was adequate for long discussions on food preparations. John, overhearing this made him cook's helper, much to everyone's approval. Word was sent and fires were started in the stoves and lamps lighted in the big kitchen and in the new little house. When all arrived, a large group of men quickly had Albert and Hilda unpacked in the kitchen and their house and the sounds of food preparation could be heard coming from the kitchen, a sound not heard before. The cattle got there and the three bulls were cut out and put with the other bulls. Two stayed bulls; the third was quickly made a steer and put back with the rest and not a very good one at that. Some people had no eye for cattle and others were just lazy so he stayed a bull for now. He was beef if he grew out, if he didn't grow, he'd be wolf meat.

Hilda saw the sheep flock and asked that four big whethers be hung up to cool; she thought mutton was as good a meat as any and better than most if cooked right. Hilda knew how to make mutton stew that would be fit for a king and tomorrow at noon they would find out just how good it was. She also planned to serve fresh baked bread with butter and a gallon or so of hot coffee with pie if time allowed. As you can imagine, in no time Hilda was loved by all, and all thought she was the best thing that ever happened at the ranch. And Albert was so jolly he could have put on a red and white coat with a white beard and passed for Saint Nick. Their apprentice, Cloud Walker, liked the name Sam, so they called him Sam Q. Walker. He would be called that forever, and his grandsons are still called Walker to this day.

Four days later John and Sam stopped at the stable livery barn in the settlement just east of the ranch some fifty miles. They had sold all the big horses but did have four good sized Morgan geldings that were matched. They harnessed them, got the bill of sale and went to the wagon yard and picked up the new wagon. They had just finished building the wagon. The manager of the wagon yard said, "I don't know, John, you keep us hopping building wagons, how many more you want?" John answered, "I need at least six more wagons - maybe ten if I can find the horses to pull them."

They drove to the general store where Sam filled the list Hilda had sent: forty sacks of potatoes, ten sacks of onions, along with other vegetables too. They bought canned goods by the case: sugar, salt, pepper, more coffee, pie filling and spices not available in the store in town and other things Sam wanted to try, and the wagon was loaded quickly. The other wagons were loaded but for one; they were waiting to see if it was needed to haul food from the store so they loaded it with cracked corn and started west.

At the stockyards a small bunch of all Black Angus cattle were for sale, ten big black three year old bulls and six milking short horn bulls. John could not buy them fast enough, for they were exactly what he wanted. Tie the Morgan to the last wagon, Sam, and help me get them started. They are better than gold -now we have beef cattle to work with. Sixteen good bulls and thirty one cows headed west; they were spooky and wild but lined out well enough. They were just not as hungry as the others had been because they had not been at the stockyard long enough to get hungry. The big cattle jogged alone for over a mile then went to grazing. Grazing cattle take grass; walk ten steps and so on, so it was easy to trail them with the slow moving grain wagons.

Suddenly, Frost was there. First he was not in sight then he was - he did it again. "Look what we found; they were by water over west some so we brought them with us." Loafer and two others got the big steers coming this way with not a mark on them. They were big red steers, good beef all of them, and they had been out a long time. "Put them with the others if their owners show up. They can have them or I will buy them."

The lead team was going up the long up hill now. The rest just followed, all pulling hard. There was no other way - it had to be crossed. Sam was driving the Morgan team; their load was lighter but they were smaller so it came out the same. Frost and Loafer had the cattle on water when the wagons crossed the stream and set up quick camp. The men fed the teams grain and put them on grass. Sam built fires and got coffee on, and Hilda had sent food so they ate that with the appetites of men who have worked outside all day long. The boys got their buffalo robes and were sleeping before John and Andy found spots to put their bed rolls down.

Long before the sun's first rays put its golden glow on the land, the feed wagons were miles west and Frost and Loafer had the cattle moving too. Two bulls were grumbling, not liking to be moved so early, and one of them had not moved at all. He was sleeping, but then he was not. Two wolves got him up and he was walking west without his quiet time or his breakfast. Bulls are not smart enough to have much to say and he wanted to look over the cows just in case one of them was in love but there was no time for that either. So he was grumbling about that.

The other bull was just mean; he thought he was tough and wanted all to know, and for sure the other bulls. So Frost told him to shut up or else he would have other things to thing about, like getting his balls chopped off. That did not impress him at all either. The cows were talking also about how dumb the bulls were, and that they should know they all were carrying calves and love making was not in their minds at this time anyway. It was their fault in the first place they had calves inside them anyway. Eagle, who was overhead, told them, "I know now why you cattle stand out in a rain storm."

"If you are so smart, eagle" a bull said, "then why do we?"

"Because you are too dumb to come in out of the rain."

"HUM. Is he right Homer?"

"Shut up and walk; how do I know if he is right - am I an eagle?"

"No, but you are not a smart bull either."

Around mid morning the big teams were having a hard time so a halt was called so they could blow and have a bite to eat. Each got a small feeding of oats and then some water to wash it down. The men each got their knives and cut arm loads of grass from the ample growth that was everywhere. The teams could eat and rest at the same time but not be unhitched and this saved time. The big red steers were trying to slip off; they were bunch quitters - you find them in every herd. That's probably why they got lost in the first place. So they would go in the feed lots with the bulls. Some of the bulls now in the lots would not be bulls for long. The ones of poor quality would be steers. Now they had better bulls to choose from.

The men had the summer calves in and put in a small place. The cows were singing their songs and some of them lost their voices. It was a pleasant sound to a stockman. Some big steers were with them and that is where the red steers would go – in an enclosure tight enough to hold calves and bunch quitters. When the cattle got there, the bulls and steers went in and seven older bulls were made into steers. They were pushed out with the main herd to go to the north range and winter. Some of them would not live; it was a big operation and they were not young, but as bulls they were not any good for breeding so it did not matter.

Chapter 39

Winter was mild this season so the stock needed little tending and did well with no help from the men. Periodically, the men just checked to make sure the wolves left them alone. Frost and Loafer had that under control and all the bears were napping. In short, wolf trapping was a thing of the past and poaching was not allowed at all. Word was out that all would answer to Frost and Loafer for violating the law and Pounce wanted to be a grandfather in the spring. No one in his right mind wanted to see Pounce looking at you on any morning for messing with his grandsons if you wanted to live. So the Moreau River Land Company had new allies to keep the peace: half Lobo, half timber wolf. It was a terrible cross if you were on the wrong side but great if you were friends. Golden Girl and Swoop were seven hundred feet up, riding the wind west.

Pounce would know soon of the mating of his two big sons. Pounce got the news the next sun and went to see Moon Boy, baby and the others to tell them that he and the rest of his family were loping east and would be gone for a week or so. Nothing on earth that I know of can run like a wolf when he wants to cover ground and nothing has the staying power or the endurance of a wolf. They have that long smooth stride that seems to be effortless and can go ten or so hours around twenty miles an hour. The wolves stop to rest and then some do it again - light or dark makes no difference - and they knew where they were going. Two eagles were overhead watching by day and owls at night. At the end of the forth day around supper time they were at the ranch.

Albert came out to put some trash in the burn barrel and nothing on earth could have prepared him to see what he saw standing in the yard. He was looking at the biggest and most dangerous looking wolf he had ever seen in his life. "I am Pounce. You know my sons Frost and Loafer, I believe. We have come far and could eat something if it is not a problem." Shaking a little, Albert answered, "Not a problem; Hilda and I will get you food right away - come on in." The dining hall was full of noise with the men chattering and dishes banging and forks and spoons making their cheery sounds as they moved over the glass dinnerware. It all fell to a deep quiet when Pounce and his family came in the room. Most everyone knew Pounce, or knew of him and his sons too, but not Mrs. Pounce or his daughter. For they rarely came with him at all. Pounce was looking at Hans and telling him to stay out of his way as he knew him for what he was: a cold, lazy, no good man and not a word was spoken because none were needed. Hans, despite his rather thick head, could sense this too, and his hunger was gone as he stared into the eyes of Pounce. The eyes were cold, yellow green like hot coals out of hell but no warmth was there and he knew fear for he saw death. Pounce could deliver it fast anytime he so chose.

"We have come to see our sons, Frost and Loafer, and meet our new daughters," Pounce said with a smile as he greeted John and Jim P Short, and Fat Legs, now known as T. L. Legs, and also Sam. "You are welcome; the boys are in the north woods getting their dens ready, and watching the cattle. Do they know you are coming?"

"Yes, the eagles have told them I think. We will find a spot in your kitchen and sleep where it is warm and go see them in the morning. We are tired; it is a long run, and we came in just four suns too. It doesn't bother the boys or my mate, but daughter and I don't go that far that fast as a rule. Before we go back I would like to see Bob and have a meal there with him - will you pay him?"

"Yes I will, in fact I will set up an account for you so you can eat whenever you want to or here with us, your choice. You have earned that and much more. Hilda and Mrs. Pounce had a long talk. She could not speak like the rest of them but Pounce helped out so they got along fine. Wolf talk is hard to put into people talk - it is much more complicated and in a shorter form and more to the point. I don't speak good wolf either, but I understand it well enough and when you get told in good wolf, you know where the poop is - they never bullshit at all. A buffalo is a buffalo, not a wild brown cow; a dog is a dog and not a tame brother, and Hans never came to breakfast either. He ate at Bob's and Pounce never missed him at all. But the rest came and conversation was brisk and continuous with many questions asked and answered over pancakes and eggs, with fried meats and black coffee.

Pounce had water because coffee was too hot and bitter for him and besides he did not lift his eyebrows or sip well, so he passed on coffee. After all had eaten Pounce and his family went north. They neared the timbered hill country and Pounce gave his long low wolf call that ended in a resounding roar. That call could be heard for miles in any direction; almost at once, Frost and Loafer called back, and all stopped doing what they were doing. A black bear was just coming out of his den, hungry as a bear can be. He stopped and went back in; a week's more sleep would not hurt a bit and coming out now might hurt. He wanted no part of Pounce or his sons either. Frost was there; he was not, then he was – "Father, how good to see you and mother too, this is Moon Glow. She will be part of us now and will be mother to your grandsons." Loafer was coming too, "Good to see you. We are fixing a den with Frost and Glow. This is Quiet One and joins us. We will be very near all of us from now on and will work with John at the ranch."

They touched noses and all knew each other, "Come mother, we will show you our den. Are you hungry?"

"Yes, girls. When is a wolf not hungry? I like my meat not cooked. The men cook it and it has no flavor. But they try hard. There is an older she man who cooks well and a he who has eaten too much food and is fat but nice; they make you laugh and are jolly. They do nothing but cook, and all love them. They are helped by a young Crow who comes from way south and west of our home. He would be a white man, why I don't know. He is a good Indian now. I think you should stay as you are now, not be something you are not. An eagle is not a fish and a fish is not a buffalo. I am a wolf not an ant, but if I were I would be good at it and not try to change. When I had the boys I ate much meat and made much milk that I gave your husbands. Now they are big as it should be and we are wolves, not trees, so I will stay wolf and be good at it."

"You are so wise mother and a good wolf. I hope I do as well."

Frost cut a young bull moose out of the moose yard and brought him near the den. He then showed off by putting him down in the exact place he wanted him to fall in the right position: legs uphill. Frost opened the hide at the back all the way to the feet then pulled it away exposing the full hind quarter. "Father, mother, sister and you boys come and eat. This is moose a big deer; we eat them sometimes but not often or all will be gone. Pounce ate a few bites then his mate, and daughter had some. The other sons had some, and it was said they thought it fine now all joined in and ate it almost to the last bite.

Six magpies sat in a tree and watched. One of them said, "They will never stop eating, I think, and we will not even get a taste. I am surprised their tails are not curled and they have no shovels on their noses the way they eat."

"Be quiet, Charlene; we will get some too and we could never have killed him ourselves anyway, just wait." Pounce heard them and spoke to them, "Come magpies and eat some; you have earned that, for you have warned us many times of danger. We have finished now so eat and no one will bother you."

"You are very kind father, why do so many think you bad?"

"Many are dead that stood against me the rest are afraid they will be next, so they think me bad. Also I am very large and quick. Frost is quick too but I am quicker.

Golden Girl came and sat in a tree, "Pounce, two men are coming over to the east and some south. They come slowly, looking always looking. They have hard things they put in the ground and cover with soft dirt and leaves. If you step on them they will grab your legs and hold you, and you can't get free, and then you will die. They also have poison they put on meat. If you eat it you will die. One is Bodkins, the old banker who hates John; he knows the wolves are friends of his so he wants to kill them but he doesn't know you are here."

"We could go bother him and make him mad," a magpie said.

"No. This is a killing thing this time. He will die - he will never quit otherwise. Come boys or some of yours will suffer from them. We have this to do. Come if you want to, magpies, you can watch and maybe warn us if you see what we don't. Thank you Golden Girl we go now." With that, Pounce, the King of Wolves, and his sons bounded softly away into the deep forest.

They were just not there. No one saw them move. "Come girls, Pounce has taught them well. The bad ones are as good as dead now - no one is quicker or more deadly." said Mrs. Pounce.

They found them setting a trap. Bodkins saw Poky just sitting there, and said "Get my gun. There's a wolf."

"And do what?" Loafer said.

"He talked!" the other man said, "It can't be." He stood there in complete amazement, too stunned to do anything but stare.

"I said, get my gun!"

Frost stood up, "Why? You can't hit anything with it."

"No! Another one! I am going crazy!"

"You are crazy already for being here," said Frost.

"We will make a deal with you."

"No deal." Pounce said and stood up.

"Pounce! No! We will go, never to bother you again."

"You are right on that one," Pounce said, "You never will. Dig a grave in the ground so they don't stink. Do you stupid men have anything to say? Last words - anything, like you wish John well, or something?" Bodkins was sweating now, and the other man cried, "Let me go, I will never tell!"

"Then why do you try to get your little gun out?" a magpie screamed.

"A talking bird too?"

"We all talk and we read your mind too," Frost said, "but yours is so small it doesn't take long to read."

"Yes," the magpie said, "You forgot to load your gun after you shot at the rabbit - it is empty."

"How many traps did you set Bodkins?"

"Oh many."

"You lie again," Golden Girl said, "This is your first one and is so plain to see a blind worm could see." Bodkins screamed "Golden Girl, I should have known."

Golden Girl continued, "I have been watching for three suns now. This is your first and it will be your last." Pounce killed them quickly and it was done. He said, "Put them in the ground and cover them.

Do it quick; I am tired of looking at them. We will tell no one of this. John is safe now - it is done." They returned to the ranch and slept soundly until the next morning's sun peeked through the window. The wolves decided to go out and look around some more.

The wolves went out over the green hillsides to look at the cattle. A few calves had recently been born and all the calves were very small. "You have two of them I see," said Pounce. "Yes," said the momma cow, "They just came yesterday."

"I think you should take them to the ranch. I will tell John, and he will make a place for them and you. You can have grain and hay. Start now and find shelter - a wind is coming in the dark time, and it will get cold. The cow got her babies up and got started one on each side. Other cows with small calves got up and went with her, and soon ten or so were moving fast toward the ranch. Golden Girl said "I will tell John they are coming and he can help them get in the barn." The eagle was screaming at other cows with young calves and soon twenty were on the high run to catch up with the first group. When they got to the ranch, the gate was open and in they went. All told, there were thirty-two cows and thirty-three baby calves. The cows fed them and put them to bed in the barn. The wind began blowing but the babies did not know it - they were sleeping snug and warm in the deep straw.

Outside the air was full of big, fat, swirling wet snow flakes - the kind that got you wet and cold to the bone but the babies didn't know that either, although eventually they would. Now they were full, warm and loved by their mothers, and that was enough. In the next pen, Homer complained again, "Now I am out here getting wet, and the calves have gotten into our barn. That is not fair." The other bull, Herman, looked over and said, "Oh, shut up Homer. If you are that dumb you should get wet and die. No one will miss you. Some of those calves are yours, and they need the barn; you don't."

Pounce and the others had made it to Frost and Loafer's dens. "You boys have made your den well, but your yard is a mess. Don't bring the remains of your kills in and just leave them. It is saying 'I live here.' You don't want that, so get rid of the bones and keep it free of your signs. Some that come will not be your friends. We go home soon. I want to see Bob and eat with him. It is a long way to the Moreau River but we will be back. I don't like Hans much - I know him for who he is. Keep the magpies close; they are good for watching, so feed them and keep them happy. They will tell you if anything is near, friend or otherwise. Sometimes they are a pest, but sometime they might save your life so they are worth having around. Now they are noisy, fighting over food but in general they are good to have around."

At the ranch, four big steers were in the cooler. Two of the red steers and two others all had put on a lot of pounds, and Bob wanted two of them. Hilda would get the other two. The men ate a lot because John worked them hard, and outdoor work builds an appetite like nothing else. Besides, the red steers were fence crawlers and always wanted out so they got out - to the cooler that is. It was certainly not to their liking but that's life. Pounce and his family had much beef leavings to eat, but Pounce still wanted to go to Bob's as there was no pie at the paunch pile. He wanted pie, and then they would start back. He was planning on running at night - the fewer that saw them, the better and the quiet one was flying west to look just to make sure no ambush was planned. None of them had forgotten Ice's close call either. John and Jared wanted pie too, and besides Pounce carried no money so they went to Bob's and looked over the group.

Two strangers were there at Bob's who thought it strange that wolves should be let into an eating house. John told them to shut up and mind their own business and that if Pounce wanted to he could buy them and sell them and never miss the change. Of course that did not set well and Pounce became irritated. He got up and went to their table and pulled out a chair, jumped up into it and sat down. "Now look boys, you can insult me and get away with it most times but never my wife or my sons and daughter. So back off now or find yourselves on the floor quick and Bob will have to wash the floor. You will not have enough blood left to walk three steps. If you want to find out, just open your mouth again." Now when Pounce was disgusted one never had to wonder what he meant; it was clear and to the point. "I know you never thought I could talk, well I can and I can do what I said, and more. Now stay out of my way or else. I am wondering how you got in here as rude and impolite as you two are. Now if you have a question, ask it but if you just want to make noise then go outside." Ice and Slayer came over too and Ice demanded of the men, "Well, did you hear our father? Ask your question and be quick about it. You were wondering how we can talk. I was thinking how you can talk as dumb as you seem to be.

The two men looked like they were about to cry then one said, "We are sorry - we did not know, no wolf I ever saw could say anything but you can. So have your pie; we will pay for it for being rude. I would like to ask a question or two if I may. Do other non humans speak?"

"Yes, but in different ways. Not all can read minds like me, or make themselves known as easily as I can."

"Can you talk to my horse?"

"Yes."

"Will you ask my horse a question for me?"

"I can. He will answer only if he wants to."

"Will you try?"

"Where is he, outside?"

"Yes."

"Then I will ask him." Everyone at Bob's came out to listen to this most unusual conversation. Pounce sat in front of the horse, "Do you like this man, your rider?"

"No. Not all the time," and he snorted loudly. "First, my name is Hobbs, not you dumb horse. Second, my right front shoe has a nail too near to my frog and it is painful. I have told him many times by limping. He picks up my hoof and says 'looks good to me.'" Pounce translated and all heard. The man put his hands on his hips, looked at his horse and said, "Hobbs I will fix this now." Hobbs bobbed his head and brushed the man's arm. Pounce translated, "He said that would be wonderful." The stranger held out his hand to Pounce and they shook. "I am glad to be your friend. I have learned more this day than any day in my life so far. Now let's get that pie." Bob was happy because he sold all the pie he had and then most of the cookies and he had to make coffee three times.

An older coffee drinker came to Pounce and put out his hand, they shook. "Because of your lesson today we have all learned much, and animals everywhere will be treated better from now on, and I thank you, sir Pounce." Pounce's mate beamed, his sons and daughter stood taller and Pounce blushed. John, Jared, and Bob grinned so much their faces disappeared, and all you could see was teeth. It was late afternoon when Pounce and his family loped down the street of the settlement to the west. A large group of people stood on Bob's steps and waved, wishing them a safe trip back. When dusk had settled into full dark they were miles west running with that smooth stride like fine silk flowing over marble that all wolves have and all others wished they had. The movement was effortless, long muscles coiling and uncoiling like velvet over spring steel, and silent like a cloud shadow moving over a far hill. A tree way ahead on the trail was soon a spot on the back trail, then just gone. Five suns later, they were giving baby a ride on the north slope of the Moreau River.

When Pounce and eleven other wolves brought baby back to Moon Boy's lodge, a large group was waiting to find out what must be done next and plan how to do it. The crowd quieted immediately when Pounce began to speak. "All who plan to go to the new lands far to the east must make plans to stay a long time; you have two choices to make. One, you can take down your lodges and pack all your things; the other is to take buffalo skins to make new lodges when you get there. You still need to pack all you have, and it will take most of your horses as pack horses. It is very far and most of you will never come back, so it will be a sad time as well as a new beginning." Pounce stopped talking and let his words sink in. "The white man's road you must walk is much different than the one you know here. There is no buffalo to go hunt, only cattle and you must own the ones you kill for meat. If you kill cattle someone else owned, they would send the law and you must pay for them. The law is like your dog soldiers: they keep the peace and all must hear them."

"The big difference is all that go will be going to lands owned by you, the Lakota, and no one can settle on it and take it away from you. You go with much wealth so you can buy the things you need or want and you still will be wealthy. But you must learn the white man's talk and learn to know money and his ways. It will take time and Moon Boy's eyes can be fixed so he sees well, so much good will come from it, and a little bad. Your crops will grow better: the soil is better and they get more rain. One thing is that if you don't like it there, you could come back and live and fight in the war that is coming and many will be killed on two sides. Hold a council and see who goes and who stays then get ready and go if you want crops this season. I and my family and eagles will help you move but do it now." Tall Elk asked Bald Eagle to fly to Tall Pine's camp of Crow and ask them to come to a council four suns from now. As long as they are coming, have them bring gold to be put in their name with J. P. Sharp's account and they could all go together, making it safer for carrying gold.

In four suns a council was held, and eighteen lodges of Crow from Tall Pine's camp and twenty two lodges of Lakota were going to move to the new lands in the east. The Crow who came to the meeting brought a large amount of gold and would bring more, but they had gone back to get their belongings and when they returned, all would go. Tall Elk was not going, but Moon Boy was and most of his body guards. Skunk was going, as was Fast Fox and more, plus some single men and women too. Lodges were being packed along with many seeds for crops. They would plant as soon as they got there and got camp set up. Eagles had gone to the ranch and John and Jim P. Sharp and L. L. Legs knew of the bags of gold to be put in accounts for the people and the land company. They asked that John buy more land if he could. The people would need work clothes and to look like white men or as near as they could with hair cuts as well. The gold would be much, a hundred bags or more, and the people would live on that and what they could grow and the cattle would be their meat. They would have to learn to the white tongue and know money but Fat Legs could help on that and Sharp Tail, known as Jim P. Sharp would also. The free and easy life on the plains was about over; the white settlers were beginning move in and make homes and the two cultures would never get along with each other, so it was time to move or fight a fight in which many would die.

In the camp of Tall Pine, the lodges of the movers were in line, ready to start. Tall Pine stood with arms folded and wished them a safe trip. When you get there, send an eagle to tell us what it is like. Many more of us may come, or some of you may want to return. The door is open both ways. They were ready so they started; they had much wealth and three eagles were air guards and ten wolves were in front and back. The sun was fine and they made good time. Four old friends saw them going and wondered why they took all the yellow gravel with them. "They must eat it," rabbit said, "to make them heavy so the wind doesn't blow them away."

"I think this time rabbit is right," fox said. "I don't know," replied owl, "He rarely is, you know." Blue Jay said "They just like to look at it because it reminds them of the sun. They are strange; too tall, I think."

Four suns more and they were in Tall Elk's camp. The Lakota were ready to join the procession, so they did. They were four horses deep and had much gold hidden among the bags and bundles, enough to start ten banks and pay for half the world. Ten eagles were high and low and on two sides. Pounce and his sons were point guards with twenty more behind and on two sides. Coyotes, bears and big cats found places to hide because they all knew the wolf king was out and that meant only one thing: get out of the way, or else - and all knew what that meant. He was feared by all, hated by many, and yet a little girl rode on his back most of the time. To her he was gentle and kind. Strange, but true; explain that if you can. They were well armed too, with guns, crossbows, and bows by Skunk with many arrows of the jagged edge kind that would cut up your insides and had poison on them to kill if they got inside. Out in front was Moon Boy on the golden stallion and Curly on his right and Cubby on his left with Shadow just ahead in the lead. They came to good water with much grass and some trees and made camp. Slayer killed two buffalo and Skunk got the cooking pot on fire and made coffee. Other fires were going now, and hump ribs were cooking, sending their delicious aroma throughout the area. Plum Leaf, Rose Bud and Morning Light were fixing stews, one with cut buffalo meat, and one of elk. Skunk was doing the elk stew his way and it was a happy camp.

Ten days later they were in camp just inside the tall trees. John, Jared, Fat Legs and others of the Lakota were holding classes on learning the white man's speech and his ways. The men, heads of the lodges, were all learning and they were teaching their families; most of them were eager to learn. They were dressed as working white men, their hair was cut or trimmed, and many could speak well enough to get by. So they got packed and moved to their new home on land they already owned and no one could ever force them to move.

Most of the gold was in accounts at the bank and they were large amounts, huge would be a better way to describe them, and T. L. Legs and Jim P. Sharp with the help of John were the administrators of it all. The ranch brought plows and disks, draft horses, and plowed their first fields and all helped in the planting and caring of them. A few of the pack horses remained the property of the ranch but most of them were taken back to the Moreau river country and turned free or used by the tribes. Some of them did not like the settled life and moved back to their home camps, while others moved eastward to join the new settlement.

In a few years farms and ranches were scattered over the land operated by Lakota or Crow and doing well. Some of the young people went east to schools and became professional businessmen others found strong drink and were lost. Moon Boy was taken further east, where eye doctors fit him with glasses, and he could see much to his delight. Skunk made hard wood bows but discovered no one needed them in the new land so he and his family went home where he was needed. White Buffalo Calf Woman went to school back east for counseling, successfully completed her education and went back west to help her people so the vision in the mist over the cooking pot came true and she was a big help to them. Pounce and his family went home to live out their lives but Curly and Cubby never left Moon Boy's side and were buried on his ranch.